"Gaige offers striking prose and layered explorations of relationship boundaries and madness."

—*The Boston Globe* Shelf Life (Pick of the Week)

"In reading Charlie and Alice's story, I was struck by three things: Gaige's crystalline prose, the three-dimensionality of all of her characters, even the minor ones, and her ability to convey the darkness in the minds of Charlie's clients, who are suffering from schizophrenia or other mental illnesses. Gaige . . . offers us something very special indeed."

—NANCY PEARL, National Public Radio

"An amazing book." —*The Philadelphia Inquirer*

"*The Folded World* is a beautifully crafted novel, from word choice to sentence construction to its unfolding plot. . . . [Gaige] presents the reader with a convincing tribute to the extraordinary in ordinary life." —*ForeWord* magazine

"*The Folded World* is more than a novel: it's a revelation, about what it means to love romantically in this problematic world. Charlie and Alice Shade's marriage . . . inspires us to consider our own attachments in a new and radiant light."

—KEN KALFUS, author of *A Disorder Peculiar to the Country*

"Amity Gaige is terrific. Once again she reveals her virtuoso ability to translate the complicated ambiguity of our most haunting feelings, and our closest relationships, into dazzling prose. For the reader who has been fortified by love's endurance, baffled by its fragility, and awestruck by the hurricane force with which it hits, *The Folded World* strikes deep and true." —CHRISTOPHER SORRENTINO, author of *Trance*

"Gaige was honored as one of the National Book Foundation's '5 [exceptional authors] Under 35' for her debut, *O My Darling* (2005). Her second time around again showcases a gift for capturing the simultaneous proximity and distance in a relationship. . . . Gaige's off-beat orientation, wit and piercing insights stand up to her first novel, this time in a more sober and less tidy narrative that offers greater breadth in exchange for sweetness."

—*Kirkus Reviews* (starred review)

"Gorgeous prose and unusual characters combine to make this an intriguing and captivating look at the ways traditional gender roles skew adult relationships. Indeed, it is exhilarating to see Alice, the horrifyingly passive wife, transform herself into a competent woman. This alchemy, in concert with a beautiful story wonderfully told, makes this highly recommended for all fiction collections."

—*Library Journal*

"One of Gaige's triumphs is her ability to sustain narrative momentum; as the story progresses and the characters deepen . . . the book becomes truly gripping. The scenes are so finely crafted, the narrative movement so fluid, it becomes impossible to resist being swept into the world of Alice and Charlie. . . . *The Folded World* entices one to read with both hunger and patience."

—*The Literary Review* (Editor's Choice)

ALSO BY AMITY GAIGE

O My Darling

THE FOLDED WORLD

THE FOLDED WORLD

a novel

Amity Gaige

 RANDOM HOUSE TRADE PAPERBACKS

New York

2009 Random House Trade Paperback Edition

Copyright © 2007 by Amity Gaige
Reading group guide copyright © 2007 by Other Press

All rights reserved.

Published in the United States by Random House Trade Paperbacks,
an imprint of The Random House Publishing Group,
a division of Random House, Inc., New York.

RANDOM HOUSE TRADE PAPERBACKS and colophon are
trademarks of Random House, Inc.

RANDOM HOUSE READER'S CIRCLE and colophon is a
trademark of Random House, Inc.

Originally published in hardcover in the United States by
Other Press in 2007.

ISBN 978-0-8129-7854-4

Printed in the United States of America

www.randomhousereaderscircle.com

9 8 7 6 5 4 3 2 1

Book design by Mary A. Wirth

i have bent my burning ear to a tulip

and it told me all about you.

—T. W.

ONE

At the moment she was born, five hundred miles away, a small boy, his mouth ringed with jam, paused in his play on the carpet. The boy was gripping a wooden block in one hand and his enormous ear with the other. He'd been suffering from a head cold, and as often as not when he worried he grabbed one of his handle-like ears for comfort, but now he looked up at the winter sun, stilled. Something had—what was it?—changed! He looked around, but his life's campaign was still the same: a playpen, a faded Persian carpet with a salty fringe, a swollen-bellied mother shuffling her cookie sheets in the kitchen. The boy pressed his hands to the carpet and stood, using his diapered rear as counterweight. Carefully, he turned around. Nothing was different, and yet the world was completely changed. He swallowed, tempted to cry. The hand went automatically to the ear—O the soft, sinewy ear. He rubbed it between thumb and forefinger. A flock of geese flew across the sun, one by one repeating the form of their shadows in a way that seemed to him now terribly worthy of attention. The sun pulsed, hot on his blond head, and the paisley of the carpet pulsed, and the room smelled vividly and wonderfully of sun damage, and he felt, all at once, like a struck match, and that was the first time he ever thought of Alice.

She herself grew up to have pale skin the erased color of a white rose. Her eyes, once blurred with myopia, became dark and arrowlike and almost Asiatic by the time she reached adolescence. By then she was attractive, slightly overweight, and a bookworm. Even after she'd been liberated from the wearing of eyeglasses, she still pushed habitually at the invisible frames. Fat as a child, she grew round in womanhood. By the time she was twenty, she no longer seemed physically incomplete. She still hid behind her hair, still wore an expression of hesitance that no longer suited a grown woman, but with her battered purse and outward sloping eyes she did not ask to be made more of than she was. In fact, at times, she seemed unaware of her own body, such as happens to people who read too much.

She had grown up nowhere but in Gloucester, and many years after she had left it, a layer of salt remained fused to her skin. She lived all her years in a tall pink house in Gloucester with her mother, an exceedingly tall woman with a wintry complexion. Her mother was full of advice, having thought long and hard about the little issues life so ungenerously sent her, when she could have been capable of thinking of great things. Instead, her mother was full of advice about little things, how to get things for free by complaining, when not to buy fish—little warnings, for example, how deceptively dangerous was the tomato, as well as public door handles, parking lots, and, most of all, the intentions of men, in particular as their corrupted art of promise-making.

Alice listened to all this advice for many years without believing any of it. Then, one day when she was just twenty-two, still for some reason living in Gloucester in that tall pink house with her mother and one ancient cat, and working as a salesgirl, she realized in one horrible, epiphanal crush that she never ate tomatoes, often avoided public door handles and parking lots, and that she distrusted fish, men, and promises. In fact, she had unconsciously added a whole new generation of niggling rules to her mother's: neither did she ever walk home the same way she'd come, or cross under ladders, or say her own name on Sunday. These precautions did not suit Alice's temperament, which was in fact much less contrary than her mother's, and which was greatly influenced by the inkling that her life had already been lived in Fate's milky blue eye. But the fact that no great tragedy had yet befallen her and her mother made their rules seem effective. As for love, it sat obediently under a cloud of suspicion. In the years since she graduated high school, several young men from her high school had come around asking for her with their broad shoulders and their damp shirtsleeves and only once had she ever accepted a date, which involved staring across the chasm of the bucket seat at a boy who had once been star of the basketball team and now worked all day installing bird barriers. She could not bear him—not he himself, he was kind—but rather the nunish feelings he inspired in her, which made her feel marked for a cool life, neat and lustless, like a woman born with physical perforations, who at the edge of her sexuality is snapped neatly apart from it.

These realizations disturbed her greatly. Still a bookworm (those million nights in the parlor with her mother), now she looked down at the book in her hand and felt betrayed by the life she was losing to it. From her earliest memories, she had lived much of life in someone else's story, so absorbed she often forgot to drink and sleep, for so pleasantly abstract was her heavy body when she read. Pleasantly abstract was her fatherlessness and the sooty-looking fishy-smelling town out the window. But perhaps, in so behaving, she had forgotten to become someone actual. There hadn't seemed to be a need to become someone actual in Gloucester. She was not modest, she simply had not yet occurred to herself. Many of her friends had occurred to themselves. Claudette was in nursing school and several others had gone thither and yon to colleges where boys sang together under arches and rode racing shells along rivers in unison, like gorgeous slaves.

So gradually, sitting by the picture window with her mother reading, Alice began to feel a kind of heat or heated opening, some beckoning accident in time. She began to feel a greater distance between herself and her mother. For she herself was only twenty-two years old, not an aging woman. She was not an aging research librarian with frown lines who collected sherry glasses and spoke constantly of the time she had once seen the Charles Bridge in Prague with a wealthy aunt. No, she was an attractive young woman with a young woman's living hungers, and after her epiphany, everything in Gloucester began to look shabby. The poor children in their yearly summer haircuts jousted in the grease-stained street with curtain rods they'd found in trashcans. The tall skinny tenement houses stood like starving girls in party dresses.

And so she decided to leave Gloucester and live on her own in a nearby city and get a job and maybe take night classes. The fact that she had never attended college was a damp, heavy clod in her heart. She did not remember why she had not gone to college right after high school. She had been one of the most promising students in her English classes. Yet all she remembered was walking arm and arm down the hallway with Claudette, and then Claudette disappearing like a bride into the glittering cosmos, and then the poor children playing with her old curtain rods.

⌒

He became a long distance runner. Slim and wiry, golden haired, the only thing out of line about him were his ears, which stuck out jughandle-like from his head. He had the energy of a coil or spring, and was often coming out of sunsets, popping out of hazelnut bushes—he was a pleasant surprise like that. In his hometown, in the heart of the heart of the Middle West, he had been the president of his high school class. Even the candidate he'd run against had voted for him. He loved to be surprised, for such was the immunity to horror that results from a completely happy and cloistered childhood. Cursed with narrow shoulders and smallish hands, he made up for this lack of burliness with a tremendous good nature and a talent for self-mockery, and in this manner became the darling of many a schoolyard bully, for at heart he had no fear, while they had much.

But for someone so cheerful, so without anxiety, he led a rather solitary daily life. After all, he was a long-distance runner, and he was busy with secret missions that were revealed to himself at the last minute. He was always running home late with a fistful of flowers for his mother to make up for lost time. And what had made him late? Some small marvel—a hedgehog, struggling across train tracks, entrancingly fat. When a thing happened, such as a hedgehog, it was the only thing that happened. Events glowed in a funnel of his attention. He was not accustomed to saying no or to not looking. Therefore he was late everywhere, waylaid by everything. He loved his grandmother, his veteran council; he loved women, but without a gentleman's stiffness. He was free-given, blank, and attracted to hilltops. He could be seen striding on his strong thin legs, running across the wide streets of Mattoon with his book bag, his hair flopping over his eyes. He was a gush of air—a pleasurable, fleeting, shudder of youth. He was Mercury running on the disintegrating edge of time.

He could have been anything. He was so cooperative and Midwestern, he could have been part of anything. His father was a successful businessman at Xerox, and his younger brother was sure to gladhand his way toward similar success once he returned from his prodigal year as a ski instructor. But he himself did not want to grow up to sell things and process things and prorate things and get great satisfaction from the plushness of his lawn. He did not want to feel alive only when traveling at great speeds. He did not want to manage life or hover above it or make copies of it. He wanted to live it, with other people. He wanted to have his hands in it.

His life had been filled with the smell of bread and laundry, he knew that. He suspected that the difference between his life and other lives could plumb an ocean. He was acquainted with few poor people and only one madwoman—a lady with a moustache who sat in the shade of the gas station. Every time he passed these people, even as a child at the skirt of his mother, he experienced a temporary, almost vertiginous thrill. For perhaps life was not nearly as knowable as it was in Mattoon. Perhaps he himself was not only a well-fed boy who slept under a handmade quilt. Perhaps he, and everyone, was more. More beautiful, endlessly corruptible—he did not know. He simply wanted to find the seam between his life and the life of the madwoman in the shade. The idea enlivened him so much that he caught each glimpse of mystery and saved it, the years racing by beautiful and four-seasoned, until one year after graduating with a bachelor's degree in history from his small Midwestern college, he felt he had a sufficient burden, and decided to move east, to a real city, and earn his master's degree in social work.

⌒

She took her two black suitcases from Gloucester to the city. Staring out of the grimy bus window, her mother getting smaller and smaller, she wondered about the future and what the future might hold. She sat at the edge of her seat, scanning the blur for this hidden majesty, until a great failure of imagination made her drowsy. She leaned back, holding a bag of carrot sticks that her mother had packed for her. Carrot sticks. She reached instead for the candy bar that lay on the floor of her big black purse. Chewing the nougat, shoving at the bridge of her nose, she took a book out of her purse. She opened the book. Comforted by the familiar smell of trapped winter in the crease, she began to read. The months previously intended for wooing the cosmos were spent instead in this bent posture.

Certain Fridays, he had long, half-philosophical, half-hysterical conversations with his friends in bars, and Charlie Shade, his fingers folded before his mouth, precociously doctor-like, listened and bargained and laughed in the center of them all. It was the fall of his second year of graduate school, and he liked it: his classes, his classmates, the gritty, bus-fumed city, his little crow's nest of a bachelor's apartment high up on a windy corner in an old gray house. He liked New England. He didn't even miss the Midwest and its river-dipped willows and its silence and all the people that he knew. But all the while he felt a nagging impatience. *This* wasn't it either, he thought, wasn't it really. He itched the back of his neck, under his collar. Where was the seam? Where were all the adjacencies? The collisions? Where did lives touch in a less casual way?

He himself did not drink. Just like his father Glen Shade, Charlie had never touched a drop. This had caused some awkward moments for Charlie in high school, but gradually he got away with it as he got away with everything. There wasn't any moral to his not drinking and he did not object to drinking in general. He got along with drunks quite well. But on Friday nights such as these, his classmates getting drunker and more confessional, falling across him like a half dozen suitors, Charlie felt such a great pull away from them that it nearly bent him backward, outside, toward the door. He wanted to run. He wanted to run a longer distance than he'd ever run, and he wanted to arrive finally. He wanted to arrive to it, whatever it was—life perhaps—life, rather than the thought of life. He wanted to feel not light but sun, not cold but winter; he wanted to be slapped by the thing standing right in front of him. It was always just over that hill, over that hill. He smeared the bar window clear with his hand. The red and purple sun was illuminating the downtown street and all the cold windows opposite, and just then a girl in bulky snow boots stepped into his view.

She was entirely overdressed for the weather in boots, mittens, and a hood. Her only visible body part was a rather petulant chin. She was causing trouble out there in the five o'clock foot traffic. It was her manner of walking. One long stride, almost a leap, followed by several shorter steps, as if crossing a brook on stones. Charlie smeared the window clear again. What the heck was she doing? Another nutso, someone nearby him slurred. We're surrounded by them. Everyone at the table turned to watch the girl's erratic progress. As she lurched past the basement bar, dark wavy hair, like steel shavings, lolled out of her hood. In recognition—a soft, private, interior popping—Charlie understood: She's trying not to step on the cracks, he said.

Why the fuck is she not stepping on cracks? somebody cried.

Charlie watched. I guess she's got her reasons.

What you so moony about Charlie, someone else crowed. You're not even *drunk*.

She's pretty, slurred Garvey Sudd.

Ya! Pretty strange maybe.

You want me to go get her for you, Charlie? Garvey shouted, standing and upsetting his barstool. I will, I'll go get her.

Charlie felt very quiet and very still. He felt something was being revealed to him. He did not want anybody to go get anybody. He just wanted to watch. He did not feel desire born but relieved. He felt something lift from the back of his head—a door—out of which a thousand bat-like metaphors flew shrieking away. He touched his hand to the glass. The girl passed out of sight.

She read books late into the night, eating stacks of vanilla crèmes. She decided that anything that didn't have chocolate in it was low fat. Sometimes she missed, especially when overhearing arguments, her mother. She missed the safety of being someone who attempted little. She even missed Gloucester, but not much. She sometimes missed her eyeglasses, for now every once in a while in the city a man would catch her gaze, say something flirtatious, and she lacked anything to hide behind. She didn't want to go on a date with anybody just yet. It would have been too awful to sit across a guttering candle from a bank teller or mechanic or volleyball coach, watching his potential melt, struggling with her own waning lack of interest: his fault/my fault. She was one of those people for whom disappointment caused a shutdown of the entire grid; it almost rendered her mute. Was she simply afraid that real people were less real than people in books? Not just people, but the world. Was she afraid of a world that spun on and on with no theme and no denouement and no author's hand to reassure her? But she wasn't afraid! she insisted to no one, kicking back the sheets on her single bed, sending a small bookslide onto the floor. She wasn't afraid! She was prudent.

She was waiting for her cosmic instruction. How else was one supposed to know how to proceed with something as bare-assed as a lifetime?

Her apartment was narrow as a shoebox and dark all day. But she liked it anyhow because it was hers and she decorated the walls with old postcards and book covers. By day, she worked as a receptionist for a dentist and listened to the distorted confessions of anesthetized patients. She tried to wean herself—unsuccessfully—of her superstitions. She saved up money for college classes. She spoke to her mother daily, then weekly, once or twice even letting the week go by, practicing a kind of emotional calisthenics. After a while, it appeared that she had successfully escaped Gloucester. And her mother did not die, and did not very often guilt her, and with a pang sometimes Alice heard new names peppering in her mother's speech. Sometimes, opening a fresh book, Alice would say to herself: This is the last book. This is the last story that is not my own.

∽

She spun around. The red-bricked buildings crowded the narrow street on which she walked, snow covering the sidewalks. No, she was right, someone was calling out. A figure grew out of the evening gloom—a young man, running. By the time he reached her, his brow was damp with sweat; his head smoked in the cold. He bent over, breathing hard, hands on his knees. He held up one finger.

"I ran—like five blocks—" He made a spooling motion with his hands, "—just to—"

She looked down at him. "Where's your coat?" she asked him.

Panting, the young man stood. He was only a hand taller than she, dressed in a sweater vest and a washer-thinned white collared shirt rolled above the elbows. His eyes glowed blue in the dusk. His mouth formed a small "o" as he looked at her, thinking.

"I guess I—left it in the bar," he said. Then he added quickly, "I don't drink myself. I was at the bar with friends. Not that I have anything against people who drink. I just don't myself. Drink. We go on Fridays. I like the peanuts. I eat the peanuts."

With that, he rolled his eyes and turned around. He appeared to be planning his retreat. His footprints remained in the fresh, thin snow. He bent to his knees again, laughing softly.

"Stupid stupid stupid," he muttered.

Then he stood, grinning.

"I'm out of practice."

"Out of practice what?" said Alice.

"Asking out girls." He smacked his hands together. "There, I said it."

Alice's eyes widened. She lifted her hood back from her face. "I'm sorry. *Who* are you?"

"I saw you through the window. Of the bar. I've seen you lots of times. Walking past. I've watched you. Not like a stalker! I've watched you out of interest. Like an anthropologist. No, not an anthropologist. Because after all, here I am, asking you out. But I'm not dangerous. I really never do this. And now I see why, too. Christ!" Charlie thrust out his hand. "My name is Charlie. I was born Charles, of course, but that didn't stick. It's the ears."

She took his hand, and let go quickly. At the last moment, she remembered to speak, "My name is Alice Bussard."

She ran her tongue around her teeth. She should speak. She should speak. Almost shrilly, she said, "In this cold you shouldn't be running around without a coat."

Then, averting her eyes, she blushed, for what raging shrew

inside her had made her say such a thing? A wave of pity for him—that he had taken an interest in her—rose in her gut. But at that moment, the same or the next, watching the snow-dusted tips of his sneakers tapping, she hated this pity, and was sick of it, and looked up straight into his face. He was still there. He had not been sucked back into the blue dusky obscurity simply because his interest was implausible to her. Rather, he was rolling his shirtsleeves down and buttoning them at his wrists, murmuring in agreement, for it *was* cold.

They stood for a moment, looking at one another.

"Oh," he said. "I have a question for you."

Alice narrowed her eyes. All around them, behind and underfoot, the snow softly quilted everything. His hair rustled; she could almost hear it.

"So," he said, "All these Happy Hours I've been wondering something about you. What are you afraid will happen? If you, you know, step on a crack?"

She stared at him. She searched her mind for an instance in which she had revealed this to someone, anyone, even once. And then, heartily, she laughed.

"Why are you laughing?" he asked.

Shy, she ducked her chin to her chest. Our lies are so treasured, she thought. Would she be able to let this one go? This lie: that while walking down slushy streets to and away from a job she so disliked, motherless, fatherless, homeless, doubt-heavy, waiting as if in prison for a bud on a tree or some small genesis or sign, she had actually been godforsaken.

～

Later, he stood in the middle of a busy sidewalk holding both her hands and looking down at his feet. Here he was, twenty-five years old and caught in the same unctuous pose as in a sixth-grade church-sponsored Virginia reel.

"Quit laughing," he said, trying to affect a teacherly expression, but the sight of her scrambled up his intentions and he laughed too, purely and shamelessly as a child.

"I can't do it," she said. "It's been too long."

"You can do it," he said. "You must! Don't be a slave to your misunderstandings. Or," he frowned, "do you *not* renounce your belief that stepping on a crack will bring chaos and disaster or apocalypse or whatever the hell?"

She drew back, wiping her mouth with the back of her hand. Her mitten dangled by a cord to the sleeve of her coat. He could see her back reflected in the department store window, her two white-stockinged legs and her hood.

"Couldn't we find a less crowded sidewalk?"

He reached for her again. "Come on, now. Don't be a puss."

She raised her eyebrows. "A puss?" She laughed, backing up against the plate-glass window itself, people streaming in between them now, bearing briefcases and grocery bags. Behind her, in the window, mannequins posed in feminine solidarity.

"What's a puss?" she said. "You should come to Gloucester some time. We'll teach you how to swear."

Charlie stepped toward her, into the foot traffic, jostled and swiped by shopping bags, feeling vaguely like a monster who had been trained for the circus. It occurred to him that sometimes a man's very maleness made him like a monster who had been trained for the circus. You didn't have to do a thing. All it took was a pretty girl to raise her eyebrows and repeat your words mockingly to you. He had known her only three weeks; she was the most beautiful girl he'd ever held in his arms. He had already kissed her once. He planned to do so again. As soon as he could get to her. He would not soon forget it. Kissing her, just on an ordinary street in the dark, he'd fallen unfathomably forward, into a space that had been wooing him in vain, it felt, for years. Afterward, he had walked home under a consummately quiet snowfall, and halfway back to his apartment he had actually begun to cry, looking at his hands that had so recently cupped her face, as if there might be bits of her beauty clinging to them like tissue.

He cleared his throat, embarrassed before himself. He now stood pressed against the department store window too, looking down into the perfumed part of her hair.

"So what *do* you believe will happen? I'd like to understand your superstition." He tapped her head. "I want to seeee into your mind."

"And what would your seeing into my mind do for me?" she asked, looking up at him, her shoulder and part of her breast pressed against his black and red checkered wool coat. "Disaster will befall me. And then won't you feel bad? It's your experiment, you see, but my neck."

He swallowed. Her use of the word "neck" discomfited him. For there it was, the white road leading down into her dress.

"Don't you know anything?" she cried, almost giddy. "Don't you know anything about bad luck?"

"No," Charlie said.

When he kissed her this time, he caught her by surprise. He drew back. Her eyes, black and narrow, widened and became large as pools. He saw this, and he saw how her eyes engorged with the knowledge of him. She loves me, he thought. He did not understand why she loved him but he saw that it was true. The traffic light changed and a fresh crowd of pedestrians streamed around them. Blue dusk coated their skin.

"Go ahead," he whispered. "You can do it. Step here. This one right here."

Blushing, she looked away.

"Listen. If the sky falls, I'll catch it. I'll hoist it back up. Whatever you think is going to happen, I'll protect you."

"And my mother?"

"Your mother?"

"What about her back?"

"Your mother's back?" Charlie laughed. "Is that what you think? You think you'll break your mother's back? Like out of a nursery rhyme? Are you serious?"

She smiled.

"You're not serious," he said. "You're wasting my time. I am a serious, highly trained mental health care professional. And you're just some flirt."

He pushed her gently away and swung himself around a nearby parking meter. He'd forgotten his gloves that day and his hands were red with windburn. She stood abandoned in the middle of the sidewalk, black hair melting over her shoulders.

Out of her immediate physical presence, he almost felt like his old self again. He felt the flaps of his consciousness closing like a box. Maybe he did not want to fall in love. Maybe he regretted even getting this far. He would have his degree soon, and Banford had already secured for him a job at the best psychiatric hospital in the state, starting that summer. Charlie had gone several times to the ornate entrance of the building to practice going in and out of the revolving door. Many men with ambition were able to restrain themselves in love: they did not *cry* with happiness, they did not let themselves be trained for the circus. Charlie's younger brother Mark had a prodigious sex life. One of his skiing pupils—a married woman, no less—had recently taken him for the weekend to Trieste. Trieste! A place so exotic it was in both Italy *and* Switzerland. Charlie shut his eyes and spun around the parking meter again, thinking maybe he did not want to fall in love with her, this Alice, this sloe-eyed, cheap-musk-wearing, hair-parted-down-the-side dentist's receptionist, but even as he thought all this, he could still see her with some third lovesick eye, an eye inside him that, Charlie realized then, he could not shut.

"Come here," he said.

She smiled, wandering over. She leaned against the cold metal post.

"Don't you have any superstitions?" she said. "Tell me you have no fears at all."

"A superstition isn't a fear," he said. "It's a compulsion."

"It's a fear, all right. It's a fear of fate. A fear of the gods. They're up there, you know. On Mount Olympus. Cruel, dangerously bored. They're jealous of us mortals. Because they can't love, and they can't die. Imagine." Her expression became sober. She looked at him. "Didn't you know?"

Charlie put both hands in his pockets and squinted up at the sky. It was beginning to snow. He felt the tight little kisses on his face. He wasn't thinking about the gods. He was thinking that maybe there had never been a more beautiful winter night in New England or anywhere. He thought maybe he had never been happier. He could not remember a time. He was glad he could not shut the eye. He did not want to shut the eye. Because she made him want to be awake all night. She made him want to be like the moon, awake all night and watching. Perpetual.

"No," he said finally. "I'm not really afraid of anything." He looked down at her and drew back her fur hood. "No," he said again, the beauty of her face strengthening his conviction. "And I'll protect you. I'll protect you. I promise."

Alice looked down. There was a break in the traffic. She raised her boot, then placed it in the space between smooth concrete planes.

"There you go," he said. "Step on it like you mean it."

She laughed and let go of his arm. She covered her bare head with her mittens.

"Sorry, Ma!" she cried.

He watched her, laughing and cringing, victorious and clumsy, her stockinged legs and boots peeking out from her big coat.

Alice, he whispered. *It's you.*

⌣

Of course, falling in love is still a falling. Though the sensation of falling might be pleasurable to the body, it is distressing to the mind. The body falls in love easily, whorishly, but then the mind comes loping behind everything, trying to make orders, blowing its shrill whistle.

As soon as she knew she loved him, she became afraid. She was not afraid she would stop loving him. She was afraid that he would be rescinded somehow. She did not know by what or whom. Lying naked on her twin bed in her apartment with the shadows of the plants passing on the wall, she stroked his head on her stomach. Her breath smelled of sex and black pepper, and she felt ruinously beautiful, her breasts tilted apart in the moonlight, the sheets threaded through her legs. Trying not to wake him, she pulled a cigarette down from the pack by the windowsill. She had taken up smoking, out of nowhere, and enjoyed it very much. It was the only thing she had chosen to do entirely by herself except move to the city and turn around when he called her name. A cinder fell from the tip and landed with a pinch on her skin before turning to ash. Who would take him from her, she wondered? What in the world was she afraid of? Had he not liberated her from those awful, burdensome working-class superstitions when he proved her wrong about cracks? Besides, she was not special enough to be in danger. She was an anonymous girl, a receptionist from Gloucester, who had never even gone to college. A bookworm, fatherless, and fond of funnel cakes.

Gloucester. Why should she think of Gloucester now, with Charlie Shade (bringer of springtime! shower librettist! thief of the landlady's *Tribune*!) sleeping possessively across her, his fine hair in his eyes, his fingers moving in his dreams? Against her will, she thought of the rows of pink and white and pistachio green tenements of Gloucester and the lack of grass and roller skates that you clamped to your shoes with a key, and men and women so old and tradition-bound that they actually hoped for another war so that they'd have to stand in butter lines again. She thought of the poor children playing outside after they'd all received their summer haircuts, the slate gray sea in the distance behind them. She thought of her mother closing the curtain and saying God save us. Alice remembered, quite vividly, her mother rolling her eyes about the poor children and their yearly summer haircuts. It was a joke. Her mother did not believe in God, so no one would be saving anybody. God would save, least of all, the grubby little children of East Gloucester. There was no meritocracy (according to Marlene) and no God, and a person could be happier if (according to Marlene) he accepted how alone he really was, alone in an oarless dinghy, lost at sea. Thusly, there was liberation—in hopelessness. Thusly night fell on Gloucester and on all the bones in the ocean, and there was Alice and her mother, stuck in a tall clapboard house oarlessly instead of in Europe where they kept the Charles Bridge. Alice often thought of this trip to Europe as the worst thing that ever happened to her mother. She wished she could reverse time and spare her mother from having to see something as beautiful as the Charles Bridge in the rain.

She laughed. Charlie's head jiggled on her belly. He wiped his mouth and fell back to sleep. But what did it matter? Why should she think of Gloucester now, and of her mother? The paper at the end of the cigarette crackled.

"Wake up, Charlie," she whispered, "you damned innocent fool."

He turned his head on her belly, murmured, and did not wake.

Why, she thought, when one is in love, does one feel least at peace? How is it that love casts damning knowledge backward upon one's lonely life? How *lonely* I used to be. How *lonely* carrying my books across the glass-shattered streets. How *bored* I was being scolded by employers, how bored going to the movies with Claudette and comparing those movies to previous movies, how bored watching holiday decorations change in shop windows, bored seeing the neighborhood children grow up—another year, another haircut. Why had life wished me to languish in this way?

Apocalyptically, she now had nothing to go back to. In her heart, Gloucester was a boarded-up ghost town. She dropped her cigarette in an empty sardine tin on the windowsill where it landed with a *pfst*. Charlie stirred.

"No," she whispered. "Never mind. Be a fool. Keep sleeping."

She drew his head closer on her bosom. How could she be hopeless now? How could she be free? For she had, in her possession, an oar.

She was suddenly possessed of a radical awareness of a god. Not god of St. Catherine's School on Quenton Avenue but a god who saw things as she did, as knowingly and as darkly—a god who was no longer in charge but was still politely consulted on hard cases.

Please, she whispered in the darkness. Please.

Leave us alone. Leave us just like this.

⌒

The little claw-footed grandmother drifted through the crowd in the auditorium. She was too short to see around anyone, so she had to trust the backside of her son-in-law. Glen Shade himself seemed a bit lost, his trademark ears panning back and forth like satellite dishes.

"Where do we sit?" the grandmother cried. "Did he order a seat for us, or what?"

Her daughter turned around and took the old woman's hand. A silk knot at her throat, her hair in buttercream waves, Luduina did not look as if she had just traveled halfway across the country at 500 miles per hour. The grandmother was much comforted by her daughter's ordered hair and appearance. As she got older and more shrunken, the grandmother often felt like a child, and therefore was comforted easily like a child. She wandered trustfully behind them into a vast hall.

"That's her," she said, pointing to a dark-haired girl holding a program.

Alice raised her hand and waved.

Smiling, the Shades scooted down the aisle and past the legs of the people until they reached the empty seats beside the girl. They shook hands. It felt very natural and very pleasant to just sit there quietly and wait for Charlie to cross the stage in his robe and mortarboard. The grandmother, however, kept stealing peeks at Alice. Every time she looked up, through wrinkled gray eyes, she became more pleased. For secretly, she was glad that, upon shaking Alice's hand, a clap of thunder had not rent the building in two and sent an iron girder down upon her.

Throughout her life, the grandmother had been plagued by premonitions. She'd had her first one, dreadful as the onset of menses, at age thirteen, regarding the collision of her favorite uncle's car with a cement truck. This collision had come to pass as airily as the premonition. Sometimes the premonitions seemed mere inevitabilities; looking into the eyes of her high school sweetheart she had felt his wartime fate as clearly as he had. But her visions were awash with perfect detail. They came with a taste in the mouth, with breezes from their own world. She had never been wrong, only once inaccurate, believing it was her classmate's sister who would disappear one day behind the school, never to be found, when it was the boy himself who was lost, infamously, a boy with a touch (when he passed backward her tablet from the teacher) soft as twice-sifted flour. She had spent days in bed afterward, ill, thinking of him, and what she might have done to prevent it. She was too old now for the costs. Yet she was plagued. She wondered which devil-marked trail had led her into this secret life. She was a Presbyterian, after all. She desired neither to be visionary nor to have highly sought-after information. But there they were anyway—stark, vivid, rippling visions of the future.

She had been in the room when Charlie was born. In those days, men considered it impolite to watch the delivery. Poor Luddy had had a very difficult time of it with Charlie, just as the grandmother had had a difficult time with Luddy. After twelve hours of labor, when the child was out, Luddy, hair pasted to her cheeks, reached out to the nurse for the bloody baby. Let them wipe him off, the grandmother had whispered. But Luddy wanted the baby right away. She reached out for him, licking the sweat off her lips. It seemed she was using her last bit of strength to reach out for him.

By the time they wiped the baby down and place him swaddled on her breast, Luddy's aspect had totally changed. Her face was the color of caulk, and her eyes rolling like a horse's, as if she were horrified by what she had done—begin a life, a life that from this moment would only be, in a way, its own undoing. Her hands wavered over the little body as if she did not know the right way to touch him. Her thin white johnny fell off one shoulder, and her eyes rolled ominously toward the nurse who had come to her side, as if to say, Don't, Don't let me have the baby.

Come now, the grandmother had said with irritation, though she herself remembered being frightened of one's own baby. Come now he's just a baby and he won't mind what you do, she said. He's tougher than he looks.

But something had gone horribly awry. Luddy's skin was gray. Can't you breathe? Can't you breathe? The baby, on the other hand, was not crying, was not making a sound, but was lying there in complete cooperation with the vagaries of life. The baby appeared to be listening to his mother's heart. The old woman leaned over and looked at him. He lay, red and in-ured and cooperative, with a little preternaturally handsome face and big ears like his father and a rather patient, scientific expression. Her daughter's breathing was by then very la-bored, and two nurses were now swinging her legs back up into the stirrups and calling urgently for a doctor. On the floor underneath them, a puddle of blood grew. It seemed to the grandmother that the earth had been kicked in casual malice by some great force, some thug of the universe, and now everything was spinning out of hand. The old woman reached out to take the poor red blind baby off her daughter's chest, as they began cutting off his mother's thin gown.

Just then, holding the baby in her hands, the old woman's sight went dark, and she was overcome with a feeling of emptiness so profound that it annihilated the hospital.

She was standing in an open field, a savanna in winter, all of the grasses broken at the stems, snow compressed by boot soles, boot tracks wending off between the frozen hillocks in separate trails. In this vision, wind blew solemnly across the snowy emptiness. In the distance, she heard a search party calling thinly. She was trudging through the snow. She was part of the search party. She was looking everywhere—under logs, bushy thickets—to no avail. She took a sharp turn into a darkened copse of evergreens. Nearby, along the banks of an icy creek, she spied a shoe, a leg propped casually on a log, as a man suns himself in repose. I've found him! she cried into the wind. Over here everybody! She approached frantically, staggering forward.

What she saw was the sort of spectacle meant to freeze all those who saw it in a kind of binding horror. The arms were carved by a knife, the belly was destroyed the same, in the reckless way a hungry animal might destroy. He was coatless, in only a dress shirt and thin sweater, the sweater torn into strips, written on with blood, damp with blood, all of him looking so cold, so tolerant, as if he had been too polite to cry out and had spent the long night dying but not screaming. She staggered backward from the body, cut as it was, lying as it was, throat cut, the head cocked and eyes staring as if appraising a last loveliness, and once again the grandmother became aware that she was standing in a white room, holding a newborn baby. She shook her head violently, keeling to the side, putting one hand against a cool wall, cradling the baby. After a moment, she felt a strong urge to get the baby out of the delivery room. She lifted the baby up and over the heads of the nurses. The baby sailed across the bright lights. Good little baby, said the old lady, in tears from what she had seen. Good little baby don't you worry.

Once outside the delivery room door, she allowed herself one glance back at her daughter, who now lay with a doctor working between her legs, working seriously but not in a hurry, as a man putters on a Sunday. The grandmother kept looking around for a nurse to take the poor swaddled thing to its crib and give it its tests. But they were all consumed with saving the mother and had lost track of the baby.

The old woman knew, however, that her daughter's life was not in danger. Yes, death had been in the room with them. She had stood there and seen its interminable distances. But that search party was not calling for her daughter.

It was calling for the baby.

And now, would you look at that, the old woman thought, there he was, her most beloved grandchild, all grown up and crossing a stage with a piece of cardboard on his head. He kept spitting the tassel out of his mouth, grinning. She remembered him at the breakfast table, his paw in a pot of plum jam. She remembered him carrying a bucket of rainwater across the yard. She remembered him hanging upside down, his hair like quills. Beside her, the girl Alice leapt to her feet when his name was called and clapped above her head. On the stage, one hand in the hand of the dean, Charlie looked for them in the audience and saw her, his dark-haired pretty girlfriend, and he clasped his diploma romantically to his chest.

Maybe I was wrong, thought the old lady. Maybe at last I was wrong! Maybe she would never see such horror in her lifetime. She would die before him, as was natural. Then and there she let herself imagine what she had resisted imagining for years: that he might marry and have children and live a good long time, live to smoke pipes and shuffle about in some old house, and that she had been wrong those many years ago in the hospital and she was just a touched old woman. The pretty girlfriend flopped back into her chair and blushed. Luduina reached over, across the grandmother's lap, and squeezed the girl's hand. Well that just about seals it, thought the old woman. Luddy approves. They might as well get married this instant. Shutting her eyes, she saw the girl in a party dress on a hot day, a large white flower in her hair. The grandmother clapped lasciviously to herself. She was very happy. She had carried her awfulest premonition with her in secret for twenty-five years, and wanted nothing more than to be rid of it.

$\backsim$

"Alice? Alice?"

"Yes?"

"Wake up," he said.

"I'm here." She drew him closer. "A bad dream?"

"No. Alice?"

"But I'm *here*."

He paused. The morning light crept upon the bed.

"Marry me," he said.

She sat up. The sheet fell in a pool at her hips. "What?"

"Marry me. Marry me today. Marry me tomorrow. Marry me every single day of your life. Ha! Will you?"

"Will I *what* exactly?" She was laughing. "Will I—"

He buried his face in her neck. Then he fell back on the pillow, his hands over his face. "No, no. Don't do anything or say anything. Don't move. I'm messing this up. Listen. Would you just—tolerate my presence your whole life? Can I just *be* there? Watch you dress and move from room to room? I'll be very quiet. Please say yes. You don't have to marry me. Just—let me watch you."

"Charlie."

"No. No, you don't have to say anything. I'll scare you away behaving like this. I'm sorry. It's just—"

"Charlie," she said.

"It just overcomes me. You. Overcome me."

"When I was a child, I dreamed of you."

He was motionless on the bed. "What?"

"When I was a child, I dreamed of you." She pulled his hands from his eyes. "I dreamed of you, Charlie Shade, thinking I'd made you up. If I had known you existed, I suppose I would have lived an entirely different life. I would never have wasted a day."

He looked at her.

He smiled. "You dreamed of me?"

"I did," she said. "I swear."

She held him.

"Why are you crying?" he whispered.

"I suspect that you are forced to lose everything," she said. "But maybe. Maybe sometimes they let you keep one thing."

"No," he said. "You don't have to lose everything."

"It doesn't matter." She wiped her eyes. "I'll hide you under my pillow."

"Yes," he said. "We'll hide."

It was July. Outside, the neighborhood steamed from a late-night thundershower. The world bled flowers. Late summer roses gaped at the sun. Alice lifted her dress off the bedroom floor. In the dim light of Charlie's washroom, she washed her hair in the sink with a bar of Ivory soap and twisted it, black and wet, into a loose chignon.

Charlie unfolded the stiff, fresh shirt that his mother had packed with cedar, meant for church. With solemnity, he fastened each button. He drew a comb across his hair. He stepped into the kitchen. Alice was waiting. When he came in, she stood. Below the dripping eaves of the house, doves overslept.

Some people are born again by God. Charlie and Alice Shade were born again by one another. After the judge married them, and they emerged from City Hall into the heat of the rain-washed city, they could hardly remember the old words for things. What was the name of this month? This hot season? What was the word for the cars that wait for strangers? Surely the words would return, but they would return back from the land of meaning, ponderous and heavysweet, like words in a poem. Walking uphill, toward the older neighborhoods where Charlie's apartment was, they tread on a soft carpet of juneberries. Children played in the streets, running back and forth under sprinklers and screaming, for they did not want to go back to school. Charlie reached for a wide white blossom that hung over a fence. What was it called, this flower? He plucked it and held it in the palm of his hand. Alice touched the slippery blossom, murmuring at its perfect smoothness.

Charlie pulled back her hair and placed the flower behind her ear. A wind came up and blew her dress against her body.

July! she remembered, finding the word exquisite. That's what they call it.

July.

Summer.

Taxi.

Husband.

Silk.

Magnolia.

⌒

The dentist died. His office was dismantled and everyone was let go. All Alice was left with was her furry boots and a hundred gorgeous afternoons of unemployment. Back then, waiting for Charlie to thunder up the stairs to their apartment after work, she came to know her own body. In this bliss and idleness she spent hours washing her hair, hours brushing it. She would lie on their bed, one hand absently naming the curves of her newly married body: hip, thigh, belly, throat. Hand on her mons, she petted the humid softness there. Only after she became tired of this would she take up a book, lift the window, light a cigarette. Hours, she would watch the people moving like soldiers and soldiers' prisoners out toward their schools and offices. She resisted pitying them, that they were not she. Then she would laugh out loud, for since when had she become so self-important? Her mother would have been horrified. Did she think that just because she was married now, there was nothing left to worry about?

They had decided to give up her apartment and move into Charlie's. Charlie's apartment was on the top floor of an old gray house on a sunny, windswept corner. It was a small one-bedroom affair with a galley kitchen. They slept in the living room because it was roomiest and sunniest. Water stains on the ceiling provided hours of lazy naked speculation. Down the hall, in another zip code, was the actual bedroom. But now that was filled with books. Books were all Alice had brought with her. Books, a reading lamp, a pair of red crushed-velvet curtains, a set of eggcups, and a large tin of Earl Grey. Everything else she left right where it lay, like a woman who'd fled the continent. Her landlord could charge her for it if he wanted. She did not care an ounce. Those days, she was content to drift about the cheerful, beat-up apartment, touching the linens and the wallpaper as newly married women do. Then she would dress and descend the two sets of stairs into the summer air. If the Russian bookseller was around the corner with his card table of dollar books, she'd say hello and touch each of his musty books while he watched her and smoked. Then she would buy as many as she had money for and hoard them, laughing, back up the stairs.

Of course she knew it could not go on forever like that. Which is precisely how she was able to do it at all. She had never been forewarned of happiness, so to her it was a complete surprise. She had a husband of the sort she never dreamed existed—gallant and tender and loyal as daybreak. It was as if she had died and gone to heaven, a heaven where you made love to yourself all day and he made love to you all night, and in between, you read.

She read anything. It didn't matter what it was. She read biographies of obscure historical figures. She read pamphlets of self-published poetry by society ladies who were long dead. She read obsolete scientific research about animal behavior. She read the demi-classics: *Twelve Angry Men* and *Darkness at Noon*, and swashbucklers, *Sarabande*. As a married woman she read more slowly, less searchingly, but with far more retention. All the love stories clicked into place. Toward every heroine, she felt sisterly.

She would have loved to try and write her own stories but in this she ran up against her long-held belief that she was not very smart. She had read more than anybody she knew and possessed a great desire to be smart, but it was still confusing to her how—if she were smart—she had missed college and ended up four indeterminate years later as a dentist's receptionist. She remembered the time at which her friends were applying to college. She remembered holding the applications herself and even taking the tests. Then the slurping sound of the dentist's suction hose behind a partition. She did not understand the logic in between. Just the applications, then the slurping. With several years in between of settling down to soup across from her mother. No college. No plaid skirts and no heavily accented professors and no confessional poetry and no secret confidence.

The fact that Charlie had found his calling made her proud of herself, in the sense that she saw humanity as one team bonded against dark adversarial forces. Two months into his first job at Maynard Psychiatric Hospital, she had come to believe in his work as much as she could. She suspected that his compassion for strangers was something she loved most about him. Did he not love her with the same heart? And yet, early on, she learned that his work was different from any sort of work she had known. It was a particular sort of work that seemed to require the use of all human faculties—the heart, the mind, the senses, the reason, and the intuition, as well as simple physical stamina. At the end of the day, she wanted to hold him as a port holds a ship. She knew that while her days were lazy with bergamot and marriage and dollar books, he had been trying to save people.

She had not gone to college, and she was unemployed, but that summer it did not matter. She wanted to give happiness all the space it needed. She saw how the shards of her life had magnetized around all this, this little apartment, this marriage, this man. For as small a thing as it was, her life felt monumental. She gave it her faith. She even fetched cold trimmings of secrets from the bottom of her heart. She allowed her mind small lapses, and in those lapses, memories arose: a poverty of love, a lost father (that great woolen absence, that transfixing hole). He took her secrets and carried them across rooms like candles. It seemed that the most guarded confession of lovers was that even at their most beautiful they had not been what they seemed, but rather, full of ache, getting on their bare knees as children with only an inkling of what might bring relief to the heart, getting on their knees and praying to God.

～

When Charlie had first arrived at Maynard Psychiatric Hospital, he found it amusing that he had ever practiced going in and out of the revolving doors. Once inside, one forgot one was even there. There was no time, no doors, no oneself. On his very first day, he helped perform a restraint, right there in the waiting room, of a ranting obese man who referred to himself as the General. The General went down almost gracefully, self-importantly, looking up with bold commander's eyes at the army of the group of them, but not before tearing the eyeglasses off the face of the charge nurse. Later, six of them were needed to help him upstairs, docile now with sedatives, just a fat man.

Charlie's job was in Admitting, where he sat in a small, dark office off the waiting room. The waiting room was large, tastefully decorated and strangely convincing. Table lamps gave the effect of a family den, copies of *Redbook* strewn about, a toy chest in the corner. The only thing that distinguished the waiting room at Maynard from that of some family doctor's was the loud engagement of the lock on the main door behind each new arrival, and perhaps also the astonished, staring-straight-aheadness of the patients once they reached their chairs. At times there were upwards of thirty people waiting in the room, but in general the suffering was quiet and ordered. Often a mother or a boyfriend came as companions, looking entirely more stricken than his or her charge. For who in the world would imagine that a person who had just been talked down from a bridge would now be asked to please have a seat in Reception?

In his small, shared office off the hallway, within earshot of these people, Charlie tried to peel through the epic stacks of paperwork as fast as possible and without shaking. Above all, it was necessary to be calm. Calm and engaged—yet efficient. He looked up, smiled. How are you? A grim nod of the head. A disbelieving laugh. A lurching forward of the tearful mother. Next, he tried to focus on the prescribed series of questions he was meant to ask: How had they come to be here today and Did they have insurance and What were they experiencing right now and Had they been to Maynard before and Did they have any history of trauma for example physical or sexual abuse or a history of hurting themselves or others? Some of the more acute patients, already having been medicated straightaway, like the General, appeared to just have been airlifted from wrecks. They were doubly remote, on a very small island with the tide coming in.

A week or two at Maynard had gone by before Charlie realized that, sitting as he was, in a crappy, unlikely office at a shared desk, he was there—at the seam. He was there. Shocked by the notion, he tried to shake off his doubt, his tentativeness, and found himself inclining forward on the front legs of his chair. *How are you?* He began to listen differently, to the shades and underbellies of the answers. He saw that even incoherent exchanges were composed of information. And, like smugglers in prison, these people were trying to give him something to take out with him. They were trying to tell him what it was like. To be crazy. Years of studying at the top of his class and students like Charlie still did not have much of a clue. His preciousness annoyed him. He was there, but could not imagine any further. In realizing this, he kept brushing up against a distrust of sane people such as himself. He remembered his history, his book knowledge: it was sane people who had developed insulin therapy, electroshock. It was sane people who developed surgical lobotomies. (And they actually gave *that* guy the Nobel Prize.) It was sane people who, upon realizing the insanity of all these procedures, eventually decided to deinstitutionalize people they had ruined, scuttling them into buses with a fifty-dollar bill and a pocket comb apiece. Greyhound Therapy. Reaganomics. (And now the news was out that Reagan himself would die demented, a man who in another circumstance might have been left weeping on this doorstep.) But now, in response to this heartlessness, a new kind of paternalism was growing: some people without a stitch of hands-on experience were calling to create new laws that would make the treatment of insanity completely voluntary. As if a psychotic person could be made free and happy by the simple, lordly permission of the law.

Was that what he could do—listen? He had ears, enormous ears. He would turn his head this way and that in the small hospital bathroom mirror. His assessments took longer than they should have, but he listened. He was good at that. There was something about him. The tearful mother leaned back in her chair. The patient sighed.

One day late that summer, Charlie found himself sitting across from a young man who looked strikingly familiar. The boy was nineteen, with handsome dewy black eyes and the physicality of an athlete, despite the fact that he was emaciated beneath his clothes, sitting upstairs in the medical wing with an IV. Charlie grinned, about to say hello—Hello, Mark—but with the boy's hand in his grip, he shuddered, for his brother Mark lived far away, in Colorado, in memory, and this boy was not he. He was a wrestler, this boy explained, well he used to be. Had Charlie read the boy's name in the sports section? the boy's father asked beside him. State champion in his weight last year. Charlie smiled, looking at the boy. Congratulations, he said. Glad to meet you.

The boy told his story. And when his parents left, he told the rest of it. Charlie had a difficult time ending the story of the boy who looked like his brother. He had a hard time turning around and heading back to Admitting, leaving the kid to the other social workers in the psych ward who did not yet know him and to whom he did not look familiar. He did not like the thought of the boy alone at mealtimes. The boy was very real to Charlie. Realer than his brother, finally. Through him, Charlie saw that darkness did not float around hunting for the weak and susceptible, but was there already, on earth, born with each of us, born within the most beautiful of us.

The patient files were right there in the break room, a wall of metal cabinets full of session notes from ward therapy and medical notes. Charlie had seen other people perusing these files. He had seen many other people perusing the files, yet he waited until he was alone to do so himself. Each day, he read approvingly of the wrestler's progress. He felt consoled that the boy was still telling his story, still talking. He read approvingly of the "strong observing ego," that self which was born when the firstborn self dies, and which could save a man. If the boy could observe himself, then he could measure himself as sane or insane—he could be like the sundial, which in combination with the sun makes time.

One day after work, Charlie paused at the revolving doors with his car keys in hand. He turned around, climbed the stairs to the third floor, and tapped on the glass of the nurse's station. The charge nurse, beset with adult acne and a crush on Charlie, buzzed him in, and noted him as a visitor, because after all, in-take clinicians weren't known to take such a continued interest in clients on the ward. "He's in the TV room," she whispered. When the boy saw him, he smiled his slight, tweaked smile and stood, offering his hand, and Charlie enjoyed watching him move his renewed body, reaching up to the TV to turn on NASCAR. They watched the race and laughed and talked a little.

One day soon after, passing a window that overlooked the parking lot, Charlie saw the boy walk across the parking lot with his gym bag in hand, his father's hand on his shoulder, get into a long, clean American car, and drive away.

And that was that. And it wasn't. He could feel these people lodged in his throat, in the shade pools of his heart. He carried them around, knowledge he had swallowed. Yet, with each click of the lock, they kept coming. They did not stop. He wondered if, deep inside, he thought they would stop coming if he was good enough. He sensed that he was rapidly using the store of strength that had been placed in his soul many years ago in Mattoon as in a granary. He only had a little fear about it. He was hoping he would soon learn the more practiced and detached behaviors of the staff at Maynard. Such behaviors were unnatural to him, although he understood them academically and agreed with them.

A woman's wet hair. What was taken away during the day was given back in the bower of Alice's crow-black, shower-wet hair. In bed, above him, she bent over his chest like a priestess, endowing a long-dreamed-of feminine absolution. Every domestic hour was a reminder. She was a wellspring of unaffected passion and sympathy. She was spiritually larger than he somehow. Quiet and uncluttered, she was free from the selfish need to fascinate. She was Alice.

She loved stories. Charlie had never met anyone with as great a capacity for hearing and standing stories. And everything would have been all right if he could only tell her the stories that were collecting in his throat and heart. Prepared to repeat each secret, he had turned to her many nights, her face orchid white in the moonlight. But aside from being an amateur's move, it was actually illegal for him to divulge anything that his patients told him in Admitting. There was a whole department in the hospital devoted to the squeezing out of information, and a law awaiting a vote in the legislature was making it worse, the hospital abuzz with the dread of it. They had temporarily locked the files in the break room. As someone who had always followed rules, Charlie had assumed that the rules were just, rather than seeing that the rules suited him.

But now, for the first time, there were two rules in competition—the rules of the hospital, and the rules of their married world. At work, Charlie sometimes looked around him, suspicious. His fellow clinicians were married. They had friends and mothers and drinking buddies. He thought that surely they must confess it all sometimes. Sometimes they must tell long, indulgent, and completely revealing stories. He promised himself that he would speak to his supervisor about this temptation. But his meetings with the famous Stephen Gregorian often took place in hallways and devolved into sports talk and their shared admiration for the Chicago Bulls. Gregorian was intimidating and Charlie wanted to appear special to him. Apparently, the man had simply accepted the rumor that Charlie could handle anything, and oftentimes clapped Charlie on the shoulder when he came down to Admitting, as if Charlie was his right-hand man, not some green recruit straight out of graduate school. He needed help. He did not need help.

At night, for months, Charlie attempted to speak to Alice in clinical generalities. But it became too frustrating. For the suffering was not in the generalities. The suffering was in the details. It was in the names. Hal—Hal Kramer. Paula Helen Lucas. Vincent Santopadre. The hometowns—New Bedford, Scituate, Ware. It was in the color of a mother's dress. The name of a cat or a car or a doll. Holding it in kept it small and tight and unreal. The telling honored it, and turned it into beauty.

        ⌒

There was a young man who had developed the habit of talking to himself. He was a striking young man, with black hair and black eyes, and a closely cropped haircut that showed the form of his well-shaped head. He was a good student and a very good wrestler. His coaches liked his focus, his timing, and his appreciation of obscure rules. He had been accepted at the state university on a full wrestling scholarship for the following September. But first, everyone was counting on him to win the State Championships in his weight.

He was popular in high school. He had girls climbing all over him like ants on a split peach, and he was cordial with them, but not encouraging, which only made them crazier for him, until walking down the halls at school he had acquired an almost mythic glow. As he passed, girls would hush and lean against their lockers thinking, Just one night, give me just one night of your life. They would have impaled themselves on swords for just one night with him, and you could almost hear all those pieces of sinew that still endeared them to notions of chastity frying up.

This boy had never been a talkative person. He preferred to express himself not through talking but on the mat, or on a field with a ball, and sometimes even with a pencil or a paintbrush. Which was why it was odd when he began talking to himself, that his downfall would be inaugurated by an urge to speak. He first experienced it that winter, at the end of long practices, Coach hoarse from shouting——a kind of lonely, far away, extra self——

Kramer! Coach would shout. Kramer! You think you can win with escapes? You going to try this horseshit with McMurray at States?

And the self would respond, not with insight, not even with an answer to Coach, but with a breathy, queer, studied commentary: right hand, left hand, your head, mat, space, moving. . . . This muttering someone was not himself, but was so like himself that he first thought of the presence as Myself. And perhaps because he was so focused, so sure to win, the coaches crowding out the sky even as he dreamt, this narrator of his life lost its ability to recede. Instead, it made itself useful during the day. Walk down the hall, *Myself would say to him at school.* Open that box. Look inside.

His habit of hearing a separate thinking self within himself was something Hal could hide. States was fast approaching. He had to cut weight. He had to focus. He had to best his best efforts. As he walked down the hallways, those hallways he lit with his own beauty, Hal looked hard into the faces of the other boys, sure that they also harbored secret soul cultures, strange private worlds, intricately folded, each man a beautifully, cruelly folded castle of paper.

Hal's English teacher was new to the school. He was a young artiste type who spent half the class turned away from the students talking miserably to the window. The young artiste looked out the window with such faithfulness that it seemed his lost future was out there in the parking lot, leering out of a car. The artiste assigned the students a writer called Proust. Proust was not on the Cross High reading list. Proust said a lot of things. Proust went on and on. Pretty much everybody fell asleep. Hal himself didn't normally listen too hard in English, a subject in which you could sew up a B just for knowing the basic and unchanging rules of grammar, but that semester, when Myself began to whisper, and States was coming, and the world itself was endowed with some astral, kaleidoscopic significance, Hal listened to Proust. One thing Proust said—and this was a line that affected Hal—he said, *It's a wonder we wake up in the morning and remember who we are.*

This statement made Hal feel better about waking up in the morning and not remembering who he was. It was hard to be precise. Because soon, the pressure inside him, having nowhere to go, started to spin, in a circular, downward, centrifugal motion, the energy inside him growing, becoming bolder, more quixotic, and less reliable, sometimes making grunting or crying noises instead of its normal, objective commentaries: Ram. Crush. Rush. Faster. Faster! Cockroach! On the mat, where he had normally felt most like himself, Hal now felt his pupils loosen, his mind expand like a lung. Across from him, his practice partner's eyes glowed like tropical fishes. The pipe-woven gymnasium ceiling had no end.

On good days, he believed himself endowed with a special power, as if he had forced his hand into the core of meaning and turned it inside out like a shirt. Endless thoughts filled the increasingly formless hours of his day. He felt himself becoming—despite his fruitlessness—a kind of intellectual. He had always liked the dampered quiet of libraries, but now he sought them out, shouldering his backpack, removing books between which he saw a very private connection. His English teacher, the miserable artiste, had noticed him hanging around after class and encouraged his reading, and Hal found that reading and then drawing little pictures of clouds comforted him more than wrestling, and so once or twice he stayed home from practice in order to read and draw pictures. When his coaches became angry, which normally would have worked with a boy as mannerly as Hal, he snapped back at them, wiping the spit from his lips and checking to make sure it was spit and not blood, such was the feeling of rupture or deflowerment by the anger coming up his throat.

After all, one could only go so long without screaming. On bad days, he felt that someone had raped him and impregnated him with spider babies. He did not want to be abandoned and left to raise a thousand babies. Soon he found he was no longer able to read Proust (for the sentences kept dropping into the binding), so he went to the library where he found an abridged version of certain Greek mythologies with pictures, pictures that depicted birthing of whole adult beings from the heads and knees of other adults. He was only slightly relieved to find a precedent for such phenomena. He was equally distressed to discover that he had begun to talk in ways few people could understand, using all those wasted literary allusions, and he came to see that knowledge might comfort a person personally but it alienates him socially.

As when, on a date with the butterscotch-haired Miranda R____, the finest of a young group of pretty and lustful sophomores, Hal tried to explain the story of the swan raping Leda. They had gone to Friendly's for dinner and then driven to an overlook where they were greeted by a cold ocular moon, the sort of moon that made people prone to telling strange stories. Looking out the windshield, Hal began telling the story of Leda and the swan, but Myself must have finished it, telling it edgewise and slantwise, and adding some things he'd been keeping to Himself, because there was something about Miranda, maybe, that was possibly sympathetic. But by the time he thought to look over at Miranda, she was crying. She was weakly trying to scratch her way out of the locked car. Instead of feeling sorry, Hal sat there and watched her, patient, surprised, as she ripped up her fingernails over nothing, over a story.

Miranda. Miranda, he said gently.

But she wouldn't listen.

Miranda, are you crying because you think that a swan is going to rape you? Listen, a swan is not going to rape you. Miranda. You should get more used to hearing crazy stuff. Crazy stuff won't hurt you because you're still so young and pretty and your hair——he reached over and touched it fondly, paternally——your hair is like spiderwebs.

He said this all very softly.

He said this all very softly, but Miranda continued to sob. She was trying to pinch up the door lock, but it kept slipping out from between her fingers.

Hal leaned his head backward against the glass, watching her. With some sympathy, he saw that Miranda was infinite Mirandas.

She herself was split and refracted and folded, one moment leaning against her locker with hawk eyes and the next moment blubbering senselessly. Maybe, he thought, everyone had a Myself, and a person was not one person but a conversation, and that maybe love and human friendship with others was not possible because how could you share that conversation, and maybe even the ultimate love was the love between you and yourself, no matter how sick and dark and suffocating, like Proust in his padded rooms with his book and his nosebleeds and his happiness.

Relax, Miranda, he said. Hey. It's all right. Just concentrate on your objective and imagine success. Demonstratively, he shut his eyes, took a deep breath, and her screams became softer in his head. Self-control, he sighed. Self-control, focus. Determination. He thought about the ancient Greeks and he heard the knuckle cracking and throat clearing of a very bored crowd waiting for him and how of course he would never win with escapes, but then he spread his arms, he pictured himself as the falcon, calling, called to, approaching.

And that's when Miranda raked him with her fingernails.

Instinctively, the pain caused Hal to perform a takedown. He pinned Miranda against the passenger door by both wrists, her hair pressed in wavy golden trees against the wet window. She stared up at him, frozen. They had one another's attention. Hal was attentive to the difference between the feel of her body and the body of a man; he had yet to make love to anybody; he suddenly felt enlightened by the body of a woman; he was pierced by the awful possibility that he could share his conversation, that probably anyone could. His eyes filled with vinegar. His arm throbbed. Miranda appeared to be holding her breath. He could not tell if she was there with him or not. He felt nauseous, imagining her there. He had her pinned, but he was the loser, awfully; the lights of the distant rowhouses glimmering below spelled out the word SHIT. Of course he was going to let her go. Of course he was. It was only that he lingered one moment too long watching her and *imagining her, not him inside her but her inside him, before he looked up and saw, through the steamed window, the horrified faces of a couple of kids from school who had come when they heard the screaming.*

⌒

How did they punish him? They punished him by pretending he was dead. When he walked down the halls now, his glow was somehow ghostly or carcinogenic, and no one spoke to him.

Little did they know, in his apparent exile, Hal was not lonely. His world merely became more tightly secured—a smaller, denser, louder world of which he was the governor, jurisprudence, and standing army. He slept deeply now—long, worried-over, nights and days, his arm thrown over his eyes.

Because he did not really harm Miranda, they could not expel him from school, so instead he was taken up to the veranda after school and beaten by some of his friends from the team, guys who had done far worse to a girl than tell her a story. They did not hurt him. That is, they hurt Hal but not Hal, and everybody was so supportive as he lay in bed with a concussion, his mother rubbing his hairless chest with Ben Gay and cooling his food with her own breath.

There weren't a lot of questions remaining about wrestling after that. Hal had not attended practice for weeks anyway. And so his mother didn't make him return to school and his father didn't make him return to school, though he did remember, in his fog, a visit from the miserable artiste English teacher, who was suddenly standing in the doorway of his bedroom, miserable lank hair wet with rain.

Bonjour, said Hal, surprised.

Bonjour, said the artiste, smiling miserably, Quel jour de merde, no?

The artiste sat awkwardly atop the radiator. He pushed back his dirty hair and looked around the dark, wood-panelled room.

Well, said the artiste. Maybe you're wondering why I'm here.

He sighed and opened his hands in a resigned teacherly fashion, and then proceeded to talk at length disregarding the use of periods. He said that he hoped Hal was feeling all right and that he would come back to school soon where he was missed (missed by whom?) but if by chance he did not come back to school, the artiste wanted Hal to know that life was school enough, and a brave enough man could teach himself by listening to himself (listening to whom?) and that many a young man throughout history had saved his life in this manner, although maybe it sounded weird for a schoolteacher to say you don't need school. It started to rain outside and Hal watched the leaves pling backward. The artiste leaned forward a little. You were a good poet, the artiste said, his eyes wet. They let it rain there for a minute.

Then the artiste said he guessed he was being overly personal here, but he wanted Hal to know that he himself had seen hard times at Hal's age, real dark times of bad thoughts and remarkable misery, and the only thing that had saved him, the only thing that made him feel that life was not a miserable franchise of hours, was the beauty of a word on a page. Everything else was imperfect.

May I remind you? he asked.

Hal scooted over on the bed and the artiste sat down, smelling of clove cigarettes and cheap Chinese food.

Sit up, said the artiste. Would you please?

Hal sat up. The artiste drew a couple words, with an affectionate flourishing motion. Then he said to Hal, Here.

What? said Hal.

I'm going to put this pencil in your hand.

I don't want it.

Go ahead.

I don't know what to do with it.

He covered Hal's hand with his own. Hal felt the heavy added weight, and fought the urge to call out for help. But the sun was

*going down, and the room was taking on its tomblike quality, and
so he let his hand be led.*

*They sat there for a long time, drawing words together, the sun
burning in its grooves. Closing his eyes, for he was so very tired,
Hal gave in to the motions and curves that created, in their innocent, blind meandering, something that meant. This one shaped
like a girl, this one shaped like a boat—were they accidents or
were they the one true salve of the burn? Something about the
artiste's fervor gave him faith, faith that when we died, we might
not vanish altogether but be buried in our poems.*

Bedroom
Headache
Mother
Evening.

⌒

Autumn came with the sound of tubas and whistles and
school buses blundering through the streets. A certain kind of
light broke across the city in the mornings that stirred conviction. Plans were laid. Locks were broken open. The tacit became explicit. The mother said to the child, I love you no
matter what. In her mind, the child swore ferociously to get a
gold star today, to be worthy. And Alice Shade stood by the
window in a calf-length plaid skirt that she had not worn
since she was a senior in high school, brushing out her hair.

She was finding it funny that just as the children in their
pullovers were going to school, so was she—twenty-four years
old and a college freshman. Her class wasn't until seven in the
evening and she was already dressed. She turned in a circle,
half-wanting Charlie to wake up. Then she could not help herself and fell into bed beside him and wanted to be looked at.

"Charlie," she said. "Charlie. I—um—I have something

important to tell you." She shook him. One eye opened. "The cigarette lighter—if you can believe it—was invented *before* the match."

He groaned, turned away.

"It's true," she said. "Just wanted you to know."

She lifted the pillow off his head. Underneath, he lay flattened against the bed, pretending to be asleep. He was wearing his favorite red long johns with the trap door in front.

"You look so cute in those jammies," she said.

He reached around and grabbed the scruff of her neck. She screeched, tumbling over.

When he was upright and had her pinned on her back to the sheets he said, "They're not jammies."

His face was imprinted with sheet wrinkles, his hair, stiff as flax, was mashed on one side. He smiled.

"Look at you," he said. "You sexy coed. Where did you get that skirt?" He let go of her wrists and sat back on his haunches. "Listen, don't let any of those Jolly Rogers near you tonight. You promise?"

Alice gazed upward. "I only have eyes for you, my love."

"You're goddamned right you only have eyes for me," he said, laughing.

He leaned down and kissed her.

"I'm proud of you," he said. "You're going to be great at college. You're great already. You deserve everything you can get in this world. It was made for people like you. You're what God meant. That's what I've decided. All the accidents, the atrocities. But you're what he *meant*."

She pulled him close. Her arms around his neck, she watched his back move with his breathing. Pigeons scratched in the gutter outside. You never knew what you were pining for, she now knew, until you had it: someone to find you incredible, just once. Not what you did, but yourself as a fact— you, on a bed, in a room. His forehead met hers. His lips, warm and chapped with sleep, found her brow, her nose, the corner of her mouth.

Beside the bed, the old rotary phone began to ring.

"Don't get it," he said.

She reached for the phone, "Hold on," she said. "Stay there. Don't move."

But as she brought it to her ear she felt the air charge with the sound of foghorns and the swiftly changing light of seaside places, and she heard the sound of cheap roller skates, and then she realized that the gust of memory was proceeding the voice of Marlene Bussard, her mother.

"Good morning, darling."

Alice sat up. Charlie slid onto his elbow. In Alice's mind, the high changing skies of Gloucester cast sunlight into the old china cabinet and its collection of sherry glasses.

"Hi, Ma. How are you? Is everything all right? It's so early—"

On the other end, the woman sighed. "Ultimately yes. Yes, everything's all right in the long run. But the short run. The short run is another matter. But tell me first, how are you? Wednesday says hello. She misses you."

"I'm good. Very good, actually. It's good to hear your voice."

As she said it, Alice marveled that this was true. She wanted to brag to her mother. She wanted to tell her mother about her night class. She wanted to tell her what it felt like to have a man say, You are what God meant. She thought perhaps she should not tell her about either, but all at once she knew it was already written that she would tell her about both. She remembered herself as a child, how she had carried her gold stars home from school as if they were cut jewels on velvet. There had always been some perversity in this, for they were only stickers, and her mother was never effusive, never said quite the thing she hoped, never a simple, nice thing that a child could see clearly without stepping backward.

"And how is Charlie? Is he still enjoying his job at the nuthatch? I feel like I haven't spoken to you in *ages*."

"You mean the hospital?" said Alice, turning her back to Charlie, who yawned and gave up waiting and slid off the bed toward the bathroom. Marlene sneezed. "Mother. If you're allergic to Wednesday, then don't pet her."

"She just leaps upon me. She *assaults* me." As if she knew they were now alone, Marlene spoke more confidentially. "Listen, darling, I have a bit of news for you. I wanted to tell you—not to alarm you—I just got a call from the doctor's office and they've told me I'm suffering from a toxic reaction from the drugs they gave me for that skin rash *last* month. The rash I got from listening to that homeopathic you-know-what. I wanted to tell you and not alarm you, mind, that I'm going to the hospital this afternoon and I'll need to be pumped out or some such thing. They take a little tube and thrust it down my nose. It's medieval. It will cost me five hundred dollars. For this, I pay them?"

Alice stopped and listened carefully. "That sounds serious."

"Serious to whom?"

"Will you be under anesthesia? Is someone going with you?" Alice fingered the back of her skirt where she discovered a silky panel of her underwear. The skirt was too tight. The zipper had split. "I mean, is someone going to take care of Wednesday?"

"The other girls are at work, of course. I've gotten the day off. I'll take a cab to the hospital. If it goes well, I'll be home this evening. But they may keep me overnight. If they like me."

"Is this—Is this related to the other thing? The mercury poisoning?"

Charlie groaned loudly in the kitchen. Alice turned toward him and scowled. The mercury poisoning was before the rash; it was from eating too much tuna fish. And before that, a possible glaucoma. Crampings, poisonings, rashes . . . Alice knew well the litany of things that had gone wrong with her mother in the past year and a half since she'd left Gloucester. Sometimes it was all she and her mother talked about. She listened carefully to her mother's health reports only because she believed they weren't the true point of their conversations. She knew they were talking about something else, some deeper subject. But what? The failure of this true subject to reveal itself made Alice insecure—perhaps the little lump *would* lead to blindness.

"I'll come to Gloucester," Alice said. "I'll drive you to the hospital in your car."

Charlie stepped into the room, his mug limp in his hand.

"What?" he said. "*Today?*"

"Nonsense," said Marlene. "It's such a long trip."

"It's not a long trip. You think it's a long trip because you hate the bus. I don't want you taking a *cab* to the hospital."

"No. Now look; I'm sorry I even told you."

Alice turned toward the window, her back to Charlie. "But what about Wednesday?" she said, almost shrilly. "Who will take care of Wednesday?"

"All right," her mother sighed on the other end. "Maybe you could sit with me at the hospital for a bit. You could hold my claw."

Alice looked behind her to see Charlie, silent, his back set rigidly, receding down the hallway to dress for work. She closed her eyes, relieved.

"It's settled then," she said.

༄

The bus lurched and backed out of the lot, leaving Charlie staring after it, his ears pink with sun. She would not get back in time for her class, he had said. But she would, she *would*, she could go straight from the bus station up the hill to the campus on her return—look, she'd even brought the English Canon with her—a textbook the weight of a concrete slab.

But now, at her feet, on the bus floor, the English Canon lay looking rather out-of-place. A man in the seat behind her was violently devouring an apple. The city receded behind the bus and the small towns passed by familiarly, and Alice began to have the sensation of traveling back in time. She would not have been surprised to see the cuffs of her shirt grow, her limbs shrink, until she was the size of a child, and ribbons would sprout from her head, and that when she got off the bus someone would have to help her with her bag.

She liked arriving to Gloucester via the highway. There was a big wind-scoured hill and then you came around it and *blam*, there was Gloucester below you, sitting at the feet of the slate gray ocean. Nothing breaking the horizon. Just foreverness. And all the milk trucks and oil trucks and bread trucks of Gloucester labored up and down the hills and hoards of seagulls hovered at the mouth of the swordfish cold sheds and covered the quayside cranes. And the working people could not stop working and winter was their favorite because it was harshest.

It was a short cab trip to the tall pink house. When she arrived, it was only midday. Over the street, the clouds passed low and fast, and the street blazed with light as she stood there with the English Canon. The windows of all the tenement houses glinted. The houses were tall and without yards, the vinyl siding white and pink and pistachio green. Then the clouds swept over the sun and the street became dark as evening. It was so familiar, so physically known, that she almost felt her mind drowse; she placed her hand around the heavy doorknocker.

But her mother was already there, behind the storm door. Alice was confused to see Marlene looking so well. Against the wintriness of her skin, her mother's still-dark hair looked almost chic, hanging neatly just to her shoulders, both sides swept back with mother-of-pearl combs. She wore a new shade of lipstick. Alice balked, looking over her shoulder. But the cab had already disappeared.

"I've made myself up!" Marlene Bussard laughed. "Isn't that an eccentric thing to do? I don't know why I did it. I was waiting for you, and so I made myself up like we were going to a party together."

Alice looked at her mother's thin, erect body. She wore what she always wore: a straight navy skirt with sensible shoes, a high-collared shirt that was cinched at the wrists, a cardigan over her shoulders, the color of almond paste. Alice glanced behind her into the darkness of the house, the plants making exaggerated jungle shadows on the far wall.

"Well," Alice said, suddenly not wanting to go in. "Shall we get going?"

"You don't want a cup of tea first?"

"Tea? I think we should go to the hospital, don't you? Isn't there some level of urgency?"

Marlene sighed. She pressed her lips together and looked out at the windswept street. She had her Charles Bridge expression on.

"Come on," Alice said. "Go on and get your bag. No need to be scared."

"I'm not *scared*—" her mother said, but did not qualify.

Marlene disappeared into the house. Alice could hear her talking in a low, threatening voice to the cat. She reappeared in the doorway with a small leatherette bag.

"Well," she said. "No need to drag it out I guess." Now her expression was that of cheerful resolve. She sighed girlishly and just then, as if in cooperation, the clouds moved off the sun and bathed the street in light. Marlene inhaled through her nose. "What a beautiful autumn day," she said. "For me, that is. Not for everyone surely. A beautiful autumn day according to me. At least for now." Satisfied that she had whittled the statement down to the exact thing she wanted to say, Marlene looked at her daughter. "Shall we?"

⁓

Thinking of moral relativism, Charlie ate his Egg McMuffin. He was wondering if, in the course of his studies and his work at Maynard, he was losing the ability to judge things. He could still judge things, but judgment itself seemed empty, symbolic, inessential. He did not know anymore what good it did to judge a man who, for example, cut holes in the walls of his house because he thought it helped release the evil spirits. Surely holes were not good for houses, but neither were evil spirits. And how could you judge a girl for stealing all the money and clothes of a salesman as he slept in a hotel bed, when he stole from her by not caring who she was or wondering how she got that way? It wasn't just his clients that made judgment seem decorative. Regarding Alice, he knew it was only her goodness and sense of loyalty that had made her do something stupid like go to Gloucester to rescue her mother again.

They had grown up so differently. It amazed him to think of Alice—fat Alice—alone in an attic bedroom in the dead of winter, her mother listening to feminist musicals downstairs. Her father lost, or unknown; in Charlie's imagination this man only existed at the diner counter in an Edward Hopper painting. Charlie's own mother, Luduina, had spent her entire days keeping house so magically that he never saw her do it. He was nine or ten before he realized why the kitchen floor was wet each afternoon. She was constantly drawing something out of the oven, and it did not matter who you were, you could have some. One summer when Charlie was a boy, a laborer named Albin had been hired to help around the yard. Sometime during the course of the summer, it became known to the Shades that Albin had recently spent time in prison for beating his wife into unconsciousness. After this discovery, Charlie's mother had treated Albin exactly the same. The man sat in her kitchen, square-headed and silent, eating her breakfast just the same as anyone. She did not call it relativism. She called it being Christian.

As for his grandmother, she had taught him to take people seriously. For she did not want to be loved in the adorable condescending way one loves grandmothers. In her stooped, sciatic figure, in her many-pocketed aprons, she possessed a kind of awesome omnipotence; she was always there to catch it when the baby fell off the tire swing, always ready with a fistful of citronella at first cough; she swatted the back of your head *before* you swore. She was the best of men and the best of women. Remorseless and gentle, wise and solid. He had grown up around such people. And in the background, a whole platoon of cousins from Springfield who came to visit every Sunday, and his happy little brother Mark, who loved to percuss on an overturned bait tub outside the supermarket for money and then spend every last red cent of it on Lik-a-sticks.

It was said that very wise men, in certain Eastern traditions, could become so peaceful that they transcended their selfhood and disappeared. When they walked, even the heaviest of them left no footstep. On Sundays, they had walked— Charlie and his father—long walks, across yellow meadows with yellow grasses, to go buy milk or butter or black licorice and a newspaper, which they would promptly shed of everything but the sports section and the funnies, and bring it back the long way, by the stream, sitting to read a while, so that by the time they got home the carton of milk was beaded with sweat, and his mother would look at them unalarmed, for she knew they had volunteered for the errand not to be helpful but to steal away together. Charlie remembered them both, his past mother and past father, as having wonderful, clear presences, strong arms, healthy appetites, and good health that was born of a lack of neurotic worry. They disliked sweets and movies, and appreciated days that were windy. At moments, they would exchange between them significant looks that connoted an enormous man-and-wife universe that Charlie stood outside of. He and his little brother would stare at this mysterious man-and-wife intimacy, their chins resting on the kitchen counter. Charlie did not know what his mother and father talked about alone. They were always quiet when he walked into a room. With his bright eyes, he kept casting from face to face to catch the secret. He kept waiting to be old enough. But now, he knew, it was nothing you could be told. It was what he had with Alice. That was the secret—love. You were a child until you felt it.

He crumbled up the wrapper of his McMuffin. He tried to believe that Alice was already back on the bus, freed from her mother, studying her textbook. Standing, he realized that across the aisle, through the leaves of a plastic plant, a girl was staring at him and had been for some time. He noticed her because her eyes were the color of amber, almost yellow.

"Hi there," he said.

She paused a moment, eyes glowing with interior purpose, her hands wrapped tight around a soda cup. Finally, she looked away. For a moment, her loneliness was bright and alive to him. A human blaze.

Although when they met again, he would not remember seeing her that day, somewhere inside of him, he remembered her eyes and her loneliness.

⟳

Alice and her mother drove downtown, passing the boarded-up storefronts and the churches and pawnshops and marquees, all of it looking pretty and cheerful in the autumn sun.

The sky snapped shut and then opened brightly above the fast-moving clouds. The hospital, with its steam stacks, manufactured clouds in the distance. The car was as old as Alice, and dragged its undercarriage against every bump. Alice looked over at her mother, whose hands were clasped on her skirt. Her legs faded into the shadows under the dashboard. The woman's face was covered with a soft down of tiny hairs, an aging woman's fur. Hanging from the downy lobe of her ear were gold clip-on earrings that glinted cheaply. Suddenly Alice was struck with a feeling of great, stupid warmth. It was as if something solid and hard in her chest had shattered into big sticky pieces and her heart had become stupid and floppy, like the soft-boiled yolk of an egg. Her eyes welled with emotion. Her mama was ill, and going to the hospital.

"I like your earrings, Mama," Alice said. "They're pretty. Where did you get them?"

"Do you?" The woman's hands went reflexively to her ears. "I ordered them from a television show."

Alice nodded, but she wasn't listening because she had suddenly become so stupid and content, a little girl, and was now only floating along in the car, herself cloudlike and quiet, as she passed the old preschool where she had learned to count. Nothing separated her from the landscape, and she did not criticize the junkiness of the storefronts and she did not remember any other incident of her mother being sick and needing rescue, and if right then someone had asked Alice, Where do you live, she would have said, Gloucester. She looked over at her mother again, her eyes wet, remembering a pretty young woman bending toward her with a cookie. They had been so often alone—no grannies, no grandpas, no cousins. The woman bending down with a cookie was so pretty, it could not have been her fault. If anyone had said it was her mother's fault, she would have punched him in the mouth. The heat of this loyalty burned up the absence of the father.

"Maybe I don't need the procedure," Marlene said suddenly. "I feel much better. I think I've flushed myself out. Do you suppose that smoke is from the morgue?"

They were across the street from the hospital at a red light, and Marlene was looking up at the steam rising out of the top of the hospital. Alice stared across at her mother in the passenger seat. The cloudy feeling tripped away and suddenly it was as if it had never existed. She felt her consciousness gather itself back to a vibrating point the size of a pinhead. Her sight sharpened, and just then the street fell into shadow.

"Absolutely not," said Alice. She pushed on the gas with her toe. "I've come all this way, and you have an appointment."

"Just, just—Just do me one favor, Alice, and drive around the block."

The light changed. Alice pulled toward the hospital.

"Alice," cried her mother. "For Chrissakes."

"Mother. You have an *appointment*."

"Just once around the block!"

The car idled in the roundabout. Above them, a glowing sign read Emergency. Marlene got out without saying a word. She walked shakily up to the entrance, holding her overnight bag, her back erect. The stupid cloudy feeling was completely gone now and Alice felt no pity whatsoever. She watched her mother struggle with the hospital door. She had come all the way to Gloucester on the first day of classes and her mother was going to get that damned procedure if she had anything to do with it. She glanced at the clock on the dashboard, noting that she was well ahead of schedule. In an hour, she'd be back on the bus.

By the time Alice entered the hospital, she discovered that her mother had left the lobby and gone up ahead of her. Alice maneuvered the corridors, passing nurses concentrating below tiny lights, until on the third floor she came quite suddenly upon her mother in a chair.

"Are you lost?" said Alice.

"No, of course I'm not lost," said Marlene. "I'm here, aren't I? Are *you* lost?"

Alice shifted the Canon in its sack from one shoulder to the other. "Have you spoken to someone?"

"Of course I've spoken to someone. What do you think, I'd just sit here?"

Alice sat down beside her mother. The waiting room was barely recessed from the hallway, just a collection of plastic chairs and a side table. A dark-skinned orderly flew across their view pushing an empty gurney.

Mother and daughter sat in a hostile silence. Alice contemplated the idea of reaching over and squeezing her mother's hand in reconciliation. She knew she should do this, but at the moment had no access to a feeling that could sincerely motivate such a gesture. If she did it (squeeze her mother's hand), she knew her mother would snap at her. Her mother was waiting to snap at her right now, but she couldn't because they weren't speaking. Her mother would want to punish her first. For something. For not driving once around the block. For having been soft and stupid and sweet for a moment over the earrings and then changing, like the daylight on the windy street, back into a cruel and abandoning daughter. Marlene would punish her for having been made to confess that she bought the earrings from a television program (*Hello, this is Marlene? From Gloucester?*), for being the sort of woman who had the time to do such things, for being so excited to see her daughter that she made herself up. Love had always made Marlene angry. Most likely, she wanted to punish Alice because she loved her.

Alice uncrossed her legs, tapped the armrest, and just as she was about to do it, to take the high road, to reach out and take her mother's hand, a nurse came swiftly around the corner and called her mother's name.

Stupidly, clumsily, Alice reached out. She nearly tipped her chair over reaching. How sincere it was now, now that the nurse in his green scrubs was calling so harshly for her mother. But Marlene had already stood at the sound of her name, and Alice's hand only grazed the fabric of her mother's skirt.

"You can come with me, Ms. Bussard," said the nurse.

Marlene turned to her daughter, who now stood beside her, pale. She smiled and then put her hand on Alice's shoulder. This was the decisive gesture. Her mother had won. She had won doubly, for now she was going to be put under anesthesia and very slightly possibly die, never to return, and Alice would always be left with her own last act of intransigence.

"Thank you for coming, darling," Marlene said. "You can go now."

"I'm sorry I didn't drive you around the block," said Alice.

"It doesn't matter."

"I love you," said Alice.

"This won't take long," said the nurse. "It's a very standard procedure. She'll be awake in an hour or two."

Alice nodded. She licked her lips. "You know what? I'll wait right here. I've got my book. If it's only an hour or two. I can catch the next bus. The three o'clock."

"Oh," said Marlene. "What are you reading?"

"Foundations of English Literature. For my class. I'm enrolled at Cross Community, actually."

"Oh, how wonderful. How *interesting*," said Marlene. "Good for you. I bet you'll get an A."

"A gold star," said Alice, smiling.

"A gold star."

The nurse coughed into his fist. He swept the clipboard demonstratively down the hallway. Marlene followed him.

Next to the nurse, she looked very tall and elegant and defined against the white hallway.

⌒

She was awoken by a different nurse some time later. She had been dreaming when the nurse clasped her arm with hard fingers. Alice jumped and wrenched herself away. The nurse stood back. She was a big-boned woman with a braid.

"Are you Alice Bussard?"

"Yes," said Alice. "I mean no."

"Your mother's been awake for some time now, waiting for you."

"She's done?"

"Of course she's done. It's a very simple procedure, really." The nurse smiled thinly. "Would you like me to show you to her room?"

Alice rubbed her eyes. She had the unpleasant feeling that the nurses had been ridiculing her while she slept. She looked down at her crotch where the English Canon lay open wantonly. Alice closed the book and stood. What sort of English student would she make, she wondered then, falling asleep over the *Canon*? She smoothed the front of her coat. Following the nurse into the hall, she passed a window that looked out on to Gloucester, and stopped short. The sky was darkening, and across the city, lights rippled windily.

"My god. What time is it?"

The nurse looked at her watch.

"Five thirty."

"Five thirty? Five *thirty*?" Alice put her hands to her head. Then she patted her coat as if looking for a wallet. "I've got to catch my bus."

The nurse stopped. "Do you want to go to your mother's room then or not?"

"I do. I do. I'll come." Alice shuffled behind her, combing back her hair with her fingers. In fifteen minutes, at five forty-five, the bus would take her back to the city and she could reach the campus—if she ran—she would run, she would make it—by seven. She followed the nurse to her mother's room, where Marlene was reading a magazine upside down.

"Hell-o," said her mother. She was propped up on a pillow.

"The anesthetic's not exactly worn off," said the nurse.

Alice sat on the edge of the bed, rubbing her eyes. "How do you feel?"

"Exshellent," Marlene beamed at the nurse. "They've tied me in a bow!"

"Who's going to drive her home?" the nurse asked, flipping a page of her clipboard and touching the tip of her finger to her tongue. "Since you're catching your bus."

"Bush?" said Marlene. Then she put her hand to her forehead. "Is your clash tonight, Alish?"

"Pardon?" said the nurse.

"Sheeze in *college*."

Alice looked at her mother. The woman had one hand on her forehead, but seemed in the cheerful dimness of her eyes to have forgotten why it was there. She lowered her hand and looked contentedly out the small window at the night over Gloucester. Alice reached over and took the magazine out of her mother's hand. She turned it right side up and then gave it back to her mother.

"I'll take her home," said Alice.

"Fine," said the nurse.

"Whash wrong?" said Marlene.

"You were holding the magazine upside down," said Alice. Marlene slapped her thigh under the hospital blanket and laughed.

"It doesn't matter," said Alice softly. "It doesn't matter. I'll stay with you."

"We always do have a nishe time together," sighed her mother, trying to effect a philosophical expression. "We always do. I wash good enough for you. Besides, he wasn't going to marry me. I never told him I wash pregnant. That wash just one big lie I told you."

The nurse clicked her pen shut.

"She's doing fine," she said. "That I.V. will come out in an hour and all you have to do is put her to bed. She'll just have to be more careful about mixing medication in the future."

Alice sat and watched as her mother fell asleep, her lips softly parting. She removed her coat and looked down at her plaid wool skirt, feeling the spine of safety pins with which she had tried to close the zipper. It was a costume. It did not even fit. In a minute, she would go call Charlie on the pay phone and tell him. She went to the window and watched the lights of Gloucester shimmering in the night. Beyond the city was the ocean. There was only one ocean in the world. It was the same big ocean, no matter how far across the world you went.

⌒

The grandmother sat straight up in bed. The strap of her nightgown fell from her liver-spotted shoulder. She looked around the moonlit room, sniffing the air. What was that smell? Pleasant, faint, long-ago. A retired smell, like that of sassafras or pepsin or rosewater. Something she hadn't smelled in years that made her well up with tender memories. The smell had woken her from her sleep, and yet now, in the clarity of night, it faded. The grandfather clock ticked downstairs. She could hear her daughter snoring down the hall. She thumped the night table for the lamp switch. Then she stopped, erect with realization. In the oval mirror opposite, she saw herself, small and cabbage-colored in the moonlight. Slowly, radiantly, in the mirror, the old woman smiled.

⌇

The apartment was pitch-black. Alice reached for the curtains, thrust them aside, and leaned against the sill. The autumn night was cool, but she was damp with sweat. Her mouth tasted sour. On the street below, under the canopy of trees, a black car idled under the streetlights. She rubbed her eye with the heel of her hand. The car pulled away from the curb, the full moon sliding down its hood.

She turned forward, suspicious of something. The black car? The rustling canopy of bat-colored leaves? She smoothed her duvet and tried to curl up against Charlie, who rolled over leadenly. From the back of the house came a soft slamming sound, a loose shutter. She propped herself up on her elbows. But just as she did so, her stomach contracted. She twisted her body toward the trash can, thinking that she would vomit. Suspended that way for a long moment, hanging off the bed with a spool of saliva on her lips, she waited, confused.

She sat up and looked out the window again. The street was empty and normal. Everything seemed normal and yet terribly changed. She felt her forehead. Was she ill? Something she'd eaten? She lay back down, comforting herself by stroking her own arms, but her skin bore a strange hypersensitivity. She could almost feel the individual hairs moaning in their shafts. The scent, in the crook of her arm, was of Band-Aids, a touch of white wine. Bile rose in her throat. She threw aside the covers and slapped a hand over her mouth. But soon the urge passed again, and she sat on the edge of the bed, swinging her feet, feeling better. Charlie was still asleep. She tried whistling a little. But the whistling sounded lonely and strange.

Then, just as she was about to get up and do something useful, for soon enough now the sun would be up, suddenly it came, all the warm viscosity, spilling into her hands. She leaned over the trash can and tried to guide the vomit into the can. It splattered on her feet and on the floor.

Charlie lifted his head from his pillow.

"Honey?"

Alice slumped down against the mattress and sat cross-legged on the floor, wet hands open in her lap. She lifted a finger, unsure if she was done. Her ears were ringing, her heart palpitating, her head ached. She felt exhausted, like a woman having worked all day and night and all day again—lifting, loving, scrubbing, crying, coddling, stirring, shushing . . .

"Oh my God," Alice whispered. Her hands moved across her belly.

Charlie threw off the duvet and came slapping across the floor to her. He knelt next to her and grabbed her shoulder. Dizzy, he fell to the side.

"Alice, honey. Are you all right? Are you sick?"

She looked up at him. His enormous ears stuck out like wings in the moonlight. His eyes were gluey with sleep. She reached up and touched the side of his face. What a strange time to meet, she thought tenderly, in the middle of the night, someone you knew so well. What strange things could be revealed to you, almost insensible things, that they should be happening to you, innocent you, who was just a minute ago asleep like child. The wind rose up, making the trees dance in the window behind him.

"Charlie," she said. "I'm pregnant."

༄

No one could understand how much pain there was in watching one's own child suffer like that, and Hal's parents loved him very much. Because they loved him so much, they did not take him to the hospital. Hal did not want to go to the hospital. He did not want to go anywhere. He lay in his bed with the covers pulled over his head and the windows shut. His parents loved him so much that they did not even attempt to open the windows. They loved him truly, but Hal knew that in order to love him truly they had to despise him as he now despised himself, and this, he knew, was the paradox. If they wanted to support him, they themselves would have to welcome his own death. They would have to become him. They themselves would have to go without bathing for days, rolling back and forth like a corpse coming overseas in a berth, as he was coming overseas in the darkness of his bedroom.

For several weeks after his concussion on the veranda, his head was silent. There was no Myself, but neither was there Hal; there was a certain black lack of meaning. But it would be spring soon, and everyone figured Hal would be up and running when the weather broke.

Then, one morning, he heard something. A voice. Not a voice like Myself but a bigger, importanter voice, coming from outside.

It said, Come here.

Hal pushed aside the bed covers.

Come here.

He sat up. The room was empty.

He waited for the voice to repeat itself, but it did not elaborate. What? thought Hal. Where? He desperately wanted to go there.

Just then his mother came into his bedroom, wearing a green dress and bearing an orange.

He asked her aggressively, Were you just standing at the door? Did you just say something through the door?

His mother smiled. She was supremely patient, and he remembered her as beautiful.

No, she said. I was upstairs watching television with your father.

You weren't standing at the door, talking to me?

No, she said.

I heard something, he said.

You may well have, his mother said. Something outside maybe.

Hal got up and went to the window. He was wearing nothing but dirtied briefs. He had a beautiful back, arched like a bow in a quiver. He must have reminded her of himself as a boy, running away from the bath half-undressed.

He put his fingers on the sill and looked out the window. His bedroom was in the basement and half underground so there was nothing but geraniums to look at. His mother joined him there. There was nothing to look at but geraniums.

I know I heard something, Hal said.

After a moment, bloated ankles appeared in the window. The old neighborwoman was stalking around in her garden with a watering can.

There, said Hal's mother. You must have heard Mrs. Z in her garden. She must have been talking to herself again.

Hal's mother raised her eyebrows. What do you think? she asked.

Hal turned to his mother and looked at her, but did not say anything about how the voice was not Mrs. Z's. He used to tell his mother everything. He did not tell her this.

Do you want to come watch television with your father and me? his mother asked him.

No thanks, said Hal.

Look, she said, I brought you an orange.

She put the orange down on the bedspread where it remained in its perfect singularity. In the darkness, it was not colored orange so was it therefore still an orange? He looked at his mother, as if she were daring him to do something or understand something with the orange, as if she were making a very significant and encoded gesture.

You used to love these, she said, gesturing at the orange on the bed. Let me tell you. I used to peel them and you would watch. You liked to lean over so the spray would cover your face. I had to sec-

tion every piece for you and take out all the seeds. You wanted it all to go on as long as possible.

Hal closed his eyes, rubbing the stubble on his chin. In his memory, he saw his mother's young hands sectioning the orange. He saw the seeds tumble down into the dark grass. But when they fell, they made a thundering sound, like the sound of a truck door sliding shut. TAM. TUM.

I'll leave you, said his mother. No, no. It's all right. I'm just in the way. I'll leave you to rest. I'll leave you with the orange.

She put the orange on the chipboard shelf above his bed, next to his sketchpad and his wrestling trophies. The way she was behaving, moving the orange around, it made him anxious. He was glad she was leaving. He got back into bed, shut his eyes, and pretended to be asleep.

But as soon as she left the room, he leapt up.

What the fuck, he hissed, pacing. What the fuck? Fucking tell me where.

He took off his underpants and threw them against the wall. They made no sound. He balled his fist and shook it until the length of his starving arm shook. He grabbed the orange and smashed it. It exploded, pouring out of his fist.

In that moment, the odor filling him, juice on his lips, Hal stood in the yard of his past, all those fireflies that used to ornament the ferns in the summer blinking at him through the evening, blinking through the dense vegetation, back when he was late, back when he was good, when there was no moon, when he was liked, when he played. When it was late, the light of the fireflies used to signal him home, and before he even saw his house, in which his parents were waiting for him, his old rat terrier would come bounding out of the ferns and run circles around his legs, crossing and recrossing the yards announcing him, as a prince returns to court—Hal, son, wrestler, half-back, doe-eyed child, dreamboat—and his mother would come to the screen door drying her hands and smile, and behind her, in his funnel of lamp-

light, his father, squinting fondly, no sound, no conversation, no need at all for words.

The seeds of the orange crashed into the grass. TAM. TUM.

∼

He was beautiful once. Everyone said as much. They used to say— he heard it many times—they used to say he looked like a Greek statue. His back was swayed, his forearms and hands were beautifully articulated, brown and clean, his buttocks glowed white in the summertime, and the whites of his eyes glowed in the dusk, and the reason he had always been the last child home in the evening was because none of the mothers ever told him to leave, they just stared at him out of their kitchen windows, hands idle over their work, as he kept a soccer ball in the air by kicking it repeatedly with his bronze knee.

His mother was beautiful too. He knew this. But one morning that spring, during his illness, during his first psychotic episode (later, they numbered it, in case there were more) on his way to the bathroom, he'd stopped to look at the photographs displayed on top of the television. There were photographs with people in them, and he knew those people to be himself and his mother and father, but he could not see the people or identify them as beautiful or ugly, and he was frightened, because he realized he had lost the ability to trust.

He stopped reading. He stopped drawing. He stopped believing in colors. He did not get up and join society. Then he stopped eating. He began to waste away in his bed. When he was a wrestler, this would have been wonderful. They always wanted him to be thin and made of steel. They wanted him to be a soldier and stop drawing. Well now, he thought, you got what you wanted. He proceeded this way until he weighed one hundred and nine pounds and was on the verge of death. And when he was on the verge of death, they carried him out to the car and took him to the hospital.

Charlie was following Stephen Gregorian's secretary up a flight of stairs. He had begun to perspire on first hearing the efficient, hostile sound of her skirt. Stephen Gregorian had been director of social work at Maynard for thirty years, through the comings and goings of trends and treatments and threats and scandals, and now had a fat neck and dark rheumy eyes, yet he still commanded tremendous respect with the staff. Charlie had studied several of his books in graduate school. How Charlie had landed Gregorian as his supervisor was unknown to him, but of course it had something to do with Banford. Charlie had been passed along hand-to-hand by these men. And now, he was being summoned, so unnaturally, in the middle of a Friday afternoon. Charlie wiped the spit from the corners of his mouth. He barely knew how to get up to Gregorian's office, and had to follow closely behind the secretary's skirt.

Walking like that, like a child to the principal, he prepared himself for trouble. Why else this formality, from a man who notoriously conducted his meetings on the fly, in elevators, in hallways? Until now, Charlie had taken Gregorian's casual treatment as the highest compliment; he felt he was being trusted. But running through his recent performance in his mind—his decreasing efficiency, his phone calls home, the time last week he had come back an hour late from lunch because he had wandered too far in his reveries—Charlie decided it was true, the quality of his work was deteriorating. When the patients spoke to him, one part of his mind was spinning selfishly on his own life, yet he would nod and say yes yes with a lying disingenuous clenching of the jaws. He had become insincere and transparent. He had become self-centered. Climbing the stairs, dark circles forming under his armpits, he became furious at himself. He was going to be fired. He deserved to be fired. And now, he would be hurting not only Alice, but that little wad of matter, smaller than a mouse's heart—his baby. The unknown personality whom he already loved too much to bear.

Or—and here Charlie actually paused on the step, shaken—the fact that Charlie had told Alice confidential patient information was somehow known to Gregorian. He tried to think of how Gregorian could possibly know. It was just him and Alice and a locked apartment, in bed. He imagined the neighbor downstairs, a taciturn schoolteacher, listening through the pipes. He imagined his mother-in-law, connected to a nineteen-forties–style switchboard. By the time he entered Gregorian's suite, Charlie's undershirt was wet. But there was Gregorian himself, standing at his office door, beckoning Charlie silently, like a playmate across a hedge. The secretary sat down and began to type in her corner.

"Charlie," Gregorian said, his faint accent making Charlie's name sound exotic. "We usually meet downstairs but—" He shrugged.

Charlie shrugged. Almost mockingly, Gregorian shrugged again, and then giggled. He turned and sat with a sigh on a hard leather loveseat by the window, then patted the seat beside him.

"Sit down, Charlie."

When Charlie sat beside the older man, a wave of docility washed over him. In truth, he was exhausted. His shock and excitement over the news of Alice's pregnancy had kept him awake for weeks. At night, he ran his fingers lightly over her side of the blanket. He planned. He wondered. But mostly he just stayed awake. There was just a sense of needing to be awake. As the man, the father, and the vigil. So now, if Gregorian was going to fire him, he would concede. If Gregorian asked him to put a gun to his head, he would have. Stephen Gregorian Stephen Gregorian, Charlie said to himself as if in a dream. He blinked slowly, overcome with an urge to rest his head against the man's shoulder. He turned and watched the man's mouth moving. He studied Gregorian's hands as they rested on his thighs. A wedding ring, so long worn it was nearly embedded in the flesh of the finger, glowed in the afternoon sun. Soon Charlie was thinking of his own father. He felt as if he was being addressed by his father, in that same ceremonial way in which his father would invite Charlie into his study to discuss some boyish transgression. During such meetings, Glen Shade would have a weary air, elegant and transfixing as a man cleaning his gun, and there was always a sense that he'd forgiven you in advance for your sins, but as your father, he had to point them out to you, and scold you, and then you were allowed to have a cinnamon candy and to sit on the window seat in your socks and ask lots of questions.

". . . which is the *point* of this meeting," Gregorian was saying. "So let's us get on with it."

Charlie perked up and smiled. He liked the syntactic construction of "let's us." It sounded hopeful.

Gregorian tilted his head. "Where do you see yourself going, Charlie?"

Charlie open and shut his mouth. Immediately the prospect of being fired came back with more force. He cleared his throat.

"Nowhere, for a while, I hope," he said, laughing stiffly. "I like it here at Maynard, very much. I'm learning a hell of a lot. You know, true psychopathology, firsthand. This is an incredible experience."

"What the hell is so incredible about it?" said Gregorian, shrugging. His neck pouched over his starched collar. "You fill out papers. You check boxes. You guide people around by the elbows. This is a very hierarchical setting. The doctors are the important ones around here. Hm? No? You don't agree?"

Charlie stared. Then, rubbing his hands, he laughed. "Have I made you think, somehow, I'm dissatisfied?"

Gregorian laughed and got up. He took a stack of papers from his desk and put them on Charlie's lap. The cover page read "Division of Mental Health and Management Services: Mobile Treatment Team Program Standards."

"You know of mobile treatment?"

"Of course," said Charlie. "Traveling psychiatric and counseling treatment. Sure."

"Now you got how many hours until you get your license?"

"Still a good number."

"And do you want to spend all that time checking boxes? Or," Gregorian sat again, smiling, "do you want to do something really challenging, really interesting for a while? Where you, as the social worker, have primary responsibilities, make decisions? Don't answer yet." Gregorian looked up at the ornate tin ceiling. "I heard an interesting thing recently. Of course you probably know that at one point, the continents were one big land mass. One land—one island—and all the oceans were one ocean."

"One ocean," said Charlie, nodding.

"Sure. That's what I heard. That means—what that means is—even though the continents just broke up and drifted away from each other, we all come from the same island. You see?"

"Yes, I think so."

"I knew you would. Nice tie, by the way. What are those, geese flying across it?"

"Ducks. They're ducks."

"Now, Charlie, you could have done anything. You didn't go to business school or law school, though I know you could have gone to the best. But no, you chose social work. Social work, you fool. To work for *society*. Your daddy was in—your daddy worked—"

"For the Xerox Corporation."

"Xerox! The ability to make endless copies, like a God! Now why would someone like you go into social work? It doesn't make a lot of sense from the outside."

Charlie shook his head. Gregorian was trying to give him an out by making him see the point himself. "All right," he said, standing. "I think I understand."

"What? You haven't even read the material yet."

Charlie hesitated. "But you said—"

"Wait, wait!" Gregorian fairly screamed, pounding the loveseat. "No! I want to send you over to my friend Bruce Zabilski for a while. The mobile treatment teams. Look—look." Gregorian waved the packet, laughing. "You. Why not? And then I want you to come back and work in my office once you're licensed—here, in administration. Help me run the godforsaken place!" Gregorian sat back against the loveseat, looking at Charlie adoringly. "Don't you know you stick out like a sore thumb here, with your sharpened pencils and your Midwestern manners? Not that we all don't need some sharper pencils around here, but I'm saying you look ridiculous. Waiting around for Goliath or something. Okay? Hm?"

"Okay."

"Read the material! Take your time! Go for a walk."

"My wife's pregnant," said Charlie.

"Well, that's *great*."

Charlie was beaming. "I always wanted kids."

"Kids are *great*. I have six! You'll make a great father. And hey, this job pays more. More work, too, of course."

"It pays more?" Charlie swatted the papers in his hand, suddenly exhilarated. "I'm really excited about having a kid. My wife and I haven't told anybody yet. You're the first person I've told. It just slipped out."

"I'm honored," said Gregorian, clasping his chest. He leaned over and embraced Charlie roughly. Pressed at last against the man's shoulder, Charlie almost cried out with happiness. He was going to be a father. And he himself was pregnant, and the extra-sensitivity that Alice had developed in these weeks—the readiness to weep, the ardor of the skin and stomach, and the ability to detect the thinnest scent out of the air (persimmon! moss! wet dog!)—were his own symptoms. For an instant, resting his head against his boss's shoulder, he let himself imagine that indeed Gregorian *was* his own father, who lived very far away and with whom he spoke infrequently and with hopeless, unshakable cordiality. When the time was right, he would call his mother, Luduina, and with one hand over the receiver his mother would tell his grandmother, and then she would go upstairs and tell his father, and then his father would get on the phone for a short time, and they would talk cordially, and Charlie would shut his eyes and pretend he was resting his head on his father's shoulder, such was the embarrassing tenderness he reserved for this man, the gentlest man he knew. His touch was so light and so gentle, sometimes Charlie couldn't feel it.

Gregorian stood. "Think about it," he said.

"I don't need to think about it. I'll do it. If you think it's the right thing for me, I'll do it. I'm really flattered by your offer to come back here and work with you. Ha!" Charlie laughed, pumping the man's hand. "This is exciting. I'm going to be a dad! It just hit me."

"Congratulations, son. You know, you have a fine future ahead of you."

"I know!"

"Don't you worry. Everything's going to work out."

"I'm not worried!"

Gregorian patted him on the back, Charlie nodding and smiling and unable to move. Gregorian gave an excited little pounce.

"A drink," he said. "A toast."

The man went to his desk and pulled out a bottle.

Charlie licked his lips. "I don't drink. I'm sorry. I'd really love to but—"

Gregorian waved him off. "God forbid, don't be *sorry*. Be happy." The man closed his eyes and lifted the glass. "To the baby. May he be healthy and happy. May he be strong. Wise. Successful." Gregorian looked over. "May he have your *wife's* ears."

Charlie laughed again, wiping his eyes with the back of his hand.

"Did I forget anything?" said Gregorian.

"May he be good," Charlie said. "That's enough. May he just—be good."

～

At the hospital, Hal and his parents had waited in a small, carpeted room with folding chairs. Hal sat in the middle, with his parents on either side, and a baggie full of sugared water hanging from a pole behind him and connected to his wrist by a tube. He'd been in the hospital for several hours and had been seen by several kinds of doctors, and gotten his head photographed and his IV connected, all of it seeming so cruel—not the tests or the needles—but the insistence that his life was this important, to be protected at all costs, when he wanted to die. Finally they were told to go to a separate room on the medical wing, where they waited for a long time. For a long time, nobody came, and the only thing that kept Hal from bolting was that he didn't want to go running down the hallway dragging a baggie full of sugared water.

His mother wore her green dress and ate, with puppetlike deliberateness, the caramels that she had bought in a package out of the candy machine, which hummed enormously in the room with them. His father ate some caramels too. They were all eating sugar together. It was an anonymous and shadowy room, and his parents appeared queer and deceitful and deliberate, moving like circus elephants, but it was also the first moment in several months in which Hal experienced a faint, faint, faint mercy toward them, toward all whose lives were small delicate violets with the whole black sky closing over them. He watched his father eat a caramel. He watched his mother. He liked them, these carnival animals. He smiled. His smile made his father blink back happy tears, not understanding.

Finally, a man came in with a clipboard, breathing heavily. He had thin blond hair and didn't look much older than Hal. His shoelace was untied, and in pulling back a folding chair he tripped over his shoelace, blushing and apologizing, and they all felt rather custodial over him, which was nice because it took the attention off Hal.

The young man introduced himself. He was a social worker, and in charge of interviewing the new patients and helping direct them to the right place in the hospital. He was new to Admitting, but he was pleased to meet with them and help them and he was very proud of Hal for coming to the hospital and for waiting so patiently, because let's face it, everybody hates hospitals, and when you are disoriented, when you are sick, you hate them especially, because they don't make sense, you know, all those hallways hither and thither. Why, said the young social worker, he himself had gotten lost on his way here, since he usually admitted people downstairs.

Do you want a caramel? Hal's mother asked the young man.

Yes, said Hal's father, holding one out. Do. Have a caramel.

Hal's father went to the water cooler and got them all little paper funnels of water.

Thanks, said the young man, wiping his forehead.

Thanks, said Hal's mother.

Hal was looking at all of these gestures and trying to perceive what they meant. There was something absurdly ritualistic about them. They all seemed like components, corollaries: caramels, cups, clipboard. For some reason, at the moment he might have burst out in injured laughter, Hal decided to go along with it. The social worker was flipping through his papers and wiping his brow when, out of nowhere, he looked up and smiled. He put out his hand.

Forgive me, he said. My name is Charlie Shade.

Hal took his hand and shook it.

You got me, said Hal. It's all code.

The young social worker looked at him for a second and then shook his head. Don't you worry about all that, he said. Some things aren't as important as they may seem right now. What's important is this: you're here. Things are going to improve.

All right, said Hal. He focused on the young man's face and eyes. The young man's eyes suddenly sort of glowed and popped out but Hal tried not to get too hung up on that. He tried to just believe. His mother reached out and put her hand on his arm. She was crying.

Do you want to know why your mother is crying? the social worker asked Hal.

I know already, said Hal. It's because of me.

His mother wiped her eyes. She smiled at Hal.

I love you, she said.

Hal knew he was supposed to love her, and yet he knew that he did not love her, but he suspected that he had loved her once. He looked back at the social worker imploringly.

I just don't see what that has to do with anything, said Hal.

Let's just take this one step at a time, said the social worker. We don't have to figure everything out at once. Why don't you tell me the story, if you can, of what brought you here. How you stopped eating. How you got sick. Tell me how you are.

And that's what Hal did.

Looking back, it was the telling of it, like a last-minute angel, that stepped between him and death.

T W O

*O*ne morning in the autumn of the following year, Alice and Charlie Shade became the parents of twins. Small at birth but extravagantly fat about the tummy, the infants were quiet, easily manhandled, and given to sighing, which endowed them with a certain air of forbearance or ennui. They were girls, one fair and the other dark. The fair one's head was a tuft of golden red, like a spring bud, and was endowed in miniature with the famous, winglike ears of her father's side of the family. The other wore a dark whorl of hair and the slanted, subtle eyes of her mother. So delicate were their features, they appeared to have been crafted under a magnifying glass. Side by side in their plastic boxes, they were the beauties of the maternity ward. The sense of conspiracy between them was palpable, and the first time they cried was when they were carried off separately.

During the first few days of their lives, they could not bear to open their eyes. They needed time for the world they had imagined to burn out of their minds. In the dappled light of the apartment's shady canopy, they rested. They preferred to be carried around in car seats rather than be left in the distant nursery at the end of the hall, and were perfectly happy to cry in order to express this preference. When they cried, they cried in unison—one sounding the first note, as with a tuning fork, the other joining in. They were like two old deaf women singing from memory. Blindly they tried to eat at their mother's breasts, pinching her white opulence, reaching with heat-sticky hands for her long hair. She would cry out, their mother, caught in the sticky trap. But just then, out of the blur, a second shape would emerge, a whole other set of hands, to disengage the mother's hair. This soapy headless energy ran around squawking and making their mother's breasts shake with laughter.

Later, at an hour no one could later remember, they opened their eyes and relinquished unreality. Their eyes were bluer than the bluest idea. Roving around the hazy whiteness, the straight shapes and corners, their gaze rested on the face immediately before them. It was a large face, with tiny pins sticking out all over it.

"Alice! Alice, wake up!"

Alice raised her head weakly from the bed.

"They're staring at me," Charlie cried. "They're *staring* at me."

Alice smiled. Her red silk robe was open, her breasts splayed to either side, as one recently ravished by love. "How do you know?"

"They can see! Holy God!" Charlie leaned over the crib, his shirtsleeves wet with dishwater. "Hello, pretty girls. I'm your daddy. I'm your daddy. Yes, yes I *am*." Unable to be still, he scooped up the fair-haired child. The infant's head swooned back into his open palm. He bent over her and told her, "Some day you'll refuse to go out in public with me, but for now I think you *like* me. Be honest. What do you think of me? Don't you sort of like me?" He lifted her into the air. She sailed across the wallpaper, contented. "Is that a smile? Did Daddy make you *smile*?"

"That's not quite a smile," said Alice huskily from the bed.

Charlie lowered the baby to his chest. "Hey, this is life. This is life, Frances Shade. Ain't it grand?"

Alice laughed. "Are you *high*, Charlie? Have you lost your mind?"

He brought the baby over to her. "Look at what I found! Will you look at what I found at the hospital?"

"Don't forget the other one," said Alice.

"There's *two* of them?" Charlie tiptoed back to the basinette. "They gave us *two*?"

He lifted out the other baby, who sailed more skeptically through the air. Up in the air, the baby looked out the window, purple blue eyes fixed on the sunlight.

"What did I say? She can see. Look at that philosophical expression. What are you thinking about, you deeply thinking baby?"

He came and sat next to Alice on the bed and they lay there gazing at the babies. Outside, an ice cream truck came down the street playing its daffy song. It wasn't summer anymore. Nights were already cold. It was as if the ice cream truck was the very last one, lost on its way home from summer.

"Yum," said Alice, collapsing backward on the bed. "Ice cream."

"Do you want some ice cream?" Charlie propped himself up on one elbow. He smelled ointmenty. "Do you want ice cream? I'll go get some for you."

"Don't be silly," she said. "You can't catch the truck in time. Look, it's already halfway down the street."

Charlie looked out the window.

"You want ice cream? You want ice cream? I'll get you ice cream."

He sprang toward the door and swung open the latch in one movement, grabbing his jacket off the hook.

"Don't be silly!" cried Alice, sitting upright. "You'll never catch it!"

But he had already begun running down the stairs, his feet making a drumbeat against the old wood. As he pushed open the outside door, he slung his arms through the jacket. The air was clean and cool. He saw the big clumsy truck in the distance, with a clown face painted on the back of it.

He ran. His strides felt miles long. The jacket made slippery nylon sounds as he pumped his arms. The air was in his mouth and he was laughing. Leaping off the curb, he tore a leaf from a tree and then whipped it to the side. The clown face pulled forward again, and the truck swung heavily around the corner, its flange swinging. *Stop!* he shouted. *I want to buy some ice cream, dammit!* Two kids arguing over a jump rope on the sidewalk stopped and watched him. He could feel them looking after him. Stumbling on a root, he bellowed, and sailed out into the street itself, pursuing the truck. He was going to get that goddamned truck. It was ridiculous, he knew it. But he wanted to run. Suddenly he knew he could do anything. He loved Alice. He was going to be a good father. He wanted to run. He wanted to catch that truck. He wanted to run after the truck and to catch it, and then walk home breathless, her sweet, cold prize in his hands.

⌒

He had been working on the Maynard County Mobile Treatment Team for five months by then. As soon as he had arrived, he had been given a modest caseload of clients with whom he had to meet at least twice a week, but because he liked them and wanted to do right by them, he called almost daily. It was his job to mediate between these people and a host of others: doctors, counselors, landlords and lawyers, bill collectors, bureaucrats, disappointed parents, disappointed children. Gregorian was right about the job—Charlie had far more responsibility. For he was a guest in their lives. He sat on their sofas and drank from their mugs. He appeared to be, in most cases, his clients' only advocate. He took them shopping, he hung drapes, he tried to explain the nuances of social expectation. With one man he even played hostage/audience to a weekly banjo concert. He was responsible for disbursing money to those with poor impulse control, this being the only role in which he felt uncomfortable, as it was often the source of contention. He did not like contention. He wanted to be the kind of clinician that clients could confide in. It was less important to him if they drank or took street drugs than that they called him when the voices were calling for the final payment. He had heard stories from other case managers who had lost clients to suicide. One-minute-too-late sorts of stories. To Charlie, the idea was absolutely unbearable. And because it felt unbearable, it also seemed impossible.

He barely had time in his day to form opinions, but it seemed to him that some of his clients were having success in the program. Therese, for example. Dressed cockeyed, spaghetti-sauced, she was a favorite among the staff, blessed as she was in her manic periods with a beatific charm. When they first started together, Therese claimed at the gynecologist that she was pregnant with Charlie's baby (a claim he was somehow too embarrassed by to write in his daily log, for she was nearly his mother's age for godsakes, and hairy under the chin). But over time, with the fine-tuning of her medication and a new boyfriend from Highgrove House, Therese's existence seemed to settle somewhere within the parameters of the mainstream. In fact, to Charlie, her extravagant ideas had a moral reflection: if she was not Saint Catherine of Cranston, then perhaps he was not everything he thought he was.

George Delgado played the banjo. All he talked about was Miami, where the girls wore nothing but cornhusks, and they all lived orgiastically on rum-soaked cherries. George was fond of making things up, but told his lies with unerring truthfulness, and Charlie, such was his natural fondness for old people, was so seduced by this Latin grandfather that it took him a while to realize George was drunk most of the time. Charlie had not easily recognized the signs: the sociable flush, the scent of Breathsin, the exaggerated spoiling of the poodle Britney. When Charlie finally got it, he was surprised. He knew all about substance abuse, but somehow it was hard to accept that it wasn't just Charlie's company that made the old man so cheerful and voluble. He wondered if he would've gotten it sooner if he knew what it was like to be drunk himself. The case managers were supposed to leave when a client was drunk or high. Leave for your own safety. Leave; write it in the log. Charlie learned to turn away whenever George staggered to the door. But it was hard to write incessantly in the damned log and it felt like tattling: *client visibly intoxicated*.

There was a handful of more challenging cases, the ones insulted by Charlie's very presence, the indictment of it, but all of them had his attention, even the ones who looked at *him* with pity, that he should be so crazy to think they were crazy. Many times Charlie had stood outside clients' houses and tenements waiting for them, knowing they were hiding inside or drinking or avoiding their medication or dentist's appointment or court appearance or haircut, all the various irritating appointments that even healthy people "forgot."

Aside from a problem with lateness, largely brought on by his inborn difficulty ending conversations, Charlie was already a success for MTT by the time the twins were born. He had become known on the team for his reliability and persistence. He was the one you went to in a pinch. There was something about him; he did not feel like a slave. He would not have felt like a slave no matter how enslaved he was. He made the most degrading tasks productive. In order to track down a particularly resistant client, he would sit on a stoop and wait, and the neighborhood kids would stand on his shoulders and pull at his ears and innocently tattle on their neighbors, and in this way, Charlie's complete approachability kept him always in the know, just as it had in the schoolyard in Mattoon. The director of the mobile treatment clinic and his new supervisor, Bruce Zabilski, had taken a liking to him. Zabilski was the sort of man who kept quiet for long stretches, in what seemed like an attempt to offset the frivolity of what most people said. After Charlie had given his first summary in the daily staff meeting, Zabilski held up his hand, giving a sort of poetic beat to Charlie, and grinned a sprung-open, large-jawed grin. Later, the team psychiatrist, a graduate of Johns Hopkins, lent Charlie a copy of *Pragmatism* and suggested they "get together for a cocktail one of these nights." The word "cocktail" was so high class Charlie didn't even demur with his usual explanations. Most of the other social workers on the team were women. They were lifers, not like Charlie, who had an air of someone on his way to something big. He liked them all. He liked women. He liked frazzled working women in particular. They were the pulse sustaining everything, and reminded him of his debt to his mother and grandmother. They drove around in their beat-up Japanese cars in all kinds of weather, reading maps, eating grinders. They had a soft, tired way of laughing at Charlie's jokes. They smoked and smelled of fruit and smoke. These women had perpetual colds, and were often, in between appointments, on the phone bargaining with their children. Pleased by the news of his wife's pregnancy, they had pooled money to buy a Diaper Genie, which Charlie now considered a finer invention than the steam engine.

Charlie's team manager was a broad-faced black woman named Harriet. Harriet had been at the clinic longer than anyone, since the inception of Mobile Treatment itself. A favorite among clients, she was otherwise notoriously difficult to work with. But even Harriet liked Charlie. She called him Champ. Making her rounds in the hallways on the institutional blue carpet, her big thighs swooshing in her panty hose, Harriet would stop by his small cinderblock office and gaze at him with a bemused, custodial look. Sometimes she'd crow, on her way down the hall, "We just can't scare you off, can we, Champ?"

After they gave him the Diaper Genie, Alice nine months huge with twins, Charlie had sat down in his office listening to the bustle in the clinic hallways and the telephones ringing, and realized, with triumph, that he morally approved of his own life. He knew that he had been handed his blessings as a child, but that he had built this adult life with Alice on his own. It was scary to love so much as they did, but they had gone ahead and done it anyway.

Of course, as with all charmed people, there was an under-current of guilt for succeeding so completely. He did not notice the guilt, but he noticed the ease.

But could he be blamed? He had never really failed at anything. Twenty-six years old, he had no enemies, he had never been fired or flunked or demoted, never even broken a girl's heart. Once, in high school, he had been snubbed by a very pretty flutist in the marching band, but thereafter he rather enjoyed circling the marching band during track practice in the spring, watching the flutist in her starched white fez perform her militant steps in the wet grass, while he got to run around and around her in circles, like some sort of guilty sexual thought she was having. In college, he ran cross-country on a team that ranked second in the state, and his teammates voted him captain, and sometimes asked him to read the newspaper out loud on long bus rides home at night.

He could not remember a particularly keen disappointment in his life. He remembered leaving college for a week to return to Mattoon for his grandfather's funeral, and how he was supposed to bring an umbrella to the cemetery but he forgot. When it began to rain, his father turned and said *Goddamn it, Charlie*, and they all stood there dripping in the rain listening to the minister, and a sodden crow had stood on a branch and yawed at his grandfather's corpse throughout the ceremony. It was such a small thing, forgetting the umbrella, but when Charlie thought of his failures, that was what came up. The crow, the rain, the death of the grandfather, all seemed retroactively caused by Charlie forgetting the umbrella. And to have Glen Shade speak sharply to you, well you never forgot it.

But was that all? Surely his life could not have been that serene, that sane. Perhaps life in Mattoon was so quiet that you could not hear the failures. What if, he sometimes wondered, after such a life, he would never really know what it was to suffer? Could he ever really touch the seam? He did not know what it was like to be exiled to the other side. Sometimes, he fingered the paper envelopes of Haldol and Ativan, thinking he should try one. Perhaps they would give him a chance to understand, for a day or so, the molasses, underwater perception of a disabled and drugged mind. A mind so wholly desperate to perceive that it *shut off*.

For he did not find his clients apathetic, even the ones who greeted him with hardly a nod and whose lips seemed too heavy to smile. He did not believe they were indifferent and without passion. Rather, he believed they were some of the most passionate people in the world. Their particular passions drove them to a form of originality that was madness, and no matter what they said, they knew they were mad. Thus the soul shut down, in a sort of self-sacrifice, so that the body might go on, empty but alive. In order not to die of heartache. Such contradiction reduced these people to mere bodies— mute, passion-broken figures, moving from room to room, hour to hour, cigarette to cigarette. He was in awe. For it was a miracle they arose from bed each morning. It was a miracle they attempted to brave a single intersection, what with voices shouting at them to die, to perish, for it would be so perfectly easy to step in front of a bus. And why shouldn't they? From their uncarpeted boardinghouses and the poorly lit back-rooms in which they worked as stockboys and envelope lickers and cage cleaners or in the buses they rode through the rain, why shouldn't they? The future lay broken in a pile of splintered planks. Late those last summer nights, beside his wife's swollen belly, Charlie asked himself, What if you knew there would be none of it tomorrow, no Alice, no babies, nothing but random days of survival without momentum, only nicotine-yellow sunlight, pill bottles, dreamlessness, the barking of a hungry dog?

It was the lucky ones who were meant to take care of the unlucky. This was what his mother and father had taught him, but it was his air and his soil, and every child knew it unless someone taught him against it. The lucky were commanded to take care of the unlucky by God or by the rule of mercy that was left of God. And here he was—a soon-to-be father of twins, a lover of his wife, a man who had said, sitting across from his guidance counselor a decade earlier, that he didn't know what he wanted to do, but he guessed *he just wanted to be good*, and years later, all his boyhood friends off to big cities and developing nations, his brother sometimes disappearing for weeks only to come home with a small vocabulary of foreign words, a gold watch, or a habit of stretching that called to mind lions, and Charlie just as happy as all of them, happier even, to be earning twenty-eight thousand dollars a year and drinking out of recycled jelly jars. Happier to live in a small city that smelled of fish, and to run sometimes, all the way home, and to have the privilege of waking up next to her, she whose love lit his way to the dark places.

⌒

Just after the twins were born, Harriet had come to the door of Charlie's office, holding a file. She pursed her lips and looked at him for a moment. Since he had returned to work, a father now, Harriet had decided to upgrade him from Champ to Chief. She'd even begun to salute him in the hallways. She sighed and tossed the file on Charlie's desk.

"All right, Chief," she said. "Here's one for you. Do you like Southern girls?" Harriet winked. "Seriously, see me Monday with some major league ideas. I don't want no *farm* team ideas."

"I understand."

"I knew you would." She straightened the collar of her blouse. "And I always thought white people said cream rises to the top because cream is white."

Charlie blushed. Harriet liked to watch it. Still, he was flattered—hard-boiled Harriet had fingered him as the primary for a tough case. Looking through the file, Charlie saw that the new client had a typical history, moving in and out of the usual systems: schools, church charities, a stint in the Army that had ended with a psychotic break, and a military hospitalization that must have been, after all that senseless chaos, a kind of relief. She had moved up north from Bellwood, Kentucky, looking for an aunt she never found, and in the process had developed an unfortunate fear of snow. Last winter, she'd been brought, psychotic and starving, to Maynard. A kindly neighbor had brought her to the hospital, and eventually she was assigned to the MTT program. Her assessment noted a host of negative symptoms: she was "apathetic," "withdrawn," and she showed "severe inability to establish or maintain a personal social support system," which was evidenced by the fact that at the bottom of that very page, she had no one in the whole world to list under Emergency Contact. Hesitating over the blank, Charlie wrote his name. He put on his coat.

There were no trees in Norris Park. A developed lowland of mobile homes, the Park ran along a remote stretch of state highway. Charlie had never been there before. He had not known it existed. Lost on the pitted, unmarked roads, crumpled directions in his fist, he tried to steer while rolling down the window. He was approaching a young girl straddling a bicycle. The girl was standing at an empty crossroads, amongst shuttered identical homes, staring at his approach.

"Hi, sweetie," said Charlie to the girl, who wore a big winter jacket and held a lollipop in the side of her cheek. "Could you tell me where Road Four is?"

The girl stared at him for a second. She took her lollipop out of her mouth as if to speak. It was one of the kinds you get for free at the bank.

"I'm looking for Road Four? Do you think you could—" Charlie glanced around the empty village, "—point me in the right direction? You think it'd be easy. You know, one two three four."

Abruptly, the girl put her feet on the pedals and rode away, glancing once over her shoulder. Charlie stared after her, resisting the temptation to think, My girls would never . . . because he knew his girls would also never have to live in a place like Norris Park. He drove on, his red Toyota bouncing in the ruts. Each house was small as a truck and cast geometric matching shadows in the same direction. One or two properties were neatly kept, with plaster gnomes or pinwheels spinning in small gardens, but many had broken shades hanging inside the windows, a trodden piece of child's clothing frozen into the yard. Finally he arrived at a low, mustard-colored structure. A propane tank sat on its side by the front door.

He pulled up to the empty driveway, got out and stretched. As he did so, a figure moved away from the window. Charlie walked across the frost-hardened ground.

He knocked on the front door. When no one answered, he

raised his fist to knock again, but a rather deep female voice just on the other side of the door said, "You're not Harriet."

Charlie lowered his hand. "No," he said to the door, smiling. "I'm Charlie. I work with Harriet. We're on the same team. I've just come to introduce myself—" He looked around. Elsewhere, a door slammed. He could hear the very loud sound of a television. "Opal Ludlow. Did I get your name right?"

The door opened. There stood a trim young woman holding a hammer.

"Hi," Charlie said again, squinting into the plastic glare of the screen door. "I'm Charlie Shade. I'm from Mobile Treatment. Would you like to see my identification?"

The young woman did not reply. She stared at him. Then, self-consciously, in the shadow of her house, she drew her braid over her shoulder and stroked it, looking at him.

"May I come in?" said Charlie. "Even though I'm not Harriet?"

The girl came closer to the door. The first thing he saw when she stepped forward into the light was that her eyes were a surprising color, goldish, the color of sunlight on the ground. She was wearing a tent dress with a man's cardigan over it. Her neck was strangely long and swannish, and her skin dense with freckles that blurred the edges of her lips. She pushed the screen door open with the hammer.

Charlie stepped into the room, which smelled of smoke and sardines.

"You smoke?" said Charlie brightly.

"Yeah," said the girl, adding quickly, "I'm allowed to."

"Sure, everybody's allowed to. My wife smokes. Used to."

The girl put the end of her braid in her mouth and lowered her eyes. She swung the hammer against her dress. She considered her own socks, then looked up. "They get that tobacco from the South, where I'm from."

"Are you from the South?" said Charlie. "I'm from the Midwest myself. Would you mind setting down your hammer?"

The girl looked at the hammer and laughed shrilly.

"I forgot to put it down!" she said. "I was hammerin' on something." She gestured over her shoulder, into the dim kitchen, where Charlie could see burnt pans piled in the sink.

"You cooking something?"

"Yesterday," said the girl.

"Already eat today?"

"Corn," said the girl. She looked at Charlie's clipboard. "C-o-r-n."

Now Charlie blushed, putting his clipboard behind his back.

"Sorry," he said. "I forgot to leave this in the car."

The girl nodded. She pointed to a chair. "Sit if you want to."

They sat. She didn't have a sofa, only a small card table and two mismatched chairs and a dim, green-glass lamp casting a dim greenness on the table. All the windows were covered with pillowcases, and in an adjoining room he saw a mattress lying flat and bare on the floor.

"Hey, do you want your mattress raised up off the floor?" asked Charlie. "I bet we could find you a frame or a box spring, so you don't have to sleep right on the floor, where it's drafty."

The girl looked up with a flash. "You know," she said. "I already told everything about myself. I came into the clinic and they wrote it all down."

Charlie shook his head. "No, you don't have to tell me anything new. I'm just the one who comes around to say hello and drop off your medication. I just came to see how you were doing." He took her medication out of his breast pocket and placed the small paper envelope on the card table.

"Good, good, I'm doing good," said the girl, looking

around, flopping her hand back and forth on the table. "They found me this house, they got me some medicine. I like the summer, but I don't like the winter." She looked outside.

"Why don't you like the winter?" said Charlie.

"Snow," she said. "And I don't like spring neither."

"No? Why not spring?"

"Rain."

"You don't like precipitation?"

"No, I just don't like things falling out of the sky."

Charlie laughed. The girl looked at him hard. He rubbed his mouth. Jesus, he thought, watching himself. You can't let down. You can't get too comfortable. Nobody around here was pretending. There was nothing charming or entertaining or artificial about it. Charlie looked around the room, imagining what it might be like to have to inhabit it day after day, critical, insensible voices poaching at you from the dirty corners. He tried to imagine it. He wanted to be able to drop down into her life.

"Does it hurt?" he said. "The rain, when it falls on you?"

"It does hurt," she said. "And it makes a racket. And when it turns to ice, it bites."

"The snow."

"Yes, sir. This is what brought me to your clinic. I hid inside one winter for two months and this lady I knew made me go to the clinic, and they gave me medicine for it. For the snow."

"Good," said Charlie, surprised she was talking so much. The assessment, he saw, had identified her so differently. Was it he who made her speak like this?

"And so I feel a little better, but I still don't like to go out in the winter. I had a nice neighbor who put salt on the road so the snow would melt fast. But that lady died. I prefer the summer. I'd move back south but you can't go home again."

"That's what they say," said Charlie.

She narrowed her eyes. "Who says that?"

Charlie inhaled and blew out slowly. "No one in particular. I've just heard it said."

"Oh," said the girl. She became absorbed in looking at her fingers, and Charlie took the time to look around the place.

"I was in the military," said the girl, taking out a cigarette. "No shit."

"Really?"

"They showed me how you land a plane on a destroyer. There were all these buttons and levers. The landing strip is only as long as a driveway. You gotta *land* the plane on that. Did you ever see it in a movie? They showed me how to figure the coordinates. Everybody's got a quarter of the sky and you had to be like All right, Pilot, you are at AR 12 approaching this or that. And then the pilot would be like, Roger AR 12, and then he'd land his plane. My God," said the girl, slapping the table and leaning in to Charlie, smiling for the first time. "It was *amazing*. You gotta see it for yourself." She nodded, suddenly pretty with excitement. "Do you have kids?"

"Twins," said Charlie. "Two months old. Girls."

"Well, I was happiest when I was a baby and couldn't put two words together. Since then, I have learned various philosophies that have confused my life." The girl stopped and looked at him hard. "My father was a philosopher."

"Really?"

"Well, he had a lot of philosophies. Mostly he used them to keep me out of sex education class."

Charlie shifted in his chair and looked at the girl's cigarette, which was almost burning her fingers. He'd spent enough time with mental patients to dread the introduction of the topic of sex. But she shook her head, moving on. He was having a hard time nailing her down. She did not seem withdrawn and apathetic to him.

"He was against the government. He was against God. He

was against love. There wasn't anything left. He crossed it all off."

"Yourself," said Charlie, suddenly uncomfortable, for he felt ill-prepared for Opal and he also felt ashamed, for he had clearly expected something different, something easy and slow and impressionable and Southern. "You can believe in yourself and your own morals. Your own convictions. Watch your cigarette."

"I'm up to my *ears* in morals," said Opal, laughing huskily. She waved him off. "That's all they talked about in the military. Look where it got me."

"I think what they taught you were rules. Rules aren't the same as morality. A person can also—follow his heart."

Opal looked at him hard again. Charlie couldn't tell if she was looking at him with appreciation or contempt. The sun came out of the clouds and lit the room through the pillowcases. He could see in the fleeting light a flash of her almost yellow eyes. With a puff of smoke, the cigarette extinguished itself.

"Well," said Charlie, looking down. "I talked to Harriet and she said you signed up for the employment workshop. She said you're taking your meds and feeling up. So now that you're doing so well, you might be able to get one of these transitional employment positions. I have a client, a cook for a university cafeteria—"

"I already worked at a university once."

"All right. I have another client who arranges flowers."

"Ha. For money?" Opal stubbed out her cigarette. "I've worked since I was five years old, okay? On my father's bee farm."

"All right. Maybe we can even see if you could do that again. If you liked it."

"Hell no." The girl leaned back and folded her arms. "I

mean, hell no thank you. Anything but that. Something different maybe. Maybe after winter."

"But you signed up last week," said Charlie, fumbling through the papers on his clipboard. "Didn't you?"

"No," said Opal, shaking her head slowly. "No, I did not."

Charlie sighed. All of a sudden he was tired and wanted to be back at his desk listening to the whirring of the soda machine in the hallway and the sound of coins falling down into it. He stood. "Seems like, with all your work experience, you'd do really well at lots of things. But sure, when you're ready. After winter's fine. I'll stop by again in a couple days with Harriet and we can talk about it."

The girl was still sitting at the table. "I like you better than Harriet," she said.

"Well, me and Harriet are a team and we'll take care of you together."

"Teamwork." The girl rolled her eyes.

Charlie stood and went to the door.

"The only thing I don't want," she said to his back, "is to live in a group home with a bunch of crazy people. I had to live with crazy people all my life. It was called my family."

When she looked up, she was smiling. Relieved, Charlie laughed.

"I hear that," he said. He pawed cigarette smoke out of his eyes. "Hey," he said cheerfully. "We could go find a box spring for your mattress some time. We could raise it up off the floor. What do you think about that?"

"Okay," said Opal. "Maybe."

"Okay? For sure?"

"Maybe." The girl returned to staring at the hammer.

"I'll take that as a yes," said Charlie.

"Take it as a maybe."

"Bye, Opal," said Charlie, smiling now. "I'll see you soon."

⌒

As the weeks passed, the twins' cheeks became rounder, as if their identities were filling them up, pustulating in their cheeks. Their cheeks got so fat, they often fell asleep from the sheer effort of having to keep their heads up, snoozing like old monks over the crooks of her arms.

She had tried to breast-feed. At the hospital, the nurse with the Irish accent had demonstrated how she was supposed to clamp the baby's mouth to the nipple, somewhat forcibly, like so! The baby clamped onto the nipple, rolling the nipple around in her mouth, considering it. Alice remembered looking up at the nurse, hoping almost irrationally to impress her—Was she fond of William Trevor's stories? Then the nipple slipped from the infant's mouth. Oh! cried Alice, cringing, while the nurse who had never heard of William Trevor grabbed her baby's head once more, put her finger in a cup of baby formula and doused Alice's nipple with it, a touch Alice felt right down the rod of her being. Did women get *used* to this? She might as well have been endowed with a hammer and wrench. The nurse grabbed the baby's head once more, rubbed the infant's lips against the nipple, so that Alice had to suppress laughter, and once again the baby's face was shoved upon the breast.

You have to teach 'im, said the nurse. Ya cahnt assume 'ee knows.

But the teacher had to be taught too. The whole idea of *clamping* the child to her . . . perhaps she was being too gentle. Hour after hour, she had sat in a chair in the converted nursery, drawn up to the window, an ache in her neck from looking down so long, while each baby slid off the target, unfocused, unambitious, starving, shriveling up. Charlie, on one week's paternity leave, cheered her on, squatting by the chair, holding the other baby on stand-by. The point was to work up to nursing both babies at once. And yet neither would attach. For days, they labored like that, the four of them, exchanging one baby for another, until finally through her tears Alice saw Charlie emerge from the kitchen with a bottle of formula. And she was so grateful. He knew that just because she had produced two babies at once she did not necessarily have two times the patience or two times the wisdom. With surprising greed, the infant swallowed the whole length of the bottle's nib and began to suck noisily.

"Later," Charlie said. "Try again later."

"Yes," said Alice, "of course."

Later, with the fidgety one across her still-swollen lap, and Charlie asleep on the bed with the other, she did try again. She knew that she was still producing the watery colostrum that was not yet milk. The babies, only six pounds each at birth, were steadily dropping weight. She was—technically—starving them. It was terrifying actually. And she did not want to feel terror but love, that famous love she had felt when they were first placed in her arms like two giant silkworms, their magical, secret-keeping faces wet with life. She eyed the bottle of formula in the warmer jealously. She had not slept. If she was going to breast-feed two babies, instead of let Charlie bottle-feed too, she actually calculated—on a tea-stained notepad in the kitchen—that she would sleep negative three hours a day, noticing that even if the day grew to twenty-seven hours she'd be left with a mere draw. If miracles were possible, both infants would adjust to a joint schedule, but what about all the other things? The dressing, the bathing, the burping, the comforting, all times two? The very fact that she had given birth to twins still astonished her. It hinted at some exceptional largesse within her for which there had been no previous evidence.

Then, in her arms, as if on a dare, the baby Frances stiffened with want and found her mother's nipple and began to suck. Alice gasped, reaching out to wake Charlie. Then she withdrew her hand. She watched the baby suckle. After several minutes, the baby stopped and rolled her blue eyes drunkenly. There, Alice thought. All right. Thank you. She burped the baby and put her in her crib. When her sister began to cry an hour later, Charlie got up half asleep from the bed and went automatically to the kitchen, and came back with a bottle.

The days after Charlie went back to work were different for Alice. They were longer and more intense. She and the twins seemed to fall into a state of deep reminiscence, their ears to the ground. The time that Alice had previously spent reading was now spent waiting, observing, doing, beyond thought or calculation. During the day, she watched them. She watched them across the small spaces—thresholds, doorways. She found that when she looked outside at the evening sky, her eyes could not understand distance. When they slept, they cast their thick dreams backward across the apartment. Their temperatures rose, the fat poultices of their cheeks flushed. They were like two human embers, and their sweet-scented sleep was a little witchy. There, with a dishrag limp in her hand, Alice was overwhelmed with a feeling of understanding that was bittersweet only in that it was so late. She remembered staring through the bars of her own crib at her mother, who was sobbing. Later, a big smile and a cupcake. Back then, it was wretchedly confusing; now, she understood. Motherhood was looking down and seeing that your ribs were blown open because your heart had exploded through your chest.

But in a reasonable mood, after a lucky couple hours' sleep, Alice could see it was a normal, everyday thing to have a baby. You didn't have to be preapproved and you didn't even have to understand it. Everyone involved would survive. And if you weren't brave enough to love them and take care of them, and if no one was ever brave enough, there wouldn't be any more babies or mothers or humankind. Besides, there were babies all over the place. They were practically giving them away. When she first ventured outside, she saw mobs of them in the nursery schoolyard, fascinated by leaves.

Small excursions were trying, and a rich territory for failure. A visit to a café had ended poorly with crying, and the very persecuted air of a businessman who seemed to feel that the twins had leached the pleasure out of his cappuccino. Later, at the post office, the lady standing in line in front of her had been similarly offended when Frances announced herself with a whole-note fart, as if this fart were somehow toxic, composed of the stupid-making gas that caused people to have two babies at once. The lady turned around with a puckered face. Alice was almost concerned for her, before realizing that the lady's mean green eyes were resting upon the heads of her children, those hatted heads with matching pompoms, looking very much as sweet and white as two pansy blossoms.

Alice had stiffened with shame. She could feel the lady's mean greenness glowing in front of her, mean like the shaggy puppet monsters on the television shows that she had begun watching in the afternoons. At first she had watched the shows casually, almost academically, but over time she had become absorbed in the bright colors of the puppets and their queer, chummy voices. She watched the TV, in a fug of sleep deprivation, while the twins played with their fingers. She saw herself as the nice little purple puppet who explained things nicely and lived in a tiny castle, and everybody who didn't understand how hard it was to have twins was the mean green rabble below. Then, standing in the post office, she was twice ashamed—ashamed for not defending her child, and ashamed that she was likening life to a puppet show. Where was this world? And who, did they say, was Alice?

But there was ecstasy, equally as strange, the quality of

which had no precedent. There was nothing at all quite so peaceful as bathing them in the sink, their soft shoulders rubbery in the water. It smoothed the angles out of you. And perhaps your sharpness and ambition were only in abeyance but you knew you had invented something genius where before there was nothing. There was nothing like their eyes. Only once you saw such eyes did you remember what love was before it was a word and an idea, and how open you were before you were warned, and it was lovelier than anything to sit on her empty pretzel tin in the evenings, drinking tea, while Charlie, still in his work clothes, bounced the laughing infants on his knees.

Once, by chance, she had caught sight of him out the window, running homeward in his collared shirt and tie and Dockers. Thereafter, she often lingered by the window at the same hour just for the chance to see such a thing again. How she loved him and missed him. How she wanted to watch him run, run straight down the middle of the street so seriously and unaware of being watched, the rapid sound of his footsteps on the stairs her favorite sound, the promise of him in the dark doorway of the nursery, listening, listening to them breathe. She loved having him for her husband, but she would have given her life for the love of a father like that.

～

"Dammit," he whispered.

Alice looked up from the edge of the bed, tying her red silk robe. Her hair was wet from the shower. "What did you say?"

"Nothing."

Alice looked past him. "Oh, it's *snow*ing. How *won*derful. About time."

He stood there at the window, looking out. The large flakes fell straight through the glittering naked branches. An infant lay prone over each shoulder. He turned away from the window.

"Uh-oh," said Charlie, sniffing the air. "I think we need to be changed."

He spun around in a circle. The babies lifted their heads, gurgled.

"Where'd I put that diaper?" he said, knowing full well the diaper was tucked into the back of his shirtwaist.

Alice covered her mouth and laughed until her gut hurt. The babies, spinning in the air, seemed to be laughing along with her.

"Behind you! Look behind you!"

Charlie spun around, looking behind him.

"No! In your pants. In your pants!"

Charlie looked down at his crotch. "*Down* my pants?"

"In the *back* of your pants," howled Alice.

Charlie stuck out his backside and looked back at it.

"*Oh*," he said, rolling his eyes.

He drew the infants gently down into his arms.

"You hold 'em down and strip 'em," he said to Alice, "and I'll wrap 'em up."

Alice stood, still laughing softly. Her hair was heavy with water. Charlie stopped to watch her rise up slowly and come to him with her arms open. He almost forgot that he had babies in his arms. So transfixed was he by her that he forgot he had babies in his arms, and when she received them and backed away, sucking that strange garden smell away with her, he almost grieved. He almost regretted that they had ever taken their eyes off one another. He was almost disappointed that they had not entombed themselves in a marble sarcophagus the day they met.

Alice lay the twins on the bed. She lifted Franny's legs as if she were a trussed chicken, and wiped her bottom. She turned and looked over her shoulder. "We're a little exposed here. Are you coming with that diaper or what?"

Charlie was looking at Alice. He was staring at her nose and the shadowed side of her cheek. Her profile was fine as the edge of a piece of paper. Maybe they should have entombed themselves.

"Your face," he said.

He was looking at her. Her cheeks, fuller now since her pregnancy, were flushed like a girl's from a fairytale.

Alice paused where she knelt.

"I love you," she whispered.

"I love you too," he said. "Whoever you are."

He stood there. He felt tall and alive. The electricity surged, temporarily filling the small apartment with lamplight.

Just then, the naked infant grabbed her feet and screamed. She was urinating, screaming with pride and happiness. The narrow stream shot out as if through a mixer straw. Alice lunged at her with a blanket.

"Charlie!" she shrieked. "Where's that goddamned diaper?"

He fell to his knees, holding out the diaper, shieldlike. "Jesus, she's like—a little *geyser*—"

"She pissed herself."

"Adults piss. Babies pee-pee."

Alice removed the blanket and peered over carefully. "I refuse to use those words. Ca-ca. Pooh-pooh. Lee-lee."

"What's a lee-lee?"

"I don't know," said Alice. "*You* tell *me*."

The dark-eyed baby who had not pissed herself looked up at her laughing parents. She looked over at her sister on the bed, jealous of the ministrations. Her face puckered.

"Oh no," said Charlie. "Oh no, Evelyn, sweetheart. Don't cry."

He smoothed her hair. Her eyes widened, watching him, and she agreed not to cry. Charlie knelt beside Evelyn now and peeled back the adhesive tabs on her diaper. The diaper was dry, but he folded it away just special for her. He lifted the baby by her legs, wiped the fat labial folds, and wrapped the diaper around her ammonia-shiny haunches. Both babies were quiet now, puffing out their chests. Alice climbed atop of the bed. She rested, stroking the fine black hair of the baby.

"This one's clever," she said, sighing.

"You're just saying that because she looks like you."

"She'll be the boss. Franny, she'll be the brawn. Look at that grip."

"I'm the boss," said Charlie, pointing a balled-up diaper at her. "*I'm* the boss."

"Are you kidding me? You're the rodeo clown. You're the dad." Alice rolled onto her back and sighed. "Meanwhile, I'll be drifting above it all like the gulf wind. Glowing. Beautiful. The mother."

Charlie smiled. Both babies' eyelids were drooping. He looked at his watch.

"Alice," he said. "I have to go somewhere."

Alice didn't move. She was looking at the ceiling.

"I have to go buy some rock salt."

"Rock salt? What for?"

"There's a client of mine who needs it for her walkway. She's afraid of the snow. She's afraid she'll slip."

Alice rolled over and looked at him, but he was looking down at his hands with a stiffened smile. He shrugged. He reached for his shoes.

"People slip on the snow," she said. "So what? That's an emergency?"

"She won't leave her house. You don't understand. She's *really* afraid of the snow."

"Call Emergency Services, then."

"They won't listen to me. They won't do anything. You have to be bleeding out your eyes—"

"All right," said Alice. "All right, Charlie. I understand."

She watched him put on his shoes. He flopped down on the bed next to her and put his hand on her head. "I can fit your whole head in my hand like a melon."

"It's Friday," Alice said, looking up. "It's eight o'clock at night. You just got home. We were *laughing*."

"I know. I guess I . . . didn't expect it to snow. Stay up and wait for me."

Alice rolled onto her back again.

"Smile for me," he said. "It'd make me happy if you would smile."

"I'm not stupid," she said. "I'll smile when you're back."

Charlie stood.

"Look," he said, pointing. "They're asleep."

They were. The shadows of snow fell down their loosened infant faces and the cartoon sheep on the blanket. Alice lay there watching the shadows, feeling the completeness of their surrender, and listened to the door go

click

⌒

The grandmother stuck a thumb in the soil and looked up at the sky. An easterly wind was picking up, the barometer dropping. By morning, the frost would finally come, and it would be time to move the dahlias inside under the sink. The weather had been cold for a while but not quite cold enough. She understood that only old ladies like herself spent time thinking about such things as when to move the dahlias inside. But everything else to do was done. She had killed all the slugs and vermin in the garden and she missed them. She had great affection for everything she had killed: slugs, gophers, and once, a deer, with her son-in-law's rifle. She had made an example of the deer and she did not regret it, but still remembered how it had stood frozen inside her sights, knowing. But once deer got a taste for a garden, they became too fancy for the roots and berries of the woods. Next thing, they'd be tapping at the kitchen window for a bottle of Chardonnay.

The old woman rooted deeper in the soil. The wind, colder by the minute, blew down her blouse and into her dead husband's wool skivvies, which she wore both for warmth and also to tell the world that she wasn't going to let grief make her impractical. She shored up the last of the asters. Then she crawled about looking for anything she'd left in the soil to freeze. Again the wind blew up. A shutter on the house swung open and she watched it. The big ash turned silver in the wind. She had a hold of something large now—a root? Elbow deep in the soil, she tugged backward. The topsoil heaved. The object was entrenched. She wiped her hands on her front, and with a rag, began to clear the dirt off it. She was still beating the thing clean with the rag when she saw the rubber sole, the shoelaces limp with rot, the dirty sock, and the leg itself, white and pale as horror. The grandmother leaned back on her heels. She did not scream. She stayed very still. The screen door opened.

Ma?

She bent down, stroking the fine reddish hairs of the leg that was buried in the garden. A small cut, a nick, could be felt on the calf. When he was a boy, he had played here while she worked, she half-watching him, not worried. She could hear Luduina marching across the yard now. The grandmother swallowed back tears.

Well, just pull it on up, her daughter scolded her.

Her daughter was bending down beside her, digging in the

soil. The grandmother looked off at the big ash tree. Her daughter stood, the beetroot in her hand.

There, she said. Now will you please come inside?

～

Charlie pulled over on Road Four and turned off the ignition. There he sat, watching the snow, thinking how pretty it was, and what a shame it was to be afraid of it. He raised the parking brake. Out in the cold air, he saw the cheap windows of all the cheap houses of Norris Park, most dark, some filled with televisions. Everybody was safe inside. Everybody deserved a home and to feel safe. If you thought about it, everybody deserved a hot lunch too and fur slippers and the opportunity at least once in life to have a bath drawn for him. Every human being deserved those things just for putting up with the basic indignities of life, but maybe it was enough to have a house, a roof that protected you from the snow, and a sidewalk you could walk on. He laughed, thinking about how, on a recent excursion to the mall, Opal had whispered—as if it was the most intimate secret—that what she really loved was a good milkshake. To watch her drink one. He should have thanked her, making him feel so tenderly, that a grown woman could still be completely consoled, as they sat in the shadeless canopy of the Orange Julius.

He dragged the large bag of salt from the backseat. He tore a hole in the lining and made a spout. The shadow of a small animal crossed into the snowy darkness. Hoisting the rock salt over his shoulder, he walked across the street to Opal's yard. The yard was covered with a thin blanket of unbroken snow and the house was dark but for one small light in the back. He shook the salt out onto the driveway and the walk. It poured out diamond-like from his shoulder. He was trying to be quiet. He felt very happy. Physical work was good. But he felt much bigger than just this. He swung the spout of the bag back and forth. The air was fresh and cold and the sky was clear now and there was nobody out but him.

On his way back to the car, he noticed that the walkway of the house next to Opal's was also untended. In fact, most of the sidewalks on Road Four were neglected, and the street itself was unplowed. He retreated back to the pool of streetlight, appraised the scene, popped a stick of gum in his mouth. Then, laughing to himself, he started in on the neighboring sidewalks. He moved up the street, pouring the salt off his shoulder. And then he just kept going, over to the next house, through the window of which an old woman was asleep in a chair. He paused, smiled at the slant-eyed cat that switched its tail in her lap. By the door was an old rusty shovel, and he put down the sack of salt to give the old lady's sidewalk a quick once-over with the shovel, and then he sprinkled the salt on top. Despite the cold, he was sweating and warm. Before turning around, he shoveled the next walkway, too. And the one after that. It took a long time. And on his way back to return the shovel, he sprinkled the sidewalks on the other side of the street with rock salt as he walked, and when he turned around and looked back, the whole block was glittering. He threw the empty sack in the backseat, dusted his hands, and got in the car.

As he drove away, he happened to glance back at the mustard-yellow house to see her face, staring at him with a strange, prescient expression, just before she dropped the curtain.

❧

Her father killed himself with a shotgun. He did it midday behind the bee cages on the farm they had shared alone together for nine-

teen years. Midday, as if it were just another chore. When she heard the shot, she came out wiping her hand on a dishrag, and knew in her heart that her life had changed. But she felt nothing—no feeling at all.

Even though the property was just a piece of scratched-up dirt and shrubbery, the old man had put up a wall around it with broken glass on the top, as if it were a palace. The old man loved his bees more than anything, and he wouldn't let Opal touch them or go near them. Neither did he touch her anymore, though he used to let her sit astride his knee when she was little and he was different and they had their breakfasts that way.

As far as Opal could remember, she'd never been embraced. Not out of love or kindness. Except by the occasional school nurse if she cried. Her father never embraced her. Nowadays, when her father had to pass her something, he was careful to be sure their fingers didn't brush. The few times they bumped into each other in that dark, close house, the old man shrieked. She began to think she had some kind of disease or contagion that her father wasn't telling her about. Whenever she went into town in his ridiculous green truck with the old-fashioned grill and headlights like goiters, she was sure not to touch anyone, lest she pass it on.

On the farm, she took care of the chickens and gave them names and talked to them in her loneliness, and when she was finished with her chores she spent the afternoons asleep underneath the chokecherry tree, watching her father tend to his bees in the smoke, like a man fighting with his imagination. At night, her father would sit in a straight-backed chair and talk about the government and the urban conspiracy and Jew doctors in laboratories and the military-industrial complex.

When her father started to get ill, with what turned out to be death, he began to destroy things. He was like a bear with a toothache. He knocked down the outhouse with his bare hands and broke it up and burned it. He burned his bed and then he burned hers and she had to sleep on sofa cushions on the floor. He said there was a plague in the house and everything had to be burned.

Then he turned to the chickens. The chickens stood there, stupidly pruning their feathers and pecking at their feet, while their brothers and sisters were butchered. He made her go to the store in town and ask for an obscure salve that made the pharmacist laugh. Finally, Opal told her father that he needed a doctor. And yet he wouldn't go to no goddamned Jew doctor.

She knew it was her fault somehow. The thing that was unpalatable or unhealthy about her had finally spread to him, despite his best attempts. After all, they shared the same air in that small, close house, they sat in the same chairs, and she prepared his food and washed his clothes. They shared the same dirty blond features, the same sorts of behaviors that made people avoid them, and she tried hard to listen to his ideas and to adopt them. She loved him. He was her daddy. But perhaps love was the agent that bore the disease.

When a position opened up at the local college to be an errand girl for a lady academic, Opal applied. She wanted to earn some money so that her father could be taken care of. He was getting worse. Once or twice, he'd even been unable to get out of bed and neglected his bees.

Her father hated academics almost as much as he hated Jews and doctors. But if there was one group of people he hated more than academics and Jews and doctors, it was lady academics. Still, Opal dropped out of high school and went to work for the lady academic. Her father promptly stopped speaking to her. He kept speaking, but he stopped speaking to her. Only she could have told the difference.

Turned out, Opal liked the lady academic. The academic was portly and her hair was laced with gray. She walked around the office and joked about her portliness and joked with the other *young researchers she had working for her and the other young re-searchers looked back up at her with shy apprentice love. The lady academic joked with Opal right off the bat and made her sit right outside her office at a little desk, and instead of making Opal get her coffee, she got Opal coffee, and took her around by the hand and introduced her by name, and Opal felt that fat warm hand in her own long after she went home in the evening.*

The lady academic was a scientist. She was studying sound waves. Opal herself felt very supportive of the project, because she appreciated sounds and music and had a keen ear. Finally, for the first time in her life, she was happy, working at the university. She was involved in something important. Out of that house and in the clear, dogwoody air of that campus, she spied the trembling image of a desirable future. Also, she loved the lady academic. No one had ever been voluntarily that nice to her. Sometimes Opal even waited across the street in her green truck, just to make sure her portly boss got across campus safely in the evening, tip-topping back and forth like a teacup full of buttermilk.

There was a dean at the college, a tall, skinny man with chapped skin, who came in to check on the lady academic and prowl around the office. He would come in and whine at the lady in his nasally, academicky voice and ask where the results of her study were and how she was spending her money and couldn't they share their Xerox machine with the philosophy department. And because the lady academic was so good-natured, she would humor the dean and sit there and bear his nasally ignorant comments. From her desk just outside the office, Opal could hear the dean whining on and on, and she would sit there making up retorts to his comments, and sometimes she would become so angry by the time he left that she'd be drenched in her own sweat.

The dean always paused and looked Opal up and down on his way out. He looked her over like she was dressed in rags. Opal was used to being humiliated, but there was something about the dean's style of humiliation that was particularly unbearable, and she came to believe that he was trying to sabotage the sound wave project.

One day, the dean came in looking particularly constipated and particularly chapped. He stormed into the office and began making threatening statements and references to some comment the lady academic had made in a meeting. Opal could hear from her seat outside the office. The lady academic was, as usual, patient and endured the dean and listened to him. But when the dean left, she came out of her office and stood there looking after him with tears of anger in her eyes.

That pencil-dicked beaurocrat! she shouted.

All the young researchers laughed. Their boss looked at them and laughed and laughed until she cried a little. They all had a good laugh over that——he probably did *have a tiny pencil dick. The lady academic wiped her eyes with the back of her hand. Then they all went back to work.*

Everybody except Opal.

That night, she stayed late at the office by herself and composed a letter. It was a letter to the dean.

The letter to the dean began very civil and articulate and altogether academic, but as the night wore on and she kept writing, it got angrier and angrier, as if she was possessed. She decided to tell the dean what they really thought of him. All of them! Everybody on campus! She recorded all the comments she'd heard in the hallways and the bathroom stalls, and she even included the comment about his pencil-dickness because it just about summed him up perfectly. As she wrote, she felt her father looking over her shoulder and laughing in agreement, and putting in a couple good zingers of his own. She wrote in a rage. She wrote in a fury. Voices from the air contributed. Late at night, she sat back, finished. Then she slipped it under the dean's door and went home to bed.

That night, she got another migraine. It was so bad that even the sound of her own breathing hurt her, and the snoring of her father sawed at her brain. She could hear the bees outside in their cages, making their ceaseless devouring noises. The next morning, she could not get out of bed. Every point of light was a green point of pain. Her father's significant footsteps walked across her body. By sunset, the headache moved off and left her wrecked.

She did not go into the office for a week. Then she returned, feeling better. But when she walked into the office, no one was there. There was a sense of abandonment in the room, and things were orderly and museum-like. Panicked, she ran into her boss's office. The woman was there, taking things out of her desk. When she looked up at Opal, her face became pale. But then, after a moment, she smiled.

Hello, Opal, she said.

Hello, ma'am, said Opal. Where is everybody?

At home, said the lady academic. She looked out the window at the campus and the blossoms on the fine, historic-looking trees. After a long moment she said, Why, they're at home celebrating. We've finished our sound-wave project!

Oh! cried Opal. That's great.

I know it. I'm going to go out and eat me an entire cow. I've gotten too skinny, don't you think?

No, said Opal. You look just right.

The woman turned back to her business and Opal stood there.

Well, said Opal. I guess I'm done here then. Got to find a new job.

Yep, said the woman.

Oh, said Opal. What did you figure out about sound?

The lady academic stopped and put down her papers.

We figured out that sound doesn't always exist, she said. That it goes off and on. Like a firefly's light.

Like a firefly, hunh?

Like that.

We keep bees, Opal said.

You told me that once, replied the lady.

Fireflies don't make honey.

No sir they don't! They don't even make fire.

Opal laughed at that. Then, straightening her sweater, she turned and walked out the door of the office. But the lady academic called out to her. Opal turned around. To her alarm, the woman was walking straight toward her. She was coming very near to her. Opal fought the urge to make fists at the ready. She did not know what to do, being this close to somebody.

The woman put her arms around Opal. Bye, Opal, she said. Opal could smell the strong sweet smell of her hair and she could feel the lumps in her figure and the movements of her ribcage as it went up and down with her breathing. The woman held onto her and even though Opal's hands were too inexperienced to respond and hung there at her sides, she felt she was still participating in the embrace. She felt that something bad was being taken out of her with that embrace. She felt she was being leeched or confessed or healed. She knew that the lady academic would teach hundreds of students, would make hundreds of discoveries and win awards, but perhaps the most remarkable thing she would ever do in her whole life was what she was doing just then.

❧

Down the hall, a baby's whine. Alice shifted on the bed. She exhaled.

"Still awake?" said Charlie.

"Yes," she said.

The clock was ticking in the kitchen. It was an extraordinarily quiet night.

"Why so quiet?"

"The snow," said Alice. "The snow makes everything quiet."

Charlie pulled his arm out from under her neck. "No. I mean you."

"Why am I quiet? I don't know."

"You're angry that I went out."

"How can I be angry? How can I be angry now?"

"What do you mean?"

Alice shrugged. "Now that I know her."

"Didn't you want to?"

"I wanted to very much. It was a very moving story."

"But—"

"But now she's in me." Alice rolled away. She put her cheek against her arm. "People are right not to want to know about what they don't see. What can you do? It must drive a person crazy, a life like that. To never be hugged. To never be touched by your own father—"

Alice paused. She closed her mouth and neither of them said anything for a moment. Alice also had never been touched by her own father. With one arm, she groped along the windowsill, behind the snowglobe, where she kept her cigarettes. She drew one out of the flattened pack with her lips.

"Hey," Charlie said. "I don't think you should smoke in the house anymore."

"Just this once." She shoved open the window, lit the cigarette, and inhaled majestically.

"I'm not comfortable with this. I thought you would quit for good after the twins."

Alice exhaled. "Do you touch her?"

"Who? Opal? Do I touch Opal?"

"Yes."

"Are you kidding? Of course not."

"I mean, in a friendly way, here and there, on her shoulder or something."

"No, I don't. I don't think she would respond very well to

anything like that. She gets very squirrelly sometimes. She's—a sick person, Alice. She doesn't trust a lot of people, with all she's been through."

"I think it must be awful, to never be touched. To only be embraced once in your whole life. That's the saddest story I've ever heard."

"But it's got a happy ending." Charlie was up on one elbow now, his expression one of reassurance. "It's about finding love and kindness in unlikely places."

Alice dropped the cigarette into a glass of water on the windowsill.

"Right," she said. "See? I just wanted one drag."

"Alice. You seem so—" Charlie licked his lips. "This—kids, parenthood—no one can prepare you. I'm dead tired all the time. And you. For months now you've hardly even been outside. And the winter. Getting frustrated doesn't mean you love them any less, you know. Why don't you get out and do something fun for yourself?"

Alice laughed, louder than she meant to. "When?"

"At night. You could even try going back to school again. Why not? I could watch the girls a couple nights a week. Plenty of parents take classes at night—"

"You're home at six, seven sometimes. Later and later it seems. It's unpredictable. And then sometimes, you go out *again*—"

Charlie paused. "It doesn't have to be school. Just something you enjoy. For yourself. A release. A book club. What do you say?"

Alice turned over, pulled his hand over her chest and cradled it there between her breasts.

"All right, Charlie," she said. "Yes, that's a good idea. I'll go out and do something for myself."

"It's a damned good idea."

Charlie lay there expectantly, ready to talk, but instead she moved his hand down the side of her body. She placed his hand between her legs. Then she pressed her hips backward, and immediately he hardened, almost fainting.

"Are you sure?" he whispered.

She didn't say anything. Turning toward him, she ignited, expanded, becoming physically enormous in his arms. He felt his words and his plans falling headlong into her like wind to a fire. There was something about her that night, the way she made it seem that they made love on an empty planet, the stars burning holes in his back.

⌒

Rain? She pressed her hand to the window. *Rain?* She turned and looked at the twins propped in their wingchair. They blinked back at her. Did rain mean, they seemed to ask, that they would *not* be going outside? Packed into their pink snow-suits, they looked stiff and bloated as starfish. Frances was sliding slowly down the cushion. Alice turned back to the window. "No," she said aloud. "Of *course* the rain won't stop us." In defiance, she hoisted the collapsed doublewide stroller and held it trembling in the air. Evelyn sighed. The rain would not stop them because Today was for Mommy and They were already all dressed and Besides a little rain never hurt anyone.

Alice opened the apartment door. The bare lightbulb on the second floor landing flickered. Looking down into the stairwell, she realized that it was impossible to prove that throughout time, a little rain had, in fact, never hurt anyone. It was quite possible that someone had been hurt a great deal by a little rain. A man on fire, for example. She was carrying the stroller down the second set of stairs. Quivering from the effort, she pushed back against the front door, holding it open with one foot while struggling to open the stroller. The stroller, she decided, was her mortal foe. It mocked her with its deadweight. She knew that when she came back downstairs bearing both babies at once, the stroller would have malevolently scooted itself some distance away, like a cur to sniff trash. It was bad enough to carry the girls down the stairs at once without having to be worried about the stroller, which tempted her to descend faster, for what if someone found it alongside the trash cans and thought it discarded? Each time she set the girls down synchronously in the stroller, she wanted to pump her fist. The girls themselves were completely unresponsive to narrative sweep. They had no favorite or least favorite moment. They were calm during even the worst parts, the worst part of all being, for Alice, the precipitous descent down the dark and narrow staircase carrying both of them. It would have been easier if they were afraid. Then at least they would cling to her.

"There." She stood back, looking down at them. The plastic rain shield on the stroller billowed with air. She straightened Frances's hat. "Let's have an adventure."

She looked at the sky, which was decidedly less gray than it had appeared from inside. It really sounded so familiar, about the rain not hurting anyone. She remembered, through the myopia of her childhood, rain on the window, how it mangled the view of trees and sky. When she turned back to the stroller, Evelyn was bent in half, reaching down.

"That's a chicken bone, sweetheart," said Alice, grabbing her hand.

The infant looked up at her, as if to say, Chicken what?

"A chicken bone. Because that's the sort of street Mommy and Daddy live on, one with crap all over it on trash day."

Alice grabbed the handlebar and began to walk. The sidewalks were herniated with roots, and the poorly tended tenements, which had been built for huge Portuguese laborer families but were now filled with students and working people like herself and Charlie, lined either side.

"We're going to the bookstore," she whispered. "Mommy is going to read a book."

In the distance, a rumble of thunder. Alice paused. In the middle of the street, a gyre of brittle leaves spun. No, she thought, she would not let a little rain stop them. She had come this far. She had come entirely down the stairs. As she marched past the shuttered houses, she saw all at once, that very morning in fact, how she had given up being wonderful, being immaculate, being the Gulf Wind, and all of a sudden was doing exactly the sort of thing her own mother would have done, marching her onward through the freezing rain for her own deep undeclared reasons and calling it an adventure. She could even remember now, her own yellow slicker, her little nor'easter, and her mother saying lightly Well, Alice darling, a little rain never hurt anyone. Even now, as Alice remembered and understood all this, and she might have been moved or astonished by life and its refrains, all she really wanted to do was get to the goddamned bookstore before it rained. The stroller took a hit from a root. The twins were quiet and absorbed by their mother's behavior. Already she absorbed them completely—her power, her moods, her kaleidoscopic face. But even that revelation, that the twins could already *feel her feelings*, was somehow too arcane for this moment made of weather, traffic, and mud.

For they were almost there. Along the lane of shops—a record store, a cheese shop, an ombudsman's reelection campaign center—people ran from awning to awning, looking at the sky. Alice was steering the stroller across a wide intersection when the sky opened up. Rain crashed onto the hoods of cars, pelted the top of the stroller. Alice shrieked and began to run. Her hair beat against the back of her slicker. She could hardly hear for the rain. A girl in an apron came out of a bakery shop sucking frosting off her finger. The girl could not understand what it meant to jog sloppily down the street in the rain with a stroller laughing tragicomically, because you could not understand such things as a young girl with frosting on her finger. Drawing a lock of hair out of her eyes, Alice looked up and saw the sign swinging in the wind.

"We're here," she said. "We made it!"

She opened the door, backed into it with her rear, and tried pulling the stroller through face-forward. The twins were silent and clammy and shocked-looking under their plastic shield.

The stroller would not fit.

Alice tried to jam it through again, the twins swaying. Finally, both babies began to cry.

"No, no," pled Alice through the plastic. "No, please don't cry. We're here. We've *made* it. Don't cry *now*."

She stood, the rain pouring under her collar, her hair entirely wet, her blouse entirely wet under her slicker, and gazed down at the stroller jammed half inside the doorway. It was impossible to move in either direction. Her children were crying. They looked like two little children in a public service announcement about child abuse. Alice covered her face with her hands.

Rain could hurt you, of course it could. She must tell her mother. She would go home and call her mother right away. And then she would add, in a hush, But please, Mother, help me. Come and take over. Do it however you like. Just save me. Help me. *Mother me.*

Somebody was brushing past her now, reaching out into the rain with bare, brown hands for the crying infants. Alice blinked back the dizziness and the rain, watching as the baby Evelyn was lifted out of her seat and into the air. Only once the child was placed over the stranger's shoulder did he turn around. It was a young man with very black eyes. Alice felt slapped by his face. The stroller rolled backward, coming unstuck.

"Leave it there," shouted the young man over the rain. "Come in."

He stepped further into the bookstore. He wore a thin white T-shirt and canvas painter's pants. She could see his spine, and the face of her baby looking back at her. Alice quickly fetched Frances and stepped inside. The door closed behind her and the rain was silenced.

The young man turned, balancing the baby with one square brown hand against his shoulder. He seemed very comfortable holding the baby. Alice stared. When she lifted her arm, a stream of water poured out of the cuff and onto the floor.

"I'm sorry," she said. "Oh God." She flapped her pruned, windbitten hands, tears pricking her eyes.

The young man gestured with his chin outside.

"It's rolling away."

Alice whirled around, dumping more rainwater onto the floor. The stroller was rolling backward into the street, the plastic sheath acting as a sail.

"Oh my God." Alice thrust Frances at the young man. She could feel her face redden. She had needed rescue from a *doorway*, and now the stroller (expensive, ridiculously expensive!) was sailing out into the street.

She marched back out into the rain, into the street, and grabbed the stroller. Through the sheets of rain she could see headlights coming toward her. She stood there in the street, staring at the headlights for just a moment.

The young man watched her the whole time, holding the babies. His black hair was closely cropped against his head, giving him the look of a monk or a soldier. His expression was level and strangely impassive as he rocked the babies, without taking his eyes away. After a moment, she stepped back into the store.

"It's all right," he said. "I've got them. Take off your coat."

Alice swallowed. "I'm sorry." She stepped forward and lowered her eyes, taking Frances from the young man, her knuckles brushing his body. "It's just—It's hard with two."

The young man smiled very slightly, revealing salt white teeth. He took Evelyn off his shoulder and held her aloft. Alice could see his navel under his T-shirt, small and tense. He made a noise like an airplane. Evelyn, usually serious and wary of being dandled, gurgled in the air.

"I don't mind," he said finally. "My cousin has four."

"Oh good," said Alice, shrugging, laying Frances down on the bookstore's old velvet sofa. "Hold her, then, why don't you? God. We're drenched." She looked at the stroller. "Everything's drenched. That fucking stroller. Excuse me."

"It's all right," said the young man.

Over her shoulder, Alice was aware the boy's swayed back reflected in the window.

"What are you looking for?" he said to her reflection.

"Oh. Well I'd like a really, really long, fat book. I want the fattest book you have. I haven't been to a bookstore in months. I haven't even read a book. I can't stand it anymore!" She laughed aloud—a silly, honking laugh—but she didn't care. At last, here they were, rows and rows of books. She took one off the shelf, opened it, and stuck her nose inside. She hefted it in her hands. "I used to read, night and day. Everything. When I was little, I used to keep a book open in my lap during dinner. I couldn't stop. Once, my mother grabbed my book and—" Alice opened her hand, remembering, "tossed it out the kitchen window. Look. She's fallen asleep on you. The baby."

"Will you look at that," the young man said. He seemed genuinely impressed, even though his expression was unchanged. He turned around, shelving a book with one hand. Alice looked at his head. It was the most finely shaped head she had ever seen.

It was difficult not to look at him. There was something

very crafted about the way he looked. He looked very created and offered. His head was so exposed, with the cropped hair and the knobs where the cranium ended at the base of the neck, and the dark brow bone sparkling with rain. One scar, like the streak of a cat's eye, ran back from his temple. He could not have been more than eighteen or nineteen, with the pliant back of an athlete. She blinked drowsily.

He disappeared into a small storeroom and came out with towels and a blanket. He spread them on the threadbare sofa. Safe in a velvety crevasse, both infants were arranged and dozing.

"Have you read *Remembrance of Things Past*? That's a fat book." He turned and began to walk toward the back of the store. "A man remembers—everything. Everything that passed."

Alice pursued. "His life story?"

"No. More than that. Everything."

He climbed a footstool. Standing there, at the top of the footstool, he opened a book from the shelf and began to read in a slow, unmodulated voice. " *'For a long time I used to go to bed early. Sometimes, when I had put out my candle, my eyes would close so quickly that I had not even time to say to myself: "I'm falling asleep." And half an hour later the thought that it was time to go to sleep would awaken me; I would make as if to put away the book which I imagined was still in my hands, and to blow out the light; I had gone on thinking, while I was asleep, about what I had just been reading, but these thoughts had taken a rather peculiar turn; it seemed to me that I myself was the immediate subject of my book;—'* "

"Yes!" said Alice. "That happens to me too!"

He looked down at her and nodded, as he continued in his slow, rather labored way, " *'This impression would persist for some moments after I awoke; it did not offend my reason, but lay like scales upon my eyes and prevented them from registering the fact that the candle was no longer burning.'* "

Alice laughed, leaning backward. "That's it," she said. "That's what it's like. To get lost in a book."

He came down from the footstool and held out the book. She took it.

"Wow," she said, making an exaggerated face. "Heavy."

The cowbell tied to the front door clanged, and a woman walked in with a large striped umbrella. The woman collapsed the umbrella, shook it off noisily onto the floor, and then clasped her hand to her heart.

"Oh," the woman shrieked, crashing over to the sofa. "How *darling*! How precious! Look at these beautiful babies. Are they *twins*?"

"Yes," said Alice, coming over to the woman. "Please. We're taking a little nap."

The woman bent down and tweaked an exposed foot. "To *die* for. Ah! This one's opened her eyes! Hello, darling. Hello, you little sugar dumpling. Don't you have the *bluest* eyes?"

Evelyn scowled up at the lady and began to cry.

Alice, wet and pruned and exasperated, looked up. The boy was looking back at her in the window's reflection. Grinning, he shook his head. She smiled back at him and the world that glowed through him. Sometimes maybe all it took was someone to say Isn't life *awful* sometimes? Because life wasn't awful. Life was on the whole gorgeous. It was awful *sometimes*. But if you spent too much time alone, you got confused. You thought maybe it was awful all the time.

⌒

The schoolteacher backed away from the door. If he looked through the peephole too often, might he permanently start seeing people as convex, with big, distorted heads? He shuddered. He should be writing poetry. He should be wearing a timepiece. He should stop eating so much Turkish Delight. He pressed his nose once again to the door. It drew him to it, the hole. Through it his womanish curiosity was channeled. But why call it that? he thought—why not call it a Byronesque thirst for love and consummate understanding? He watched her shining hair fall in a curtain over her shoulder. Everybody felt Byronesque when looking through a peephole—that was the *point* of a peephole: you appreciated them but they didn't appreciate you. They only stood there (the UPS man, the local Ombudsman on campaign) turning their huge ears slightly toward the door.

Byron had died at 34. Sometimes the schoolteacher wished he had died at 34, too. Then he probably wouldn't be ABD and driving a used Taurus. It wasn't healthy for a man to drive a Taurus. And the Turkish Delight, well, that was a hard-to-shake fetish that he had acquired while in love, as a boy, with his piano teacher's mother. Again he drank with his eye at the hole. She had the front door open now and was struggling to open the enormous contraption with which she pushed around her children. But how did she manage to look so lovely (he wanted to know) even through the unkind lens, her barrettes slipping down her black hair? The daylight snapped shut behind her and she disappeared back up the dark stairwell.

He sat down in a chair. He put his finger to his cheek. He put his finger to his lip. He spread a book on his knee. He let his slipper dangle from one toe. Sometimes he could not get comfortable. It didn't have to do with any one thing. He couldn't get comfortable *on earth*. When he heard her footsteps coming back down, he became irrationally excited. It wasn't just about watching, it was about not having to think (for one moment) about his essential physical uselessness. O to be a clarinet. To have one's body covered with keypads. To produce sound when touched.

She had her babies with her now. She was coming down the

staircase like Diana of the Harvest, her small feet sensing each stair. Standing before the outer door, the white light met her face and she sighed. The babies swayed in her arms. What (he held his breath) did she need, in her soul? He craned to hear her soul. She put her shoulder to the door and shoved, meeting his gaze without knowing it. He backed away from the peephole instantly. The draft sucked itself under his door.

By the time he looked back—thirstily, with regret—she was gone. Bubblegum wrappers settled on the dirty floor. A little help, he scolded himself, *that* was what she needed. Something as simple as a little help with the door. So why was his hand still clutching the doorknob, when she was gone? Why, he thought, gritting his teeth, why lie to yourself? You are completely alone. There is no one here to listen to your fucking intentions.

～

He startled at the sound of the telephone. Still asleep, he pressed it to his ear.

"Charlie?"

"Christ," he laughed. "Alice."

He looked outside. The view was pitch-black.

"What time is it?"

"It's seven-*thirty*, Charlie. I was worried."

He laughed again—his most natural defense. "Shit. I fell asleep on my work." He looked around at his desk, the palette of folders, the voluminous papers stacked beneath the desk lamp. He smeared clean his mouth, patting the desk. "It's just—last night—I hardly slept. Did you sleep? When do you sleep? Standing up, like a horse? I'm—I'm an idiot."

"Oh, Charlie." He heard her voice melt around his name. "Come home. The twins are asleep now finally. Be with me. I'll make you some dinner?"

"How do you do it? How do you manage?"

"Well, we actually had a wonderful day," said Alice. "We went to a bookstore!"

"You did?"

"I bought a fabulously fat book and I'm looking at it right now, in the kitchen. It was so wonderful, to go out. Thanks. For encouraging me. Although we got absolutely *drenched* in the rain—"

And then, gradually, although he was helpless to stop it, her voice became somewhat like background noise to other thoughts he was having. What GAF should he give the new guy? How the hell was he supposed to fit everything wrong onto Axis IV? He was hopelessly behind on his progress notes. The meetings with Dr. Hsu about Therese, was that yesterday or today? Did it matter? He saw a shadow in the hall. It was Bruce Zabilski, putting on his coat, walking toward him. Charlie waved. Bruce stopped, zipped his coat, and paused at the door.

Charlie covered the receiver. "Do you need to talk to me?"

"Take your time."

"—sailing out into the street, with a mind of its own—"

"Honey, listen," Charlie said. "I've got to talk to Bruce for a minute. Can I call you back?"

"Call me back?"

"Or, no—" Charlie slapped his forehead, smiling at Bruce. "I'll just come home right after. Don't forget where you were in the story about the rain and the bookstore. I was listening."

"All right," said Alice.

"The stroller was sailing into the street," he said.

Charlie hung up the phone and clapped Bruce's hand. "Hey, man. Come on in, come on in. I'd offer you a drink but—"

Bruce stepped in, gestured with his hands in his pockets. He was wearing, as usual, his long gray trench coat and his Patriots cap. His skin bore its usual sallow color, hairily shadowed around the jaw line. He was a huge tree of a man.

"You'd be surprised," Bruce said, rubbing his jaw. "Once or twice a day I'm on the verge of scrapping it all. Throwing off the whole idea—the whole fussy, clichéd, recovering alcoholic's mindset, all twelve steps of it, and just having a little drink. Just a nice little drink in a nice little glass. Sitting at a nice little bar some girl has just rubbed clean. Once or twice a day I can't understand for the life of me why I should not do this. You've really got to find a powerful reason—something better than living long enough to grow old because who wants to grow old? Sometimes alcohol just doesn't have a powerful enough enemy. At around five o'clock it doesn't. The sun setting, the cold air. The crack of a bat—Do you know what I mean?"

"No," said Charlie. "I'm one of those people. I'm not tempted. Never have been."

"Aw, screw you, then. You are a waste of my verbiage."

"Do you want to sit here, Bruce? Until it passes? You want to talk?"

Charlie folded his hands over his shirt. Bruce looked down at him, his broad-featured face underlit by the desk lamp.

"You're cute," said Bruce. "I love it when you practice on me. But I'm not having the jones right now, thank you anyway. Not today."

"Oh, good," said Charlie. "Well, then?"

Bruce sat down in a chair and exhaled. He fixed his cap over his bald head.

"Nope," he said. "I just wanted to sit here with you, tell you a thing or two about myself. You're so—" Bruce looked Charlie up and down, not unkindly, but without reserve. "White. I mean, like snow. You're light. I mean it. In the best way. You're some kind of guy. I'm glad Gregorian sent you over here. I like being around you, Charlie. You're like a little campfire. I like looking at you. I mean that in the very best, most heterosexual way." Both men laughed. Bruce's big square shoulders went up and down. Charlie thought passingly that Bruce was nice to look at too, like a big rough oak, and he also thought Bruce was sort of full of shit, and that Bruce wanted him to know it. It was different being supervised by someone so like Bruce—a man's man, weathered, an alcoholic at fourteen, a bachelor from Fall River who on at least one occasion in his past had been thrown through a bar window without feeling it. Charlie uncrossed his legs and stretched.

"I've noticed that you've been staying late," Bruce said. "Why are you staying late, Charlie? Your duties end at five. We don't pay you enough to stay late. This isn't Morgan Stanley, sweetheart. You know that, right?"

Charlie nodded, rubbing his eyes.

"I know you went to visit a client after hours."

Charlie lowered his hand. Blood rushed to his neck. "Excuse me?"

"Opal Ludlow. I know you went over there to help her out. She called ES when it started to snow and by the time they got over there, she was all happy because you'd come yourself. She told the guy."

Charlie opened his mouth to speak.

"No," said Bruce. "Don't say anything. Don't worry about it. It happens. The sense of personal responsibility gets too great. You start to see there is a standard of humanness that can't be written as a rule. But I don't want you to say anything right now, though. I want you to sit there and listen to me. All right?"

"I'd like to explain," said Charlie.

"No," said Bruce, whose face had grown solemn, and whose shoulders grew in the tiny chair, emphasizing the terrible impressiveness of his body. "Just listen. Before I lost everything, I lived in a rented house two blocks from the ocean. The house was so damned cute, there was even a goddamned weathervane on top of it, and this sign by the front door that said 'Home is Where You Hang Your Hat,' which between my wife and I was a joke, right, because I never hang my hat. Corny shit, right?" Bruce paused, his gaze fixed. "Well listen, I *loved* it. Amy bought these seedlings and we were actually growing an herb garden in the backyard. She was a very gentle human being. You could practically *hear* her love you, the signal was so strong. We'd met in rough times, she had her share of troubles, but she was trying to show me—I think she was trying to show me a vision, something—real. But it was a risky proposition with me. I was a huge gamble. I'd only been dry a couple years—"

Bruce stopped. He lifted his cap off his head and put it back down. "Anyway, we lived like that for a while, being married, drinking ginger ale, planting herbs. Each one had its own little sign, you know, 'I'm basil, goddamn it!' 'I'm rosemary!' I remember I was planting one in the garden, a tiny green tree, and I just started shaking. I was—I think I was—*happy*. Was it a good feeling? No! It was terrifying. I still can't explain it. I got in the car, drove to a bar, and just like that, I was back at it. And love was this useless frilly decoration on the big black lack of importance that was life. The drinking life. During that first bender, I went out there and looked at those herbs I had planted, and they cracked me up so bad! What useless, gay shit! Flavoring. *Accent*."

Bruce moved his large leg. "Charlie. Do you know that until two months ago I lived in an apartment over my sister's garage? Do you know that most nights I sleep sitting upright in a chair? I own one fork, one glass. The last time I saw Amy was five years ago. Sometimes I pretend that my nephew is my son when I watch his ball games. I wanted a son of my own so badly."

"No," said Charlie. "I didn't know that."

"Go home, Charlie," said Bruce, pointing. "Go home to your wife. Watch yourself. You think what you have is easy.

What you have is the most endangered thing in the world. It draws threats. You might think, what freak storm is going to come over the horizon and take all this away? Well, the storm might come, but it won't come from the horizon."

Charlie raised his finger, as if to speak.

"If you don't call Emergency Services next time," said Bruce, "I'll give you a written sanction. You know very well what you did was improper. I won't keep turning my head just because you're Gregorian's sweetheart."

Bruce stood. He lifted his cap again and put it back on his head. "But for now, carte blanche. I trust you. I'm kind of sweet on you myself. I know your problem is that you're too nice. I won't give you another single AA testimonial, I promise." He reached over and grabbed Charlie's ear, smiling. "Deal, Jughead?"

"Okay," said Charlie, nodding. "All right, Bruce. Deal."

Bruce flapped his hands in his coat pockets. He looked around at Charlie's office. "You're the only guy around here with plants in his office. Plants are good. They make oxygen. You got a green thumb."

"All they need is water," said Charlie. "It's not a talent."

"Oh, it's a talent all right," said Bruce, "You just don't know it." He flicked off Charlie's office light and walked out into the hall. "Are you coming, or what?"

Charlie groped for his coat in the darkness.

৶

She turned the page, jostling the drowsing infant on her knee. In the distant town of Combray, at noon, the steeple bell of Sainte-Hilaire sounded twelve times, and the cook trundled out to collect her goods—the fresh brill from the fish-woman, the cherries, the almond paste, and the chocolate cream. Word spilled into word infinitely, page into page. Careful to keep the bottle fast in the child's mouth, she turned another page. A draft washed across the floor.

"Charlie," she said, looking up. "I didn't even hear you come in."

He turned around, hanging his coat, lips pursed. He came over and pushed back the attention-damp hair on her forehead. Then he knelt, his chin on her knee, and watched the baby.

She looked at him for a moment. "Everything all right?"

"Sure," he said.

They looked at the baby together. Charlie took the bottle and held it there at the baby's lips.

Alice found herself searching his face. She gave his ear a tug, and he smiled, if not a bit wearily.

"I've got it," he said. "Let me do it."

But peering down with such concentration at the baby, his expression took on a peevish quality. His skin looked wan, leached by fluorescence. He smelled of lunchmeat. He did not look young or anything like a long-distance runner. He sat there squatting on the threadbare carpet in stark contrast to the men and women who had just then been populating Combray, carrying basketsful of cherries up and down the streets of Alice's mind. Suddenly the bookstore clerk with the shorn head rose up in the crowd, walking toward her with an armful of books, his smile almost perceptible, almost in sight.

"Dammit," Charlie said, leaning back on his heels. "She keeps spitting it out."

"It's all right," said Alice.

"No, it's not," snapped Charlie, pushing the nipple back into the baby's mouth, and the baby's eyes flared, wakening. "I'm not doing it right."

"Gentle," she said. "Be *gentle*."

Suddenly, she experienced the sensation of missing him.

She was missing him even as he was there. He squatted over the baby. She looked away. The flatness outside of the book made her lonely. Not too long ago, they could be lost in their own thoughts or reading separate books and yet still be together, the tangle of invisible threads that connected them vibrating live with a billion transmissions. He nicked himself with a razor and she would wince. She laughed to herself and he would share the joke. He stumbled in a dream and she would stir. Now perhaps they were attuned that way to the babies, and to other things. She reached out and put her hand on his shoulder. He did not look at her. She knew the vibrations between them were still there, as stars still exist behind cloud cover. She leaned down over the baby to hide the tears in her eyes.

"Mommy loves baby," she whispered. "Mommy loves baby and Daddy loves baby."

Charlie stood, holding the empty bottle. He walked several paces off, rubbing his neck. Discreetly, Alice wiped her eyes. It was the book. It was her adolescent temptation to feel exceptionally isolated. For there he was, right there. Charlie Shade. Bringer of springtime. Shower librettist. Thief of the landlady's *Tribune*. He turned around, leaning against the kitchen counter.

"Listen," he said. "I'm sorry I've been late."

Alice fingered a strand of hair. "I know it can't be helped sometimes."

"Yes, it can be helped." He stepped toward her. "Here. Let me put her down."

He came back from the nursery with his tie off and shirt undone. His pants retained their creases and slight, first-day sheen. He sat beside her. By then, she was leaning sleepily against the wing of the chair.

"Are you asleep?" he said.

"No."

His shirtsleeves were rolled to the forearm. He pulled a string of hair from the corner of her mouth.

"I'm failing you," he said.

"What?" Alice said, opening her eyes, sitting upright. "No."

"Yes. I'm trying to do too much. I shouldn't be trying to do so much at work. There's no need to be late. I could be more efficient. My primary responsibility is here," he said, pointing at the floor.

She grabbed his hand. "Don't *coach* yourself like that, Charlie. I want you here because you want to be here." Alice paused, grimaced. "You know what? I'm doing better now. Maybe I—scared you before. It takes a while to get used to being a mother, but I'm getting better at it. Like today, we went to the bookstore." She blinked. "But I guess I've already told you that."

Charlie was looking down. "I think we could afford a sitter, now and again, so that you can get a break."

"We can't afford a sitter, Charlie. Have you seen our stack of bills?"

"Now and again. We can give up something else."

"Oh, Charlie," Alice whispered, terribly sleepy now, "I just want you. Just you. Yes, come home to me. Don't be late anymore. I—love you."

She leaned back and shut her eyes. She saw him running down the snowbound street after her, coatless; she felt his hand stroking her hair, like some never-possessed father; she saw a magnolia blossom, a guttering candle, and then her mind clouded over. Her arm jerked off the armrest.

"It's all right, Alice baby," he was saying. He was covering her with a blanket. "Go to sleep. It's all right. I'll be better. I won't be late."

In the distance, a baby whined. She was vaguely conscious

of Charlie moving away, away across the room. Mommy loves baby. Mommy loves baby and Daddy loves baby, and baby loves Mommy and Daddy.

∽

"So," he said, rubbing his hands together. "Where shall we start?"

The girl looked straight ahead at the vast, brightly lit warehouse. Stacks of mattresses surrounded her. She wiped her nose with the back of her hand.

"Opal? What do you think?"

She pulled her cardigan around her, pushing a piece of paper with the toe of her sneaker. Then suddenly, her head jerked backward. Charlie stepped toward her, grabbing her arm. Her eyes rolled toward him, shocked, as she stared helplessly for a moment at his hand.

"Jesus, are you all right?"

She nodded.

"That ever happen to you before?"

She shook her head no.

Charlie ran his hand through his hair. Tardive dyskinesia was the one side effect, besides all the other side effects, that made patients stop taking their meds. And it was a good excuse too, he thought. The twitching below the tongue, the base of the neck, he had seen this at Maynard and he knew there were drugs to counteract it, but that it could also become permanent, a muscular scar. He would talk to Hsu immediately. It would be fixed. Charlie glanced at her again, she standing right next to him. Nothing else betrayed her illness. Otherwise, standing there in the mattress store in her green cardigan, she looked exceedingly normal. For she had done her braid neatly today, and in her bright green sweater and new Reeboks she looked normal and fresh and young with her freckle-blurred lips. The hairs that were too short for her braid formed a humid halo of airy curls around her face.

"I'm sorry," he said. "We'll fix it."

Opal nodded. She wiped her nose with the back of her hand.

"I'm cold," she said.

"We'll be out of here in no time. Just as soon as we get someone to help us."

Charlie craned his neck around the absurdly high stacks of mattresses. He heard footsteps somewhere nearby.

"Hello?" he shouted. "Anyone here?"

"Be right with you!" replied a voice.

Opal's teeth were chattering. Charlie frowned, stuffing his hands into the pockets of his own warm jacket.

"Feeling cold could be just a side effect of your medication. Why don't I tell Dr. Hsu about that too? See what he says?"

"It's because I'm skinny," muttered Opal. "Always have been, always will be."

"Better than being fat."

"I'd rather be fat," said Opal. "Harder to break a fat person."

"I hadn't thought about it that way." Charlie fingered a piece of candy in his jacket pocket. "I'm skinny, too." He sat down on a low stack of mattresses. "Runners are usually skinny. I'm a long-distance runner. Well, I used to be."

"Why?"

Charlie cocked his head and looked up. "Why what?"

"Why do you run long distances?"

"I don't know," he shrugged. "Because I'm good at it?"

The girl rolled her eyes at him. Charlie laughed, happy to be teased. He had never thought about it really. He liked to run. Why not? Opal began to rock back and forth, her limbs now moving rhythmically. He assumed she was dancing to her own internal radio, before he heard, softly, actual music over the store's PA system.

"That's good. What's that, a waltz?"

"Contra dance," the girl said, smiling a little.

She danced slowly over to a cardboard cutout of a man leaning against a mattress.

"Hey, stranger," she said, dancing in front of the cardboard man.

Charlie looked on, entertained, pleased, until the clock on the wall sobered him. He was supposed to be at a med drop a half hour ago. The salesman came jogging around the corner in a burgundy polo shirt and ill-fitting black jeans. The salesman leapt toward Charlie and shook his hand greasily. He stepped back and wiped his hands on his slacks.

"Just finishing lunch," the salesman said. "That's no excuse for making you wait. Very sorry. We're short a hand today." The man noticed Opal hanging back. "Good morning, ma'am."

Opal looked at him straight on. Charlie had come to know this look of hers. She was deciding whether or not he was "just another mickey-mouser" or the rare sort you could actually believe.

"We're looking for a box spring," said Charlie. "For a twin bed. Something simple and cheap. And quick." He leaned forward. "I'm running pretty late. If you could—"

The man started jogging away.

"Follow me," he called over his shoulder.

Charlie jogged behind him, the sleeves of his nylon jacket swishing.

"Come on, Opal," he said, running backward now. She sighed and began to follow with what looked very much like a military lockstep. Charlie smiled and turned back to the salesman, who was surprisingly farther away.

"Hey," called Charlie. "Wait up, will you?"

But the salesman turned a corner and proceeded to jog down the aisle in a different direction, head bobbing over the tops of the mattresses. What the hell was the guy trying to do, Charlie thought, outrun them? Charlie snorted and then, unable to resist the challenge, began to run in earnest, pushing off the linoleum with the tips of his sneakers. Coming around the corner, he saw the guy at the end of an aisle, even farther and smaller, gesturing encouragingly.

"Jesus," said Charlie. And then, over his shoulder, "Over this way, Opal!"

At the end of the aisle, he entered a small clearing, where the salesman was bent over into a box, rummaging around, as if he'd been there for hours.

"Jesus H.," said Charlie. "Big place."

The man stood up. "We're the biggest mattress warehouse in the Northeast."

"I'll bet." Charlie stepped backward, looking for Opal.

"You want to wait for your wife?"

Charlie bobbed forward, laughing, waving his hand. "No, no. She's not my wife. No. She's my friend. We work together. We're partners." He waved his hand again.

The mattress man nodded. "Doesn't matter to me what people do," he said.

"Well. I'm just telling you she's not my wife."

"I'm not one to judge," said the mattress man.

"Like I said—" Charlie stopped. "Why don't you go ahead and show me what you've got."

The salesman showed Charlie four or five box spring models, which only varied in terms of price. Once Charlie picked the box spring, the salesman explained that of course you couldn't put the box spring straight on the floor on account of air circulation problems, but you could buy, for example, in an end-of-the-year closeout sale, this very simple metal bed frame on self-locking wheels. Charlie stepped backward into the aisle again, but Opal was still nowhere in sight.

"Fine," he said. "I'll take the frame, too. Okay?"

"Good choice. All for one low price."

"Fine," said Charlie, dusting off his hands. "So how do I get back to where I came from?"

The salesman stepped into the aisle and explained it, gesturing. He ripped off Charlie's bill, and Charlie carried it flapping in front of him as he ran back down the aisle, stopping momentarily at two identical crossroads, lost.

"Opal?" he shouted.

He jogged back in the other direction. Then he tried jumping up to see over the stacks of mattresses. Jogging to the end of what seemed like an impassable aisle, he heard quiet, strangled breathing. He stopped short, coming slowly around the corner to see Opal sitting on a low metal shelf.

"Jesus!" Charlie knelt in front of her. "Are you all right?"

Her face contorted and turned pink. She put both hands on her head.

"Oh. No, don't cry."

"I have a *headache*," she said.

"Oh, man," said Charlie. "I'm sorry. I guess I—I—"

His hands itched. He didn't like seeing her sitting there on a shelf like something for sale. It wasn't right—it wasn't *Christian*—not to comfort somebody weeping like that. He put one arm around her shoulder and gave it a squeeze.

"Hey, it's all right," he said gently. "I'm sorry I left you behind."

She sniffled, suddenly erect, as if struck with a new and pleasant idea.

"You left me behind," she said, not unkindly. It was as if the small truth of what happened had entered, shouting down the larger illusion.

"That's all. I'm sorry. But it's all right now. I found you. Plus, congratulations. You got a brand-new box spring and a frame with self-locking wheels."

He took off his jacket and put it over her shoulders. Opal looked down at the jacket, toying with the zipper. Charlie heard a cough and looked up.

The salesman was gazing down at them. With a tight, unpleasant smirk, the man winked.

⌒

Back in Norris Park, Charlie leaned across Opal and pushed her door open.

"All right," he said. "I'm really late for my next appointment. So I want to tell you that your box spring is going to be delivered next week by somebody named Mario."

Opal nodded vigorously. "No problem," she said.

"Is your headache better?"

"Oh, yes," she said. She did not get out of the car.

"I've—So I've really got to go. But listen. If you need help setting it up, you can call me. But Mario will probably do it all for you. Okay?"

"Call the switchboard for you?"

"Yes, call the switchboard."

Opal looked down at her nicotine-stained hands.

"That was fun," she said.

"It was?" said Charlie, surprised. "Well, that's great." He laughed. "That's great." He chucked her on the shoulder.

He watched her as she got out.

"Oh, hey, Opal," he called. "Sorry. Can I have my jacket back?"

She pulled the jacket off and pushed it through the window.

"Hey thanks, man." Charlie waved. And then—looking

clean, fresh, *happy*, completely normal, almost like a sister, fair and skinny and duck-toed—she marched up to her house and disappeared inside.

He pulled out toward the highway. After driving for a while, he realized his eyes were moist. In his heart, a feeling of redoubling gladness, almost as he had felt as a child in church, or at the end of a movie wherein the world is narrowly saved.

⌒

At the beginning, when they give them to you in the hospital, you cannot believe they intend to entrust such things to you, and sometimes when you first go out with them in the world you forget to pull the stroller along. And then (this is what she was realizing) there comes a point beyond which you cannot function naturally without them. The only pose that feels comfortable is the pose of holding a child. Walking alone and aimlessly, hugging her coat closed, she felt like a teenager, casting about for a struggle or a temptation. The precious hour she had wrangled to arrange the babysitter now became an hour to kill. The girl, Joanne—a serious, peach-complexioned girl who lived next door with her parents—was studying child development at the same community college where Alice had once registered for Foundations of English Literature. Although Alice had lingered for a long time in the apartment explaining things, it appeared that Joanne was completely adept with the twins, moving in the dim nursery light between the cribs and the changing table, testing the warmth of the formula by dropping it soberly on her wrist. The girl was at least more academically qualified for mothering than Alice herself.

She walked with her emptiness past the record store, the cheese shop, the campaign office. Her jeans chafed her thighs.

She wondered how long the feeling of bereftness would linger if you were to be separated from them permanently. Motherhood destroyed, in a way, one's ability to be alone. The threads between her and her babies stretched and sagged but would never snap. In fact, the more they sagged, the less likely they were to snap. All humanity, then, was bound each to each by an infinity of stretched webbing. Even he, she thought, looking so isolate and so beautiful, even he had a mother. Through the cold glass window, she could see him sitting at the cash register, working a pair of scissors across a sheet of acetate.

"Hi," said Alice, pausing inside the shop door.

"Well, hi," he said, his scissors open. He looked at her for a moment in the doorway, then with slightly more recognition said again, "*Hi.*"

"Hi. I finished the book."

He narrowed his eyes.

"The book about remembering, by Proust?"

"Oh." He nodded. Then he said, "You finished that?"

"Yeah."

"You finished that whole book?"

"Well, you know, the first book. Took me two weeks." Alice wiped her nose with her hand, then stood there, too embarrassed to turn back conversationally, for she saw that she was bragging. "I loved it. It was really—Everything was so—" She kicked at the floor with her clog. She had yet to really look into his face. When she did, she was alarmed by the complete levelness of his expression, and how it looked exactly the same as last time, how she had not exaggerated it in her memory. He was dressed in denim overalls and a loose white undershirt. His eyes, crow-black and steady, had not left her face.

A man in a hunting vest walked up to the register. "Where's your military history?"

The boy got up and walked slowly across the room and pointed at a shelf with his scissors.

"Don't you know the rule about scissors?" Alice said.

He looked down at his hands. She walked up to him. Taking the scissors out of his hands, she closed the blades, and returned them to him handle out.

"Hold them like *that*."

He stood looking down at the scissors.

"It doesn't really matter," she said. "It's just something they tell children."

He looked up and nodded. Then he smiled.

"Where are those babies of yours?" he said, pointing at her with the scissor handle.

"With a babysitter. Our first time."

"Don't worry about it. Everything's okay." Abruptly the young man turned around and began to walk toward the back of the store. "I have something for you."

Alice pursued. "You do?"

He ducked into a small storeroom. She stood at the doorway watching him dig around in the boxes, his shoulder blades working. The room was painted blue and glowed like an aquarium in the winter light. It smelled of must. She leaned against the doorway, watching him. A black cat leapt off of a shelf behind the register and walked around her legs. She knelt, rubbing its silky head.

"This is where my uncle keeps new books that I haven't shelved yet." The young man peered at her under his arm. "Keep an eye on the store, would you?"

"Oh," Alice said. "Oh no. They're looting the place."

He stood in alarm.

"No. It was a joke."

He came out of the storeroom and looked anyway. Then he handed Alice a large, water-stained volume.

"*Clarissa*," she said.

"You can have it for free. It's a duplicate."

Her eyes widened with pleasure. She opened the book and

then put her nose inside and took a long sniff. He looked down at her, shaking his head.

"Don't smell it," he said. "Read it."

She was laughing. She laughed for a long moment, aware that her laughter was odd, sourceless, but she couldn't help it, clutching the heavy book to her chest. She felt so entirely grateful.

He said, "Your hair is like oil on water."

Alice stopped laughing and stared at him with an open mouth. His face grew serious. He edged past her, out of the doorway. He went to the register and popped it open. He withdrew a sleeve of quarters and cracked it like an egg against the drawer.

Alice walked up to him. She put *Clarissa* on the counter.

"Have you read this?" she asked him softly.

"No."

"We could read it together. At the same time. Like a book club with two people in it. You said yourself it was a duplicate."

"I don't know," he said, spilling out his quarters. "I don't think I could concentrate that long."

"Come on, if *I* can read it—with twins—you sure can."

"I'm more of a writer these days. I'm not much of a reader anymore."

The door opened, and a gust of cold air poured in.

"What do you write?" she asked.

"Poems. Tiny ones."

"You write tiny poems and I read large books." Alice leaned forward. "What are your poems about? I'd genuinely like to know."

He looked up. "How I went crazy," he said.

"Sweetheart?"

Alice whirled around, one hand to her chest.

"Hey, baby," Charlie said, grinning, rubbing his arms. "Whoa, it's cold out there." He looked back outside, then he smiled at the other customers in the store as if they'd been expecting him. "Great place. No wonder you like it so much."

He walked up to her and gave her a full-mouthed kiss. Alice neatened her hair. She pressed at the bridge of her nose.

"You surprised me," she whispered. "Where'd you come from?"

"I saw you through the window. I had an appointment around the corner and when I saw you I couldn't resist. I thought," Charlie grimaced, "maybe I'd give you a lift home, if you wanted, it's so damned cold."

"Oh. Sure." Alice looked down, tucking a strand of hair in her mouth. "I'll take a lift. Thanks."

Charlie leaned over.

"Hey," he whispered. "I missed you, is the truth of it."

Then he leaned back, holding her by both shoulders. She was looking fixedly at the cords of his neck and the reddish hairy tuft of his chest hair when he exclaimed, "By God. *Hal*? Is that you?"

Alice spun around. The young black-eyed clerk was smiling at her husband, reaching out a hand. She gasped hoarsely.

"Jesus, you look great," said Charlie, moving past Alice to shake the boy's hand. "Damn, how *are* you? It's been a long time."

"I don't remember your name," said Hal.

"I'm Charlie. Charlie Shade."

"I remember *you*," said Hal. "I remember you a lot. Just not your name."

Charlie clapped the young man's shoulder. "You look great, man."

"I feel good." Hal nodded his head and put his hands in the pockets of his overalls. He looked quickly at Alice. "I remember you. How's Mattoon?"

Charlie laughed. "I told you about Mattoon? Jesus, I was fresh out of school when I met you. Totally green."

"I thought you were good. You were a human being. My mother still talks about you."

Charlie laughed, motioning for Alice. She came and stood under his arm.

"Hot damn," Charlie said, looking around the bookstore. "What a great gig. Surrounded by books. Now you can read all you want. Hal here is very well-read."

"Well," said Hal. "My uncle runs it. I just help out Mondays and Wednesdays. Sweep. Shelve."

"That's excellent," said Charlie. He stopped, smiled down at Alice. Her mouth was open and she was blinking rapidly. "Hey. Did Hal here help you find what you needed?"

He kissed her again, rather demonstratively this time, and then looked at Hal and immediately felt bad for kissing the pretty woman that Hal kept stealing glances at. Somehow, he felt very tenderly toward her, to see her caught flirting like this, her face flushed with the pleasure of books and attractive company. He preferred seeing this Alice to an Alice sitting cross-legged in front of the television, folding onesies, hair pulled back unevenly with barrettes. Besides, she was his. He could understand how Hal felt. He had seen her through the bookstore window himself. He kissed the top of her head.

Alice was looking down at *Clarissa*.

"She reads a lot of books," said Charlie to the silent pair.

"Good for business," said Hal.

"She reads a hell of a lot. She'll read everything in here, I bet you."

"Yeah," said Hal, laughing. "Maybe."

"Well, this is incredible," said Charlie, shaking his head. "Running into you, Hal. It's a real pleasure to see you."

Hal scratched the back of his neck, nodding.

"All right, my man," said Charlie, holding out his hand to the side. The boy put his pencil between his teeth and reached sheepishly for the hand.

Charlie turned to Alice. "Ready to go?"

Alice nodded.

"Thanks a lot for the book," she said, not looking up.

"All right," said Hal.

They walked toward the door.

"See you," said Alice.

"See you," said Hal.

Charlie turned. "Hal," he said. "Great to see you, man. I mean it."

⌐

"Well," Charlie said, laughing shortly. "I'll be. *Hal*."

He held the door as Alice bent into the car and sat down. He came around to the other side and got in. He pulled the car into traffic.

"I'll be damned." Charlie shook his head at the passing landscape. "What a good-looking kid, huh? He looks—" He raised his eyebrows, thinking about it. His face was fuller now, elastic, comprehending. "—perfectly healthy. No kidding. If he's lucky, if he takes it easy, he may be completely out of the woods. A fair number of people who have a psychotic episode don't actually develop a full-blown illness, you know. He's got a damned good chance, looks like to me. Don't you think?"

Suddenly Alice turned from the window. "Dammit, Charlie. I wish I didn't *know* what I *know*."

"What do you mean? About Hal? He'll never find out that you know."

"*I* know," Alice said, pointing to her chest. "*I* know that I know. I know everything about him. I know that his mother has a green dress!"

"It's all right. Hey now, calm down. It's not a problem. Hell, I might have made some of it up. The green dress, I probably made that up."

"You couldn't have made it up. It's too good."

Charlie opened his mouth, then closed it.

"I shouldn't have asked you to tell me about people," said Alice. "It was selfish. I know you're not supposed to tell me. It's not right. Now look. It—collapsed."

"Hey, everybody does it sometimes. It's all right. You're not some stranger. You're my wife. Everybody does it sometimes. It's just a weird funny thing that it all came together like that. That's just the danger of working in the same town for a while. You start seeing your clients all over the place. In fact," said Charlie, turning down their street a little wildly, the wheels whining, "Hal's a success story. He's back. Do you think he looked ashamed to see me? Not at all. Proud. When I met him, he was half his weight, terrified. *Crazy*. Now look at him, standing so straight. A working man."

"And his college scholarship?" asked Alice. "His wrestling career?"

Charlie pulled up to their apartment building and turned off the car. He put his arm over the back of Alice's seat and looked at her.

"You're a good person. You have deep, genuine love for all people, real people and people in stories. I forget sometimes how deep you take it all in. I'm sorry I put you in an awkward position."

Alice turned away.

"Listen," he said. "I miss you, Alice. When I passed by that store, I have to tell you the truth, I didn't recognize you at first. I thought, Who is *she*? Damn she's pretty. And then I realized you were my wife. And I felt so—" he shrugged. "Outrageously lucky."

She looked down at her hands.

"And then I felt sad. Because I missed you. Be with me."

"I am with you."

Charlie grabbed her hands and pulled her toward him.

"Listen, I love you. I want to be like you. I want to be worthy of you. You make me want to be good."

"You already are good, Charlie," said Alice, her eyes wet. "You don't have to *try* so hard."

"I just want to tell you. I never forget you. All day, you're with me." He smacked his thigh. "Marry me."

"We're already married."

"All right, then how about a date?"

"What?"

"This Friday. Ask Joanne to sit for us."

"We can't afford to have her but once a week, Charlie."

"Yes we can. Just this once. Alice, I'm begging you," Charlie made exaggerated bowing motions.

She pushed him away, laughing. "And what are we going to do on our date, poor as we are? Go lick salt off rocks?"

"Let's not be poor for one night. Get a new dress and everything. Will you please? Get a new dress?"

"I don't know," said Alice.

"Please? Go up and ask Joanne."

He leaned over to kiss her, but she leaned back, scrutinizing his face.

"Is this for sure? I mean, you're sure we should make a plan? Something could come up at work."

"Alice—"

"We could keep it flexible. Sometimes you can't predict—"

"Alice." Charlie took her hand. "I promise you."

⌒

It was hard to imagine telling things to people. What if he were to tell her, or someone like her, about the voice in the bedroom? About the smell of hospitals? About the absence of color and Myself and oranges and verandas and nosebleeds and geraniums glimpsed from a corpse's point of view? About the folded world. For you could not reveal it. It was you. It was all that you could not say. It was why you chose to arrive yourself instead of sending a letter. They could not know you, but whenever you came, when you were there, they could be happy enough because your riddle was nearby. Hal was sitting straight up in the chair with a book open on his lap. Soon he realized he was trying to mimic the posture of a person reading. He shut the book and waited.

Or could you reveal it, yourself-as-world? Sometimes, he was not sure. For in its unfolding, it was no longer a world. The revelation was the disappearing. He always got to the same point in the riddle in which love was death. The death of the world of oneself. The hanging-by-a-threadness of oneself.

He contemplated getting up to shelve, but he felt excessively delicate, in the sort of way that used to be fine, but now always had some fear in it. A red car drove down the street. Hal winced. It was so red. He checked the front pocket of his overalls for his relapse list. He was supposed to keep his list with him at all times. Working at bookstores, admiring women, was he growing too confident for who he was?

Hal had done very well in the hospital. Everyone said so. Two weeks in and out, made it seem like a bad flu. Maybe because he was an athlete, and maybe because he had been a pretty normal person before it all went to hell, Hal had instinctively followed the rules. He'd met variously with doctors, psychiatric and otherwise, and he went into a room with a young woman who instructed him to make things out of multicolored pasta shells, and he recognized in this woman's eyes the same transfixed expression of women who had looked at him all his life, and she would blush when he walked in wearing his overalls and carrying his clipboard on which he was supposed to check off his various daily successes, and his mother and father came every single day to visit him. His mother would look at his clipboard and make impressed noises. A couple times, the social worker—Charlie Shade—had visited, and they sat together in the TV lounge, and Hal was more forthcoming than he'd been for a long time, and even told the heretofore-untold story of Miranda R_____ and what really happened at the lookout.

Within days, the medication began to take effect, and two weeks later Hal had been sent home with his mother and father, and treated as an outpatient. On Tuesdays and Fridays, his father drove him to a clinic where he got his pills, and there were new doctors and new therapists and social workers, and all of them were very nice, and as he got better he also became more lucid of mind, and he tried to accept what they told him, that they'd have to wait and see, but until then he just needed to relax and follow his progress for a little longer, and that he might not be able to do some of the things he wanted to do, and that they would have to wait and see about college, but a deferment was probably in order, and that wrestling was really out of the question, and anything particularly stressful was just out of the question—so much lost so quickly! But coming from where he'd come from, Hal didn't mind that much. The Spring of Miranda had exhausted him, drained him. He himself now found it quite ridiculous to be so preoccupied with turning an opponent over on his back and forcing him against a rubber mat, and he looked back at his old sketches and drawings, made of dark, disturbed graphite clouds, and wondered rather impartially what in hell they were supposed to represent. He held a dead pencil in his hand. The books on the shelves were dead too. He finally joined his parents in the den and watched television with them. Sometimes he laughed at the right parts, but it was still really a vast moving aggregate of pixilation and cultural reference. He would have to be rebuilt, down to the smallest screw.

Still, over time, he had begun to sense, in the far distance and approaching, a reasonable solution, a reasonable moment, coming along, calling out for him without yet knowing where he was. He felt—if you could believe it—lucky. He was told that he was. But also, he knew it. He had not been too much destroyed. He did not want to be any further destroyed. He understood: the threat had him pinned. He understood he was pinned by something that could kill him with just one more tight clutch to the throat. And so he liked watching her hair and the arrival of color but he needed to step slowly, carefully, leaving breadcrumbs.

Beside him, Uncle Bob's cat mewled, flashing her delicate fangs. The cat leapt righteously to his lap, compacted herself against his legs, and shut her eyes.

Uncle Bob was not Hal's uncle. Uncle Bob was his fan. An acquaintance of Hal's father, the old man had played football for Yale years ago, and was a great fan of wrestling and all the sports that they played at places like Yale. The man now was half-crippled, and could be seen hobbling up the bleachers at all of Cross High's wrestling matches, pressing familiarly on the shoulders of all the people he passed.

And down below, on his blue foam moonscape, Hal had reigned in every match. When it was his turn, he stood up from the bench, fastened his headgear, and just this action prompted the bleachers to erupt in scattered applause. It was as if they were clapping for his existence. To exist, to exist so perfectly. To stand at five-eleven but appear seven feet tall, to stand in the complete candor of a blue jumpsuit, which articulated the very disks of the spine. The other boys on the benches crossed their legs when he stood. Everyone became a girl. Everyone became a girl when Hal walked out onto the mat. Even his opponent momentarily fell in love with him, then had to shake it off, shake it off and try to think of smashing his head, try to think of destroying him. But Hal was always the protagonist. He didn't even have to win. Hal was the winner even when he lost. And he had only lost three times—

once when he wasn't thinking, and twice to the state champion, a square-headed boy strong as an ox who had been killed in a motorcycle accident during the Spring of Miranda. The death of the square-headed champion and the psychotic break of Hal had removed the two top wrestlers in their weight class in one season, and it was just too much for everybody, for all the fans, especially for Uncle Bob.

By the end of the summer, many of Hal's classmates and teammates had gone off to college, but Hal had not. He was still helping his mother with the garden and doing what they told him at the day hospital and otherwise trying not to think too much. One evening, an evening of a particularly rosy summer sunset, a sunset that Hal noticed but tried to be careful with, Uncle Bob showed up. This was when he was still Mr. Green. He knocked on the door and Hal's mother let him in. He sat with his elbows on his knees, and spoke at great length about his days at Yale and how when you get old it doesn't matter what really happened, just how you remember it. After some more of this rather one-side discussion, Bob Green turned to Hal and said he'd been thinking, he was wondering if Hal could help him out at the bookstore.

Hal's parents looked at him hopefully.

I can only pay you six dollars an hour, said Bob Green, but on the other hand, you don't have to do much but put books in the right place and sweep up, and reach the high places. Have you seen the store? People just come in to yak about books and old times, buy a dollar paperback. You know much about books?

Hal knows a lot about books, answered his mother. Go look at his bedroom. They're all over the place. He writes poetry sometimes, even.

I won't lie to you, I already knew that, said the old man. Son, I—And here the man stopped and tried to resist some affliction, some great painful affliction, that had overcome him.

Hal knew then that Bob Green was having a harder time letting go of Hal than Hal was. What would he do this winter, with only a group of children in bunchy jumpsuits? Bob Green wanted to be near Hal. Hal knew it. Although Hal could never figure out why anyone wanted to be near him, he was quite used to allowing it, to rolling over to it like a bitch to her pups, and he didn't begrudge it anyone. Besides, he was pleasantly overcome with what seemed like a whim—refreshing, slight: Why not work in a bookstore?

Hal put up his hand, as if to protect Mr. Green from what he was about to say.

I'd like that, he said. I accept your offer.

Hal glanced over at his mother. She wrinkled up her nose at him and pressed her hands against her skirt.

What are you doing Monday? said Mr. Green.

Is that a trick question? said Hal.

Mr. Green squinted.

Working for you, said Hal.

Everybody laughed. No one harder than Uncle Bob.

And now here the old man was, hobbling into the bookstore with a candy bar stuck out of his mouth. He hitched his thumb over his shoulder.

"Dinya see your mom out there, Champ?" He pasted his white hair down against his head. "She's waiting for you."

Uncle Bob came over and pulled the black cat off Hal's lap.

"Poor girl," he said to the cat. "You in love with the kid? Well, get in line."

Hal walked outside and got into the car. His mother was sitting with her hands on the wheel. Her hair was aglow with sunlight, and she was wearing a plaid skirt with a large gold safety pin on the side. She smiled at him and they drove along in silence for a while. He flipped on the radio, and the dashboard lit up green. Listening to the soft music, the queer frightened feeling receded. The threat of color receded. He smiled and bent his head. All those girls . . . he missed them. It had hit right when he was ready for them. He missed having the chances. He missed the time before love was death or anything else but love. Maybe this was it for him now. Maybe the rest was over, and maybe he could have some of it back.

"How are you feeling?" his mother asked.

"Good," he said.

"Good," she said. "I'm glad."

Hal looked over at his mother. He remembered how, those first days in the hospital, she had tried to adopt the RIGHT Attitude: Reasonable expectations, accurate Information, et cetera et cetera, how she had poured over their catchphrases, when if you asked him she was born with the right attitude— her own. She was his mother. The colors blurred past outside the window. Closing his eyes, Hal smoothed his hand over the seat of the car, feeling the dimples in the fabric. Soon he was thinking of her again. Her face appeared in a pear-shaped drop of water in his head. Oil on water. Oil on silk. He smoothed his hand over the door handle. Then he opened his eyes, ashamed. He did not know what he was ashamed of. It was not good for him to fantasize. Take it easy, he cautioned himself. But this shame felt pleasant. He was ashamed of his wrist where she had touched it. He was ashamed of the cat where she had scratched it.

"What color was your hair when you were young?" Hal asked his mother.

Her hand went up to her head. "Well, it was dark brown. Like it is now, but without all the gray."

"There's not so much gray," said Hal, peering over.

His mother touched the side of her hair. She glanced at him, tears in her eyes. She looked very happy and almost beautiful. He knew what she was thinking, that he was getting better and that he was going to love her again and become Hal again, and for once he let her think this and did not yank it away.

～

"Hey," said Charlie. "You wanted to see me?"

Harriet looked up from her papers. Squinting, she patted the top of her desk. He took her glasses off the bookshelf and handed them to her. When she put them on, her broad face relaxed.

"Cupcake," she said, leaning back hugely in her chair. "We got a problem."

Charlie sat down quickly in the chair facing, where the clients sit. "What is it?"

"Miss Ludlow. Seems she got an unexpected visitor the other day. Some guy tried to deliver a mattress—"

"A box spring," said Charlie. "And?"

"—and she came at him with a hammer."

"What?"

"The guy's all right. Lucky for us he has a strange sense of humor. And good reflexes. You got a comment about this?"

"What?" said Charlie. "Jesus."

"You're surprised? You shouldn't be surprised. It's your job not to be surprised. Why weren't you there for the delivery if there was this potential? You were what, trying out for the Red Sox?" Harriet raised her eyebrows and looked at him over her glasses. "Is this unprecedented behavior?"

"Yes. This is definitely not baseline. Jesus. The guy's all right, you said?"

"The guy thought it was funny."

"It's not funny. Where is she?"

"Miss Ludlow is at the hospital. The policeman took her in. She was pretty acute at the time, but he took a report."

"What'd it say? What'd he think, the cop? I mean, maybe the mattress guy provoked her. Maybe the mattress guy should be evaluated."

"Maybe, Charles. But that's not how we approach things here. It's not us versus them."

"But last time I saw her she was perfectly—I can't—It doesn't—"

"Oh, stop," said Harriet. "I know you're concerned. I've already spoken to Miss Ludlow. Dr. Hsu and I met over there right away with the police. He's got her on new medication and she's already feeling better. I asked her—"

"When did this happen? I mean, I could have gone with you, right?"

"It was over the weekend, Charles. I was *on call*. I'm the team leader?" Harriet narrowed her eyes, pausing a moment. "I asked her if she liked living alone in Norris Park or if she'd prefer to live with other people, in a more supervised situation. If that would make her feel safer."

Charlie cocked his head back, as if struck. "What'd she say?"

"She was very upset. She said I could take her dead body to a group home."

Charlie rubbed his jaw and looked out the window.

"But it's all right now. I told her nobody's sending her to a group home. I was just asking for her preference. She was very upset. But you know, Charlie, if this is something that comes up again—well, it's untenable. For *her*."

"Well," said Charlie, laughing a little, fingering the shrinking space between collar and neck. "She's going to feel threatened with that now, the group home idea. Don't you think?"

"You got an objection to my handling of this?"

Charlie licked his lips. He shook his head. Then suddenly he said, "I feel she's improving rapidly. She just started to come here for the employment workshop. She meets Carter religiously. Her physical appearance is improving. She takes her meds."

"All this, and she *still* beat on a guy with a hammer." Harriet sat back and folded her hands under her breasts. The phone rang, and she let it ring, sitting there until it stopped. "She's got a lot of negative symptoms, Charlie, you know that. She's very withdrawn. Antisocial. And she's not med-compliant, obviously. I mean, do you watch her take her meds? Are you trying to be singularly responsible for this girl? You have the time for that with all the other clients who need you?" Harriet shrugged, and took a candy out of the dish on her desk and unwrapped it slowly. She put it in her mouth, and leaned back. "Charles. How do you think you're doing with this case? You feel like you're able to maintain your objectivity?"

"Yes. Absolutely. I think I'm doing well."

Harriet narrowed her eyes. "You one hundred percent sure? You're not being too influenced by your own—hopes for her? They're *your* hopes, remember." She leaned forward. "Be honest with me now."

Charlie wagged his head, swallowing. "I'm *sure*," he said. "I'm sure."

But suddenly he was not sure. He looked up into Harriet's strangely solicitous face. He tilted his head, as if listening for the Midwestern sincerity, which had not, until then, ever truly forsaken him. He felt something drain from his fingers. Blood? Confidence? He remembered a time the week previous when Opal had complained of the Radio, how it was louder than usual. And then, passing an old man in the grocery store, the withering, murderous look she had given him for no reason. This was not her usual mickey-mouser look. This look was something else. He gave her her meds. He observed. Didn't he? But he could not remember one exact memory of her placing the pills in her mouth. He only remembered being gratified by her smile behind the screen door whenever he came for a visit, by her neat braid, by the squeaking of her new sneakers on the linoleum of the mattress store.

"Do you think she thought it was you?"

Charlie looked up, his heart pounding. "What?"

"The delivery guy," said Harriet, rolling the candy in her mouth. "The man she assaulted. Did she think the guy was you?"

"What?" Charlie laughed. "She probably assaulted him because he *wasn't* me."

"You sure?"

"I'm sure. I'm probably the only person in the world she trusts!"

"Well, it's painful to trust. It's painful for a healthy person to take that risk. Let alone someone who's been messed with a thousand times. Her affection for you could be causing her pain."

"I know, Harriet. I understand those concepts."

"But they're not only concepts." Harriet pursed her lips. "You know, I'm just talking with you. That's my job. If you've got any more ideas, you could share them with Bruce. Maybe you boys are more comfortable together." She put her hands on her knees. "Opal will be discharged in a couple days. Let's see if we can stay on top of this one, all right, baby?"

"Absolutely."

"How about we go see her together next time?"

"Sure. All right. If that's what you think."

"That is what I think or I wouldn't have said it. Hey. I ever tell you about my brother Odine?"

"No," said Charlie, checking his watch. "I'd like to hear about it, but I have a med drop."

Harriet stood, revealing the rumpled seat of her skirt. She took her big beaten purse from a drawer.

"I'll come with you then," she said. "Lucky you."

~

The morning sky was huge with sun. The bedroom glowed. He turned over, body sleep deprived and belly rumbling, and looked into Alice's face. Her cheek was pouched against her hand. He remembered her on a ship's deck. High, black seas. Her white hand clutching the gunwale. It's only a storm, he had called out. But when she turned to him, her face was calm. We're in a storm, he said. He expected her to be afraid. But she was not afraid. In the dream he understood that she was not afraid because he was there. Smoothing the blanket down over her body, he licked his lips, hoping for the taste of salt.

Later, outside in the clear, late winter brightness, passing the children waiting for their school buses, the dream clung to Charlie, cheering him up. There was nothing a man wanted quite so much as to be looked at like that by his wife. Girls could excite you, fortify you, but only your wife could blow you away. Behind the driver's seat, his good suit swung from a hook, pressed and clean, ready for the date. After work, he would dress at the Y, pick up some roses, and arrive not as the man who left his whiskers in the sink, but as the lover. This thought excited him, even though it was a put-on and she might even roll her eyes. He moved through his morning duties swiftly. The staff meeting went through at a clip, and then they all dispersed into the city.

Then, at noon, the switchboard paged him. Somehow, he knew it was Opal. She had been out of the hospital two days. Just the day before, he had gone to see her with Harriet. Harriet had plodded alongside him, as if he needed her protection. Knocking on the door, calling out familiarly, he was thinking, *Just you watch.*

But it had been awkward. Opal was withdrawn, virtually

silent. She sat wrapped in a blanket, chain smoking. She offered him not a single smile. It was as if they barely knew each other. Once, while Harriet was helping herself to a glass of water in the kitchen, the girl's eyes flared meaningfully. *What?* Charlie whispered. But Harriet came back in and sat there drinking her water, one big hand spread on the card table. She was too big for the place. Yet they stayed nearly an hour, Harriet talking softly, Opal's eyes cast down.

Charlie checked his pager and then fumbled for his cell phone. But it wasn't in his coat pocket. Neither was it in his shoulder bag. He almost ran a stoplight checking for it in the glove compartment.

"No way," he said, smacking the dashboard. "You've got to be *kidding* me."

Swearing, trying to laugh, he pulled over at a gas station to make the call from a pay phone. He turned up the collar of his coat.

"I am *not* going to *no* group home," Opal said when she answered, her voice lower and huskier than usual. He heard her drag on her cigarette. "She can take my dead body to a group home."

"Opal," he said. "You do not have to go to a group home. That's only if you want to. Didn't Harriet explain that pretty well yesterday?"

"When I get angry, they think I'm crazy."

"I don't see it that way. It's okay to be angry sometimes."

He tried to assuage her, telling her it would not happen, not if she showed up regularly to Carter and took her meds and simply stayed out of trouble. Not if she kept her house clean and ate right and if if if. But that day, his heart was not in it. Part of him, he realized to his shame, hoped that she might agree to a group home. If that would do it. If that would help. But mostly he was thinking of how in the hell he was going to finish everything on his docket, including his paperwork, and shower and change at the Y by six o'clock. Scratch the roses, he thought.

Opal could sense his distraction. She breathed evenly on the other end, and then said, in almost a whisper, "You can't break me."

"Break you? What do you mean? You feel like I'm against you now? That's not true." Charlie turned and checked the car, which he'd left running.

"You know what I mean."

"Nobody's going to break you. We care about you."

"Slice me up. Stuff me into *rooms*. With *groups*."

"No. Nobody's trying to go against you or hurt you in any way."

Opal took another drag on her cigarette. Charlie stood there, listening. She did not sound good. Not good at all. But his heart was not in it. His gaze, absently focused on a leaf skipping down the sidewalk, sharpened only when a gust came up the street and washed over him, smelling of metal.

"When are you coming today?"

"I just came yesterday, Opal. I'm coming to see you again on Monday."

"What if it snows? It smells like snow."

Charlie looked up at the bright blue sky.

"It's one hundred percent not going to snow," he said. "I guarantee it. There's not a cloud in the blessed sky. Look out your window."

He heard the cigarette paper crackle. He told her that he was sorry she was having a hard day, and that if she said the word he'd call someone else to come be with her. When she refused, he told her to take it easy and rest and light some candles and don't forget to eat lunch.

And then, at just about three o'clock, in one complete sweep so total it was almost like an eclipse, a low dark cloud rolled across the sky. The temperature plummeted. By then, his anomalous efficiency had forsaken him and he was late yet again, hustling George Delgado across the parking lot to the pet store to get dog food. George had waited outside for Charlie for an hour, and his face was white with cold. George did not like it when Charlie was late, and often took the opportunity to scold him in his heavily accented voice and compare him to the numerous other social workers he'd had in his long tenure as a mental patient. George refused to quicken his pace across the parking lot toward the pet store. By the time they crossed under the awning, Charlie had felt, on his face, the cold wet kiss of a snowflake.

"*Shit*."

The old man turned inside the door of the pet store and glowered at Charlie.

"Don't swear, okay? I'm your elder."

"All right," said Charlie, following the old man into the cavernous store.

But as he watched the old man finger every single ridiculous item on the racks, he couldn't help but grit his teeth. Why so slow? he thought. Why so *slow*? George paused over a little tartan vest that he said he wanted to buy for Britney.

"Just the food, George," said Charlie, gesturing forward.

His pager vibrated again. The switchboard. Leaving George to his reveries in the aisle, Charlie trudged up to the register.

"Could I ask you a big favor?" he asked the girl in her red apron, who turned and looked upon him with a sanguine expression. "I've lost my cell phone. I've got to make one quick phone call. If I could just use your phone for a second, it'd be a great favor."

The girl pointed out the window with a long plastic fingernail. "Out there's a pay phone."

Charlie had to squint to see it, clear across the parking lot—a single booth standing amidst acres of tar.

"Yeah," said Charlie. "Listen, I'm a mental health care worker. I've just been paged. It could be an emergency."

But the girl was already shaking her head, as if to some sad, distant ballad.

"Nu-uhn." She waved her plastic fingernail in the air. "I'm not supposed to let no one use the store phone. You can head on back and ask the manager to use his."

The girl pointed. The back of the store and the manager's office seemed almost as far away as the pay phone in the parking lot.

Charlie clenched his jaw. "Thanks," he said to the girl. "Thanks a *hell* of a lot."

He walked back to George, shocked at himself, but also enjoying the bitterness in his mouth. He wanted to swear some more. They paid for the dog food, and Charlie led the old man out by the elbow, the sack of food over his shoulder. The old man pointed at Charlie's car as they passed it.

"Charlie. You lost your own car."

"No, I didn't," replied Charlie curtly. "We've got to go to that pay phone way over there. I've got to make a call."

At the pay phone, Charlie stabbed at the numbers in the cold. George stood beside the booth, shivering and white-faced. This time, Charlie called Margot, the receptionist.

"Another page from Miss Ludlow," said Margot. "She's called here three times in the past twenty minutes. Where've you been? Would you like me to page Harriet?"

Involuntarily, Charlie's fists clenched around nothing.

"No," he said. "Wait. Let me think about it." He checked his watch. It was a quarter to five already. "It's the snow."

"What?"

"Let me call her back first," said Charlie. "I'll see what's up. If there's any problem, I'll get right back to you."

But when he called, there was no answer. He tried twice. Then he slammed the phone down on the receiver. Just as he was calling Margot back, he noticed that George was gone. Charlie charged out of the phone booth, squinting toward the street. Nothing. Panning the parking lot, he spotted the old man halfway across the lot, making for the steps.

"Mr. Delgado!" Charlie ran, slipping on the thin coat of snow that was already beginning to cover the lot. "George! Where are you going? Wait up!

"Where are you going?" said Charlie, coming up to the old man, trying to smile.

George shrugged, his large chapped lips pursed. Charlie held him lightly by the arm as they walked back to the car. Once inside, Charlie leaned over and checked the old man's seatbelt.

"Okay?" he said. "Everything okay?"

George said nothing. He shrugged, looking miserably out the window, where the snowflakes were swirling and falling like exploding plaster from the vast grayness of the sky. Why today, Charlie thought. For god sakes why today? The car windows were becoming completely opaque with their breath, and with George's nervous sullen energy. Turning the corner at the bottom of a hill, the car fishtailed, arighting itself only as Charlie gunned it uphill, inching forward up the steep incline.

"I can't see!" George shouted, his hands clawing at the steamed window.

Charlie glanced at the old man. "Just sit tight, George. I can't talk right now, okay? I've got to control the car. It's very difficult to see right now."

"I stand outside too long! While you make a phone call. I *freeze*."

"Just hold on a minute. We'll talk in a minute."

The old man slumped over and looked philosophically out the window. "Why you always got to make a phone call? Why you always got to be late? Why you got to—"

"Because I have a goddamned million appointments *every day*." Charlie drew a breath. The windshield wipers beat the snow back in the silence. "Please just be quiet for a second. Please."

There was quiet as the car squealed up the hill. The pedal was completely depressed now. Charlie leaned forward, as if it might help. Visibility had shrunken to yards, and all he could see with certainty was the glow of the taillights in front of him and the traffic lights on the top of the hill ahead. He checked his waistband. His beeper was still on, but there were no new messages. Why would she call him three times and then not even wait twenty minutes for his response? Maybe she had finally called Emergency Services. Maybe by now everything was fine and he would be able to go home, where he was expected in thirty minutes. Scratch the shower, he thought. Scratch the roses, scratch the suit. So I won't be the lover.

Miraculously, the old Toyota made it up the hill and into the right driveway. Charlie unzipped his jacket and leaned back against the seat. His hairline was drenched with sweat, and the air smelled of burned rubber. He looked over at the old man.

"Hey," he said tenderly. "Sorry to be short with you. I just wanted to make sure I got you home safe." He touched the old man's shoulder. "I'm really sorry I was late to come get you. I'm sorry you were cold. I should have done better."

The old man looked over. "Wanna come in for a little? Come see Britney?"

"No, thank you," said Charlie. "I'll run the bag up, okay? But then I have plans with my wife."

"Good for you," said the old man. "I was young once, too."

"I know you were."

Whereas he normally would have been touched by the old man's nostalgia, Charlie felt dread creeping up his neck, a dampness.

He slapped George's hat on his head and walked him up the

steps to his apartment by the arm. When they had finally climbed the steps and made it inside, Charlie ran back out for the dog food. In the kitchen, he could see the old man holding up a biscuit for the dog. The little dog was jumping up and down as if on a string. Charlie snatched up the phone by the door, dialed Opal's numbers. The phone rang and rang on the other end. No answer. Call Emergency Services, he said to himself. Call right now.

The dog jumped up and took the biscuit.

"Listen," called Charlie, hanging up the phone. "I've got to run. I put the dog food right here by the door. Okay?"

"Wait! Don't forget to say hello to Britney!"

"Hello, Britney," called Charlie.

The dog came to the doorway and dropped her biscuit.

He was off again. The Toyota backslid several feet down the hill before moving forward. At the top of the hill, he veered toward the highway. It was five thirty already. Already the trees were white. People were pulling into driveways, getting out, looking up at the sky. In front of him, a salt truck chugged slowly along. He turned on the radio . . . *a surprisingly low number of hair loss patients . . . Time for new furniture?* He slammed it silent with his fist. He was missing a headlight; only the right side of the road was dimly illuminated. It was then, squinting at the road, he realized that he did not know what he was doing. He felt completely out of control. Why was he driving onto the highway, away from home? Bracing his body against the seat, he tried to talk reasonably to himself, as he might on a very long run when his mind would try to tell him to turn back, telling him all the things of which he was incapable. But it wasn't right, to be paged five times and then nobody answers. His throat felt thick. He smeared his snow-wet hair back with the palm of his hand, swearing softly. As soon as he got there, he'd call Margot or the answering service or whoever and do the right thing.

But it was worse than he had imagined. When he pulled up to her house, he felt terror inside. Was it the glow through the pillowcase curtains? The tattling of that single crow from the roof? Was it what he had begun to see through her eyes—the horror of snow? He ran from the car, leaving the door open behind him, the car bell dinging softly. Something was wrong. Slipping on the unshoveled walk, he fell down hard, his left wrist shooting through with pain. He stood, painted white with snow, and beat on the door with his other hand.

"Opal!" he shouted.

But he already knew. He staggered to the kitchen window and looked into a crack between pillowcases. The first thing he saw was her small, clenched hand, forefinger pointed at the wall, gun-like. She lay on the carpet with her head on her arm, facing away from the window. That dusty blond head that had become familiar to him, its braid unraveled. He crashed across the frozen garden to the door. He turned the doorknob, but it was slippery with snow. His wrist throbbed as he tried and failed to grip it. He pushed instead with his shoulder; the door gave. Lunging across the room, he removed the blanket from her body.

He stood there, holding the blanket. The hand. The braid. The pill bottle.

"God*damn it*!" he shouted. He lunged to the telephone. It would all be recorded by the dispatcher, his voice, breaking on the word *ambulance*, as if he were her husband or brother, or somebody who knew her secret childhood hiding place (behind the woodpile) or her favorite food (milkshakes), and not just some caseworker, paid less than thirty thousand dollars a year, who was never supposed to visit her after five o'clock and who already had been warned against doing exactly this sort of thing, but who now held a blanket (knit by her grandmother, the only person who was kind to her, besides himself) filled with her vomit, and was now slapping her cold cheek and shouting into the phone *No, no she isn't conscious* and being told to put his finger in her mouth and clear away the vomit. He did so, closing his eyes, feeling the bile rise in his own mouth, feeling along the hard teeth to the tunnel of her throat. With his numb fingers, he dug out her mouth. He was now crouched atop her, one hand on her shoulder. He leaned back. Her mouth closed stiffly and slowly around his absence. *No*, he whispered into the phone. *Nothing yet.*

They told him to pick her up and give her the Heimlich. It was there, embracing her from behind, his ear against her shoulder blade, her small hard rump in his lap, that he heard the sirens.

Abruptly, he placed her on the sofa and went out the door. There he waited, thoughtless before the alternating lights, until two young men leapt out of the ambulance, nodded, and walked inside.

Charlie stood outside watching through the open door. From there, he saw the men lift her off the couch and he saw her bobby socks dragging along the carpet. Her braid swung back and forth as they pumped at her, one standing by holding a defibrillator and watching, his expression that of a young man thinking about something else entirely—a song he liked, the advantages of a better bicycle. Charlie closed his mouth and swallowed. He was supposed to be like them—calm, disengaged, effective. For example, if he had been smart, if he had been good at this job, he would have called Harriet himself as soon as he got the first page.

He looked at the watch on his throbbing wrist. A cry escaped him, both from the physical pain and from the time. His wrist bone protruded, broken. And for what? *For what?* Because look, there she was, sitting upright on the couch, her eyes fluttering back in her head, the front of her dress a dark wet circle. The young medic had his hand on her shoulder, and was rubbing it softly. The other medic came to the door, peering out into the night at Charlie, who was revealed by a single floodlight.

"You all right?" the medic asked him, stepping out into the night.

"Yeah." Charlie put his left hand in his pocket.

"You coming with us?"

"Yes," said Charlie.

They lay Opal on a stretcher. Charlie held the screen door for them. As her small face passed by, blurred with freckles, she stared up at the sky, where she must have seen, through her death-haze, the snow. Perhaps she thought she had made it and was dead. In death it would always be snowing. Death would be full, perhaps, of whatever you feared most, except you wouldn't be afraid anymore. Scorpions. Doberman pinschers dragging snapped chains behind them. Beheaded Arabs. Your own uncle raping you, bees in his hair. The people who once loved you most, loving you no more.

⌒

Alice and the babysitter sat in silence. The girl was studying the carpet, rubbing her hands together between her legs.

"Are you cold?" said Alice.

The girl looked up. She had hair the color of amaretto. The Christmas lights still left up on the windows illuminated her hair in snatches. She wore a fuzzy pink turtleneck sweater.

"No," said the girl. "I'm fine."

Alice turned away. A car approached, then passed away down the street. She stood and smoothed the front of her dress. Brightly, she went to the shelf where the snow globe sat.

"Ever seen one of these?" she asked the babysitter, shaking it.

She held the globe up in front of the girl. Inside it, the eternal snow swirled. Two figures appeared—two children— building a snowman.

"Neat," said the babysitter sincerely.

Alice put the snow globe back on the shelf. "So you're all set with the bottles and things? And you know how to turn on the mobile?"

The girl nodded.

"The song is a little annoying. Ba-deedee ba-dee. But after a while you just don't hear it."

The girl smiled, shrugging her shoulders. "I know."

"Sorry we don't have cable. But you're welcome to use the phone or read any of my books or anything you want. The twins really should sleep almost the whole time, since I just put them down. They sleep a lot, babies. They just—sleep."

The girl once again said nothing. She bent her head and pulled the tube of her turtleneck over her glossed lips, teething it gently.

Alice looked out the window. "The night tonight," she said softly. "Sort of like a snow globe. Isn't it?"

She did not wait for the girl's reply. She stood and walked into the kitchen and bent over the sink, clenching the taps. Her knuckles were white. She was having difficulty breathing. Out of the presence of the babysitter, her heart ached, groaned, as lake ice groans when it melts. She was sobbing into her hand. He was more than an hour late. It was dark and snowy. There would be no date. She looked down at her new dress, and clawed at the knot on the waist.

"God*damn* it," she whispered.

In the bathroom, she undressed. She hung the dress on the back of the door.

"Joanne," she said, emerging in a sweatshirt and jeans from the hamper. "You can go home now, okay?"

Joanne peeled her sweater from her mouth. "Go home?"

"It's snowing pretty hard. I think my husband and I will be staying in tonight."

The girl, standing, seemed resigned. "All right," she said,

accepting the twenty-dollar bill that Alice placed in her hand. She walked across the room to the door and opened it herself.

"Good night," said Alice.

The girl turned around on the landing, and a look of concern flitted across her young face, a look that suggested she had just understood something about being a woman or being a wife or wanting things at great cost. Her brow furrowed. She ran her hand across the top of the staircase railing.

"Have a good night," the girl said.

"You, too," said Alice. "Say hello to your mom and dad for me."

The tenderness of the girl's naive concern softened something in Alice. Alone, waiting, she suddenly became calm. He was now so late that she could give up hoping.

In their bedroom, in the moonlight of their first January, the twins were sleeping deeply. Their chests rose and fell so slightly. They appeared so motionless as to be painted, the light from the nightlight glowing moonlike upon their faces. Frances's arms flapped once, and then the infant fell back into her timelessness. Alice's envy of them made her sad. To envy a being without knowledge or experience! She tried to resist it, yet she envied them, and even though she resisted it, she had the wish that they would never grow up. How trite the thought was, and how inescapable. To be that still, to be without expectation, to sleep that deeply, nothing but a watery darkness to dream about, perhaps the sound of footsteps, a cough, a church bell. The pleasant shameless warmth of urination. The smell of your sister's head. A shadow passing across the room.

Before she knew it, she had the phone in her hand.

"Mother," said Alice. "It's me."

"Alice? Alice. My daughter Alice? That charming little girl who used to live with me?"

Alice ran her finger across the top of the old kitchen wainscoting, smiling. She could almost picture her mother waking up from her evening nap, wiping her mouth, pouring the cat off her lap.

"I just wanted to say hello."

"Hello." Marlene yawned on the other end. "This is an unexpected pleasure, to hear from you. It's been a while. Not that I'm complaining. I *never* complain." Marlene snorted. "It is, however, wonderful to hear your voice. I was just dreaming about the pond where, as a girl, I used to chase bullfrogs. Aren't memories funny? Piano keys you never play. Is it snowing there?"

Alice looked at the floor. She covered her mouth with her hand. In a moment, the urge to cry passed. Don't cry, she instructed herself. You are twenty-five years old. A mother and a wife. At this same age, her own mother had raised her all by herself, unmarried, penniless, and disowned by her family. Alice steadied her voice.

"I was just thinking of you, is all. I was thinking maybe you could come down soon. Not just for the day. Stay a week or something. I know you hate the bus, but—"

"For Chrissakes," cried Marlene. "What took you so long? I was *waiting* for you to ask. I'm a grandmother, dammit. The girls at the library think those children are a figment of my imagination."

Alice laughed. "I was trying to do it by myself. I wanted to do it myself."

"You don't need to do it all by yourself."

"You did it by yourself."

"And it was hell. I nearly tossed you in the Bay."

"Mother!"

"Of course I'll come. Give me time to arrange it. It will be so lovely, us girls hanging about. I'll take care of them, while you get to have some time to yourself. Take a bath. Read a book. Have you been able to read, Alice darling?"

"A little." Alice bent her head. "Not much." In her memory,

the big pink house arose again, this time covered in shadow. The big, rangy seagulls of Gloucester circled the cold sheds. "Are you sure you want to come? I mean, you have your own life."

"But I don't *want* it," protested Marlene, laughing.

Just then, the door opened at the foot of the apartment stairwell.

"Thank God," Alice said without meaning to. "Mother, I have to go. I have to go."

"Call me soon, dear. We'll make a definite plan. Call me soon, Alice!"

Alice hung up the phone. She ran to the top of the apartment stairs. Below her, down the dark staircase, the door opened with a gust of snow. She realized that no matter how blatantly he had broken their date, no matter that he had not even taken one moment to call her, she just wanted him to come home now, to come home.

The figure below looked up at her in the flickering hall light.

It was the schoolteacher, the short little miserable-looking schoolteacher who lived downstairs.

The schoolteacher stared up at Alice with a mixture of irritation and hopefulness. It was almost as if he hoped Alice was there waiting for him, although he also knew that she wasn't.

"Oh," said Alice. "Hi."

The schoolteacher sniffled, rubbed his nose with his wrist. Of course, he thought, there you go, she thought I was someone else. The expression on her face was one of such disappointment. He wanted to hide from that expression. Of course she was not waiting for him. No one was waiting for him. Not even a dog or a cat. Not even Beckett. He had loaned his copy of *Watt* to the boy who'd had a nervous breakdown. The schoolteacher jammed his key in the lock.

Alice opened her mouth. The man disappeared inside his dark apartment. Just before he shut the door behind him she saw, beneath a bald lightbulb, a tall shelf of books. She stepped down one stair.

"Wait," she said, her voice echoing in the stairwell.

The door to the schoolteacher's apartment slammed, sending a rain of paint chips to the hallway floor.

Alice shrank back into her own apartment. Hand on the doorknob, she stood frozen for a moment just inside. Then she took the snow globe off its shelf and heaved it across the room. It landed with a crash against the wall, but did not shatter.

January.

Ice.

Distant music.

Christmas lights.

Car wheels spinning.

In the nursery, a baby whined, awoken. Below, a key scratched in the front door. Footsteps pounded up the first flight of stairs. Alice, lying prone on the floor, her head on her arm, was watching a small pool of water form beside the glass globe. Inside, the snow fell sideways, but the girl and the boy and the snowman did not seem to notice.

~

It had taken a long time to read and understand the menu. The effort of this and of being in a place they could not afford had cast them into silence. Now Charlie was eating his salad energetically, making appreciative sounds and wiping his mouth with his good hand. The other hand lay bandaged in his lap.

After a while, Alice set down her fork.

"For god sakes, Charlie. It's just a salad."

He looked up, vinaigrette on his lips. He set down his fork. They both looked out the window at the glittering darkness. The waitress came to take their salad plates.

"I showed a lady a picture of you. She said you had kind eyes."

"Oh yeah?" Charlie smiled. "What lady?"

"You don't agree?" Alice held a spoon before his face. He saw his face cradled in a spoon, his features distorted and not kind. "A lady who tells the future. A psychic."

"You did not," said Charlie.

"I did too. I went and got my future told this week. Ten dollars."

"Where?"

"A little place in between the shoe store and the Italian bakery. She sits at the window behind a heavy purple curtain. It's all very theatrical. Sometimes you can catch her reading a detective novel." Alice took a sip of water. "To test her, I took off my wedding ring, and I made up a fake name and a fake birthday."

"Where were the twins when you did all this?"

"Oh I just left them crawling around in the street." Alice rolled her eyes. "They were in the stroller, Charlie. In the *stroller*."

"All right."

"There was this—this kind of jingly jangly music in the background, and I expected a bunch of concubines to come out and fan me with palm leaves. It was weird. It was sexy."

"Jesus, Alice. What the hell do you mean by that?"

"Oh, not her. The whole gesture. Submitting like that. Laying your hand—your bare wrist—across a table—" Alice paused, her napkin to her mouth. She remembered the tremble of the psychic's lips, tasting a bitterness, and the twins beginning to cry, invisibly afraid, and how she grabbed her coat and ran, ran ran ran. She did not tell him this. She had wanted to make the story better than it was.

"What a racket," Charlie said. "People like that prey upon people less intelligent than yourself. Because of course there is no prewritten fate. You, me, that fortune-teller, God even, nobody knows. It's black out there."

"It's pink."

"Mm?"

"The color of the universe is pinkish, actually. Not black. If you average all the colors. So I've read."

"You know what I mean. Arbitrary."

"What sort of arbitrary universe takes the trouble to be pink?"

Charlie squinted at her.

"Oh I ag*ree* with you, Charlie. All right? I agree! It's a racket. That's what I started this whole thing by saying. I just want to tell you about my stupid adventure."

They were quiet. Again, the waitress came over. She filled their glasses with water. Charlie kept his eyes in his lap.

"You confuse me," he said softly. "When I leave home in the morning, you're nice and warm and familiar. And when I come home, you're all razzed. You're like freaking Elizabeth Taylor. 'Clink! Clink! Clink!' Sometimes I don't know where you get these ideas. Do you get them in books?"

"There," Alice said, leaning over the expensively white table, "You just gave yourself away. You think I have to *steal* my ideas from books. You don't think I can make them up all by myself?"

"Of course I do. Of course."

"I decided, last week, that if I had to live inside a house, if I had to live *inside*, I would live way inside. I would live the life of the mind. Of the imagination! I could become a true eccentric."

"You bring up last week because I didn't show for our date."

"I bring up last week because I had a great realization," sniffed Alice. "And because you didn't show."

"I'm sorry I made you unhappy."

"Oh stop," Alice said. "Quit poking around for the soft spot."

"I'd like to comfort you."

"I don't want to be comforted by you these days."

"By your husband?"

"You can't have both, Charlie. You can't make me feel bad and then make me feel better. You lose credibility."

"*You* make me feel bad sometimes. *You* make me feel better."

"Well, then, I guess a marriage really takes four people. Two people to put it together and two more to tear it apart." Alice picked up a piece of bread. "We'd better eat this bread," she said. "It looks free, but its cost is actually subsumed by the rest of the menu."

"No," Charlie said, pointing. "We don't finish conversations like that. Other people can talk like that. You're starting to care too much about how our conversations *sound*. It's like, it's like you write them while I'm away."

"Then how do you know the lines so well, if *I* write them?"

"See, there you go. When did you become so clever?" Charlie tried to smile. "You know what they said about Cassius."

"No, I don't know what they said about Cassius. I never went to college, remember? Who was Cassius? Wasn't he some boxer?"

"Don't. Don't," Charlie's fist struck the table, making the candlelight gutter. "Don't lie about yourself. I know you!"

Alice looked around. She smoothed her hair.

"Lower your voice please," she said.

"When I am working with clients, with anyone, somebody

suffering because, say, voices have told him to freeze himself or burn himself or walk into the ocean, or some woman is so ill she can't move—cannot move—from the floor of her apartment, do you think I am thinking only of that person? Of that freezing man or that woman on the floor? Do you?"

"I don't know," said Alice. "I guess I would hope so."

"Then you don't know a hell of a lot about me."

The waitress came then, setting down their dinner plates. No one spoke.

"I understand about them," said Alice. "The man freezing, the woman. It's hateful for me to be jealous of them. When I found out about Opal—I felt terrible, being angry you were late. What did I matter in the face of all that? I feel terrible and small-hearted when I'm in competition with them."

"But you *aren't* in competition with them. It's you, you, everywhere. Everything I am capable of doing is because of this. Because of love. And I have to believe love increases—hope increases—when you give it—"

"—Away?"

"You can't give it *away*. It's love. You make more by giving it." Charlie took her hand across the table, firmly. "We do the same things when we're apart. We both take care of other people. Maybe you can think of our time apart as time spent parallel to each other. Maybe you wouldn't feel so lonely."

It must have been the word *lonely*. The combination of *low* and *only*. Alice began to cry.

"I wanted to live a life *with* you, Charlie," she wept. "Not parallel."

"I know," said Charlie softly, his eyes wet. "I wanted it too." He looked down. "But we have our babies now. And I don't— make enough money to give you more opportunity, at the moment, for yourself."

"You'd make more if you had a private practice. And make your own schedule. Wouldn't you?"

Charlie leaned back. "I would. I will. I—Or I could go back and work for Gregorian. But by then, the twins would be in school—"

Alice smiled, sniffling. "Seems far away. The twins in school."

"I know."

"Charlie."

He looked up.

"Did you fall in love with me because you thought I was crazy?"

"What?"

"When you first saw me, and you chased me down the street? And you wanted to know why I wouldn't step on the cracks?"

"No. *No*, Alice." Charlie smiled ruefully, leaning forward on the table. "I chased you down the street because I thought you were gorgeous." He moved his untouched dinner plate aside, now reaching out with both hands. "If anything, you reminded me, in your solitary world, of myself." He bent his head close to hers. "Hey. We can let it go now. We have each other. We *found* each other."

Alice pressed her fingers to her eyes.

"Keep believing in me," he said. "Please. I'm right here."

"I'll try."

"What would make it easier? What would make me more believable?"

"Well." Alice rubbed her eyes. "Could you try, could you at least try to be home when you *say* you will? I can't stand the sight of cold food. It's every woman's nightmare."

Charlie nodded. "Absolutely. No cold food. What else?"

"Don't bring me flowers when you're late. If you're late, heaven forbid don't stop and buy flowers."

Charlie laughed. "Thank you. I've always felt stupid about the flowers."

"One more thing," Alice said, dabbing her mouth with her napkin. "I spoke to my mother. I asked her to come and stay with us for a while and help me take care of the twins. Give me some time off, some help."

"Well, I think that's a great idea," Charlie said, slapping the table.

"You do?"

"I think that would be fine."

"Really? You and Marlene, you don't get along that well. Well, no one gets along with Marlene that well."

"Not true! Your mother and I don't know each other. I'd like to get to know her. Sure! Why doesn't she come for a little while? What else?"

"And don't take me to this damned hoity-toity restaurant again. I know you hate it here. We belong at a place like Snakey's."

Charlie laughed.

"Take me to Snakey's instead. Where we used to go."

Remembering, Charlie's eyes stung. The waitress was approaching through the candlelight. He thought of how they had stood at the counter, shoulder to shoulder, eating junkyard dogs with relish.

"I love you, Charlie Shade. You know, I really do."

"I love you too, Alice," he said.

When it got hot and crowded in Snakey's, the windows steamed up. Standing at the counter before the window, the city disappeared, the view disappeared, and after a moment of feeling crammed in, you realized that you didn't care if anything else existed anyway. You had the girl next to you, that was enough. And if you made promises to her there and did not keep them, or she made promises to you and did not keep them, they were still, years later, your promises. They still belonged to the two of you.

THREE

*T*he bus. How she loathed the bus. Outside, New England went by in a gray smear. A collection of strangers, together they were borne through tunnels of blasted rock, while an Indian lady ate an entire stinking banquet from her lap, and a child smeared her hand down the window, ridding herself of something viscous. Below, in their cars, people stared. The bus always made one feel captured and displayed—no, worse—poor, Third World; she might as well have been carrying a pineapple on her head. Beside her, a young black man wearing an enormous dress-like T-shirt and headphones large as coffee rolls feverishly genuflected to his beat. *Bat* du *bat bat.*

"Could you turn that *down*, please?" Marlene said.

The young man's eyes remained shut. He bobbed his head. *Bat bat* du *bat bat.*

"Excuse me." She prodded his arm. He jumped, surprising them both, and his eyes snapped open. He smiled handsomely, a slight space between his teeth, and lifted one of the headphones off his ear.

"I'm sorry?" he said.

"Could you turn your music down, please? I can barely hear myself think."

The young man fumbled with his Walkman, his large thick

fingers spinning the tiny dials. The music sank to a dull roar. He turned and looked inquiringly at Marlene.

"Better?" he shouted.

Marlene turned back to the window. She folded her hands back over her skirt. It was not the music that bothered her, but rather the young man's complete indifference to her company. He hadn't even said hello when she sat down. She turned her chin this way and that in the window. Hello, she said quietly. Soon, beyond her reflection, the metropolitan horizon came into view. Whenever she saw the city, which she had often visited as a girl for parties and dances, she felt a pang in her heart. Cities always made her feel hopeful, and hope made her uncomfortable. Tall buildings stood clustered together like gossips. Amongst them, doubtless people performed their complicated modern ablutions. She remembered going into the new public toilet in the city with her father, when she was small enough to need to be dragged along, and how she had reached down for the beautiful brass drain in the middle of the urinal, before her hand was slapped away.

Against the bus driver's orders, Marlene stood before the bus came to a complete stop and squeezed herself into the aisle. When she fell forward at the last lurch, the young man beside her had to grab her arm to keep her from tumbling forward. She looked down at his black hand on her rose-colored overcoat. Pleased, but with her resentment now directed toward the bus driver, who was whistling sadistically, Marlene gathered up her bag and her *Redbook* and dropped her apple core in a baggie, and stepped down the aisle. How she hated the bus. Behind her, her pal followed, now chanting out loud with his music—*Goin through the emotions of gun holdin whicha whicha yao long shotguns down my pants limpin killer be who still livin*—all this in the hassled and depressing silence of the bus, which she hated, the lone voice—*and through all of that a nigga ain't scared of death* (and finally she thought—

it's for me, he *is* talking to me)—just as she was thinking this and was pleased, she stepped off the bus and was shocked to see, coming toward her with a grin, big ears aglow in the sunlight, her son-in-law.

Marlene gaped as Charlie took her purse. "I didn't know you were coming to get me," she marveled. "I was going to hail a cab."

"It wasn't any trouble," Charlie said. "Is this your only bag?"

Marlene whirled around. The largeness of her suitcase beside the bus now embarrassed her. She had only been invited for two weeks.

"It's full of secondhand baby clothes," she said. "The girls from the library."

Charlie slung her purse over his shoulder. A bus passed, blowing his fine-sifted, sunlit hair into his eyes. Standing there in the wet light of the bus station, untouched by the city itself, he appeared heroic to her, with his premature laugh lines and his blue parka and his Brut deodorant and the manful, secure way he held the purse, and unconsciously Marlene leaned toward him, hypnotized. As a librarian and a spinster, she was rarely around men, and she sometimes tired of it, all that sovereignty. She was tired of being feared, and would have liked just then to be told what to do by a man. Charlie put his arm around her and gave it a squeeze.

"You look tired," he said. "I know you hate the bus."

She allowed herself to lean her cheek against his parka. She did hate the bus. In the distance, her young friend disappeared into the crowd. Singing. Gesturing. Promoting himself to the city. Give her a million years, she'd never be able to stride into a crowd like that.

"No," she said, straightening. "I'm not tired. Let's go see my grandchildren."

They walked together toward the parking lot. They did not

really know one another. Their relationship had thus far been awkward. It was difficult to know where to step, with Alice prostrate between them. Many of their interactions had involved Charlie lying to Marlene over the telephone. But in another lifetime, who knows? They felt then that they might have been friends.

"You look well," called Marlene to Charlie's back. "For a father of twins. What's your secret?"

He said over his shoulder, "Your daughter."

"She'd well say the same of you."

"We have a blessed life," said Charlie. "Our children are the most incredible babies in the world. To tell you the truth, I don't know what I did to deserve all of this. I think they got the wrong guy." Dragging the suitcase across the parking lot, which was wet and rocky with melted slush, Charlie laughed at the idea, although it seemed true. "Here we are."

They stood at opposite doors of the beat-up Toyota. Marlene gazed across the wet roof at her son-in-law's face. She felt very generous. She wanted to say, You do deserve it. She had never been picked up at the bus station by anyone. She did not say anything. Charlie winked at her in the sunlight.

"Thanks for coming, Mom," he said. "We could use the help."

She was so stunned by the word—*Mom*, reborn extraordinarily of a man's mouth—that he had disappeared into the car before she could reply. She stared at the shimmering space where he had stood.

But what she did not ask was, why was he home from work on a weekday? Charlie faced forward in the white winter sun, the world framed by windshield grit. He gripped the steering wheel of the Toyota, whose headlight he had still not had the time to fix. He *was* blessed. And to show that he knew he was blessed, he had kept his word and come home on time for a run of several weeks now, even though it was hard to just pack up and leave the office with the phone still ringing. He was blessed more than anything to see Alice laugh again, at him, trustfully, her head thrown back. Just last night, in an attempt to make dinner, he'd melted a spatula, and she had found even this charming. When he embraced her, she accepted, softening, not waiting to be let go. So he was happy and he was pleased, because he was blessed, but he had also noticed with displeasure that his happiness had a little grit in it. Was it necessary to sacrifice certain things to happiness? Every time he paused at a stoplight or stood in his undershirt before his open closet, the words of his supervisors echoed back at him. *But why didn't you alert Emergency Services right away Charlie? She says she spoke to you right beforehand. Margot easily could have paged me.*

Charlie comforted himself by feeling misunderstood. The individual is always misunderstood by the group—he was beginning to believe—and is often asked to conform to the erroneous image the group has of him. When one works alone, there is no misunderstanding. A man has an unimpeachable personal morality, which is his instinct. No matter what he does within this frame, the action is, amoral or moral, right. Rules—he thought—are different, made for order, for the ordering of groups. Charlie looked steadfastly at the gritty view, sure that all this was infallible. But there were the voices anyway:

Seems like we could have headed this off somehow.

Margot easily could have paged me.

We almost lost a life, Charlie.

And himself, protesting: *Don't you think I know that?*

Charlie almost laughed aloud at the realization that he was, in effect, hearing voices. It was useless to keep going over things. The matter of Opal's suicide attempt was weeks past, ancient in his line of work. She was in good hands at Maynard. It was very common to go in and out of the hospital like that until one truly accepted the facts of one's condition: medication, monitoring, "pleasure surveys," slow progress, halfway house dances. As for him, the review meeting he'd had with Harriet and Bruce had seemed like a pure formality. It happened after any particularly grim event. How many interviews had Eugenia given when her client went plunging overboard a ferry? A client of Peter Carter's slipped away into the crowd at a Red Sox game, one gleefully disappearing giant foam finger. Charlie had even convinced himself that in the course of the meeting, Harriet and Bruce weren't so upset at him for not following the rules that fateful day, but that they were genuinely, narratively interested: Uh-huh? And *then* what did you do?

But after he told the story, in that shadowed conference room, they had sat there far too soberly. Harriet wouldn't look him in the eye. It was clear to Charlie they had been talking about him. He became frightened with the possibility that Gregorian would become involved. Sitting there, holding a paper funnel of water in his hand, the evidence against him mounted in his own mind. Even the half-drugged account that Opal had given from her hospital bed did not do justice to the amount of negligence that Charlie had actually shown that evening. On the one hand, he knew it. He didn't have to be told.

But then, on the other hand, staring down at the circle of water and the shiny veneer of the conference table, he heard himself speaking eloquently in his own defense, preempting all their suspicions: ES *never* would have gotten there before he did. What if he had spent the time trying to persuade ES, or to track down Harriet or Bruce instead of just driving over there himself? He'd lost his cell phone that day, right? So what if those minutes to stop and find a pay phone and make the phone call had been the difference, and what if they had really lost her then? Because they *didn't* lose her. He'd gotten there in time.

But wasn't there an opportunity to call someone once he'd arrived at Mr. Delgado's house? Harriet wanted to know. Because they wouldn't even be asking this, see, if it wasn't for Opal's comments (Harriet had gone to see her again, he noticed, without him), and look, they were just confused as to what transpired in the hour and a half after which Opal last tried to reach him and the arrival of the ambulance. Because there was a system, a whole phone chain set up in anticipation of . . .

He *did* return Opal's call, he objected, just like he promised. But there was no answer. And then Mr. Delgado tried to escape, so Charlie had to chase him! He tried to run out onto the highway because he was mad.

Why was he mad?

He was mad because he had to wait by the pay phone while Opal was contacted, Charlie explained. His cell phone was lost—didn't he already say that?

And suddenly, sitting in the conference room telling the story, Charlie had felt abjectly sorry for himself. Everybody wanted so much from him—George, Opal, Harriet, Bruce, Gregorian. They wanted his 100 percent exclusive attention, and in this perhaps they unconsciously were setting him up to fail, in order to be relieved of their optimism. He covered his face with his hands, and there, in her silky Japanese robe, pulling the brush through her wet hair, was Alice. He'd chosen not to fail Alice. Why should he be made to feel bad about it?

Just then, Bruce had patted Charlie's knee with his large slab of a hand. "Hey kid," he whispered. "Hey. It's all right." With this sympathetic touch, Charlie's eyes stung. Through a crack in his fingers he saw their faces, greasy and fatigued by this hour of rule-following, the sun completely gone down by then, both of them wanting to be home and watching *Access Hollywood* with their feet up. Charlie saw that they had followed him down all of his explanations: Delgado's fault, the fault of the system, the fault of bad luck. Bruce's trench coat was crumpled in his lap. He looked tired. Whenever they lost somebody, it was Bruce who had to explain it to the Department. Sometimes they even sent a bureaucrat over to conduct an investigation, taking hours out of everyone's day for interviews, as if when someone was dead it truly mattered what the Department thought about it. Charlie knew that more than anything Bruce didn't want a visit from the Department, and for him, Charlie would keep it from happening.

"Listen," he said, pressing his eyes with his fingers. "I'm sorry. I think it's clear that I let you both down. I wish I could explain how much I care what you think of me. That, while I'm here, I'm a credit to your team. Also," he looked away, down at his lap, but it was the truest thing he'd said yet, "I care about her. Ludlow. It's surprising. The gap between how much I care about her and how I handled events that day. I should have been more sensitive to where she was coming from, with the mattress guy and the hospital and all that. I really cared, but maybe I just didn't—" Charlie shook his head, "care enough."

"Don't be foolish," said Harriet. "You care enough. This isn't about caring."

Bruce opened his hands in a gesture of inevitability. "You haven't been around here long enough to know how frequently I've met in this conference room with caseworkers less gifted than yourself," he said. "This line of work has all sorts of traps built right into it. It's a tremendous responsibility to take on, guarding the lives of people. I'd be an idiot to blame you for this. We *all* saw Opal. We all work together as a team. Hsu, Carter, you, me, Harriet. If there was evident suicidal ideation, we all should have seen it. Sure, maybe she had a special trust with you, but you never have to shoulder that responsibility all by yourself. That's what a team is. We're a mobile treatment *team*." Bruce removed his trench coat from his lap. "Goddamn I want a drink. A nice cold Bombay gin martini with a single pearl onion."

Charlie looked up.

"I'll have a drink with you," he said.

Bruce laughed. "Sure, Bud," he said. "Anyway, I've heard enough on this point, and to me the case is closed. Opal's where she belongs for now. Monday will be a new day. For us. For her. A new day, shiny as a fucking penny."

Charlie looked over at Harriet, who was nodding absently, staring at the carpet.

"Listen," Bruce said to Charlie. "You look tired. Take tomorrow off. It's Friday. Have yourself a nice long weekend. I will personally check in with your clients."

The big man stood. Charlie remained sitting, staring at the table.

"I don't need to take tomorrow off," Charlie said. "Seems like I should be working more, not less."

"We don't blame you," Bruce said. "Okay? I understand the situation to my satisfaction. I'm not sanctioning you."

With that, Harriet looked up at Bruce. Her face betrayed surprise, as if the plan had been changed midcourse. As Bruce slapped Charlie on the back, Harriet bent forward to fetch her purse from the floor. When she looked up, Charlie saw for the first time, her mask of niceness. Her eyes met his briefly, then she smiled with a tight, boardroom smile. She did not like him anymore. She did not trust him. If she trusted him, she would have yelled. If she had thought he was worth it. She did not call him Chief. He was on the other side of something now and he knew it. He would have to prove himself somehow. It was his reputation that was being sanctioned. Whether or not Bruce said so.

Yet here he was, on a Friday morning, *taking the day off*, dragging his mother-in-law's gargantuan suitcase up two flights of stairs. Just to think of it all together gave him a stomachache. He felt that someone might have forewarned him as a child that one day relief and trouble and love and loathing would huddle together on the same inch of territory. In the stairwell, on this dark morning, it was guilt, too—guilt for the fact that it might be possible to extract forgiveness unjustly, which cheapened everything, the music of Alice's laughter, love, love, fatty fistfuls of it, late-night sex, intimacy so convincing it was as if they had never left off and he had never come home late once, and she was childless and ticklish and untold.

"It's too big," Marlene said. "The suitcase."

Below him on the stairs, his mother-in-law looked up at him, tapping her lips.

"I can handle it," Charlie said.

"It's too heavy. You're going to strain your back. Put it down."

"Can't put it down now," said Charlie, grunting up the second set of stairs.

"Use your legs," she crowed from below. "Use your abdominals."

Then, for a moment, Charlie imagined letting go. Just, letting go. The black suitcase, barreling down the stairs. *Seems like we could have headed this off somehow.*

◡

Not until they all crowded around the little wooden table for dinner did they realize how tiny the apartment really was, with its tiny lamps throwing tiny light. They loomed over the table. How large they felt, each one, how large especially the things they were not saying, for Alice did not really believe that Charlie had taken the day off just to fetch his mother-in-law from the bus station, and Charlie knew she did not believe it, yet there it was, affected quite nicely, and wasn't the chicken delicious? He reached over to her. She leaned toward him, her eyes shiny with some sort of emotion. *What?* he whispered silently. *What is it?*

"Cinnamon," said Marlene, wagging her fork. "That's the secret ingredient."

Charlie turned away from Alice. "Well, it's delicious," he said.

Alice yawned. "God, I'm tired."

"Of course you are, Alice darling," said Marlene, pushing more chicken on to her daughter's plate. "I was wiped out with just one baby."

"You had to do it alone."

Marlene paused, her fingers greasy. "Sure, but with Charlie away during the day—" She nodded respectfully in his direction.

"True," Charlie nodded. "Alice takes care of them on her own all week." He smiled. "That's why you're here."

Marlene's emptied suitcase sat in the corner of the living room. It was too huge to fit in her corner of the nursery, next to the twin bed they'd set up there for her. Marlene kept stealing glances at the suitcase. Abruptly, she stood and covered it with a blanket, then sat down with satisfaction.

"Goddamned monstrosity," she muttered.

It was all going very well, Marlene thought. Very well by her count. But what sort of count was her count, the mathematics of a lonely woman? Gradually, sawing at her chicken, she worried that she might have been overconfident about her performance as a grandmother. She was worried that she wasn't qualified to care for a baby after all these years. In Charlie and Alice's brief visits to Gloucester, she had only hours to dandle her granddaughters, not enough time to do any harm.

Perhaps now she would err in some terrible way and Alice would never forgive her. She would make them sick. She would all smother them, living in the same small room. She would take their oxygen.

"So who's taking care of Wednesday?"

Marlene looked up. "Denise, the archivist."

"The archivist?" said Charlie, vaguely amused.

"From the library," said Marlene, raising her eyebrows a touch, annoyed that she should have to remind him where she worked.

"That's nice of her," said Alice.

"Well, she's an archivist. She's good at taking care of old things," said Marlene.

They all chewed in silence. A cry pealed out from the nursery. All three of them stood at once.

They laughed. It was a relief. The baby crying. The three of them standing.

"Eat, both of you." Marlene moved toward the kitchen. "Allow me. That's what I'm here for."

They could hear her opening the cabinets and mixing bottles of formula, just as she had been instructed only hours before.

"To me, it's exotic," Marlene called from the kitchen. "Wipes and nipples and boppies. Binkies." Then she sang a few bars of "My Favorite Things," substituting these words, and Charlie and Alice looked at each other and laughed with weariness, and held hands across the table.

⌒

They spent that weekend shopping and walking through parks, and sitting together—the five of them—in an outdoor café, warmed by the tea-weak sun, growing more comfortable with the arrangement. Sunday was unseasonably warm, smelling of the green, living smell of deep thaw. The tops of the trees were dusted red. It was February. Their shadows grew long by four o'clock.

Walking home under pink shadows of dusk, Marlene guarding her turn at the stroller, Charlie chased Alice down the sidewalk doing his impression of the elephant man, back humped, one leg dragging behind. She ran away screaming, her hair beating on the back of her coat. He chased her into the street.

"Watch out for cars!" called Marlene.

He tackled Alice as soon as they were within reach of grass. He bit her earlobe with his teeth, making ghoulish noises. Tangled in the hard dry grass, she struggled and screamed, and tried to roll away. He leapt after her, seizing her by the ankle, and dragged her back to him.

"You guys!" said Marlene, "That's someone's private property."

He had her pinned now by the wrists, chips of leaves in her hair. Her small eyes disappeared in laughter. The air felt cold and fresh in his lungs, and *God* how he wanted to run just then, run with her in a fireman's carry, all the way down time and back around to the beginning, when he first pushed open the pub door and stepped out coatless into the blue winter to chase her. If he could just have one moment back, then the whole rest of his personal history would come floating down behind it. He would be Charlie Shade from Mattoon again, class president again, cross-country co-captain again, someone who always pretty much knew what he was doing again, someone with a certain private honorability. He lay down beside her, panting.

"Do you remember—" he said. "That old bar inside the VFW where I—once took you dancing? You wore a dress— very low-cut. Those guys. You gave them all—strokes."

"Everything—was borrowed then. Or stolen—"

"Stolen?"

"You stole—" said Alice, "my landlady's—newspaper. Every Sunday."

"You knew about that?"

"We were poorer even than now—"

"We swore we'd never be rich. Remember?"

"Stupid kids!"

They laughed. Then Charlie's face grew serious, and he pressed one hand firmly against her temple.

"So," he said. "Do you still believe in me?"

She raised her head to look at him, then set it back down on the grass.

"Yes."

"Good." He lowered his face to the stiff, vaguely sweet surface. "Because I need you to. I really need you to."

On the other side of the street, Marlene passed by, pushing the stroller. The twins were asleep. The street was thick with dusk. Marlene smiled. She watched the figures on the grass. She was embarrassed and yet touched to see them sprawled on the grass, embracing and whispering. If she hadn't known better, she would have thought they were just two kids, young lovers, just starting out. But then again, she thought, wasn't that what they were? She called over her shoulder, waving them on.

"Remember to check yourselves for ticks!" she cried.

～

People passing by the campus often mistook it for a prep school, expecting to see boys jogging out across the fields, carrying lacrosse sticks. But the only figures that crossed the perennially green lawns were doctors with name tags, social workers, and nurses in their short haircuts and big blousy shirts covered in flowers or paint strokes. Maynard Psychiatric was one of the oldest psychiatric hospitals in the country. It occupied one of the more desirable plots of real estate in the area, sitting abreast of a wide, lazy river, a river that had figured prominently into the suicidal ideations of generations of mental patients.

Nearly a month now separated Opal from her suicide attempt. Bruce had kept his word—the review was dropped. In gratitude for this, Charlie focused on being more effective with his other clients, checking in on them with the regularity of a ward nurse, scribbling in his daily log, all within the bounds laid out in his Mobile Treatment manual. Each time he was helpful to one of them, got them to the doctor's office on time or carried their groceries or talked them home from their demons, he felt he was redeeming himself on the issue of Opal. Gradually, the old fond feelings for Opal had returned, no longer fogged by guilt but by a sense of having learned from his mistakes, and Charlie sometimes caught himself planning her promising future—a fresh start, a job in a flower shop, a bicycle with a basket.

He climbed the hospital steps three at a time. In his jacket pocket he carried a package of sour balls, a pack of Newport Menthols, and his mother-in-law's rolled-up copy of *Redbook*. He whistled as he pushed through the hospital doors, winking at the receptionist. He was excited; he was excited to see her. He wanted to tell her she was missed. And forgiven. And maybe he was hoping a little bit that she would be glad to see him too, because wouldn't that mean he had generally done right by her?

He saw a familiar colleague walk down the hall with a mug of coffee—an old face from his days in Admitting. Those days seemed a long time ago to him. Back then, he thought, it was all pretty much academic. Academic and medical and prefigured. If he kept going up two more flights, he'd be right back on Gregorian's loveseat.

In the two weeks of Marlene's stay, Charlie and Alice had finally slept, more than they had in the entire past five months. They slept as if they'd just been rescued together from a wreck on the open sea. Marlene, never much of a sleeper herself, did not seem to mind playing the nanny. She was good with the twins. Charlie suspected that the care of infants satisfied her need for exacting performances, and that this was the secret motive of all grandmothers. He was, despite this, hysterically grateful. It was Marlene who was helping him put in some extra evenings at the office, which he needed just then toward his redemption in the eyes of the team. When Charlie had gotten home late several times the previous week, post-dinner, Alice had not objected. Alice looked up at him from her lamp-lit book and he could see at least she wasn't lonely, at least she had company, and that she still believed. Loneliness, Charlie thought, the loss of love or the never finding of love, that's what drives people crazy.

He entered the ward and knocked on the glass door of the nurse's station. A pretty young nurse with red hair looked up at him and put down her pencil. She came around to the desk.

"Can I help you?"

"I'm Charlie Shade, from the Maynard County MTT. I'm here to see Opal Ludlow. I was her primary, before she came here."

"*Oh*," said the nurse, smiling with a cute, crinkled nose.

"I just wanted to drop by. Say hello. She doesn't have any family up here, so—"

"Yes," said the nurse sadly. "We don't get anybody but you guys. Nice for Opal, though, to get two of you in one day."

"Two of us?"

"Another lady this morning from the MTT. A heavyset black lady."

"Harriet," said Charlie.

The nurse pointed at him with her pencil. "That's her."

Charlie stood there, nodding, looking at the nurse's clean and empty face.

"She didn't mention it to me," he said.

He took the sour balls out of his pocket.

"Sour ball?" he said, holding out the package.

"No thanks," the nurse replied. She squinted down the hall. "She's right there in the TV lounge. Enjoy your visit."

Charlie had seen a lot of rooms in the past year. He learned to expect that the rooms he entered would be dark and smoky and disorganized, or worse yet, clean, undecorated, and prepared for long absences. But these ward hallways, today, took on a particular chill for him. The successive, identical rooms were all empty, as if suddenly evacuated, except for one figure, breathing shallowly in his bed, facing the window, the sheets twisted around his body exposing his buttocks in worn gray underwear. Charlie turned away and kept walking. Entering the TV lounge, he saw her. Maybe it was the familiar braid fastened with a glittery pink elastic, the sort he would someday use on his daughters' hair, or maybe it was the rigid set of her frail shoulders facing toward the TV. Or maybe it was the TV itself, gazing down from its cage high in the corner, showing a young couple embracing on a soap opera set, but he felt in himself an overwhelming feeling of desertion, as if he were her, sitting there, squared in a chair, no sentient soul nearby.

"Opal?"

A grate covered the window, graphing the world outside into tiny sectors. His attention settled on the wall, where several pieces of children's art were hung. Crude drawings on pieces of red construction paper. A flower with eyes. A heart with tentacles.

"Opal?" he said again.

She did not turn around.

When he came and stood in front of her, he saw that she was not in fact watching the TV, but staring at the wall in front of her. She lifted her eyes, and moved her gaze delicately until it reached his face.

She began to cry.

He knelt in front of her.

"*Jeez*," he said gently.

He took her hand. It was ice cold.

"Opal. Why are you crying?"

Her head was bent almost to her lap. Tears were being squeezed from her eyes. The small curls of hair that had slipped from her braid ringed her face.

"Opal. You won't be here much longer, you know. They want to discharge you in a day or so. Soon. Wouldn't you like that?"

Squatting, he tried to look up into her face. Her chin was pressed to her chest.

"You can go back and be in your own place. Wouldn't you like that?"

She inhaled sharply, held it, and just like that, the grief in her weeping hardened into something else. She clutched her hands together so ragefully that the fingernails made white crescents against her skin. It appeared as if she was trying to squeeze herself to pieces. Or was she trying to resist striking out, smashing him? Her face was beet red from the strain.

"Opal? Can you hear me?"

She shook, she looked through him, her eyes burning. He stood.

"Nurse!" he called. "Nurse, please!"

Down the hall, the redhead came out of the station, wiping her fingers on a paper napkin.

"We need some help over here. Right away, please."

He knelt back down and tried to lift her face with the tip of his finger. Surprisingly, she yielded to his touch, and when her eyes met his again, the rage left them and was replaced once again by grief, as if he himself were changing into different people in her eyes. Despair washed across her features. The expression was so desperate that Charlie leaned back, feeling physically struck. She looked at him as if she were dying of pain—not a physical pain, but a pain of the core of the self. Her look almost begged him: Let it end! *Let it end!*

The nurse was upon them. She was checking Opal's pulse. Opal was docile, and let her eyes and hands be manipulated. Then she offered Opal a pill, and Opal took it between her fingers and the nurse got her a Dixie cup.

"Go ahead, honey," said the nurse.

"Swallow it, Opal," said Charlie. "Go ahead."

Opal's eyes met his again, and this time the will to be angry or sad went out like a light, and she tipped back her plastic cup of water and swallowed.

"All right?" he said to Opal, bending down. "We're right here next to you."

The nurse's hands slid from Opal's head, leaving her braid mussed. With a shaking hand, Charlie smoothed the hair back down.

"Jesus," he said, standing. "They want to discharge her?"

The nurse made a huffing sound.

"Well, she was doing all right before," she said. "She wasn't even on half-hour checks. Looks like she got upset, seeing you." She clicked the end of her ballpoint pen and thrust it in her pocket.

Charlie looked up at the nurse, whose pert red hairstyle and creamy complexion suddenly annoyed him. What the hell did she know?

"Well, it's upsetting," he said. "Sitting in a room all day by yourself. Where is everybody? Aren't there *activities* or anything on this ward? It's goddamned lonely in here."

"Everyone else is on a trip to town. But Miss Ludlow didn't want to do any activities," said the nurse, folding her arms. "And maybe she doesn't want visitors, either."

Charlie swallowed. He laughed, rubbing his jaw.

"Ha!" he said. "I'll get out of your way, then. Sure. I certainly don't want to be in your way. Since everything was going so nicely."

He pulled the package of sour balls out of his pocket and tossed them on the chair next to Opal, along with the *Redbook* and the Newports. Opal's eyes were closed, and she was leaning against the chair. He spoke anyway.

"I'm leaving some things for you, Opal. I'll be back soon. You let the nurse know if you need anything. Bubble gum. Cassettes, maybe. Anything." He put his hands in his empty pockets. "I'll see you soon," he said, softening now that he was turning tail like this, chased away by a twenty-year-old nurse. "You take care and try to just take it easy. Listen to the nurses and doctors as best you can. And when you're ready, we'll be there for you. And you can go back home and take care of yourself and do whatever you want."

He stood there another moment. Opal did not move.

"But whatever happens, we won't forget you." He wiped his nose with his sleeve. "I won't forget you."

When she still did not open her eyes, Charlie nodded at the nurse.

"Okay," he said, rubbing his hands together. "I'll go."

⌒

The breeze smelled of moss and trees and police horses. The park grounds popped and thawed around her. Spring would come. One day, soon, it would be here, flowered, offered, complete in itself. Alice took off her jacket and folded it beside her.

A squirrel pounced across the path and rested its paws inquiringly on the foot of her bench. She lifted the grocery bag onto her lap.

"Are you kidding?" she said to the squirrel. "No, you can't have my stuff."

The squirrel persisted, rose on his haunches, sniffing.

"Get lost," said a voice behind her. The squirrel darted into the underbrush.

Alice stood, reflexively clutching her groceries. Standing beside the bench was a motionless figure.

"Jesus," she said, heart pounding. "You surprised me."

As he peered down into his lunch bag, she stared at the familiar white-scarred temple, the close-shaven head, a brow bone like a burnished wooden beam.

"Salami," Hal said, looking up from the bench. "Do you like salami?"

Alice swallowed. She pushed at the bridge of her nose. "I don't know. I guess."

"Want to trade?"

"Trade? I don't have anything to trade," Alice looked into her grocery bag. "Saran Wrap? A bottle of Drano?"

The boy smiled. "You should never offer a mental patient a bottle of Drano for lunch. He might accept." He gestured beside him, at the bench. "Sit."

"I actually have to get home soon," Alice said, pinching her arms where they met around the soggy bag. "My mother is watching the twins for a bit—"

Hal looked at her, sandwich in hand. "I'm sorry," he said. "Did I make you uncomfortable? I mean, about the Drano?"

"No."

"A dumb joke."

"No."

"Hey, it's all right."

"Please. I'm just a generally clumsy person."

"Will you please just sit down already?" said Hal, mouth full.

Alice sat. She placed the bag of groceries at her feet.

"All right," she said. "Okay. To tell you the truth, I feel awkward. Now. Knowing you, through my husband."

"Knowing—"

"About you."

"About my visit to the nuthatch? Hell, everybody knows about that." Hal laughed. "I was All-American."

Alice squinted.

"I was an All-American wrestler. You don't just—slip away."

"I see."

"In fact, they say—they say I'm supposed to talk about it now. You know," Hal withdrew a juice box, rolling his eyes, "to air it out."

Alice leaned against the bench with her elbow, facing him. "So then, are you better now? Do you have to—go back?"

He gazed at her with his even, uncompromising expression. The juice rose up the straw and into his mouth.

She looked away. "See? Those are insensitive questions."

"Hey, don't be—hard on yourself. Sometimes it just takes me a minute. To—hear things." The young man weighed his remaining sandwich in his wide, flat hand. "I'm not otherwise specified. Psychosis N.O.S. It doesn't count unless it lasts. You've got to be crazy for a long time before they take you seriously. I'm crazy on a—probationary basis. You?"

"Am I crazy? I don't think so." She smiled. "But there's always time."

He looked at her fondly for a moment, his expression softening.

"Sure," he said. "Don't rush it."

He tossed the soggy sandwich up and down lightly in his hand. "Where's that bastard squirrel?"

"I think he's over there," said Alice. "In that tree."

Hal threw the whole sandwich into the tree. The squirrel scampered away from it.

"You've got to break it into *crumbs*," Alice laughed.

"Who says?"

"I do. I say."

"He's too good to eat it whole?"

"Well, it's just, like, a courtesy. Like cutting a child's meat. Haven't you ever fed a duck or a pigeon or anything?"

Before she knew it, he was up and scaling the tree. He clawed at the slippery trunk with his sneakers and then he was up, up crouching in the branches, collecting the parts of the sandwich. With his jacket hitched up, Alice saw the band of his white briefs glowing in the afternoon shadows. He jumped down, flushed, happy to be given a physical challenge. He returned to her side on the bench and tore the sandwich into bits, laying them precisely and clownishly in the grass.

Alice leaned back and folded her arms.

"You're very disarming, you know," she said. "It's nice."

"I'm disarming?" He stood up and moved just to the other side of her on the bench, where there was hardly any room for him. He squeezed in between her body and the rail.

"Yeah, you are. Disarming." She giggled. "Why did you move just over there?"

"I wanted to look at you from this side."

Alice bent her head. He was looking at her, breathing from the climb. She felt his ribs go up and down against her arm, his breath on the side of her face.

"This is your good side," he said after a moment. "The other one's pretty good too."

"If you say so," she said softly.

He leaned back, spreading out his legs. She moved over an inch.

"Your hair is almost as pretty as my mother's."

"Really," Alice said. "Only almost?"

"Almost. She was a beauty."

"Is she still alive?"

"I think so. I mean, I haven't seen her since this morning."

"God," Alice said, elbowing him. "Don't joke about stuff like that."

He leaned forward on his knees, smiling. "I got you. Look, you're smiling. You're not going to have any arms left at this rate."

And then, suddenly, without warning, he kissed her face. On the cheek, softly, as if somehow it could have been accidental.

"Sorry," he said immediately.

Alice's mouth fell open. She was unable to respond or to look away. His shoulders were squared toward her. He held the rolled top of the lunch bag, looking like a huge man-child in his varsity jacket. He leaned forward again. She turned away, catching her breath, his lips to her skin.

"I'm sorry," he said into her ear, this time with a touch of insincerity. "I just wanted to kiss you on your good side."

Abruptly, he stood. He looked down at her, his thumbs in his jacket pockets. He flapped his jacket open and closed.

"Don't worry," he said. "I'm crazy. Remember?"

Then he smiled, a smile so sudden and explosive and foretelling it was like getting smiled at through the leaves of a jungle. It made her speechless. He fell back and began to jog away. She was overcome with an urge to laugh. He jogged across the shadowy park, *Cross Hill Varsity* stitched across his jacket. Hands in his pockets, trotting along athletically, he seemed completely free of conscience or memory—memory, even, of her. He picked up a stick and whipped it into a bush. It was as if she was not there at all, behind him, her head full of pudding. And perhaps she was not. Perhaps with a kid who looked like that, he only dreamt you up. She pressed the palm of her hand to her cheek. She might as well have been leaning against her high school locker, still afraid that the heat running up her thighs was some sort of black magic that would be her ruin, as if she had no will, no reason.

"Jesus Christ," she said, catching her breath.

Marlene dried her hands at the sink and replaced the damp dishcloth to the faucet. Beside it, the bottles were drying upside down on their racks, the nipples floating in warm water. Passing the nursery, she peered in once again.

Her daughter lay, still asleep, on the narrow bed. She had been sleeping there for hours, as if under a spell. Marlene could smell her buttery body heat, which she remembered well from all those years of cohabitation, all those years in high school, those deep sleeping years, those pajamas-all-Sunday years. Paused there, Marlene smiled at the sleeping figure, trying to affect the roll of Loving Mother in the Doorway. And yet, underneath, a growing gloom. For secretly she dreaded the idea of going back to Gloucester now. A tall empty house. The company of an irascible cat. Rows and rows of library books, long ignored and smelling of malaise. She scratched her chin. On the other hand, of course, she couldn't stay forever. Perhaps she was encouraging some strain of laziness in Alice. To be able to sleep like that, like a teenager, in the middle of a weekday afternoon? With two infants in constant need of care?

She brought two bottles into the nursery and sunk them in the warmer. As if in collusion with their mother, the girls were sleeping deeply. She picked up Evelyn and sat in the rocking chair, slipping the nipple into her mouth before the infant had a chance to cry. Frances awoke, her wide purple eyes watching dispassionately through the bars of her crib. She was a cooperative baby. She did not care overmuch about herself.

Alice, Marlene remembered, had been sweet too. White as a sack of flour, with a whorl of black hair. Aside from her fair skin, the infant had claimed every other trait of the Portuguese in her. Marlene's mother had been Portuguese, her father Quebequois. Marlene herself had wanted so much to be blond, strawberry blond like her father. But instead, she was dark-haired, dark-stained, her skin tanned easily, and for this she was always being banished to the shade by her father. She was bequeathed only his tallness. She remembered his reddish blond head bobbing up and down on the far side of a box-wood hedge. Always going somewhere with such resolve. Always tall. With a pale, aristocratic, consternated forehead, dented at the temples. His speech was touched with an elegant accent, for he sometimes emphasized the odd syllable, as in, Put on your jack*et*, Marlene. And although he was not a warm man, she knew in her heart that he loved her, if only as much as he loved himself, for in substance they were much the same. In groups they pretended to be sociable and gay, but alone together they watched all things with the same silent intensity. She never loved him more clearly than when the circus came to Gloucester: Watching the sequined man lower his head into the jaws of the great white tiger Albermarle, all the children squealing and their parents clutching them to their breasts, her father had known not to touch her or to exclaim or pretend to be frightened, and, driving home afterward, their identical satisfactions fused and shimmered in the silence.

But it was lost, all of it. The adorable stories caught in the throat. She had not spoken to Robert Bussard in as many years as Alice had lived, for he had disowned her when he learned of her pregnancy. She was nineteen; the front window curtains had been gently drawn closed against her. Among the Catholic immigrants of their particular circle in Gloucester, this action had been looked upon as just, somehow necessary. She was a girl with a good head and better things had been meant for her, but even if her father could have ignored the illogic of this going-to-wasteness, she was unmarried, and her sin was absolute. Small communications—secret packages, visits—were exchanged between herself and her mother, until Inez Bussard had died some fifteen years ago. But with her father, whom she had loved the most, an absolute, history-annihilating break. He still lived in the old house just out of town. She often heard of his reputation for moral clarity, as if his banishment of his daughter inspired utmost respect, it was so pitiless and unremitting. Once, not long ago, she had driven past the house to see if the curtains were still drawn. She had not planned to; her hands drove her there. Sailing past it—small, vinyl sided, geraniumed—she caught her own face in the sunlit car window, a smile so solicitous and pure it took her years to recover from glimpsing it.

And for all that, what? When to this day, she had only ever been intimate with one man. Only with one man, in one place for one week—a dark-paneled boardinghouse that smelled of Brylcream. Better to have been a whore, to drown herself in a short happy life of sex and silk and grease. Instead, how earnest it had been, how pious, even in the way they undressed and folded their clothes to the side. It was as if they were lovemaking for the pleasure of God. During, on her back, she had watched wasps fret in the eaves of that great, dark house. Somebody was practicing violin down the hall. Her lover dented the bed with his largeness, his broad back spangled with moles. A friend of a friend from a dance hall. She remembered his back but not his face. She remembered the wasps and the dark-paneled walls and the sense of being in church, but not his face. Sometimes in Alice's face she sought his face. She could no longer summon his mouth or ears or habits, and what did it matter? What in the world did they have to do with one another?

"Mother?"

Marlene looked up. Alice was sitting upright on the bed, rubbing her eyes with the heel of her hand.

"Hello." Marlene walked over to the crib with Evelyn. She scooted the child, who had sunk into a milky trance, back up into her arms. "You slept like the dead."

"How are the girls?"

"They're fine. I'm going to miss them when I go."

"You can come back and visit again. Soon, I hope."

"It won't be the same," Marlene said. Then, quickly, in concession, "Are you going to have a bath? Would you like me to draw it for you?"

"No, thanks," Alice murmured. She bent down into the crib and touched Frances's cheek. As if remembering something else, something private and smooth, she closed her eyes and touched the side of her own face.

Marlene cleared her throat. "So. Where did you go this afternoon? What sorts of errands did you run?"

Alice opened her eyes. "Little things, here and there."

"Like what? What sorts of things? Tell me, for fun."

"Just things."

"Like what?"

Alice raised the child from the crib and pressed her nose against her scalp. Her hair tumbled out of its loose knot. "And what a good girl you are, Frances. Did you have a nice afternoon? Did you have fun with Grammy? Aren't you lucky to have Grammy to watch you and to play with you?"

"Well," said Marlene, hoisting Evelyn onto the changing table, and snapping open her onesie. "I don't know if they feel lucky. But they like me all right. It's you they love. So, where *did* you go? I'm just curious. Tell me."

Alice sat down in the chair with Frances. "Is this bottle for her?"

"Yes. I fed Evelyn already. And now, obviously, I'm changing her."

The two women worked in silence. Once the dark-haired child was cleaned and snapped into a fresh onesie, Marlene placed her in her crib and flipped on the mobile. The infant's eyes lit up as the shapes spun predictably overhead. Alice lay her sister down beside her.

"Two sweethearts," she said, yawning. "Isn't everyone happy now?"

"And what about you?" Marlene hadn't quite meant to vocalize it, but there it was, said. "Are you happy?"

Alice froze, leaning over the crib.

"Happy enough, of course. Before, just last year, I never saw a couple so much in love as you and Charlie. Nowadays. Well, honestly, it seems a little strained. You're both rather—" Marlene shrugged, "distant with each other. Does he always come home so late? What does he do? I mean, is it work exactly?"

Alice leaned back, cinching closed her robe.

"Now please don't get huffy, darling. Why can't I ask you questions like normal mothers do? You've always been so private—" Pausing, Marlene smoothed the back of her daughter's hair. "Of course, with newborns, it's just impossible to be as moony as you two were before. But I wonder—Sometimes you seem so distant, darling. Melancholy. You used to write such dark poems when you were a child. I was afraid I'd come home one day to find you swinging from a beam." Marlene placed a hand on her daughter's arm. "It's all right to be sad. Sometimes, after childbirth, the hormones make one very emotional. You can feel—out of your head. Why won't you talk to me and tell me things? Confide in me."

"Because I don't know what you're talking about." Alice drew away, eyes bright. "I don't have anything to confide. I love my children. And I couldn't ask for a better man than Charlie."

"But that's not what I'm asking."

"I think I will have a bath," said Alice, stepping past. "If you don't mind."

⟲

"I love the smell of you wet," he murmured, wedged between toilet and sink. "I mean shower wet. Dark and wet and secret."

"Charlie," she said. "It's too small in here for the both of us."

He stroked the arm of her silk robe, which parted slightly in front. Slyly, he pressed his nose into her hair. "I'm having very, very indecent ideas."

"Sure." She smiled at his reflection. "Now that *you're* home, it's party time."

"That's right. You said it."

He came up close to her ear. He drew one finger across the steam on the mirror, writing her name. She could feel the reddish burrs of his evening stubble, and she trembled. She trembled having him so close to it—her good side. She turned her head away. It was nothing. But if it was nothing, why did she turn her head away?

"Actually, I had an interesting day," she said, forcing a laugh.

"You did? Tell me about it."

"You sure you want to hear about it? I'd like to tell you."

"Sure I do. Yeah, tell me." She could see him through the letters in the steam, blue eyes open and waiting. She smiled back, relieved that she could tell him anything and that he was himself. "Wait," he said. He wrote with his finger, *Charlie loves* above the *Alice*. Then he seemed to change his mind and drew a heart instead, until the mirror was rather jumbled, the letters dripping. Through these spaces, she saw his expression change, become distracted, afflicted, as if the problem of drawing a heart on a mirror had become merely the first clue of a larger, more complex problem. She recognized the expression, familiar to her now this past year: he was elsewhere. He was with her, but he was not.

"I had a pretty damned interesting day myself," he muttered.

Sighing, he pulled back, and sat on the toilet seat.

"Alice, listen." He took both of her hands in his.

"Uh-oh," she said. "A two-hander, huh? What is it?"

"I know we were supposed to go to the lake Saturday, for the Valentine's picnic, but I can't. A client is getting released from the hospital and if I don't go, nobody will be there with her. She can't—come home by herself."

"So it's a work day? Can you take off for it during the week?"

"Not exactly. I'd go more in the capacity of a friend." He bent his head. "I know what you must be thinking."

"No, you don't." Alice pried her hands free. "You can't possibly know what I'm thinking if I don't know myself."

"Dinner!" Marlene called, down the hall.

"Which client is it?"

"Opal."

"Why didn't you say her name? Why did you call her 'a client'?"

Charlie stared up at her, blinking.

Alice shook her head. "It's a Saturday, Charlie. One of your two days off. In fact, this whole week you got home late. Marlene asked me why. We hardly saw you."

"One or two nights."

"*All week. Please* don't pretend I'm exaggerating. That's the worst part."

He looked down at the bath mat. "Okay. I hear you. I don't want to seem like I'm going back on my word. I won't do it, then. You know," he laughed, "I don't even want to do some of the things I do. Since what happened, I have a hard time, I don't know—judging."

"Dinner, I said!"

Alice slumped back against the bathroom wall and looked at herself in the mirror.

"Oh, Charlie. I don't know. I can't make these decisions for you. I don't even understand the situation. What if something terrible happened again?" She touched her hand to her temple.

"Do you have a headache, Alice baby?" he said, reaching up.

"Don't," she said, pushing his hand away, "—touch."

Marlene's voice boomed through the bathroom door. "I said *dinner*, godddammit!"

~

When they entered the room, like two kids in trouble, they saw that the table was set with candles.

"Voilà." Marlene pulled out the chairs for each of them. "I wanted our last dinner to be special. Inez Bussard's famous Portuguese fish stew."

Marlene lifted her chin, tightly, proudly, secretly wanting recognition for saying the name of her own beautiful, cowardly mother aloud. She wanted recognition for also having a mother. She sat down and smoothed her skirt, her dark hair hovering brushed and shiny on her shoulders. "Eat. Eat while it's hot."

Charlie and Alice looked down into their bowls.

"Smells delicious," said Charlie.

"It simmered for four bloody hours," said Marlene. "But

it's the least I can do. You two have been very kind to me. I've enjoyed my time with my grandchildren. I've taken twelve rolls of film. If I stayed any longer, they'd go blind."

"Well, we've enjoyed it too. You've been—" Charlie gestured with his spoon, "a real lifesaver. Because of you, we both feel like normal human beings again. Isn't that right, Alice? We're indebted to you, Marlene."

Marlene waved her hand, about to demure, when Alice looked up.

"I think you should stay."

"What?" Charlie said.

"I think Mother should stay," said Alice. "Just another week. Saturday, Charlie—Your client—Mother can go with me to the lake instead. I don't want to go alone."

Charlie smiled expansively, shaking his head. "But I'm not doing anything Saturday, Alice. I changed my mind. I said I'm going with you to the lake."

"Don't. Please. I mean it. It's too shabby in comparison, the lake. Besides, we would only worry." She turned to her mother. "Would you like to stay another week? It would be nice to have your company. I'm asking you."

Alice bent down to her soup. They both watched her as she sipped from her spoon.

"Well," said Marlene. "Of course. Of course I will. If you both agree."

"I don't know what to say," said Charlie, trying to smile. "It's up to Alice. I guess I don't really have any reason why not. Sure. Why not? Stay then."

"All right, then," said Marlene. "I'll call Denise after dinner."

Alice finished her soup. She stood, dabbed her mouth with a napkin. She leaned down toward Charlie, and then paused, as if she did not know quite where to place her kiss. She placed it—somewhat generically, he thought—on the top of his head.

"I'm so sleepy today," she said. "I don't know what's wrong with me. I want to fall asleep for days or weeks or years like in a fairy tale. I'll feed the girls and then go to bed."

"Don't wake them now," said Marlene. "It's too early. I'll do it later."

"All right." Alice went to her mother and hugged her shoulders, as if she had chosen, publicly, a favorite. "Good night."

She disappeared down the hall to the bathroom. They could hear the faucet. A toothbrush tapped against the sink.

Marlene turned back to the table. She wanted to be sure what happened had actually happened. She wanted some form of corroboration. She was radiant with daughter-love. She'd been asked to stay! But Charlie was bent over his soup, shoveling it into his mouth distractedly.

"So," Marlene said. "Alone at last."

Charlie looked up and smiled.

"Fantastic soup," he said. "Is there cinnamon in here, too?"

"Saffron."

Marlene pushed the breadbasket at him. He took another two rolls. As he ate, she studied him. She settled back in her chair. She would stay another week. She suddenly felt very confident and very much like talking.

"So," she said, placing her spoon beside her bowl. "Charlie. Tell me. Are you still thinking of a private practice? One of these days? I'm just curious. I know it was a plan of yours. To have a practice. Regular hours. More money—"

Charlie looked up, over Marlene's head, and ripped at his roll with his teeth.

"I really don't know," he said.

"You don't know what?"

"I don't know how—vital that sort of situation feels to me right now."

"What do you mean? I thought this job was a kind of training. Temporary." Marlene bit her cheek. "Besides, it's very vital. There are many people—I have many friends who go to social workers like yourself for family counseling. I think it's quite vital. I think you could be quite helpful—instrumental—to regular people. Once or twice I myself have considered going to a counselor."

"You should," said Charlie.

Marlene winced, gripping her spoon.

"There are several thousand of them in this state alone," Charlie said.

"Good ones? Skilled ones like you would be, or mediocre ones?"

"All kinds. Red ones, blue ones. In a box. With a fox."

Marlene did not laugh. "I think it's silly to dismiss such work."

"I don't dismiss it. I may well want a practice one day. It's just that I like what I'm doing now. Nobody wants to do what I do. What I do is out in the middle of it. It's *vital*."

"It's trench work."

"Listen, Marlene," said Charlie. "You may not know it, but you are talking right at the root of the problem. An attitude like yours is the same one that forces the mentally ill into unsafe places. So they don't upset us." The faucet was turned off in the bathroom, and Charlie lowered his voice. "It's all right to be a little bit crazy, to see counselors, but once you cross the line, forget it. We disown you. We don't recognize you. You're not on the human continuum."

"That's not how I feel."

"That's not how you feel consciously. Unconsciously maybe we hope that they'll all just off themselves and solve the problem. If they would only kill themselves already. Then the rest of us could all have a good old-fashioned cry without being scared of seeing ourselves in them. Right? And if all the weirdos die off, then one sunny day we will have succeeded in creating a completely comprehensive, unchallenged mainstream."

"I don't see it that way."

"Of course you don't. Because you don't really understand what I do," he said. "Compassion for strangers takes a certain amount of imagination. Maybe you don't have the imagination."

Marlene's mouth fell open. Just then, Alice walked out of the bathroom, crossed the room, and fell onto the bed.

"You guys keep on talking," she said drowsily. "It won't bother me at all."

The two at the table said nothing.

After a little while, inert on the bed, Alice began to snore lightly.

"The word I meant was *understanding*," said Charlie. "I meant that you just don't know enough about mental illness. I'd be happy to explain—"

"No," said Marlene. "I wish I hadn't brought it up. I've overstepped my bounds. I see that."

"I mean, you haven't wondered what it would be like to be *desperate*." And there in the candlelight, her face rose up. Opal's shaking, red, bottled-up face. What was inside that mind? God, he could hardly stand it, sitting there in this stupid filmy candlelight, eating saffron. It was so idle, it was cruel.

"Well." Marlene stood, her bowl in her hands. "I think I understand. Thank you for explaining it to me."

Charlie looked up at her helplessly. "We separate, too much, caring for those we know and despising everyone else. Some of the most evil people in the world love their families."

"And what about caring for everyone else *except* your family?"

"I love my family," Charlie said, at almost a whisper. "I can't believe you'd suggest—"

"More than anything? More than everything put together?"

"Everything already *is* put together." Charlie looked over at

Alice sleeping. "Besides, she wouldn't love me if I were different. If I were different, if I didn't care, she wouldn't love me."

"Oh, Charlie. You're so young." Marlene snatched the bowl from in front of him. "You're so young. And let me tell you, this is an old world."

Turning, she took the dirty dishes into the kitchen.

∾

The lake was known in local lore for being home to a rarely glimpsed magnificent fish, but it was difficult to imagine how any sort of fish would exist in such a lake, least of all a magnificent one. Algae throttled the banks. Yellow swans paddled between floating car tires; a small gang of children was throwing bread at them. The Valentine's Day party organizer was teaching a second group of children and adults how to make paper boats, and another was leading a game of Red Rover. Above them, on the hill, Alice could see her mother, Evelyn lodged between her knees. The child was squinting out into the sun from under her pompom hat. Alice walked farther on.

"Awful," she said. "Do you see that, Frances? That is called littering."

The child blinked down at the offending beer can. Her hair was lit lemon yellow in the sunlight. She grabbed her mother's necklace and played with it thoughtfully.

"People. People are so fucking thoughtless, sometimes. I have half a mind to—"

To what? The child looked up at her mother's lips, her blue eyes like those of a student respectfully attempting to concentrate. Fucking? Alice bit her lip. She would have to let it go, she thought. You couldn't crash around angry all the time. Children would drink your poison right up. It was unimaginable to Alice that she might become a bitter woman. Was she not herself the cowed result of such parentage?

But they had planned this for *weeks*, she thought. It had been *his* idea. Besides, it was embarrassing, to show up at a Valentine's Day party with one's mother when everyone else was in the traditional homo- and heterosexual pairings. Worst of all was that she was not so much angry, but disappointed. He would have made this fun. He would have made her laugh. He would have done something subversive with his paper boat. He would have fomented a game of chase. Out on the lake, several planks of dirty ice were in slow transit across the surface.

"Sorry, baby," Alice whispered, kissing the child. "Mommy didn't mean to swear."

"*Aaaaaliiiice*," called her mother in the distance.

She turned. Her mother and Evelyn were still up on the hill, on the fringes of the picnic, smaller now. Her mother's voice echoed: "Don't go too far, Alice!"

Alice waved and turned back to the lake. Two kids on dirt bikes came rattling around the corner. Frances laughed, watching them come and go.

"You like to see people enjoying themselves, don't you?"

The child once again studied her mother's face. Alice sought comfort in its blank receptivity. She swore to herself that she would not base all her life's philosophies on first-hand experience alone, which would only offer her daughters a postage stamp–sized view of the world. She swore that she would not have a Gloucester-sized mind. She would let small grievances go. Besides, Valentine's Day always put her in a foul mood. In fact, didn't everyone sort of hate it?

"*Aaaaaliiiice*."

"I'm right *here*, Mother!" she cried, over her shoulder. And then, for spite, she moved farther away, down the lakeside path. Turning a bend, she found herself in a small copse of straight, bare birch trees, lit brilliant white by the sun. The birches reached heavenward, delicate monuments.

"Look," she whispered to the child. "That's beauty, darling. That's what you should look for. Wherever you go."

"*Alice!*"

She turned on her heel. "Chrissakes. What *is* it, Mother?"

"*Oh my God!*"

"Mother?" Alice lurched forward. "What's wrong?"

"*Come quick! My God, come here, Alice!*"

Alarmed, Alice stumbled back across the frozen ground. She came out of the copse and turned the bend, emerging now into the sunlight. Her mother, on the hill, was standing with her hands covering her mouth.

Beside her stood Evelyn.

"*Look! Look she's—*"

It was amazing. The child, in her bundled stoutness, upright! One tiny hand fluttered atop the picnic basket, then, moth-like, flew free. She stood intently, face fixed at the distance, a young woman studying the sea. She lifted a tiny sneaker.

Alice began to run. In her arms, Franny's head bobbled.

"My God," said Alice, laughing. "Oh my God!"

Up the hill they went, past the bread-throwing children and the boat-making children, toward the bundled figure, the upright wobbling standing infant, who had just now placed one sneaker forward on the grass. When the child could make out her mother's face, she smiled gummily. The knee of her standing leg collapsed, and a wave of awareness crossed her features. She grasped for something solid in the sky, but instead fell back heavily on the blanket.

"Why, Evelyn Shade," said Alice, falling to her knees. "Look what *you* did."

"Did you see that?" cried Marlene. "Did you see her stand all by herself? Unprecedented. I didn't do a thing. She just— got up. What a moment! What a fucking Kodak *mo*ment."

Marlene dove into her purse. "Where's my camera? Where's my goddamned camera?"

Alice was not listening. She was stroking the child's cheek, crying. She pressed her thumbs to her eyes.

"What's wrong?" said Marlene, one hand in her purse. "What's wrong? Why are you crying?"

Alice spoke to the child, who was now tugging on a handful of brittle grass.

"We'll have to tell Daddy," she whispered. "We'll have to describe it to Daddy. Won't we?"

⌣

"So." Charlie folded his hands around his Styrofoam cup. "Here we are."

The donut shop was a cube of sunlight. Charlie looked around, then cracked his neck. A group of day laborers entered the donut shop. They looked up at the menu board with dirty, serious faces.

"Isn't the smell of baking nice?" he said. "I like the smell in here."

Opal continued to stare down at her lap.

"On Sundays, in Mattoon, my mother would let us go down to what we called the Sip and Dip. Me and my brother Mark would get a whole dozen donuts. Then we'd eat them all in bed together." Charlie rubbed his nose. "I guess that sounds a little weird, to eat donuts in a bed together with your mom and dad."

Opal smiled a little.

"Isn't that weird?" said Charlie, heartened. "To eat donuts in bed?"

Opal's fingers writhed in her lap. She wasn't really smiling about that. She wasn't hardly listening, and when she did she didn't think it was all that queer. She thought it was nice. But she wasn't thinking about donuts or families or the smell of donuts. Her hands were clutching one another, secret enemies. For what she was thinking now was I have been doing this for six years Six years now Six It doesn't get It doesn't get *better*. Bread and butter bread and butter. The sunlight was coming in from all angles. The sunlight had her in its kiln. She squinted. Kiss and kill. Show and kill. Why so bright? What in God's name did the sun have to be so *bright* about? LITE-BRITE. Here, Mrs. Miller, this is my LITE-BRITE. Well, why don't you plug it in Opal and show the class now wouldn't we like that class?

"Opal," Charlie asked her. "Are you all right? What are you feeling?"

She squinted. She squinted at the sun. It was so hot it was green. What was she feeling, she thought. What was she feeling? What an obscure question. What a prissy little question. What a drop in the bucket. What a pebble what a slit what a speck what a *fleck* of a question. What did it matter? The muscle of her mouth was now contracting around a sound in an attempt to say a word, but it was such a distant obscure tiny word that it was difficult to see how the word mattered. Her father would have called the word Academic. The word describing what she felt. Any word that represented something that couldn't be measured or sold for a dollar amount was Academic: Pain. Want. Perhaps. Sometime. Death. Chance. Love. Punishment. All of it Academic and Obscure and Quaint and Jewish. What was she feeling? *What was she feeling?* Why didn't they go dig up his grave and ask *him*? He was just sitting there, underground, like a bum in a dark train car, fiddling with the buttons of his burial suit, going on and on and on. She could still hear him. All the time! Talking about the military-industrial complex and rats and Jews and—

"Headache," Opal said finally, touching her temple.

"A *head*ache," said Charlie, leaning back with satisfaction. "You have a headache? That's it?"

She closed her eyes, to indicate agreement.

"I'll tell Dr. Hsu first thing Monday," he said, and she felt his cool shadow pass in front of her. "No need for you to be having headaches. I'm sorry about that."

He was bringing her a cup now. A cup of what? She peered inside.

"Apple juice," he said, proudly.

Apple juice! Apple juice! What they feed children. What they feed children to make them take naps little potions little tricks drink it up. Little apples, pressed to pulp. She felt like an apple herself. Her head, in a press. Her life juice, in a cup. Urine yellow. Thick as spit. Stinking of kindergarten.

"No thank you," she whispered.

"No?" He bent down to look in her face. "You don't like apple juice?"

She closed her eyes again, agreeing. No, she did not like apple juice. It was around the Time of Apple Juice, in fact, the Time of Kindergarten and of Show and Tell and of Tire Swings, when her life had been taken from her. Destroyed. Dismantled! Brick by brick. Screw by screw. Bore by bore. Taken apart like a cheap tricycle. She had died then, behind the toolshed. This scent was the scent of death.

"No," she said, turning her head away. "I don't like it."

"Well, that's all right if you don't like it," he said, moving the juice out of her sight. He leaned forward on the table a little. "You seem to be struggling, Opal," he said. "Are you having difficulty? It's really hard to come out of the hospital. The first day is absolutely just the worst. It's all right, if you are. Having difficulty."

And then, for the first time that morning, she looked at him. Really looked at him. His face was just there across the small table. She liked his ears. They were funny. They had minds of their own. His nose was small and red around the nostrils. His blue eyes were red on the rims. He looked like a blue-eyed boy with a cold. He was like a childhood beau from a childhood she never had. Temporarily, the thought of him being her childhood beau made her cheerful, but then like a passing shadow she became morbid and hated him. She broke up with him in the childhood that she never had. She struck him on the head with a hammer and he covered his bloody face in the childhood she never had. She marched away from him leaving him to die, never knowing him. And then she ran back to tend his face but he was not there because neither was the childhood. All the tire swings of the world swung empty. The black enormous force washed over her, practically sucking the breath from her lungs.

It's all right, said her beau said his soft beau voice. *However you feel is all right with me. We can just sit here quietly for a little.*

She closed her eyes, and there they were again. On tire swings. Some other girl was getting raped behind the toolshed. Poor girl, she thought. And look at me, sitting here with my nice beau and not a care in the world!

"You haven't touched your donut," he said after a while.

Opal looked down, startled. The donut looked back at her, startled. She pushed it toward him.

"You want it?" she said.

"No thank you," he said. "What kind is it?"

She turned it this way and that. From all angles, it was the same.

"A round one," she said.

He smiled. Was that funny, she wondered, what she had said? His eyes were blue like good news. His expression was the expression of somebody enjoying a joke made on him. He wasn't mean and tough like a man. He was a little Quaint. Oh how Daddy would have hated him. A thin gentle guy with hair the color of a wood pee-wee. A real Yank. An Academic sort. The sort that turns clear away from you when he coughs. That your beau? hollered Daddy. That all you can come up with you unclean piece of shit?

Shut up, she said.

Charlie leaned forward. "What?"

Quickly, she pointed out the window. "Look at that dog," she said.

There was a spotted dog in the back of a truck. The dog was looking at them through the plate-glass window.

"Now you'll just have to wait," Opal chastened the dog. "You'll just have to wait out there in that car until your owner gets his donuts. Then you can eat them in a bed or wherever you want."

Charlie laughed. It was a nice, natural laugh and Opal was pleased. He was a good beau, she thought. Real and polite and miscellaneous.

Fuck him, said Daddy. Screw him! Hit him in the face! Hammer him!

"What a cute bugger," said Charlie.

Shut up! *Kill him!*

"No use barking," said Opal to the dog. "A waste of breath."

"That's right," said Charlie, laughing. "No shoes, no shirt, no service."

The dog wagged its tail, barking at them.

Then she listened: nothing. The sun became mercifully shady and a man came out and got in the truck with the dog. And just like that, she saw, it had turned into a nice, happy moment. A spotted dog. A round donut. Laughing with a beau. She listened. In her head, a reprieve. A nice moment. She felt fairly sure it was a nice happy moment for everyone within range of it. Also, she had survived another hour.

"Well, then," said Charlie.

"All righty," said Opal.

They got up and dusted the crumbs off their pants. Then they walked outside and he took her to the bank where she cashed her Social Security check and then she bought cigarettes.

～

"Now, darling," said Marlene. "*You* look like your father."

She crossed her legs and scrutinized the child in her lap. The child clapped again. The skin on her round face was taut as if the very bones of her face were a loom or a drum. She had a robust, outdoorsy beauty, with hair like gusts of beach wind.

"Now your sister, she looks more like your mother. She'll be dark and voluptuous and probably a touch—Machiavellian. And maybe a little smarter than you, dear. No offense. It's just Evelyn's almost ready to walk, and you're pretty much a quadruped."

The child spread her fingers apart, pressing her hands together.

"You sure do like to *clap*, though, *don't* you? *Aren't* you good at it?" Marlene pressed her nose against the child's shiny nub, feeling in the very density of her waist her generous good nature. The child was a scoop of love. "You know, you've got a very English nose. You'll have a blond, English confidence. And confidence matters more than intelligence. That's the secret. Why else do you think the English ruled the world for so long?"

The child wrinkled her nose and laughed.

"I wasn't a confident child," said Marlene. "My daddy used to tell me all the time I was too dark and too skinny. He used to make me sit in the shade, so I wouldn't turn brown. He made me wear Mary Janes until I was eighteen because they were flat. My chest was flat. At school they called me Olive Oyl. Oh they used to tease me awfully. Now," Marlene shifted the child to her other knee, "If I had been satisfied and confident, like you, I would have saved myself a lot of tears. A *lot* of tears—"

Down the hall, the telephone rang.

"I'll get it!" cried Alice.

Marlene looked out the window. "My mother—your great-grandmother, is dead. Your great-grandfather says I don't exist. And your grandfather disappeared. Poof. He blew away, like a feather."

Through the baby monitor, she could hear Evelyn stir in the nursery.

"Alice, darling!" she called. "Evelyn's up. Are you still on the phone? Would you like me to get her?"

After a moment, the child began to crow. The bathroom door swung open down the hall.

"No," came Alice's voice. "I've got her. You just stay put, Mom. Okay?"

"Fine by me," muttered Marlene. She looked again at Frances's face. Flawless. Unremonstrative. Stay-put. In a matter of years, she would be sporting a beach ball on the Jersey shore, signaling to her friends.

"Now where were we?" Marlene said.

But then her daughter's voice rose softly above the monitor static. *Hush, hush*, she was saying in her husky voice. *Mommy's got your bottle right here, brown baby.*

Marlene listened to her daughter's voice through the monitor. Why did she have to call Evelyn brown baby? She wasn't brown anyway, but white as a sheet. Like Alice herself. Marlene was sure Robert Bussard would have approved of Alice as a woman. If she hadn't been illegitimate, of course. But she wished he had gotten just one look at her fair skin—not Portuguese skin, but the skin of some cloistered princess—and her roundness-in-the-right-places, if not even a little fatness, and that fullness of her lower lip that cast a shadow on her chin. Her father had an artist's eye for women.

No, no . . . please don't apologize again . . . please don't . . . make this awkward.

Marlene tilted her head. She reached over to turn off the monitor. Instead, she withdrew her hand, listening. Through the static, she heard a sigh.

No. It's nice of you. I'm flattered. But I really don't want it to feel . . . I wouldn't want Charlie to think . . . Exactly.

After a pause, Alice's laughter filled the room. The quality of this laughter made Marlene sit upright. It was a deep-throated laugh. It was sexual. She twisted up the volume knob of the baby monitor. In her lap, Frances bleated.

"Stop that," said Marlene to the child. "Hush."

. . . Yes, well. I really am flattered. . . . I don't get a hell of a lot of invitations . . . I'm stuck—

The child screeched again, amused, perhaps, at the projected voice of her mother.

"I said *be quiet*," snapped Marlene.

Static. A long pause.

But please . . . Please just don't say anything else like that. I can't say it . . . back to you. Okay?

Then, as if in dismay, the child in the nursery began to wail. With the monitor volume on high, the scream filled the room. Frances turned, seeking her sister. Through the screaming, Marlene could still hear scraps of her daughter's voice, filled with a kind of forced jocularity.

. . . Ha, I know . . . when the boss says it's time . . . Watch yourself with . . . those . . .

The rest of it was lost to screaming.

Marlene snapped the monitor off. She sat there several moments, swallowing back the acid in her throat. In her lap, the infant raised her hands questioningly, as if to confirm there was nothing in them.

⌒

Harriet was pointing a finger in his face.

"I want to know what the *hell* you were doing with Opal Ludlow on Saturday."

"What?"

"Are you lovers?"

"What?"

Harriet shook her head, her expression livid. "Don't lie to me *again*, now."

The point of Charlie's pencil, still pressed to the page of his daily log, snapped. He looked down at it, stupefied. The big shambling figure of Bruce was coming quickly up the hallway, hands out in front of him, saying, "Hey, wait a minute, now." A pair of nurses who'd been talking there pressed themselves back against the wall, staring.

Harriet still filled the office doorway. "*Sev*eral people saw you. That's one *hun*dred percent unacceptable. You got *some* balls. What exactly do you think your role is here? *Jesus*?"

"All right," said Bruce. "Let's take this inside."

"—And I didn't even find out 'til today. Like some fool!"

Bruce put one hand on Harriet's back. Violently, she shrugged him off.

"I'll move when I move," she shouted over her shoulder. Then, as if on second thought, "*You* been covering for him since day one, Bruce! At the expense of *my* work and *my* clients. People's lives!"

She stood, panting in the doorway, looking hard at Charlie, who was still transfixed by his pencil point. Her face was shiny with sweat.

"Harriet," said Bruce softly. "Go in and sit down."

She was not moving. She was glaring at Charlie with a look no one had ever shown him before.

"Harriet, baby," said Bruce.

Finally, the broad shoulders slumped. She sighed and walked in slowly, taking a chair on the far side of the room, joints cracking.

"All right," she said. "I'm ready. I'm ready to talk."

Bruce shut the door behind him. Turning, he said, "What in God's name is going on, Charlie?"

    ∾

Alice pushed open the glass door.

Hal looked up. Seeing her, the opacity left his dark eyes.

"*Hey*," he said. "Hey. Hold on."

A fortysomething redhead stood at the register, wallet in hand, wearing a wry smile. The woman looked Alice up and down. Her gaze made Alice's face hot. She walked with great intention across the store. A young girl in a Catholic school uniform sat on a footstool, intent on her book. Nearby, a man in a baseball cap appraised the shelves, hands in pockets.

"Ten dollars fifteen cents," said Hal behind her.

"Phooey," said the redheaded woman. "I've only got a dime, darling. Could I owe you the nickel?"

"Don't worry about it."

"Oh wait. Here. One, two—two pennies."

"It's all right. Really."

"All right, Hal, darling. I'll *owe* you then."

Against her will, Alice turned. The woman was combing back her stiff hair, looking evenly at Alice. She cast a long look at Hal, and drew herself reluctantly out the door.

Hal sprinted around the counter.

"Hi," he said.

Alice looked down. "Hi."

"Are you upset? You look upset. Do you want to take off your jacket?"

"No," said Alice. "Thank you."

"Why are you upset?"

"I'm not upset."

Behind them, the schoolgirl sneezed.

"God bless you," said Hal.

"Listen," whispered Alice. "You really, really, really shouldn't call me at home."

"All right."

"All right? Just all right?" She laughed. "It's not all right. I know you just want to be my friend. But it doesn't look right, really. I wouldn't want Charlie to think anything was going on. You understand that right? How it looks inappropriate?"

"Looks?"

"Is, I mean. Is inappropriate."

"Why is it inappropriate?"

Alice opened her mouth but said nothing.

Hal stepped back slowly, nodded, and sighed. He moved away, back behind the register. He shoved a stack of books aside, and began to sort them on the counter.

"What's wrong?" she said.

"I don't."

"You don't what?"

He looked up. "I don't just want to be your friend."

He was gripping the spine of a book. He set it down next to the register.

"Come here," he said. He grabbed her by the wrist.

He pulled her into the blue storeroom. Pushing her shoulders back against a file cabinet, he stood squarely in front of her, the sun lighting his closely shaven head.

"I think about you all the time. I think about your hair. I think I love you."

"No, you don't!" cried Alice.

Hal's brow wrinkled. He shook his head, his mouth open.

"No," Alice said, pushing repeatedly at the bridge of her nose. "You're—you're like a gosling."

"A what?"

"You were sick, and now you're better, and I was just the first person you saw. You just decided it was me because I was the first person you saw and liked when you could see. It's not me."

Hal cocked his head back, as if struck.

"But that's not it," he said. "I can't believe you'd say that. I'm like a *duck*? My love is like a duck?"

Alice put both hands over her face.

"I can't believe you'd respond like that," he said. "You certainly—don't have to love me back."

She took her hands from her face. "Well, okay, then."

"Fine," he said, shrugging. He took a stack of books in his arms. "Then get out of my storeroom please."

"Don't," Alice said, astonishing herself. "Don't go."

And just like that, he put the stack of books down.

"See?" she said shrilly. "You're so young. You don't even know how to act."

"What? I should play hard to get?" Suddenly he winced, and covered his temples with his fingers. "Jesus."

She stepped toward him. "Are you all right?"

Under his hand, he was smiling.

"Gotcha," he said.

"Damn you."

"Seriously," he said. "You're hurting my brain." He gestured for her to move out of his way. Then he stopped and ran one hand over the bristles of his hair. "I've been feeling like something else lately. I mean I've been feeling—unlike a corpse. I don't want it—to stop. You might not understand. I could try to explain. But I can't explain. If you could live every day over again with me, then maybe—" He paused. "I'm alive. I *feel*."

He sat back against the radiator, smiling with quiet amazement. His head and the side of his face and the plants in the room were lit with sun. Alice nodded slowly.

She settled on the far side of the small room, leaning against a file cabinet.

"I like you very much," she said. "But from a certain distance."

"Well, I like you up close," he said, looking at her.

"I like you as a friend."

"I like you up close."

They looked at one another. The bell clanged at the front of the store. He stood on the other side of the room, completely straight, completely unguarded, completely facing her. He faced her and watched her as if deaf. She could see his breastbone rise and fall with his breath. He was staring at her. He was perfectly created. He was facing her completely. And then, swiftly, without further comment, he came toward her. Just the two, three steps it took to cross the small blue room. He reached one warm hand inside the back of her parka to her naked back. He gripped her there, by her stem.

"Don't," she said.

"Please," he said. "Just once."

He bent down and put his nose against her nose. Standing there together, she felt his breath in her mouth. And then it was like drinking. Her eyes slid closed. She was drinking muscle and silk and salt. She heard him breathe thirstily through his nose.

"Oh," he said. "Oh God."

She felt his hardness against her. Suddenly this filled her with a physical passion edged with rage. He was up inside her parka now, inside her nest. She clawed at the sides of his arms, his shoulders, as if looking for the switch that controlled him. In response, he pressed her nearer, reaching further in. He kicked her sneakers apart. He was fumbling now, with one hand, down her pants. She grabbed his wrist. He pushed down anyway. She could feel his cold fingers and his relentlessness slide through all the barriers of mind and body and hem and was overcome with the annihilating physical desire to accept. When he reached into her, she gasped, opening her eyes. It was as if they were both coming upon the same sweeping view. He moved his hand slowly in the silence. Her body paused, expanding. The walls fell as curtains, soundless. She waked herself.

"All right," she whispered, turning her head away. "That's enough."

He exhaled, putting his mouth to her neck. His lips were warm and soft.

"Okay," she said. She put one hand gently on his chest.

Slowly, he withdrew his hand. She closed her eyes. She saw him disappearing down a tunnel of time, spinning away. It felt good to be in his arms and it felt good to see him disappear spinning down the tunnel.

Then she heard a voice: "Good God."

Someone was standing in the doorway of the storeroom.

"Who's there?" Alice said hoarsely.

Hal stood, large and inert, in her way. All at once she felt strangled by him and by his proximity and his power and his stupid youth and by herself also. "*Move*," she shouted. He lifted his hands from her as if from something burning. He stepped aside.

Marlene took a step back from the doorway.

"Mother?" Alice said.

The stroller was between them, the engorged purple blue eyes of her children staring up at her. Their eyes moved philosophically from face to face—mother, man, mother, man. The man from before! Evelyn smiled, thinking of Airplane. She lifted her arms.

"No," Alice gasped.

"I—" said Marlene, shaking her head. "I didn't—"

The older woman was withdrawing from the doorway. She was being sucked away. The infants' fuzzy heads went backward into space. Their eyes, searching, could no longer locate their mother. By the time Alice straightened her clothes and came stumbling out of the storeroom after them, she saw Marlene making haste out the door, a tall man in a raincoat helping to lift the stroller out sideways.

⌒

He stepped into the frigid afternoon. The air was raw and cold. His lungs contracted; he bent over coughing. Then, straightening his coat, he tried to breathe normally. A siren rose up and died in the distance. He walked several paces and stopped. He turned, and walked back to where he'd been standing. He was shoved from behind by a man exiting the clinic.

"Sorry," the man mumbled.

"No problem," said Charlie. "My fault."

The man, his eyes widening, stopped and looked at him. "Who wins a tie? That's what I want to know. Who wins a tie?"

Charlie nodded. "I don't know," he said.

He watched the man as he strode away down the street, talking aloud. Then Charlie discovered, like some cheap souvenir, a smile frozen on his face. The same disbelieving smile he'd been wearing just now, in his office.

Charlie blinked city grit out of his eyes. A bus came grinding up the hill and pulled toward the stop on the side of the road. As if the bus itself wore the news flashing on its sign, the impact of the moment finally registered. The shock of being forced out, banished, the failure. The shock of the cold air. The freefall. The terror of it. Dead of insincerity, the smile dropped from his face. His heart went dumb. How in the world would he be able to say it out loud? He would not be able to say it out loud. He did not speak this language.

"Oh, Jesus," he said, his own voice drowned out by the traffic. "Jesus, help me."

Numbly, Charlie began to walk. The wind blew his coat open, but he did not move to close it.

Streetlights glowed through the curtains. The hallway light cast a path across the dark apartment floor. In this twilight, the objects in the room were shadow colored, the two sitting chairs, the bed, broad as the sum of two bodies. Alice laid her keys on the side table and shut the apartment door. Like a child coming out of her bedroom from a nightmare, open to the meagerest signs of rescue, she was gladdened to see the light on in her mother's room down the hall, and to hear the sound of a cough, zippers.

Stepping forward into the darkness, she struck a large object with her foot. She bent down—the suitcase. She looked down the hall toward the lighted nursery.

A room with a mother in it was always a changed room. The lights a mother turned on were different lights. Brighter, further. And a mother's smell: perfume, sherry, wax. A smell so singular it broke the heart, for there was only one mother, and you did not ever get another one or another chance. And it was never right and never enough. When she was sad, you would wilt up and die for a little while, and when she was happy and dressed up in her blue silk dress, it made you yourself feel dressed in a blue dress, and thusly in your pajamas you floated, beatific, until the electrician or the volleyball coach came to the door to pick up your mother. And when they left you just got very small and waited. Much later, credits rolling over the treacherous face of J.R., she would return, the mother. And once (it had been the final date in memory, the electrician) you pretended to be asleep because she was sobbing. Walking across the flickering room with her hands over her face. You opened your eyes a crack just to see how horrible to see. For now and always would the color blue be twinned with this weepy march of the mother across the darkened room, as would silk, electricity, pajamas, couches, doorbells, and Larry Hagman, catching in its web of associations almost everything obliquely, until the taint of sadness formed a nagging little footnote to every memory of her, and sometimes even broke free of all context and became a rogue memory, doing senseless violence to others in the middle of a day.

Alice stood in the nursery doorway. Her mother was bent over her small, leatherette bag, stuffing in socks, a book, Kleenex, a neck pillow.

"Mother," she said. "Why are you crying?"

"*Shh*," said Marlene. She pointed at the twins. "I will speak with you *outside* this room."

Alice backed away from the doorway, watching her mother's final, angry movements. Her throat burned. She rubbed it with the fat of her hand, following her mother down the hall.

As soon as they reached the living room, Marlene spun around.

"What took you so long? Were you with *him*?"

"No," said Alice. "No, Mommy. I was walking. I was thinking."

"I should have known. I'm dis*gus*ted. I'm disgraced."

"Don't leave," said Alice. "Sit down."

"I'm *not* going to *sit* in this *place*. And since when do you call me Mommy?"

Alice reached out her hand. Marlene's face was shining with sweat and tears, her eyes wide with a crazy look.

"Mother," she said. "Please calm down."

"How could you? How *could* you?" Marlene's arms flapped at her sides. "Have you been using me as a cover? Is that why you asked me to stay?"

"Please just listen to me. I barely know him. It was just that once."

"I *saw*."

"What you saw, that's all there was. I swear to God."

"He's your lover! I heard you on the telephone."

"He's not. I swear to you. And it will never happen again. Ever."

"I don't believe you. Why should I believe you? I didn't raise you to be—" Marlene felt the woosh of air, and she knew the word was irrevocable, and yet it brought such acute satisfaction, "—a *whore*."

Alice pressed her chest with her hand. "A what?"

"A whore! What you did was what a *whore* does. I should have seen this cheapness in you and this—" Marlene clawed the air for the word.

"Me?" Alice took a step toward her mother. "Me, a whore?"

"Don't. Don't you shirk this."

Alice stepped closer, whispering now. "I was conceived in a hotel."

"You were not conceived in a hotel!"

"No, that's right. A boardinghouse. A boardinghouse."

With a sharp cry, Marlene turned, raised her hands to the ceiling. Then she collapsed into a chair, unable to speak. Alice went to the window and looked out to the damp blue street, a damp blue tongue licking the city. She spoke quietly.

"I don't want to offend you, Mother. I don't even blame you for calling me a whore because maybe I am. And that's my own fault. My—shame. But Mother, you've never loved anyone, so how can you pretend to know what it's like?"

Marlene's eyes flashed. "I did too love people!"

"Who? My father? You loved him so much you forgot to tell him he was the father of a *child*?"

"He left, Alice. He was gone."

"But you never even *told* him about me. Maybe he would have stayed! If he knew about me!"

Alice's voice broke. Marlene looked away, through the wall and backward, to where the broad back still dented the side of the bed.

"I didn't have enough time to love him. If I did, it was for such a little while."

"Exactly. There are people you love for just a moment." Alice started to cry. "And then there are people, people you love too much. People who break your heart when they leave the room, you—love them so desperately."

Marlene looked up. "Charlie," she said.

"Love like that *kills* you. You hang by a *thread* from it. You wouldn't know!"

"I do know."

"How do you know?" cried Alice. "Tell me how you know. You spent your *whole life* warning me against people. I thought I was disrespecting you if I cared for anyone! It still feels shameful. What did you want me to do?"

"This is unendurable," said Marlene, standing. "What does all this have to do with anything? *I'm* the one who should be upset. I was the one hanging around cleaning bottles while you were off with—"

"He's not my lover!"

"You can't control what I think, Alice." Marlene grabbed the doorknob, and flung open the front door. "I'll believe whatever I want. That's my right."

She pulled the suitcase out onto the landing.

Still crying, Alice tried to help, but Marlene swatted her away.

The suitcase sat on the landing. It filled up the doorway and the space between them. For several moments, breathing hard, they both stood, staring at it.

Marlene sighed. "You have to tell Charlie."

Alice wiped her face with her sleeve. She stared at the suitcase.

"Tell Charlie. He would want you to. If what you're saying is true, he'll get over it."

Outside, the horn of a taxi sounded.

"You're really leaving?" said Alice. "You actually called a cab?" Her voice was suddenly shrill. "Please don't leave Mother. I need—I need—help. I *need* you."

Marlene stepped over the suitcase and faced her daughter. She brushed Alice's hair back over her shoulders and smoothed it. Through her tears, Alice smiled gratefully at this tenderness. But then, just as quickly, Marlene withdrew her hand and stepped out into the lighted hallway, her purse over her shoulder.

"Perhaps you're right, Alice," she said. "Perhaps I never loved a man. Not even for a little while. I was never half the woman you are. But I know the pain of love you're talking about." Trembling, Marlene drew her wrist under her nose. "Because I love *you*."

Then, as she had a thousand times, Marlene Bussard straightened, drawing herself up to full height. She grabbed the suitcase handle and lowered it down in front of her, stair by stair, and was gone.

⟿

The schoolteacher threw his coat on a chair and collapsed into it. He rested his big, curly head against his hand, lacking the strength to remove his shoes. Under his feet, the patterns in the shabby Persian carpet seemed to have faded even more since yesterday. Such was the exhaustion of Fridays. Such was the way he saw things on Fridays, after a week of teaching the youth of this country. *But why's it called* Portrait of a Young Artist? *one of them had crowed that afternoon. I mean, I don't get it. The guy doesn't make any art.*

The schoolteacher kicked at the fringe of the carpet.

"Hey, fuck you, kid," he said aloud, pointing.

He heard a crunching outside the apartment building. Weakly, he raised his disheveled head. Through the streetlit curtains, he saw a figure pass his window in the growing darkness. The figure came around the front where the schoolteacher left the curtains open a crack.

It was the husband from upstairs. He was walking slowly, almost morosely, thought the schoolteacher, like a boy bringing bad marks home from school. The schoolteacher watched him. He heard the key scratch in the front door. Then the husband made his way, moroser still, up the old creaking staircase to his wife. He imagined her up there, at the sink. For he could hear the couple's plumbing whenever they used it. The water scooting up and down the ancient pipes. In fact, he could hear everything about them, if not most constantly their footsteps. Such heavy footsteps for such average-sized people. Up and down all night, to the keening of babies. The sounds of the couple upstairs had become such a part of the schoolteacher's life that they interfered with his dreams. He used to dream grand dreams: Rimbaud once visited him and sat on the bed reciting a recipe for bouillabaisse. And once he'd met Papa himself—old Hemingway—whittling on a stump, and Papa had said to the schoolteacher, "All this time, I was trying to look with my eyes. But my leg hurt. And then I couldn't see anymore, and I realized I should have been looking with my leg."

Now he dreamt only of water and toilets and jewelry box music.

He heard the husband's key scratch in the upstairs door. What would it be like, wondered the schoolteacher, to come home to the arms of somebody like her? She appealed to some Muse-seeking thing inside him. She looked somehow French. He would have liked to see her in a corset. He had watched them both, many times, through the peephole, through the window, even on the street, walking on the opposite side.

Sure, he himself had once had a serious girlfriend. It was the worst thing in the world. She was a short, button-nosed girl from Philadelphia. A virgin and a graduate student of advanced mathematics. A wonderful girl with clear dark eyes, intelligent counting eyes. They were supposed to get married. But then he'd seen this girl cry. She had bought an ice cream on the boardwalk and it had fallen off the cone, and she had looked at it for a moment, and began to cry. Just like a child! When the schoolteacher remembered the series of events, he sometimes forgot which had come first—her crying or his realizing that he couldn't marry her. A grown woman, crying over ice cream. He didn't think he could stand a lifetime of that.

So he had told her that he didn't love her anymore, or that he never had, in the deepest sense. Not true love, as was necessary. He loved parts of her and surely she loved parts of him. He loved her little nose that took on a shine in the heat, and surely she loved things about him—his poetry perhaps—but there was something missing between them. Think of mathematics, he'd offered. True love was like a prime number—rare, indivisible. They were not indivisible.

The girl from Philadelphia stared at the ice cream in the puddle. So that's that? she had said. Then she began to cry harder. Like a child! It had made him feel a million miles away from her. It was the worst thing in the world.

And now, overhead, he heard the couple upstairs stomping, fighting. The schoolteacher sat upright. What on God's earth could you count on? Shocked and offended, he stared up at the ceiling. A piece of plaster drifted down onto his arm. A shout. Crying. How could he stand it, the husband? How could he stand it, whether it was his fault or not?

He himself had been grateful that he'd cut it off with the mathematician. He decided it wasn't practical to be married to a temperamental woman. That night, after she dropped her ice cream and was gone forever, he stayed awake in bed for a long time. When he finally slept, it was a very, very deep sleep. He slept as a man sleeps moving into a new lifetime after death. In the morning, he awoke with a terrible realization: he was no longer a poet. What sort of poet breaks up with a woman because she shows *emotion*? All of a sudden he understood that he had always been a terrible poet and always would be. He wrote poems of sanity. And as Socrates had said, all the poetry of sanity would be brought to naught by the poetry of madness, and behold, at the end of time, the sane poets would not matter.

Then he had gotten out of bed and showered and shaved and went to the concrete high school at which he taught English. And he took many rights and many lefts to get there, and he ceded many rights-of-way, and he taught as he was supposed to, and read essays by students who wrote as they were supposed to, and he would've killed himself that afternoon, that very day, in the teacher's lounge, with a penknife across the throat, if the kid hadn't come up to him in the hallway.

Excuse me, the boy had said. *I'm in your fifth period. I was wondering . . . Could I show you something?*

The boy was a wrestler, the star of the team, and the red hood of his team sweatshirt formed a red corona behind his plainly handsome face. He had wide, saucer-sized hands, with which he touched his teacher's arm with surprising gentleness.

I've been writing . . . he said, haltingly . . . *poems. Like we read in class. Will you tell me if they're any good?*

He drew his fingertips across his black sketchbook and opened it. Underneath his fingers were drawings of thunder-clouds and shadows, done neatly with a pencil, and short ax-iomatic poems written in the tiniest lettering:

"Poetry is directions on the box of your thinking."

The poet stared at the book. And there, with the boy, the rest of the students draining into their classrooms, he became wild with happiness. What a mistake it would have been to kill himself in the teacher's lounge, simply because he had broken up with a wonderful girl and wrote sane poetry, when boys like this would keep coming, keep bearing him up from below, just as perhaps when he was young and beautiful somebody had been borne up by him. Was he not, after all, the boy's teacher?

Yes yes, he had said to the boy, laughing. *They are good.*

The boy looked up at him with his handsome look. *Should I make corrections?*

No! shouted the poet, his voice echoing in the empty hall. *Don't make any corrections, dammit. Just write. When you're my age, you can make corrections.*

Laughing, he grabbed the boy's elbow, this boy much larger and stronger, and drew him over to the light and wrote down a list of poets for the boy to read and study. He was ecstatic. He pressed the piece of paper to the boy's cottony chest and the boy took it and looked at it, and the poet could perceive the curves of a smile on his lips. He would tutor the boy. He would read anything the boy wrote.

Just don't make corrections and don't worry what they'll think of you, he told the boy in confidence. *It doesn't matter what they think of you. Prepare to be misunderstood.*

The boy nodded and walked away.

Several months later, the boy had a nervous breakdown.

The news was all over school. He was in a psychiatric hospital. He was nuts. The State Championship would be lost. No one could believe it. No one but the schoolteacher, gasping for air in the teacher's lounge.

Now, he coughed and sat up in his chair. The couple had progressed to throwing things. It was upsetting. He could hear the man yelling, and the woman yelling back and then pleading, like a child. Something heavy (a chair?) fell onto the floor.

He arose. He cleared his throat. He went to his apartment door and opened it and stood in the hallway. From there he could hear their shouting more clearly. *Paint me a picture, why don't you!* He climbed a stair, the voices dropping again, then rising: *Don't! Don't say that!* He hoped they would stop soon so that he wouldn't have to do anything like call the police. It wasn't his business. It wasn't his fault they got married to each other. Look, he hadn't gotten married because of exactly this sort of crap. He had spared the world his graceless venture.

Suddenly, he wanted some credit for it. He wanted someone to thank him for not crapping on the institution of love. He wanted someone to thank him for not being yet another dilettante. He wanted someone to thank him for quitting poetry. He wanted some great poet to thank him for quitting poetry instead of desecrating it with his amateurishness. He wanted some unborn child to thank him for not conceiving her and not leaving her a hope chest full of mawkish villanelles. He wanted some sort of organization of martyrs to give him an award. He wanted to be decorated for not putting up a fuss. He wanted to be the president of forgettable people. He wanted there to be a competition for the least competitive person, and he wanted to win that competition. He wanted some sort of badge or outfit or medal or key or hat. He wanted to be asked to stand. He wanted to be considered. He wanted to be considered in earnest before being ignored. He wanted all the insane and beautiful and passionate people in the world to take one moment of silence in gratitude for the ones who had ceded them the stage—he, the unread poet, the sacrifice, the schoolteacher—he wanted one goddamned moment of appreciation.

Just then, the door to the second-floor apartment flew open and the husband came thundering down the stair. Pulling on his coat as he came, he almost collided with the poet in the darkness of the foyer. They stared at one another for one moment. Mumbling an apology, the husband pushed through the front door. It slammed behind him. The sound reverberated in the hallway.

The poet turned. The wife was standing at the top of the stairs, watching. Her shining, dark hair was mussed, and she held a glass globe in her hand, as if just having used it to defend herself.

"Are you—" said the poet.

She stared at the closed front door behind him. Absently, she touched her finger to her lip and looked at it.

He cleared his throat. "Are you all right?"

The young wife blinked slowly. She tamped her hair back with the hand that held the glass globe. It glistened and snowed in her hand.

"No," she said. "I'm not all right."

And then, without another word, she disappeared back into her apartment.

Well, thought the poet. So that's that?

He liked the couple. He didn't have anything against them. He didn't even mind dreaming about them. He would continue to watch her through the peephole, and to dream of long conversations they would not have together. Surely they would work it out between them somehow. For there had to be some upshot, didn't there? There had to be some persuasive reasons to fall in love, or else nobody would do it. Surely love had to hold some secret wonders that he himself was not gifted to see. Perhaps he himself was not desperate enough to find the wonders. Perhaps he himself lacked the gift or the madness or the talent. But if no one could find the way, and we all began to die alone, our brittle, discrete worlds dying with us, surely love itself would have to take pity on someone—one last survivor, one remaining prophet, false or true, to go forth into the next civilization with these rumors of paradise.

She is waiting and she has the knife. She is waiting and the knife is here. The knife is waiting. The knife is her wife. The knife is a life. The knife is a slice of light. Turn it this way, turn it that. You can make a rhyme out of it. You can sing it in a round. You can marry metal. You can marry earth. You can make a rhyme out of it. There is reason inside it somewhere. You can knock and no one comes to the door; you can stand there not knocking and someone comes. You can be—as she has been—invited. (She stopped and hesitated, for sometimes her thoughts burst apart like a field of quail at a gunshot, the quail taking even bits of the field with them, the field which was her mind falling to puzzle pieces with the gunshot.) Because what she wondered now was, Can you be disinvited? Can you disinvite yourself? Can you refuse to make a rhyme out of it? Does the universe get mad at you? If you change direction? If—like a bird in the sky that tacks sharply away for no known reason—*you change your mind*? She knew the universe to be wrathful (night is only a cover for the witchhunt). There is a strict order. You can only fall into it. You can fall out of it, but it will still be there and will always be. Just as you can tumble out of your crib but you'll still be a baby. You can tumble out of your coffin but you'll still be a corpse. You can say "that's not my coffin!" but they'll bury you in it anyway. Blind, unhappy men read books in every doorway. You want to tell them, You might as well go along with it. Be the baby or the corpse or blind like you are. You might as well accept the invitation.

So you understand! You understand! cried the nighttime. *Will you obey?*

She was lying on her new bed. Well, not on her bed but on the floor next to her new high bed. She knew it was time for sleeping but since she was not asleep she made the gesture of lying on the floor. She was trying very hard. She was a Hard Worker. She had Good Intentions.

She'd been invited to take up the knife. She was asked to take the knife and wait, there in the dark, like a burglar in her own house. She felt flattered to have an invitation, but beyond that. . . . The ink runs in her mind. She is Good. She has Good Intentions. But beyond those the ink runs. You can make a round out of it. How do others take actions and how do they reply to invitations? She was not used to watching civilizations. She did once have a friend Bethany and was invited to the lake with Bethany for a week and she said yes and it was a success—logs and bogs and singing in a round and those round rubber rafts you drift down rivers in. She had said yes, then, even though she was scared. But had she ever been invited and said no?

She sat up, feeling suddenly nauseous, spinning, enclosed. She heard footsteps crunching outside. Was it him? She got all excited until she remembered the knife. She picked it up and held it in front of her pointing out. He was not going to like it. She knew the knife was not good for him. But it was his. It was special like he was.

She listened—nothing.

Nothing but, *So you understand!*

No, she could not remember ever saying no. Maybe no thank you, as in no ketchup thank you. But not ever when she was commanded. Not when it mattered. All anyone ever had to do was get mad and she would say yes, yes! And the universe was furious now. Maybe if God had just once asserted His or Her gentle existence over the course of the evil of her life, she would not fall to pieces whenever somebody raised his voice:

Will you obey?

A soft knock at the door.

She sucked in her breath.

The witchhunt has begun!

Opal? his voice was strangely slurry. *You there?*

A soft knock at the door.

You can make a round of it.

You can marry a knife. You can marry earth.

You can marry a ghost too but with whom as your witness?

She was dallying. She was wasting time!

Sparks flew all around; time was afire.

Will you obey?

She gripped the knife hard with soldier-like zest. She rose to her knees.

A soft knock at the door.

Opal?

And suddenly, her body rigid, she understood that she was going to change the universe. She was going to yank the universe inside out like a shirt. She would NOT rise from the floor. She would say NO. She would NOT accept, as she should have done years ago, the concrete cast still wet. NO! she might have said. No, no, no. Don't!

The disappointed knife clattered to the linoleum.

Speak for yourself, she said to the knife. Do it yourself if it matters so much.

She collapsed to the floor.

She was glad. She knew the universe was right there, waiting with its greasy brown lunch bag of punishments. Once he left, she would be alone with it. The hot opened mouth. But she didn't care.

That's right, you heard me! she hissed. I said no, dammit!

After a moment, she got up, remembering, and ran to the window. She parted the curtain.

No one.

No—there. There was someone. Staggering away. Look at him! So skinny and without a coat on. Walking in a zigzag as if fate were still fighting over him.

～

He struck the door again.

"Open the door!" Charlie cried, his voice breaking. "Open the door!"

He felt no pain, but the butt of his left fist had blood on it. He listened, tilting over on his toes.

Suddenly he was on his hands and knees, staring at concrete.

The intricacy of concrete! The most solid thing made out of the littlest pieces. Shattered glass. Rock. Horsehair. Colored sugar. Broken pencils. Irregular verbs. He spread his hands across the rough surface of the concrete. He realized he was now kneeling upon it like a penitent. Was he praying? Or had he dropped something? Was that why he was down there, examining the concrete? He raised his head. Through his damp parted hair he saw a door. Still shut. He hiccupped. Was he having an idea? Was he trying to peer through the mail slot? Because that was a good idea! Still on his hands and knees, Charlie raised one arm to the mail slot. But this disturbed a certain balance, and he fell forward softly upon a hairy, flat thing.

"Wel-come," Charlie read aloud.

He rolled over onto his back.

"Why, thank you," he said.

Was everything more true or less true when you were drunk

and lying on a sidewalk? For now the stars were twinkling, but they did so out of order, and they signified nothing. The night sky was meaningless, Charlie decided. Completely without meaning.

"Wallpaper the whole damn thing," he advised God.

Some time later, he woke up. He did not know how much later it was. It could have been seconds. He did not know how he had gotten from wherever he was before to here. The wind was picking up in the trees and vermin crashed in the under-brush and he was staring at the multitudes of grasses, the vast gathered masses trying to see the felled giant. He turned onto his side. Again and again, he felt liquid running up and out of him. He was malfunctioning. He was felled. The force of his gut expelling was so great that it busted something in his eyes. He gripped the grass, trying only to survive. He didn't want to die here. He wanted to die, just not right here. He opened his mouth and gagged, but only sour bubbles came up.

Someone had him by the collar now.

"Don't," he said to the figure in the darkness, "—touch me."

He wanted to tell the person that he was going to die after this so could he just please wait? He wanted to tell the person he thought his neck was broken and don't touch him because did he want to accidentally end up with manslaughter charges? He wanted to say, Don't waste your crimes on me, Buddy. I'm already going. I'm going willingly.

"Good God, Charlie," the figure was whispering.

He felt the cottony brush of cloth on his face. A hairy breastbone loomed overhead, exposed by an open robe.

"How the hell did you get here?"

Charlie reached up, fingered the robe.

"Dad?" he whispered.

All went completely black.

The pain was astonishing. It was a killing cramp. A cramp that began just under her ribs, in her seed, where she was born. The pain parted her lips. Her fists loosened. She felt her ribs split and bloom open like a fruit. Frozen, her back arched, she was now completely submissive to the pain. It was something like a rape. The rape of oneself by death.

How fitting, the grandmother thought, for death to enter into one sexually. Eighty-nine years old and sex a distant memory. The touch of her husband had once made her radiate like this. The windows blew open. The larks on the wallpaper flew out into the night crying. Next, though it did not seem possible, the vice tightened.

"Luddy!" she cried out at last, unable to bear it. "Luduina!"

But even as she cried out, the grandmother knew she would not be heard. Her daughter was asleep with her eye mask and cucumber cream down the hall. The old woman would have to die alone. In the middle of the night. In the middle of the island of her bed. At the end of the twentieth century. Yes, it was all coming due, converging, her own death the only one she had not troubled to envision.

Her eyes snapped open.

Wait, she thought. But what had they done to him? To Charlie?

She struggled to sit up, but lacking the strength, only fell back.

Where was Charlie? Was he alive? Or was he, just moments ahead of her, flying to God? Charlie. Her first grandson, her spiritual and eternal favorite. The world's most beautiful child—if beauty is measured by the relief it brings—with fine golden hair and a pure face like an open aperture, Charlie running in between tomato vines, the child who had healed her of her widowhood. The curse of her life was that she had spent so much of it with his death, knowing he would die, die so horribly, so unnaturally, and young, she had *seen* his cut body. She had waded in the bloody grasses. She *knew* this. How long and how silently and shamefully she had known this! Sitting in church, clutching her purse, she only hoped that her thoughts were not transparent, with Luddy singing beside her, happy and young and muscular.

She had seen him buried in the garden, she had smelled a violence in the air that winter, presaged with the first frost. But now, dying herself, it seemed not to be; it seemed some great reversal had taken place, some merciful, mysterious bowing out, some *un*happening . . .

The wallpaper larks, impatient for her, had returned and perched on the sill. The whole cosmos was still.

Could a man turn about his own fate, that enormous ship coasting into port with its engine off? She loved him dearly, but knew not even he had the talent. So?

Well?

Did the cosmos have an explanation for her?

She listened. All she could hear was someone slathering honey on her toast in a distant country. The grandmother paused there, hanging from death by a silken thread knotted to her sternum. There, arms outflung, she smiled.

Fool, she thought. What did you know? For you are dying. Nobody's dying but you!

Hurry, she thought, Hurry!

She rejoiced. She wanted very much to step into the straightforwardness of death. She was relieved to let go of the folly of being. She was, at last, relieved of her dark talent. For death was the teacher, the defrocker, the eraser, and would ask of one at the last—of course—that single, remaining conviction, the thing one is so convinced of that one does not recognize it as completely arguable—all this so that she could stride out to God lacking all assumption. She could go to Him now with a face like a sky, never having heard of Him, His newborn baby.

The old woman readied herself. She felt the urge to neaten her hair. She would put on her coat and glasses. She lifted a finger, as if to say to death, Please, just let me get my glasses.

⌒

The nursery was quiet. Alice stepped into the room crookedly, stopping to put one hand over her eyes and concentrate. Exhausted and made monstrous by her crying, and by the one hour of nightmarish sleep sitting upright in a chair, she doubted she should allow herself into the nursery. But she wanted to look at them. Just one look. Her silhouette darkened the nursery window, her hair a tousled shadow.

In the darkness, the green darkness of the nightlight, she leaned over the cribs, and was startled by two eyes staring back at her. Frances was awake. The infant gazed upward, silent. She was never awake at this hour; they had begun to drop off—eight o'clock—off the face of the earth. But now, the infant smiled, completely awake, content. She pressed her hands together and looked down at them seriously. Tearfully, Alice laughed. She reached down to touch her daughter. She drew her hand away.

"Can't sleep either, can you, sweetheart?"

The infant stared at her mother. Nearby, her sister slept. The infant reached up.

"No," Alice said. "Stay where you are. Where it's safe and warm."

But the child had already reached up far enough to grasp a lock of Alice's hair. Caught, Alice bent over into the crib.

There, she remembered her nightmare: she was watching them, in the crib, flames licking up through the floorboards, the match in her hand.

"Let go," she whispered. "Let go of Mommy."

The child did not let go. She pulled back harder, reeling Alice in.

"Let *go*!"

The child let go. The corners of her lips pulled down. She filled her lungs.

"No," she whispered. "No. Don't cry."

Tenderly, repentantly, Alice lifted the infant from the crib. The child's sandy hair was aglow in the nightlight, as was her white throat as she struggled to hold her head up.

"Don't cry. Don't cry."

The baby felt hot in her arms. Hot. Delicate. Alice bounced the baby. The baby stared at the nightlight. She had recently grown one tooth on her lower jaw; it sprouted upward like a small white turnip.

"Oh, Frances Shade," Alice whispered into the child's hair. "What in the world do you want me for? Should I lie for you?" She looked into the baby's face. It seemed to say Naturally, yes, you should lie. Alice's chin buckled, but she did not cry. She looked out the window.

"I've failed. I have poisoned everything. You don't know now. But someday you'll know. You'll know who I really am. And then you won't—you won't—"

In her arms, the infant hungrily tasted her mouth. Alice sighed. The warmth of the child was making her sleepy, finally. The innocence and incomprehension of the child was making her sleepy. She lowered herself into the rocking chair. Of course, it was not confessions the child cared for now. It was milk, warmth, wool. Reclining in her lap, the child tasted her mouth again, eyes bright with desire. She placed a hand on

Alice's breast and twisted the shirt. Alice turned her head away, unable to bear the look.

Someday you'll know who I really am. And you won't love me.

Outside, branches clattered in the wind. The moon gazed at the apartment building and the apartment building stared back with its old, myopic windows. She did not go get a bottle. Instead, she found herself moving the child's hand, that soft, searching animal, and lifting her shirt, exposing her breast to the bluish white moonlight. She cupped the child's soft head, saying nothing.

The child stretched her lips toward the nipple, remembering. Alice bent forward, leaning over the child. The small, protuberant mouth sought, fell wide. Alice felt the child's lips slide across her breast. She tried again, pressing the head forward. Again the mouth fell wide, and Alice gasped, the small head in her hand like an egg. She could feel the tendons of her neck protrude, tears gathering in the corners of her eyes.

Then, below, a pinch. The child was reaching out. She was clutching the breast in her hand, burying her downy head. Alice felt the mouth around her nipple, like a small, warm mitten.

The infant suckled. She smacked at the dry breast. Alice knew she was offering nothing. Alice was not innocent. She could not pretend that she didn't know what it was like to be alone with a weeping woman, or to miss one's father, or to be presented with the gift of wreckage. But the infant ignored all this. It seemed an incredible kindness. It seemed the kindest action anyone had ever taken in the world. Alice covered her face. The tears ran down her face and breast. Yet still the child, somehow confident, somehow Christly, pulled and pulled, gently, with her warm mouth.

Charlie stared at the coffee table in front of him. He wore a blanket around his shoulders. They had been silent for some time.

He was trying to steady himself. He felt so light and so empty that he was afraid he had ceased to exist. Across from him, in an easy chair, wearing a flannel robe, Bruce sat with one huge leg crossed over the other. His shins were hairy, and one slipper hung from his toe. Under the track lighting of the apartment, Bruce's scalp, big and round as a globe, shone through his thinning hair.

"I've never seen you without your baseball cap," Charlie said. "You look naked."

"Well," said Bruce, finally. "I've never seen you rolling around in your own vomit on my doorstep."

Charlie coughed into his fist. His head throbbed. A clock ticked in the kitchen.

Bruce stared back at him. "So why did you come here? Did you want to have a physical confrontation with me?"

"What? A fight? With *you*?" Charlie laughed.

"Well, you were drunk. And belligerent. Pounding on my door."

"I was? I honestly—ha—don't remember. In any case, I'm not angry at you."

"Really?"

"I don't blame you for firing me."

Bruce nodded, squinting. "So—"

"You might be surprised to know I don't really have a lot of places to go to at the moment, Bruce. I guess I needed someone to talk to. I don't really have a lot of friends."

"Come on. You must have a lot of friends. You're one of the most likable guys I've ever met."

"Sure. I'm like a lot of men. I have tons of friends and not one single friendship. It's a way—It's a way to stay liked."

Bruce uncrossed his legs and paused. "I have several intimate friendships," he said.

"Good for you."

"Like you said, some guys have a hard time being genuine."

"I bet you learn to be pretty damned genuine at AA meetings."

In the kitchen, a buzzer marked the hour.

Charlie did not look up. "I'm sorry," he said.

"Don't be sorry," said Bruce. "Be different."

"Can't I just be sorry?"

"You have no boundaries, Charlie. With no boundaries you have no self and no accountability. Who are you? What comes first and last in your life? You can't have everything. What do you need most? *Need*, you know, with your gut? If you need everything equally, it's an insult to life. It's indiscriminate."

"Come on." Charlie rubbed the side of his head. "Please. I'm not quite ready for this, Bruce. For revelations."

"No." Bruce leaned forward. "You're in the perfect place."

"How's that?"

"You're in the vise. You're either going to break or push back. It's the perfect place for revelation. For some people, the only place." The big man sat back. He rested one square hand on the armrest, and with the other, he scratched his lushly whiskered face. "Listen, I can reduce this to a sanction. You can easily find another job until you're licensed, and it'll just look like you moved on. I thought about it all day. You don't have to be fired. Nobody needs to know. After the weekend, I know Harriet will soften up. She's just hurt. She really liked you, Charlie. You can even go back to Maynard, take your position with Gregorian. That's my final decision. Okay? Everything's going to be okay."

"My wife," said Charlie. "She's seeing somebody."

Bruce dropped his hand to his lap. "Jesus."

"She just told me about it tonight. She didn't spare any—details." Charlie swallowed back bile, gesturing for the trash can. "Could you please pass that—"

"Take a deep breath, kid."

Holding the trash can, Charlie's eyes fluttered closed. But the blackness behind his eyes had been colonized by the image of them, and they looked good together, his wife and Hal—dark-eyed, dark-haired, embracing in the shadows. Charlie opened his eyes. Bruce was handing him a washcloth.

"Here, kid. Put this over your right eye. It's totally bloodshot. I think you burst a couple blood vessels."

Charlie pressed the washcloth over his eye. There the image burned again.

"I can't," he said.

Bruce nodded. "You can see them."

"Yeah," said Charlie. "How did you know?"

"I know."

They sat there for a while. Bruce leaned forward. Blinking, Charlie looked at the man across from him, sitting attentive and hairy-chested and hairy-legged in a bathrobe in the middle of the night. And with just that simple act, the attentive leaning forward of a friend, the last stanchions collapsed. Sheets came off Charlie. He felt his very identity clatter in bolts and screws to the floor. The raw, fetal nakedness of himself remained, recoiling, untouched by sunlight. Shaking, Charlie pushed the washcloth into his mouth. His shoulders were shaking. He wept. He dropped the washcloth and ran his hands through his hair again and again.

"Oh God," he said. "Oh God oh God oh God."

He was really crying now. He looked up helplessly at Bruce in his chair, trying to explain. He wanted to say, This'll be over any second now. This has got to end soon. Right? But his body had taken over. There he was, cross-legged under a blanket, punching his own leg with a balled-up washcloth. Even when Bruce stood and went into the kitchen and turned on the tap, Charlie kept crying. He could not stop. Bruce came back into the room carrying a glass of water. He stood there, patting Charlie a couple times on the shoulder.

"It's all right, Bud. Take a deep breath."

Charlie began to hiccup.

"It's all right, my man."

"Give me," said Charlie. "One of those—Klonopin or something. Would you? I know you must have some around."

"No," said Bruce. "Absolutely not."

"Wish I—could stop," said Charlie.

Almost magically, with a hiccup, the sobs turned to laughter.

"Shit," Charlie said, laughing uncontrollably.

Bruce sat down heavily across from him again, looking weary. Charlie tried to raise the glass of water to his lips, but it rattled against his teeth.

"Just imagine," said Bruce, stretching his arms over his head. "Become a drunk and every night could be just like this one."

"I—am such—a *prick*," said Charlie, wiping his eyes with the back of his hands.

"Why? Because you ignored your wife?"

"No. Because I didn't really know how hard it was to be unhappy." Charlie sat back against the couch. He licked the tears from his lips. "I was going around pretending like I understood everybody. I had no idea!" He laughed. "It's *hell*." Bruce laughed too, shaking his head. "Just to think of myself with my clients. Thinking any minute now they were going to snap out of it. I thought if I got a smile, they were cured. Like I could tap-dance it out of somebody. What a narcissist. What a fucking circus animal. I've always been that way. And with Alice. Was it any different? She was saying 'I'm scared. I'm lonely.' And I'd waltz in with *carnations*. I'm a pretender."

"Don't be too hard on yourself, Charlie. You were born,

well—" Bruce shrugged, "—golden. It wasn't your fault. How could you know?"

"But you saw this coming. You tried to warn me."

"I suspected. The gods are cruel gods. They had a bead on you."

Charlie smiled. "That's what Alice used to say. She used to talk about the gods. She said she wanted to live a small life that the gods wouldn't see."

"Well, they saw."

"You bet they saw."

"But maybe now?—"

Charlie swallowed. "But now what? What the fuck now? I feel like dying."

"Nothing has changed in the world. Only you've changed. The world will be waiting for you to come back, changed. Besides, listen. I've been working in this field for years and all I can come up with is that either all of us are crazy or none of us are." Bruce rose from his chair. "Hey. How about some sleep, Charlie. Go to sleep, friend."

"No. Not yet. I can't even—close my eyes."

Charlie stared down at his lap.

"You've got a nice place, by the way, Bruce. It's nice."

"All these condos are new. We're the first people in them."

Charlie pointed with the washcloth to a photograph on the mantel. "Who's that woman?"

Bruce did not turn to look. "My ex-wife, Amy."

"Why do you still have her picture up if you haven't seen her in years?"

"Don't know."

"She's pretty." Charlie nodded. "Pretty smile."

"Listen," Bruce said. "I have to go in tomorrow. I'm on call. And besides, I'm going to have to find someone to replace you. You can stay here if you want. Sleep, clean yourself up. Check the cupboard to see if there's anything to eat. Have whatever you find. Okay, Bud? Make yourself at home."

Charlie smiled gratefully. "You know what your problem is Bruce? You don't have any boundaries. Always giving giving giving."

Bruce pressed his lips together. He took his baseball cap off the sideboard and put it on. Cinching his bathrobe, he walked out of the room.

"You wear your baseball cap to bed?" asked Charlie.

"None of your business."

Charlie could hear him now, walking up the stairs, the boards creaking underneath him.

"You saved my life," Charlie called. "You know that, you bastard? I could have died."

The creaking paused. He could hear Bruce breathing in the stairwell. Then the big man proceeded up the stairs to bed.

～

Having dirtied their clothes, having dug a trench for rainwater, having chased a tomcat up a tree, the neighborhood children wondered what to do next. They had already dammed the sewer and stripped all the birch bark they needed for their secret club documents. The light of the Sunday afternoon was draining back into the horizon. In his house, a father looked out, folding closed his newspaper. What to do? he thought. Should he drag the trash cans to the curb, or take another nap? He smelled his empty juice glass, having forgotten what he'd been drinking. Rye, was it? His wife coughed in the adjoining room. Outside, in the shadows between houses, the children watched the tomcat in the tree, flicking its tail. Even the tomcat looked bored. He began preening himself on his branch. For he liked the onset of night because that meant moles and mice in their stupid intrepidness and their fresh delicious eyeballs, but he himself wished for the longer days to return, the light, his summer coat, glossy and handsome. He coughed, hair in his throat. The children stared up at the tomcat. A boy dropped the rock in his hand. It was Sunday. They were impatient for spring. There was nothing left to play with in winter. Under the porches of houses, the dirty snow hunkered, willing itself to melt.

Leeeeeeeeeeeuh. Your mother wants you inside please! Leah!

What, already?

I said come here. Now.

And with this, Alice awoke, as if she herself were the child being called. She looked wildly around the room, scrambling to sit up in her chair. In her lap, a sleeping infant. The child's bottle had long rolled across the carpet. The floor was covered with objects: rings and rattles and mirrors, a stuffed panda bear faced down, a trail of Cheerios, a crusted bowl, a dirty diaper that was coming unrolled like some awful night flower. The stench hit Alice—her own child, in her arms. She waked the child.

"Franny, for god sakes, you're *filthy*."

Alice clawed her hair out of the way, swearing. She swung the child off her lap, but the child had already clutched a lock.

"Goddamn it. Goddamn *use*less hair."

The baby sneezed, speckling Alice's face. Alice bent over the child. Her nose was red around the rims; her face, damp and hot.

"Oh *please* don't be sick, Franny baby. Please don't be sick."

The child on her hip, now beginning to cry grumpily, she strode down the hallway to the nursery. She lay the child on the changing table and, with one hand, steadied her there, pantless. The dirty diaper was heavy with urine and feces.

"Stay," she said.

She moved to the second crib, but it was empty. The sight took her breath. She burst out into the hallway.

"Evie? Evelyn!"

She lurched into the bathroom, looking—crazed—under the sink and in the tub, as if the child might have stored herself there. She ran back into the nursery and grabbed Frances.

"Evelyn! Evelyn!"

They ran down the hall. There were only so many places to look. The key was in her memory somewhere—how could you misplace a *child*? Below the window, in a pool of sunlight, in the middle of an unmade bed—fingers! Alice climbed across the bed; Evelyn squinted, whined, and turned her head away, wanting to be left in peace. Her sister, unwatched for one second, casually ate a Kleenex, proffered by the box on the bedside table.

"Don't," gasped Alice. "Don't *eat* that. Jesus!"

She took the two infants in her arms and waded down the hall through the colorful debris. Evelyn shrieked, clawing at her mother's arm. Frances, the meat of the Kleenex still in her fist, spread her legs, and when replaced upon the changing table, relieved herself, the urine rainbowing out over the carpet.

It was then the telephone rang. Alice lifted her head, one child twisting the flesh of her arm, and the other one gripping a Kleenex in her mandibles. She hefted Frances over her shoulder, urine moistening her shirt. *I must*, she thought . . . *At all costs* . . .

"Hello?" she shouted into the telephone. "Hello?"

"Alice?" It was a foggy voice, a voice from far away.

"Yes? Yes? This is Alice." She pinned the phone against her shoulder, shutting her eyes, hoping, listening.

"Alice dear? It's Luduina."

Alice froze. "Hello, Luduina! How *are* you?"

"I'm not—I'm not well, Alice. May I speak to Charlie?"

Evelyn was now pulling her mother's hair, pulling back with all her strength, in grief for the loss of her sovereignty, and her sister thrashed on her shoulder. *I must at all costs* . . .

"No," said Alice. "I mean, no, I'm sorry. Please. Could you hold on? Don't hang up. Please. I'm so sorry."

The telephone slid crashing to the floor and she stepped back into the nursery and thrust both children into the same crib, Frances naked from the waist down, and Evelyn convulsing with outrage.

"There," she said. "Devour each other."

Catching her breath, pulling her unwashed hair from her mouth, she fetched the phone from the floor.

"Luduina? I'm sorry."

Silence came through the receiver. Alice froze.

"Mrs. Shade?" she whispered. "Are you all right?"

"I'm afraid I have some sad news. It's about Charlie's grandmother."

"Gran?"

"She's passed away."

"No."

"She has."

"Oh. I'm—sorry."

"Yes. We all are."

"Charlie will be—"

"He'll be sad."

"Heartbroken." Alice paused. "He loved her. So much."

"She loved him the same. He was her favorite. They were best friends, when he was a little boy."

"I know. I've heard so many stories. He talks about her all the time. All of you, really, together—" Alice walked slowly down the hall to the front windows. She put one hand flat against the windowpane. "I never knew mine. My grandmother. We never met."

The woman paused on the other line. A screen door slammed in the background.

"Yes," she replied. "One doesn't—get the chance in this life sometimes. To be with whom one wants. It can seem unfair."

Alice drew a breath and held it. "But if you love someone very much, a million years with them could still seem—insufficient. Couldn't it?"

"So," the woman cleared her throat. "Can I talk to him?"

"To Charlie?"

"Yes."

Alice turned, took three long steps across the room and brought her feet together. "He's at work."

"On a Sunday?"

Alice laughed. "Is it only Sunday?"

Mrs. Shade paused again. "Well, yes."

Down the hall, the girls were murmuring at their toys. Alice walked back to the cold window. Outside, on the street, a group of children stood idly around a tree. A tall shadow approached, and out of the dusk came a man in slippers. He grabbed one of the children by the arm and marched her down the street. Alice put her cheek against the glass. Her eyes slid closed. She had tried to call Joanne; Joanne was on vacation. Her mother was gone—lost? Not answering. She knew no one. Her inborn bookish shyness, and the circle she and Charlie had drawn around themselves in their joy, now revealed her as a floating, unallied thing. The only person whom she could think of to help her was the boy she had destroyed everything with through touching. She heard herself speaking softly:

"What does it feel like?"

"What, dear?"

Alice's hand slid slowly down the window, leaving a disappearing trail. "The end of knowing someone."

"The—Well—" On the other end, the woman hesitated,

confused. In the background, the sound of a man's voice softly asking a question.

Alice blanched, shaking herself awake. She took her hand from the window.

"I'm sorry. I'm sorry. I haven't slept in a couple days. I'm not—making any sense."

"It's all right—"

"I'm sorry."

"Alice. Is everything all right there?"

"Everything's fine. Except this, of course. Charlie will be—" She pawed her hair from her face. *I must at all costs go on.* "I'll have to tell him."

"Alice. We would like very much for you and Charlie and the children to come home for the service. We were hoping we could talk to Charlie about arrangements."

"Of course. Absolutely."

"Might you—get in touch with him?"

"Absolutely. Right away. When is the—"

"Friday."

"Yes. I'll have him call you right away."

Alice turned and crossed the living room and stopped in the middle of the wreckage. She had no idea where he was. He'd been fired, so he couldn't be at work. She turned around in a circle. She tried to feel his consciousness in the world. She closed her eyes and hoped for it, but ended up choking on the emptiness. For he was still too angry to reveal himself to her. And this, in her fate-haunted, gray-skied Gloucester-born soul, was as death. She sat down, in the middle of the carpet. Evelyn, remembering herself, began to scream again.

"I'll have him call you," she said, controlling her voice.

"Thank you," said her mother-in-law. Then she added, "And yes, by the way, you're right. A million years would be insufficient. Completely insufficient."

In her distant kitchen, the woman began to cry.

Alice sat, listening to the sound, wishing she could cry like that, faultlessly and deservedly. She could hear birdsong, too. A bird on a telephone wire in the Midwest. She went to the window again, to watch the children in the street.

But the children had dispersed. Instead, standing in the middle of the street, looking up steadily, was Hal.

Seeing her at the window, he waved. He returned his hands to the pockets of his jacket. He seemed prepared to stand there a long time. Just, to stand.

"I'm sorry," Alice whispered into the telephone. "I'm so sorry."

Standing in the door on Monday morning, watching Bruce leave for work, Charlie's heart dropped, sliding loose and sick and frightened in his chest. He wasn't sure if it was the state of his marriage or the fact that it was his first workday as a fired person or if it was simply the prospect of a day spent alone in a strange house. Or was it some genuine, almost wifely attitude he'd developed living with this man for three days, a kind of indebtedness at being taken in and being tolerated, despite the shipwreck of who he had claimed to be; he would even miss the sound of hacked-up sputum. Wincing at this thought, he lowered his hand from the screen door, and with a twist to his chin, cracked his own neck. In the driveway, Bruce gathered the folds of his trench coat and got into the front seat of his Jeep. He rolled down the window.

"Have a good day, honey," Bruce said, touching the bill of his baseball cap.

"Ha," said Charlie. "Yeah. Don't forget to wear your galoshes, asshole."

The gears ground to reverse. Bruce stuck his head out as the car rolled backward down the driveway.

"You know what I've always wanted for dinner? Pot roast. Nobody ever made me a pot roast once in my whole life. Can you make pot roast, Charlie honey?"

"How about a bowl of Fritos if you're lucky?"

Bruce pulled the Jeep onto the road and flicked on the windshield wipers. It was starting to rain. Up and down the street, the suburban architecture wore the gloom poorly.

"So. What are you going to do?" Bruce called.

"I don't know." Charlie squinted up the street. "Stick my head in the oven?"

"Well, it's all clean for you. I never use it."

The Jeep revved, rolled backward. Nearby, a dog barked.

"All right. So, should I be worried about you?"

Charlie considered it.

"I don't know, Bruce," he said sincerely.

"Stay in the game, Charlie. Stay in the game."

But an hour or so later, still sitting unmoving at the breakfast table, cereal untouched, Charlie's lungs were crushed by a force of grief so great he felt he was being driven over. He looked down at his sweater for the tracks. His mouth filled with spit. He was frightened. He considered phoning Bruce at the clinic. But it would have made it worse to call, since everyone would know about his dismissal by now and he would have to *say* it. So instead, he pounded on the table. Beating the table, like an enormous demanding baby, he felt better, and the pressure moved back off his chest.

"*There*," he said, slamming the table, standing. "Motherfucker."

He rifled through the kitchen cabinets. Surely Bruce kept a stash of something. For guests maybe? Some kind of fruit cordial? Or maybe he was the sort of guy who liked to keep a nice big bottle of the hard stuff around, as a kind of challenge? A nice broad-shouldered bottle of whiskey? He stood on a kitchen stool, rummaging with one arm in the uppermost cabinets, when, seizing a jar of canola oil, he began to laugh. If they could only see him now, the town fathers of Mattoon. His track coach, the police chief, or the Rotary president himself, Glen Shade, who at sixty-eight still repaired his own roof. Charlie stood laughing on the kitchen stool for what seemed like a long time. Then he came down and pulled himself out of the kitchen and up the staircase. He passed Bruce's bedroom, and was lulled by the downy-looking comforter. He fell on top of it, mouth open. Another hour passed.

He would go on, he could go on this way, hour by hour. Soon, time would collect into buckets of years. He tried to lie very still, practicing.

The sun came in at an angle. He rose on his elbow. There was a huge armoire in the room, in which he discovered only three plaid shirts and one tie dangling. Across the room, a small desk, with a cartoon thumbtacked to the wall over it. On the desk itself sat an empty can of Shasta, a pen, and a stack of peach-colored papers tied together with a piece of twine. Charlie stood there over the desk. He plucked at the twine that tied the envelopes. With a jerk, the letters slid loose across the desk. Why the hell leave them out then? He picked through them coolly, not caring, finally lifting one up and reading the front. The envelopes were addressed to Bruce, all of them five years old and postmarked within weeks of each other. Charlie lifted one to his nose. Faint, lingering perfume.

Slipping one open, he removed the letter itself. He sat.

" 'Dearest Bruce,' " he mumbled, then read on silently: "You have done everything to me including hit me with your hand but I was never so amazed by you as I am now. Why haven't you written back? Everything is growing over. Mostly the garden is weeds now. I am less angry. I would be reasonable. Dont you believe it? If you are truly sorry you would want to comfort me well then come hold me. I feel the same. I am the same woman and you are the same man that once was happy. Please come home. Forever Yours With Love, Amy. P.S. As an afterthought to my last letter, I would like to change the word 'betrayal' to 'disappointment.' Please, ladies and gentlemen of the jury, strike the word 'betrayal' from the record in the case of Zabilski v. Zabilski."

Charlie swallowed. He folded the letter back in its sleeve and picked the next.

"Dearest Bruce,

"A blue jay flew into our deck window this morning. I heard it and there was this exploshion of tiny feathers. I went out onto the deck and it was there with its neck broken. I threw it out into the garden and am hoping more blue jays grow where I planted it. Ha. Ha. What would you like me to do with your Bow Flex because my brother wants it. It's worth a lot of money. I could sell it and give you the money and you could buy liquor with it. Or I could. All this to say I'm drinking again too. Come on! How can you avoid me now! Now that I've fallen back to earth and broken my little neck? Forever Yours With Love and a Couple Other Things, Amy. P.S. I would like to reinstate the use of the word 'betrayal.' For now I've betrayed you too I have started to doubt you. <u>Please come home.</u> Don't do it because it's the right thing. Just do it."

Charlie stood, tugging at the collar of his sweater. He stuffed all the letters back into a pile, and retied the twine. His face was burning, as if in shame. Shame of what? Of which? He stepped back and looked out at the view through the small window. But there was no view. There were only the gutters of the next condominium and the gutters after that. Again, he sat.

The following letter had no salutation:

"I wont yell. I wont scream or yell if you would just write or call. I know they have a phone at the Y where you're getting these. Are you staying there or just picking up mail? I went there yesterday but nobody would tell me. They say on the street that the third floor of the Y is liquor and the fourth is heroin and up and up like that, and the top floor is death. Meaning, if you stay long enough at the Y to make it to the sixth floor you're probably dead. Then you just step right off into the clouds heaven. What floor are you on? No seriously I know somehow you'll make it out OK. You are resilient and smart. You are strong and alone. Me maybe I was actually always worse off than you. Turns out right underneath everything is this layer of fire. This thing you never saw burning me up because you were busy worrying about you. Women have it worse because they live for other people. And maybe they are happier briefly but that only means they will be sadder longer. I might go stay with my brother so would you come by the house and water the plants while I'm gone? The potted palm and the jade both need a gallon every other week the rest should be watered every other day or when dry. I enclose herein my brothers address. I know what your thinking. From the frying pan into the fire, right? Well I'm already on fire. But even on fire I will be Yours Forever With Love, Amy."

Charlie rubbed his eyes, his chin. He shuffled through the remaining letters, but they were all dated before this one. This one, then, was the last. He turned the letter over. The back of the stationery was covered with a final postscript.

"P.S. In the future you will have to try and see through the anger in these letters. You know I've always been shy about the intensity of my feelings because I was pretty much made to feel like a freak show when I was a kid. I just want you to know Bruce you were the only one who never made me feel like that. You were the only one who ever really knew me as much as I could be known and I had a very good time with you on earth. You were it for me. Magic. Even when you were drunk you were just a little less magical. You loved me and I always knew it. And whatever I was in reality, however drunk or skinny or ugly I really was, you know what? I wore a ball gown and dimonds when I was with you."

Charlie pushed the stack of letters aside and put his head down on the desk. Of course, he thought. The mantel—that's where we put photographs of the ones we lost.

And the top floor is death.

He sat like that with his cheek against the desk for some time, the sun warming the side of his head. It took him a while to realize he was crying. A collection of water on the desk beside his eye. If he had to admit it, he couldn't really take the news. The news of life's obscurity. He did not know how to stay in the game when the game ceased to be about winning or losing it. For example, love. You fall down from heaven together and you're separated for all those years until you find each other again. In some AA meeting. Some snowbound alley. You love with the intemperance of people waiting an eternity for the chance. But that force itself is a force too great. You buckle. You run. You go hide somewhere where you can't be found. Then before you know it you're running your finger over a face in a photograph and it doesn't feel like her skin and you will never, *ever* recover. How can you recover from that? That you lost it all for vanity? Trying to be the clear winner. Trying to be king. Trying to trade places with the gods when there they were, up there, desperate to trade places with you.

Charlie sat upright. Outside, the cooing of a bird, and the dewy dropping of moisture from the gutter to the roof. He stood, his throat tight, his hands open and loose, as one preparing to catch something. The chair fell backward behind him.

He ran. He was crashing through the house, snatching his jacket from the couch, cramming his feet into his shoes. He left the cabinets open, the bed in disarray. He snapped his watch onto his wrist, for suddenly time mattered. Pausing in the kitchen, he dialed his own number. *Don't don't don't,* he whispered. But no one answered, and he did not feel her consciousness in the world responding. Don't what? Don't go? Don't leave me? Don't go to him? Don't forget. Don't suffer. Don't give up. Don't worry. Don't die. *Don't let go of me.*

He flung open the front door, slamming it shut behind him, diving off the steps where he had lain drunk three days before. He ran. He flew. He felt shocked awake. Forsaking the sidewalk, he leapt into the street. The horn of a dark-windowed SUV sounded, and the car swerved away from him, taillights glowering. But still he ran, the street underneath him slick with rain and motor oil, a wet fog obscuring the suburban houses, smelling of bones.

Run, he thought. You better run like you've never run. He sprinted. He'd been hiding, idle, watching television, but what if now his world ended where this fog ended? He began to fall into the trance of his pace, the suburban development giving way to coarse woods, and suddenly he remembered himself as an infant, in the sun-warmed parlor of that milk white house, pulling himself across a paisley carpet, pulling himself up like some evolving animal, in his diapers and short pants. His mother in the kitchen. His father in his den. And the whole unspeakable possibility of his life, suddenly known to him in a flash. The birth of his heart. The assignation of his fate. But this fate, he saw now, was never a given, was never irrevocable, but was merely the gentlest of suggestions, and could be attained or lost depending completely upon one's capacity for joy and for suffering, depending completely upon one's endurance, one's ability to keep running. Fate was the countryside in which one was lost.

Shit! he shouted, lungs burning. Alice!

In his memory, the time passed, his gums pained him, his face roughened. And still later, how many afternoons spent running, just running, for no reason, just because he could. . . .

The school bell would sound, and like a shot he was off, jumping over roots, skidding around corners. He would run past the P.O., the Sip and Dip, he would run past the beauty salon over which lived a hairdresser's daughter whom he always hoped to catch half-dressed in the window. He would just run. He never knew why. He assumed he ran because he was free. He assumed he ran because he was good at it. But now, running around the fog-bound bend of an empty road, he understood. It had been practice. Every run to prepare to run for his life.

The road drifted upward; he ascended. Deep into his second mile of sprinting, he was pushing the limit of what his body could bear. The fog had thickened. He could see nothing until it was upon him. The trees on either side of the road bowed in and out of whiteness, dark and wet. He could hear a car whirring toward him in the distance, the sound echoing off the walls of air, seeming to come from all directions at once. He shed his sweater and dropped it by the side of the road. A flash of color parted the fog, and Charlie jumped away from the spray of gravel, crying out as he stumbled into a ditch, one knee down, his hand opened against the black street, a man crawling out of the ground. The car sped back into the fog before he even saw it. Coughing into the crook of his arm, choking now on his own dry throat, he pulled himself upright and resumed, running crookedly up the hill.

He clutched at his undershirt, then yanked that off too. Behind him, tires screeched. He glanced over his shoulder. An accident? He could not stop now. He looked up to where the road disappeared into whiteness, and he looked down to where the road disappeared into whiteness. Panting, turning, he squinted back down the hill. What? What was it?

Someone was coming. Someone was coming around the bend of the road toward him. The figure disappeared again into a patch of fog.

Blindly, Charlie called out, swatting away the thick air.

Who's there?

The figure again emerged nearer. Charlie stopped.

Who's there?

Charlie?

His eyes widened. He opened his eyes with the hope that if there was any chance that it was her, he could will it so. Through the whiteness Charlie Shade began to run again, this time back the way he'd come—at first doubtfully, then faster, then at full stride, making a whooping sound despite himself, despite his heaviness, or because of it. She was his city, his conspiracy. She was his wife. The miles rolled off his shoulders. He could have run forever.

Crying out, she ran sloppily, her sore breasts swinging, her hood falling backward, exposing her face. She glanced back to the idling car where the babies waited, in their sloppy outfits, amazed by the miracle of an icicle out the window, gossiping softly—how much they already knew about love from one another. She pushed her hair from her eyes; she could see him now, shirtless and rubbery legged, wobbling in and out of the fog. Suddenly, within sight, he sank to his knees in the road, laughing, if not a little crazily, his face red as a beet. She got on her knees also and crawled to him and pulled him close. She was joyful for whatever tiny turn she had taken since, whatever small correction she had managed, that treasured, final conviction that had struck her up in that cold window, the conviction that made her come down and tell the boy that she wished him luck, that she had to go, and that she hoped he would discover for himself someday what she too had discovered just then—that the universe was treacherous only in that it would outlast you, and knew your death and slowly breathed you in your whole life, but that despite all this, there were small ruins all over the territory, the posts and beams of people who built there regardless, on fog, on blackness, on starlight, houses in which they were safe merely by being in them together.

⌒

At last. At last she had broken backward into the great intention of her life and could see it all with such magnificent sweep. She could let go now. She could step into the furthest realms. It was so easy now. It was so quiet. She leaned back against the headboard. The pill bottle went rolling to the floor. Just as a part of her leaned back, giving in, another part of her began to move, possessed of a great energy. She sat up. She was up and running now. She was bursting out the door. She was moving fast, her cardigan flapping. She was running so fast that the street underneath her lost its hardness and turned to a kind of buoyant, rubbery surface. She ran down Road Four stumbling and laughing and, with the help of a slight tailwind, her hair pulled back from her face and Opal was flying.

The tongues of her sneakers caught in some bushes. Pumping her arms, she kicked herself free. Soon, she was sailing higher. Lifting her feet, she cleared the top of the tallest tree. She remembered being born all sticky and gooed up. Everybody, uglyborn the same way. It seemed almost lovely to her now, almost sweet, even being pulled out of her mother with forceps. All of it, even Uncle Ad and his laughing outside the toolshed. Flying, she remembered every day of her life: the day she wanted a candy cane so bad that she pushed off and went after it herself and the lady her mother cried Well, I'll be damned, Dave, look she's *walkin'*, she remembered her first burn, her first correctly lettered word, the surprise of salt, the first time she was frightened when she came across a claw-footed bathtub, the first morning she heard music, the first time she saw a black man, riding up past her on an escalator, the first day she sinned, the first joke she laughed at, her first fistful of silk. Oh the feel of silk. Oh the little girls from school who were so doted upon that ribbons simply sprouted in their hair.

Sailing over the trees, Opal realized she wasn't even jealous anymore. She wasn't even curious why not her. Why no silk for her. For she loved them all: the black man on the escalator, the spoiled girl with the ribbons, the rapist, the horse, the ant, the bee, the dust mite, the worm, the politician, the mistress, the saint, the marauder, the Indian, the Chink, the Jew, dead men, living men, babies, the dean of arts and sciences, the devil, Jesus, Daddy, Mommy, and even Opal herself, that girl back there in the bed lying so still, she loved even her, with her freckled lips and her hair all crooked on the pillow. And she loved the cold day as she slipped upward into it. For now she stopped her kicking and realized she no longer had to try. The time of great effort was finally over. Underneath her sneakers floated the peaceful world—the rooftops the color of rust, the brittle gardens, the dogs in their yards, seagulls, slope-shouldered grandmothers in galoshes being helped into cars, the traffic, the traffic, the soft blinking of the lights.

She flew over the city park. Below her, she spied a girl and a boy on a bench. The girl wore a Catholic school uniform and her knees were bare. But the boy—just as Opal flew overhead—looked up and drew his breath. His dark handsome gaze followed her path across the sky. Why, he could see her! She waved at him. Hey, boy! He looked a little alarmed. Her shadow crossed his face.

Don't worry! she shouted. I'm fine! I thought I'd regret it, but I really don't!

The handsome boy stared up at her, the girl beside him chattering on. Opal laughed. She loved them, she loved them both, loved them all—the sane and the insane, for they would all, in their own time, sit at the same great table. She didn't regret it and she didn't pity or envy anyone, most especially not herself.

She turned forward just in time to dodge the TV tower. The tower blew past in a cacophony of voices and corny music, then receded. Below her were the outskirts of town, obscured now by encroaching clouds of fog. Patches of fog skidded by underfoot. In snatches, the view of the ground was hidden then revealed again. Below her, she saw a lady at her mailbox, looking in, looking hopeful. On the straight road that led back to town from which she'd come, a red beat-up car puttered along, one headlight missing. A man and a woman sat in the front; she could see their knees. The car slipped into the fog.

Hey! Opal cried out. Hey, if it isn't Charlie Shade! Hey Charlie! Up here!

But just as quickly she smothered her words with her hand, and the familiar car swept past underneath her feet, rustling her pant legs. To her relief, she'd gone unseen. For what she realized was that she did not want him to see her, he who had already dragged her back once before, dragged her back inert like a body across the field of surrender, waving his hanky. He for whom she had defied orders. It could only go on so long. She could only protect him so long. That's what she suspected anyway. He looked nice enough from up here, but down there he was somehow horrifying.

She sighed and turned forward, a little sadly, sailing through the silence and peacefulness, the air completely opaque with fog now, the wind growing stronger. Some day— tomorrow, never—he would understand.

She grew thoughtful. The fog had healed itself up behind her and now she was sailing up out of it, into an inky atmospheric darkness. She realized now that she was flying away from the sun. The further she got, the sky grew darker and the wind stronger. The thin moon was a lick in the sky. The stars gazed at her frankly. The wind howled.

The wind blew the braid from her hair, and blasted the clothes from her body, and soon she was flying naked and white through the darkness. The wind was polishing her edges. Sparks shot from her feet. Her veins glowed pink underneath her white, wind-polished skin. And then she saw that she was becoming not flesh but stone, the rarest of stones—the iridescent stone, in fact, for which she had been named. Finally, her body was a gem, a treasure, an exception. She was a completed moment of beauty.

～

"Cut it all off," she said. "I mean it."

"Mar*lene*," replied the woman standing behind her, lowering her scissors and putting one hand on her hip. "Are you in a funk? A girl should never get her hair cut in a funk."

"I don't want my hair cut, Judy. I want it cut off."

The two women stared hard at one another in the mirror. The hairdresser—Marlene's age, but with orange lipstick and large breasts snug in a white angora sweater—raised her opened scissors. Behind them, a lady under the dryer coughed into a Kleenex. The hairdresser tenderly adjusted the plastic cape.

"Quit stalling," said Marlene. "Just cut it off, for Chrissakes. Use a razor."

"I'm not a *bar*ber, Marlene. Only for the neck."

"Fine, for the neck then." Marlene leaned forward. "Well?"

When she felt the first cold snip of the blades at her ear, she sighed. She leaned back and closed her eyes. The sense of relief was overwhelming. She had worn her hair exactly the same her entire life, hovering bluntly and conservatively just over the shoulders, just as she had worn the most conservative and unrevealing clothes and still covered her shoulders with a cardigan. So with every snip, evidence fell to the floor in tiny piles. The evidence was memories—memories of tugging, twisting, properness, communion ribbons, French braids (those sadistic French), the hands of her mother Inez brushing, digging, looping, talking with the particular accent of a woman with bobby pins between the teeth. This ritual Marlene had performed herself with Alice many times. _Sit still._

No.

Don't you want to look pretty?

No.

Yes, you do.

No, I don't. You want me to look pretty.

Well, hang me for that.

I like it snarly.

I'll bet you do.

Marlene exhaled. She felt the blades now right in front of her eyes. The cold blade on the bridge of her nose, then, _snip._

"Well," she sighed. "Goodbye, hair."

"Oh, don't be so dramatic," Judy crowed. "This is ridiculous. Women pay loads of money just to get it black and perfect like yours. What in the name of Mike are you so upset about, anyway?" The hairdresser stood large in front of her now, working her elbows. "Huh? What's stuck in your craw, Marlene? A spat with somebody? What?"

"My daughter," she muttered.

The woman scooted to the side, revealing Marlene to herself in the mirror, uneven, crazy looking, half-shorn.

"My daughter is a Jezebel."

"A what? You mean Alice? The girl who put up with you for twenty-odd years? The girl who gave up going to college to just to keep _you_ company? That girl?"

Marlene blinked. Hair rolled silently down the plastic cape.
Chignons. Ponytails. Pigtails.

I hate pigtails. Pigtails are for pigs.

Well then, darling, how shall I please you?

Leave it down.

Down?

Down, like a lady.

Like a lady. You're only eleven.

I want to look like a lady. I want to look like you, Mama.

Oh cara. You don't want to look like me.

I do. I want to look just like you always.

Oh Marlene.

Leave it down, Mama.

Eu te amo, Marlene.

Eu te amo, Mama.

And now the salon was spinning, the ladies staring out at
her from under their conical hats, daubing their lips and
brows, until she was facing the mirror again.

"Voilà," said Judy.

Marlene stared, silent. Judy bent over.

"Hello? What do you think?"

Marlene blinked rapidly. Her eyes were wet.

"No more pigtails," she said.

"No," said Judy. "No more pigtails for the big girl."

"My mother used to put it in pigtails. I hated pigtails. But I
wanted to please my mama. She was beautiful. I miss her."

Marlene ran her hand over her head. Then she ran her hand
to the back of her neck, and up, where the bristles were short
and amazingly soft. She smiled.

"There you go," cooed the hairdresser. "Isn't it soft? Doesn't
it feel—"

"Free," said Marlene.

"That's it. It feels free." The hairdresser appraised herself in the mirror, pulled a shank of her own ash blond hair over her shoulder. "Maybe I could go short myself. What do you think?"

Marlene pulled the plastic cape from her body. The floor around her was covered with a ring of black hair. She was ready now. She was emerging from the chrysalis new and sleek and brave, better able to maneuver, ready for a less freighted life, unmoored and unburdened, forgiving, unfussy, wash and go. When she got home, she would pick up the phone, and she would call. She knew where he was. It was his turn to listen. She would clear her throat when he answered. She would speak clearly. And she wouldn't be afraid. She would say, Hello, Daddy? It's me, Marlene.

Epilogue

Certain mornings, the fog moved like ghosts. It curled up off the sea in human shapes. Other days, the sea was clear as a fact. Flat sea, flat sky. The sight could clear the mind. Once, that winter, the small bay had frozen, catching several small craft cockeyed in the ice. Next to the sea's cathedral vastness, certain doubts did not cloud the mind. Why were we here on earth? What were we doing? The sea answered that. It was enough to watch its surface strain and foam in the wind. Along the grass between the road and the bulrush, two little girls threw breadcrumbs into the wind. The crumbs blew back over their heads into the road. Seagulls, elegant white scars, held themselves aloft in the air.

Their mother lifted the window. Paint chips fell onto her desk. "Evelyn!"

The little girl looked up at her, squinting.

"Keep *off* the *road*. You are not to stray *one inch* from the grass."

"She dropped her bread," said her sister, stepping into the shadow of the house. "She had to get her bread off the road."

"What bread?"

The little girl standing in the shadow bent her head. The dark-haired girl in sunlight continued to blink up at the attic, licking her lips.

Alice rested her elbows on the sill.

"Are you girls feeding your lunch to the seagulls again?"

"No," said Evelyn.

"Just a little," said Frances. "Just the crusts."

"And what will you eat for lunch?"

"We'll trade," said Frances.

"Trade what? What will you have left to trade if you feed it to the seagulls?"

"Look, look, here comes the bus!" said Evelyn, running to her post, her dark hair shaking glossily in the sunlight. She hugged the signpost as if it were a boyfriend. She waved up at her mother. "Bye, Mommy! We'll miss you! Have a good day!"

"Study hard, Mommy!"

"*You* study hard," Alice said.

"We love you, Mommy!"

Alice waved. "I love you too. A trillion times I love you."

She closed the window. The school bus came, took them in, and thundered away down the road. She stared down at her book. The house was quiet. It always took a while to adjust to the twins leaving. A kind of maternal cramping always came with the withdrawal of the bus. She removed her glasses, placed them beside her book. Sometimes it was hard to concentrate on her studies. The reading was extensive and dense; she not-so-guiltily wrote stories in her notebook for fun. Her handwriting, graceful now that it was practiced, filled pages. She stood.

The house was old and beautifully decrepit. It stood shoulder to shoulder with a row of motley houses overlooking a poor man's glimpse of striking blue ocean. Down the road stood a processing plant and a pile of scrap metal upon which cranes snacked at night. But always in the air was the sea. The sea roamed throughout the drafty house. In the summer, the air smelled of fish and rot and swamp, but she loved even this smell. She stepped softly down the attic stairs to the second floor.

She drew her hand along the wallpaper of the hallway. On the wall she had kept, for the sake of intrigue, an oval framed photographic portrait of a woman that had been left by the previous owners. The woman had a small, curled mouth, an expression of suppressing laughter. Alice leaned toward the photograph. And what are you laughing at, she whispered. She moved on down the long narrow hallway.

Finally she reached the bedroom door. She placed her hand against the lacquered wood. In the distance, the sound of a ship cutting toward the Bay. She pushed open the door.

And there he was. Fixing his tie. Trying to get the ends even. He stood before the tall, tilted mirror. The mirror was tilted but his image was straight. Sun broke recklessly through the window, upon the wood floor, the unmade bed. She pushed the door open all the way, but still he did not yet see her. He was completely absorbed in tying his tie, his face twisted in consternation, chin up, lips pursed. His hair had thinned enough at the top to reveal his scalp under the golden strands—now, with a slight, disapproving grunt, he licked his hand and smoothed the hair down.

How stunning, sometimes, the accidental, strange-making glimpse of the husband. She pictured him during his day, out in the world, at a staff meeting or a luncheon counter, this stubborn, stray hair drying and becoming happily erect, re-vealing him as the sort of person—just that sort of person—who made other people feel that in the final analysis, everything was going to be all right. He stepped back, apprais-ing himself in the mirror. If she said something now, he would be startled. He would be startled, and then he would smile and say How long have *you* been there? And she would say, Years. Years. He swore softly; now the tie would not lie flat. If she said something, he would be flustered. He would have to start all over.

On the other hand, if she didn't say anything, she could

keep watching. Just like this. She could have one more moment like this, watching him without his knowing.

The ray of sunlight, thick with dust, lit him and made his dress shirt glow. If she did not say anything, she could hover there like an angel who spies upon those he loves. For one moment longer, she could love him as an angel loves, without hunger, without injury, without ambition, without self. She could love him impossibly, as if she herself were not even present. And he could be only exactly what he was—one man: human, divine, lonely, courageous, and engrossed by small puzzles. She rested her head against the doorway. All she really wanted was one more moment to love him like this. One more moment, and then she would speak.

THE FOLDED WORLD

Amity Gaige

A Reader's Guide

Random House Reader's Circle: Was there something in particular that prompted you to become a writer? Did you choose writing as a profession or did it choose you?

Amity Gaige: That's a hard question to answer, because I began writing so young that I can't remember an actual starting of it. I don't remember making a conscious decision.

RHRC: Is there a specific writing philosophy you follow? Describe a typical writing day.

AG: My personal writing philosophy is to try and write better every day. I certainly want people to like my writing, but I know that if I write with the intention of trying to please people, the writing will not be good, because it will not be authentic. So, ironically, I have to be willing to write something strange or unlovable in order to write anything truly good.

My typical writing day has changed dramatically since I wrote *The Folded World*, because I now have a baby. But back then, I would take my days off from work and split them in half. In the morning, I would write. In the afternoon, I would research. I would hunt for interviews, try to get people on the phone, or simply drive around Rhode Island to some of the outer reaches —halfway houses, hospitals—in order to learn, down to the smallest detail, about what it was like to lead lives like those described in the novel.

RHRC: What sparked the idea for *The Folded World*? Did the plot flow from beginning to end or did you write segments and tie them together?

AG: For several years before I began *The Folded World*, I worked at an urban college campus, and had a job in a tutoring center, and people would come into the tutoring center, and for some reason they just kept telling me their life stories. Liberian refugees, recovering alcoholics, ex-convicts, you name it. At that point, I was struggling to finish and to publish my first novel, and not getting far. Perhaps because of this, I identified with the people who talked to me and sought in them some greater wisdom or perspective. But I was young and I did not always know how to behave, nor did I always know whether or not my interest in them entailed an obligation to them. I had one student who became violent and scared me. About this same time, a local social worker was killed on the job. I think I was basically interested in the question of what one should do with all one's good intentions and one's hopeful dreams in the midst of a gritty, unfair world. Although that sounds like a difficult space, it was definitely one of the most creative psychic spaces I've been in. For this reason, the book was written pretty fluidly, from beginning to end.

RHRC: The characters in your books are always just a little bit quirky yet easy to relate to. How much of yourself and people you've encountered in your own life can be found in your characters?

AG: If you ask me, all the characters are completely invented. No one in *The Folded World* is based on a real person. But of course your unconscious gets influenced by people you meet over the course of your life.

RHRC: Which character in *The Folded World* is your favorite? Why?

AG: I have a soft spot for the small role of the "poet/schoolteacher," who lives below Alice and Charlie and likes to look at Alice through his peephole.

One of the sections of the book I like to reread is where the poet/schoolteacher talks about wanting to be given an award for being average and unnoticeable. Alice and Charlie are having a very serious fight upstairs, while he stands there imagining winning the competition for "least competitive person." It was fun to give voice to the feelings of the frustrated artist, working a vaguely related job for a dream of art. On the other hand, that character also represents, to me, a caution against giving in to one's cynicism. He is so afraid of the risks of intimacy that he is only comfortable when looking through a peephole.

RHRC: What kind of books do you like to read? Who is your favorite author and how has he or she inspired you?

AG: I like the greats—Virginia Woolf, Hemingway, D. H. Lawrence are some of my favorites. I also like to read poetry to remind myself how inherently beautiful words are. I often read poetry to "warm up" before I write. I read Rilke's *Duino Elegies* several times a year. Some contemporary books I've loved this year: Ken Kalfus' *A Disorder Peculiar to the Country*, Christopher Sorrentino's *Trance*, and Tom Bissell's *Chasing the Sea*; I love John Updike's stories and Janet Malcolm's nonfiction.

RHRC: What do you like to do for fun?

AG: I love to play tennis, though I have a rather limited talent for it. I also like to cook. With my son, we do a lot of abstract "dancing" around the house. My husband and I go on long walks with him in the woods. I like to go out with my husband, and talk about all the places we've been and what we would do if we were rich.

RHRC: Have you begun your next book? Can you give us a sneak peek?

AG: It's in such early stages I can't yet really see its plot, etc. I can say that it is definitely one of the most personal things I've ever written.

1. Which of the characters in *The Folded World* do you most relate to? How and why?

2. Discuss the mother-daughter relationship between Alice and Marlene. How did Marlene's relationship with her father, and the fact that Alice never knew her father, play a part in their relationship with each other?

3. Charlie Shade lost his job, nearly lost his family, and almost lost himself trying to be all things to Opal — to help her. Yet when Opal sees him as she's flying over the earth at the end of the book she says, "He looked nice enough from up here, but down there he was somehow horrifying." What does she mean by this? What about him is "horrifying"?

4. As a child, Charlie sensed the moment Alice was born. The author writes, "Some people are born again by God. Charlie and Alice Shade were born again by one another." Do you believe in "soul mates"? Were Charlie and Alice destined for

each other? What choices could they have made to change that destiny?

5. At Charlie's birth, his grandmother had a premonition about his death. Her other premonitions had all come to pass. Why didn't the one about Charlie? Or did it?

6. Many of the characters in *The Folded World* are mentally ill, but others are eccentric or lost. What do you think *The Folded World* says about mental illness? What is the fine line that separates the sane from the insane?

7. When Charlie decides to train in social work, he does so because he wants to find the "seam" between his life and others, the place where lives "touch" one another. Is this impulse to find this place a good and noble impulse? What exactly leads him astray from his original intention to help people?

8. Alice is a bookworm. She reads so much she hesitates to make real contacts. At one point, she fears that she believes real people are "less real than people in books." What are the pitfalls of being a bookworm? Is it true that sometimes characters in books seem "more real" than real people? How or why?

9. Why doesn't Alice go to college, the first time when she graduates high school, and the second time when she has another chance after signing up for night classes?

10. At one point, Charlie has the thought that Alice is "spiritually larger" than he somehow. Do you agree? And why are the spirits of each character limited? Which character in the book is spiritually the largest? The smallest?

11. Hal and Opal are both diagnosed with mental illness, and spend time in psychiatric hospitals—the same one, in fact. Both their lives are damaged by the illness, and yet Hal, at the end of the book, seems to have made some type of recovery. Opal, of course, does not. Why do you think their lives end so differently? Why do some mentally ill people flourish despite their illness and some do not?

12. Discuss the italicized sections in the book. Are they literally spoken by Charlie to Alice? Or are they some other form of storytelling?

13. In Part Two, when Charlie is reflecting on his satisfying life as a father and now a mobile clinician, he wonders if, after a life of successes, he can ever truly understand what it means to suffer. Do you agree? Do you think a person needs to suffer himself to understand another person's suffering? Why or why not?

14. Discuss the concept of "the folded world." What is it, and why is it the title of this book? When Hal becomes attracted to Alice in Part Two, he fears that his folded world might disappear, "For in its unfolding, it was no longer a world." Do you agree that this is a predicament in loving someone else?

AMITY GAIGE is the author of the acclaimed novel
O My Darling. In 2006, she was selected by the
National Book Foundation for the prestigious
"5 Under 35" honor. She currently teaches
at Mount Holyoke College and lives in
Amherst, Massachusetts, with her family.